SURRENDER YOUR SONS

SURRENDER

YOUR

SONS

ADAM SASS

Mendota Heights, Minnesota

First Edition
Second Printing, 2020

Book design by Jake Nordby
Cover and jacket design by Jake Nordby
Cover and jacket images by aarrows/Shutterstock, Yuliya Shora/Shutterstock, xpixel/Shutterstock, Brusheezy.com

Flux, an imprint of North Star Editions, Inc.

This is a work of fiction. Names, characters, places, and incidents are either the product of the author's imagination or are used fictitiously, and any resemblance to actual persons living or dead, business establishments, events, or locales is entirely coincidental. Cover models used for illustrative purposes only and may not endorse or represent the book's subject.

Library of Congress Cataloging-in-Publication Data
Names: Sass, Adam, 1983- author.
Title: Surrender your sons / Adam Sass.
Description: First edition. | Mendota Heights, MN: Flux, 2020. | Audience:
    Grades 10-12. | Summary: "Connor Major and other queer teens trapped at
    a conversion therapy camp work together to escape—and expose the camp's
    horrible truths"— Provided by publisher.
Identifiers: LCCN 2020008091 (print) | LCCN 2020008092 (ebook) | ISBN
    9781635830613 (hardcover) | ISBN 9781635830620 (ebook)
Subjects: CYAC: Sexual orientation—Fiction. | Sexual reorientation
    programs—Fiction. | Camps—Fiction. | Adventure and
    adventurers—Fiction. | Murder—Fiction.
Classification: LCC PZ7.1.S26477 Sur 2020 (print) | LCC PZ7.1.S26477
    (ebook) | DDC [Fic] —dc23
LC record available at https://lccn.loc.gov/2020008091
LC ebook record available at https://lccn.loc.gov/2020008092

Flux
North Star Editions, Inc.
2297 Waters Drive
Mendota Heights, MN 55120
www.fluxnow.com

Printed in Canada

To my husband:
you never stopped believing in me.

To my parents:
my coming out only made us stronger.

To the surrendered:
find each other, and survive together.

AUTHOR'S NOTE
WITH CONTENT WARNINGS

This book is a thriller. But just like with any thrill ride or roller coaster, there are some safety precautions we need to go over before we can all have a good scream. First, I want to acknowledge that you'll find queer pain in this book. However, it's not *about* queer pain. It's about what queers *do* with pain. Queer pain is something we've seen either too much of in the media or bungled in some way. Pain is something queers deal with regularly, even if it's just occasional feelings of isolation and otherness. In my experience, queer people process pain in many ways, but a big one is through humor. In *Surrender Your Sons,* you'll find queer kids put through bad experiences, and then sometimes, they'll make a joke about it.

Yet there's no universal queer experience. That's why I wrote a variety of different kids into this book. Being part of the queer community is like the ultimate group project in school. Don't be the one who lets the others do all the work! No one likes that person!

One last thing to acknowledge is the "S" word. Feelings of self-harm can be upsetting to even hear about. As badly as I wanted to make *Surrender Your Sons* a suicide-discussion free zone, I was committed to showing the consequences of conversion therapy and I couldn't fully tell that story without bringing up suicide. It's not the whole book, but it does come up.

I promise you, the reader: in the pages of *Surrender Your Sons,* there's light in the dark.

You'll find scary things in this book, but just like in life, when the trouble hits, you'll also find humor, good friends, and courage you couldn't imagine in your wildest dreams.

Now that that's out of the way, I am happy to present *Surrender Your Sons*.

—Adam Sass

MOM'S ULTIMATUM

This war has gone on long enough, but not for my mother. Even though she's been in an upbeat mood since she arrived home from work, I know better than to drop my guard. It's a trap somehow. Her cheeriness lingers over our home-cooked meal like the Saharan sun—omnipresent and pitiless. She thinks I don't have the guts to ask the question that will blow apart our fragile cease-fire—the question that has dogged me for over a week—but I very much *do* have the guts:

"Hey, so...when do I get my phone back?"

I ask calmly, without demands or tantrums. Nevertheless, the question ignites a fire in my mother's eyes that has been kindling underneath our brutally pleasant dinner. Mom shoves away her plate of half-eaten chicken and asks, "Your phone?" My question is the scandal of the century, apparently. "Are you serious?"

I'm dead serious, but I shrug: it's crucial that I project an aura of casual indifference, even though my heart sinks with each day I'm cut off from Ario and my friends. Mom would keep my phone forever if she could. Last Thanksgiving, my uncle scolded me, *"You treat that thing like it's your second dick!"* He's not wrong, but I've been phone-less for almost two weeks and this battle for my sanity has reached D-Day levels of slaughter.

"It's just that..." I begin cautiously, remounting my defense, "...could I get a *time frame* of when I'll get it back?"

"Are you kidding me?" Mom's conviction grows as every muscle tightens in my neck. "You are being *punished*, Connor—"

"I didn't do anything wrong!" A reckless energy seizes me as I leap from my chair in a foolish attempt to intimidate her with my height (as of my seventeenth birthday, I've accepted the reality that I'm tapped out at five and a half feet).

"Don't come at me with your trash attitude! And you're not excused." Mom grasps the silver cross hanging outside of her nursing scrub top and kisses it—no, *mashes* it to her lips; her typical plea to Christ to help her out of another fine mess her heathen son has dragged her into. She fans her hands downward for me to sit, and—with an extra loud huff—I oblige. Mom and I take turns sneering at each other, a performance battle to prove which of us is the more aggrieved party. She blows tense air through "O"-circled lips, and I pissily toss a sweat-dampened curl from my eyes.

Our clanking swamp cooler of an air conditioner doesn't provide any relief from the latest heat wave tearing through Ambrose; however, the stench of hot July chicken shit from the farm next door manages to travel on the breeze just fine. I ladle peppermint ice cream into my mouth at a mindless speed until a glob of pink goo drips onto my shorts next to a hot sauce stain...which is from yesterday. It's the same Mercedes-Benz Fashion Week-worthy outfit I've donned all summer: gym shorts and a baggy hoodie with the sleeves chopped off.

What do I care how I look? Because of Mom, I might never see my boyfriend again.

When I was closeted, all my boyfriend, Ario, squawked about was how important it was to come out: it would save my life; food would taste better; fresh lavender would fill the air. Well, I did that—I've been out for months, but I'm starting to think he was only repeating shit he heard from YouTubers who were either lying or lucky.

If this is what being out is like, he can keep it.

When I first came out to my mom, I didn't mention having a boyfriend. I enjoyed a frigid—but unpunished—summer of Mom dealing with my queerness as nothing more than some unpleasant hypothetical. But then she found out there was an actual *boy* involved, with lips and stubble and dirty, filthy, no good intentions. That's when she confiscated my phone. The rest came rapid-fire: laptop—gone, Wi-Fi—cut off. My friends have been banned from coming over—all except for Vicky, my best friend (and ex-girlfriend), aka my mother's last hope for a straight son. Not that that matters. Vicky stopped having time to hang out as soon as her son was born—I don't know how she's going to handle our senior year while taking care of a newborn. The baby isn't mine, but try telling that to my suddenly desperate-for-a-grandchild mother.

Gay? Jesus wouldn't like that.

Knock up your girlfriend? Well, babies are a blessing, and at least you're not gay.

Scowling, I lick the drying peppermint off my fingers, where remnants of electric purple nail polish still hide under my cuticles. Mom stripped off my color when she took my phone—it was a merciless raid. She was weirdly violent about it too. Plunged my hands into a dish of alcohol and *voilà*: no more purple fingers. Just manly, pale white sausages, as the Lord intended.

If Ario were here, he'd repaint them. Ario makes everything okay again.

"I forgot to tell you earlier..." Mom says, commanding her voice to soften. "It turns out I was right—your dad's birthday present for you did get turned around in the mail."

I roll my eyes and scrape the last dregs of ice cream from my bowl. My birthday was Memorial Day, and we're currently well past the Fourth of July. *"Turned around in the mail."* Clearly, the man forgot. I've made peace with Dad missing, ignoring, and forgetting every single thing about my life, but, like...don't try to trick me into thinking he gives a shit.

A puffy, yellow envelope with my name scrawled across the face lies propped against a candle in the center of the table. Whatever Dad left for me in that envelope, it'll be something half-assed. I'm ignoring it.

"You know what probably happened, it's that international shipping. You can't count on it," Mom continues, eager to sell me on this lie—whether it's her own feeble creation or something Dad made her swallow.

"Sure, yeah, international shipping," I say. "Everything takes two months because it's the 1900s. They still send mail across on the *Titanic*—"

"Connor—"

"You'll believe anything, won't you?"

Mom's smile freezes and then dies. *Victory.* An evil warmth fills my lungs as I savor finally landing a hit. Unfortunately, as usual, guilt follows. Dad put Mom through the wringer for years—lying, raging, drinking, disappearing—and I just squeezed lemon juice into her most painful wound. I don't relax my scowl, though. If she stays vulnerable, there's a decent chance she'll give up and return my phone.

"This is too much fighting," Mom says, swallowing another bite off her trembling fork. "I'm trying to be civil with your dad. Can't you just...be my buddy on this?"

A fire grows in my belly. More guilt. She does this: she makes herself pathetic, and I end up feeling like a bastard for asking for any kind of decency or dignity. In the end, the guilt is too overpowering and I'm forced to nod. "I'm your buddy, Mom." She laces her fingers under her chin and, on the crest of an enormous sigh, weeps into her meal. Guilt consumes my entire being like an inferno. "Come on, don't cry..."

"It's so hard raising a boy on your own," she squeaks, dabbing a napkin under her eyes.

"Momma, not this again," I groan, my guilt evaporating from a renewed rage.

"You don't know what you're putting Vicky through, not making it right—"

"I'm not the dad!"

"Then who is? It's a miracle birth?"

"I don't know. It's not my business—"

"You were her boyfriend for a year. Suddenly, she's got a baby and you tell me you like...men..."

"You think I made up a boyfriend so I could duck out on her—?"

"Did you?"

"Gimme my phone and I'll show you pictures; my boyfriend's real."

"Your dad didn't want the responsibility of a child either. Not that I blame either of you. It's a hard, hard thing, being a parent. You're constantly over a barrel—"

"Mom, STOP. You're like a broken record!" I growl under my breath and poke at the coagulated remains of ice cream in my bowl.

Nothing will ever convince her because she doesn't want to be convinced. I could put that baby through a paternity test and wag the results under her nose, and she'd think I faked them in Photoshop. This baby thing of hers is just a fancy coat she's wearing over her total discomfort with who I am. It's not even the same situation as Dad; Dad didn't deny I was his. He stuck around eleven years, then blew off to England to be with his ex-girlfriend. He sucks, but to my mom, me coming out is just as unforgivable.

These last few weeks have been torture for both of us. I miss Normal Mom.

"All this fighting's no good," she says, mopping her wet cheeks with a third napkin.

"We're buddies, okay?" I close my hand over hers, anything to quiet this storm. She shuts her eyes and smiles.

Now's the time, Connor.

A lump rises in my throat as I ask, "Can we just get past this? Can't I get my phone back, and then the fighting'll be over?"

"CONNOR," Mom moans and yanks her hand out from under mine, suddenly disgusted like I sneezed on her. The unexpected obliteration of our truce sends pins and needles of anxiety up my spinal column. She presses prayer hands to her mouth. *Prayer hands! Marcia Major, bringing out the big guns.* "Please fix your priorities. If I were you, I'd worry less about my phone and more about these grades I've been seeing. Retake the SAT. Prep your application essays. You should be sick to your stomach thinking your friends'll go off to good colleges while you end up at home, watching TV, giggling, or whatever it is you do all day while Vicky goes it alone raising Avery. I'd worry about being twenty-five someday, doing that same thing. Thirty. Forty years old, mouthing off in *my* kitchen about some boyfriend you think you got—"

"I *do* got a boyfriend—"

"You do not. If you live in my house, you do not."

When Mom finishes, I whip my head away with a flourish not seen outside of a telenovela—she doesn't deserve my eye contact. My neck is boiling, and I can't summon the breath to yell back at her about how much everything she is saying *sucks*. I stare out of our enormous picture window onto a country road and the vast farmland where I'm trapped. The only two houses on our street are ours and the Packard Family chicken ranch. The man who runs the farm is also our local reverend...and my mom's only friend. She refuses to hang out with the other nurses after work. She excludes anybody in her life who might warn her about what an out-of-control zealot she's turned into.

Above Reverend Packard's soybean fields, storm clouds mutate into a single, nauseatingly yellow mass. The Packard farmers rotate crops each year—one year corn, one year soybeans. Corn, soy, corn, soy. On corn years, there's a hint of magical possibility in the air. When I was a kid, I'd imagine blue, scaly creatures and elves hiding between the massive stalks, plotting mischief. But on soy years—this year—the view is low and clear, and Ambrose, Illinois, is exposed for what it really is: grain elevators, churches, and that's it.

While I gaze, hypnotized, at the road separating our home from the endless soy fields, a black minivan sails past. It's the only car I've noticed since dinner began, but this is the third time I've seen it. The black van—its windows also blackened—has been circling our street like a buzzard. Probably lost. Nobody comes to Ambrose on purpose (except for me and my duped mother).

"This came for you," Mom says, tapping the yellow envelope on the table.

"From Dad," I say, sneering. "You told me already."

"No, his present is still stuck in the mail, like I told *you* already. You remember Ricky Hannigan? You delivered his Meals on Wheels?" Pins and needles swarm into my fingers like fireflies over a marsh. Normally, I'd be grateful for the subject change, but it squeezes my stomach just to hear Mr. Hannigan's name. Ricky Hannigan was an older client who received hot meals at home from yours truly every weekend since school let out.

But that's all over.

"I remember Mr. Hannigan," I say, shaking my head out of a stupor.

"Well, he died."

"I know he died. Hi, that's why I haven't been going on deliveries. You think I want to hang out here all day, getting under your skin?"

"Anyway, it looks like he left you something in his will." Mom taps the bulging envelope again. "Isn't that kind? The Reverend brought it by. He wanted to give it to you himself, but you were busy in the *shower* for a long time."

My cheeks burst into flames that my mom would inform the frigging Reverend about how long I'd been in the shower. So what if I was in there for a while, imagining Ario next to me, our bodies pressed tightly in the rushing water? I have no phone, no friends, and nothing to do all day but look forward to a pathetic shower wank—dreaming of Ario's perfectly furry chest...his curly hair...his feet up in the air...

"Thanks," I say, plopping the envelope beside the sweating ice cream carton. Ricky's package is feather light—is it cash? A check? Rare stamps? Ricky Hannigan lived in a shitbox home and every spare cent went to his medical care, so I shouldn't get too excited. Still...he didn't have to leave me anything. I'm kind of embarrassed he did; I barely knew him.

"You're not gonna open it?"

"I'll wait 'til I'm alone." I turn to her, hands folded, and don't dare to blink. She's not getting one iota of whatever is in here. It's all going toward Connor Major's New Phone Piss-Off Fund. "Mr. Hannigan was a nice guy, but he was private. He wouldn't want me opening this in front of anybody."

That's a lie. Ricky Hannigan was best friends with anyone who walked in his door. A few weeks before my junior year ended (and I unwisely came out), Mom arranged with the Reverend to get me into the Meals on Wheels program, so I'd waste my summer doing Christian things for Christian people. Most of my customers were cranky old dickheads, but not Ricky. He always smiled when he saw me.

I don't get smiled at a lot.

Ricky wasn't any older than the Reverend, but he needed meals delivered because he'd been in an accident forever ago. He could barely talk, so I never pried much about his injury. Then last weekend, I showed up at Ricky's house with his usual tray, but his hospital bed was empty. He was gone. After that, the Reverend stopped my deliveries altogether, as if Ricky had been the only customer who mattered.

Outside our window, the black van cruises by for a fourth round. This time, Mom and I both spot it. Startled, her hand jumps, her fork and plate clattering, and the sudden noise stops my heart.

Clearly, I inherited the panic gene from her, so thanks a bunch, Marcia. When she finishes blotting the gravy stain out of our plastic tablecloth, Mom pulls back a curtain of dark hair and announces, "Connor, your punishment's over."

Honey and sunshine flood my heart for the first time in weeks. *For real? Just like that?* After this long and bloody war, her 180-degree turn takes me by such surprise that I can't stop myself from blurting, "Why?"

"You don't want it to be over?"

"No! I'm sorry I said it rude like that. I just...What changed your mind?"

Mom closes her eyes, leaving me to twist in agony until she reopens them. "Because my punishments aren't changing anything."

Holy sanity! Don't sass her back, Connor; just smile and nod.

At long, long, *long* last, Mom slides it across the table to me— my phone, encased in a turquoise shell. My portal to worlds other than this one. I close clammy fingers around my old friend; its cool, metal touch is bliss and already slowing my rapid heartbeat. Without another word, I lift the phone to nourish my eyes with dozens of texts, pictures, and "I miss yous" from Ario.

But there aren't any. The display stays black. Mom didn't keep it charged.

Exhaling slowly, she unfolds a crinkled scrap of notebook paper, flattens it beside her uneaten meal, and scans the page. As Mom reads to herself, she inhales deliberately deep, calming breaths. I have no idea if I'm supposed to stay or get out of her sight, so I mumble "Thank you" and slide back my chair.

"I've got one last thing to do," she whispers, eyes still on her paper. I drop back to my seat with nothing to focus on but this ominous pulling sensation in my gut. "I've been reading about set-ting boundaries and ultimatums,"—she swallows—"and I'm gonna read mine to you now."

"All right," I say without breath. *I'm being kicked out.* She's never been nervous to chew me out before, but all of a sudden, she hands me my phone and can't stomach eating dinner?

This is it. Ultimatum time.

"Connor," Mom reads, "it's clear you're choosing to reject your responsibilities so you can be with another boy. Whatever you might think is fair, this choice has consequences. This boy, or any boy or man...I won't meet him. I don't want to know him in any way. If you...marry a man, I won't go to the wedding and he won't belong to our family. If you have more children someday—you buy them or whatever—they won't belong to our family. You're always welcome here. But nobody else you're married to, unless it's Vicky. These are my terms, and that's the price of this phone. Do you accept this?"

She looks up, her eyes stained pink.

"Um...fine...sure," I say, swirling my filthy fork around my plate. Why couldn't she have just screamed? I don't even want to cry. The twisting in my stomach has vanished, replaced by a great, big, empty nothingness. Raise a baby that's not mine—and force my best friend to marry a guy who likes guys—or be alone forever. These are the only choices Mom will allow for me.

"That wasn't what you expected me to say?" she asks, fluid clogging her eyes and nose. "What *did* you expect me to say? That none of this matters? That it doesn't change how I feel about you?"

"Does it...change how you feel...?"

A blank stare greets me. Anxiety drives hard and fast through my limbs like I'm wearing vibrating armor. I'd rather text Ario than have a meltdown at the dinner table, so I collect my phone and Mr. Hannigan's envelope and leave. I'm rounding the breakfast island, almost to the stairs, when Mom charges after me with brand-new, furious energy:

"And don't go online and talk about me! I know you do it."

"I don't."

"You do."

"How do you know? You don't know my account!"

"Gina sends me screenshots."

Gina. Beneath the kitchen archway where the tile meets carpet, I spin around with shock. *BE-TRAY-AL.* My cousin Gina, with her condescending, asshole lawyer husband, has got nothing better to do but snitch on me and breastfeed her fugly baby. *How come everybody in my family wants to literally kill me?*

"You're all scum!" I roar. But anger never works on Mom; it only makes her more self-righteous. Her tears have already dried.

"Do not discuss our private business with anyone else or online. Am I clear? And you're gonna take down your kissing pictures."

"No."

"You have to take them down or you can't—"

"THEN I'M OUT OF HERE!" I don't give her the satisfaction of finishing her threat: *—or you can't stay.* I kick the kitchen tile so hard, I think my foot might crack it.

Still, Mom never blinks.

She's really doing this to me. I'm really getting kicked out? Where will I even go? Dad lives in a totally different country, and he cares even less about me than she does, if that's possible. Maybe I could crash with Ario...I'd hate to burden him with my family drama more than I already have, but I don't have a choice and his mom would jump at the chance to help me.

She's so nice. She's so normal.

How come everyone else gets a mom who's nice and normal, and I get this mess?

I fight for a full breath while pins and needles unfurl a cape of anxiety down my back. *Don't faint.* I need music—Carly Rae. Ariana. I'd take anyone at this point if it would pull me out of my spiral. Finally, I nod—numb from head to toe—and drag myself upstairs. I pass a wall of glazed, ceramic crucifixes and framed portraits of my parents' wedding—colorful, tacky dresses and dapper men in suits. A true collision of Floridians and Englishmen. I'm somewhere in these pictures, a four-month-old fetus. *The secret wedding guest.* And my parents, the happy liars. They've been split up almost half my life and she's telling *me* what's cool and not cool with God.

This isn't forever, Connor, I remind myself.

I have time to change her mind.

—

Finally, I'm alone in my room. My charger slips in, and after thirty eternal seconds, my phone wakes from its coma. This oasis of privacy. I haven't felt private in weeks (lonely isn't the same as private). In my bottom desk drawer, an overlarge SAT prep book rests where my Nintendo Switch used to be. A sticky note on top reads:

"Switch" to this instead.

My life is one big crime scene. Mom helps herself to my room, my phone, and my gaming shit any time she wants so she can hunt for evidence that yeah—I'm not the son she thought I was.

A barrage of texts pop like fireworks on my phone's display, but I assemble my backpack before checking them—*before I have the chance to talk myself out of this*. I stuff a raggedy JanSport with T-shirts and socks until it's bursting. The gym shorts I have on will be enough to last me the summer, pants-wise. I can go weeks wearing these puppies. And that's everything. Mom still has my laptop, so I don't need anything else but my bike outside to take me to Ario's. I'll wait until she's asleep and be gone before I ever have to hear the words *Get out of my house*.

I put on Kacey Musgraves. "High Horse" is a good bop; if I play "Space Cowboy" or any of her slower stuff, I'll break like an egg yolk. Downstairs, Mom sings along—*flatly*—to Karen Carpenter while she washes the dishes, and I crank Ms. Musgraves up to my phone's maximum volume. A cool night breeze flies in my open window, but still, I flick on the oscillating fan attached to the windowsill. When I get worked up like this, I overheat. I peel off my sleeveless hoodie, curl next to my wall charger, and let the coarse carpet fibers give me a back rub while I text my traitorous cousin Gina:

> *ur a goddamn snitch*
>
> *ur baby's ugly*

A job well done, I block Gina's number and her accounts everywhere on social media. Knowing her, she'll create a fake account to follow me, so I set myself to private. Next comes the real business. I send identical, separate texts to Ario and Vicky: *Got back my phone finally*.

The "I'm typing" bubbles appear instantly.

Ario: *omg are you okay???*

Me: *I'm so wiped out. I miss you.*

Ario: *I miss you! Did she hurt you?*

Me: *What? No she doesn't do that. She's just, like, mean, I guess.*

Ario: 😔

sorry hang on, my gd sister won't leave me alone brb

Me: *Okay! No worries!*

All the worries.

I want to tell Ario I've already packed a bag to run away to his place, but that plan is already curdling. Am I really going to run away for my whole senior year? Is it even legal for the Navissis to take me in? What if his mom ends up saying no? She would never. But if she says yes, what do I do about school? Ario and I go to different ones, but his is a lot nicer. Maybe I could switch to his school—he's out there and totally popular. He's always hanging out with, like, a million people! Nobody gives him shit. He graduated last month, so we couldn't be open, cutesy boyfriends who kiss in the hallways between classes, but at least I'd have an easier time of it over there.

Ario lives in White Eagle, a much nicer town fifteen miles away that has actual civilization like movie theaters and bookstores. We met at his local bookstore; he marched right up to me while I was huddled in the LGBTQ section like a frightened cat. This beautiful older boy with dimples and the smoothest skin introduced himself, but all I could do was sweat like he'd caught me shoplifting. He noticed how freaked out I was, both to be spotted in *that* section and to be approached by someone so...magnetic. He asked for my number, and in my shock, I couldn't remember the whole thing (*was it 4731 or 3471?*). He took my phone gently, his fingers briefly grazing across mine, and made a new contact for himself under "Ario Bookstore Cutie" (which I renamed to "Ario Bookstore" to deter any investigations from my spying mother).

When I met Ario, it felt like a longstanding curse was finally breaking. My life was going to be a dreamy gay teen movie, just like it was always supposed to be. That never happened. Ario brought light into my life, but it only made the shadows stronger. Navigating around my mom, the Reverend, school, Vicky, her baby drama, the physical distance of simply getting to Ario...these obstacles didn't make my new relationship exciting. They robbed me of energy and joy at every possible turn.

That's when Ario thought me coming out would be the solution. It wasn't.

What is it that's so wrong with me? It's like the whole entire universe is telling me I don't deserve a boyfriend. Pretty soon, these obstacles will get worse. Ario and I don't have much IRL time left—next month, he's leaving for college in Chicago. A three-hour drive away.

Finally, my phone vibrates with Vicky's response: *Hi!! Sorry, I was napping. My mom was giving me a break from Avery. Are you okay??*

Me: *I'm sorry! Go back to your nap—I'm fine. You never get to sleep.*

Vicky: *Stop it, I'm up. This heat is totally wretched!*

Me: *My mom's convinced herself that I'm Avery's dad and that I'm ditching you—she's totally projecting her shit with my dad.*

Vicky: *Oh God.*

Vicky sends a *Real Housewives* GIF of Bethenny Frankel rolling her eyes.

Vicky: *You didn't tell her about Avery's dad, did you?*

Me: *Of course not.*

Vicky: *Because I know how she gets. It would be ok if you had to tell her to shut her up.*

Me: *Vicky, stop, I swear I would never tell anyone for any reason.*

Vicky: *Thank you.* 🙁 *I'm sorry. I know it would be easier on you if she knew the truth.*

The thing is, it would. We both know who the real father is: when Vicky and I were together, she "cheated" on me (although I was fully neglecting her, so who cares?) with Derrick, her supervisor at the AMC theater in White Eagle. Derrick is twenty-three and she is hardcore in love with him. Even after he suddenly left town, leaving her to give birth alone, she didn't tell anybody. Her dad would have Derrick arrested. She refuses to do that. She truly believes Derrick is going to have a change of heart and come back any minute.

I want to scream that she's D-E-L-U-D-E-D and Derrick deserves everything that's coming to him, but it wouldn't reach her. All it would do is alienate me from my only ally in Ambrose. I'm the only one Vicky trusted with the truth. Unfortunately for me, I was dating Vicky when she got pregnant, so the longer this mystery goes on, the more I look like the Big Gay Deadbeat.

Me: *Maybe everything would be easier if we got back together. People would leave me alone, and you'd have help...*

Vicky: *lol what about Ario?*

Me: *Well, you'd just have to be cool with me seeing guys on the side lol*

After an eternity of Vicky typing, her response is simply *haha*. I shouldn't joke (maybe only half-joke). Vicky, like me, is up to her neck in shit, and if I offered to be Avery's unofficial father, she'd say "I do" just for the extra naptime.

Vicky: *I gotta go, but I love you. Text whenever.*

I switch back to Ario, who as it turns out had been texting me the whole time I was talking to Vicky, but my asshole phone never buzzed. He sent a GIF he made of himself—doe-eyed, with curly black hair, making a heart shape with his fingers.

Me: ♥ *Do you think I could stay at your place for a couple nights? I'm kinda nervous here.*

When he doesn't respond, I notice that I missed his last message following the GIF: *brb I'm heading out—promised my sis I'd drive her and her demon friends to the county fair. Blerg, it's like an hour away. Text me later, okay?? Hang in there!*

GOD DAMMIT.

I missed my window to text Ario my most important ask. The tops of my ears burn. I flip my phone facedown and stroke the pendant lying across my bare chest. It's a recorder the size of a finger, handcrafted from bamboo; gripping it always brings me closer to Ario. I need him to text back or I have literally nowhere to go. I can't burden Vicky with this. She's got enough on her plate, plus me shacking up with Vicky would cancel whatever remaining doubts Mom might have about us.

Meanwhile, Ricky Hannigan's envelope sits on top of my swirly, untucked covers, almost forgotten. Mr. Hannigan, that sweet, sunken-eyed man, left me a present in his will. I undo the envelope's brass clip; inside is a folded booklet. No money. I'm not sure what I expected; the envelope was way too light. I recognize the booklet's bright yellow cover immediately—a Broadway Playbill. Ricky's room was covered in them. Old ones, mostly—*Chicago, Dreamgirls, Sweeney Todd, A Little Night Music, Into the Woods*—all from a time when Ricky was still able to go out. This Playbill is for *South Pacific*. On its vibrant, chalk-drawing cover, sailors dance around a tropical island. Ricky was always playing showtunes when I walked in, but

I don't remember this one. I flip open the booklet's cover to a rude sight: the pages have been vandalized with black Sharpie in large, scrawling letters, so uneven they don't even resemble words at first.

Then I understand: Ricky left me a goodbye note. He couldn't comfortably hold a pen, so his letters are different sizes with tremorous shakes in the lines. Still, his message is clear:

HELP CONNOR.

My lips open but no breath comes. I flip to the next page. Across the acknowledgments section, Ricky has scribbled another word:

NIGHTLIGHT.

It doesn't stop. On every page, splattered over the cast bios:

NIGHTLIGHT. NIGHTLIGHT. HELP CONNOR. NIGHTLIGHT.

The Playbill falls onto the tangled shirts in my open bag, and I scamper backward as if it were a bomb. Pins and needles flood my fingertips as goose bumps sail across my shoulders; the night breeze coming in my window isn't cozy anymore. I try to pull on my sleeveless hoodie, but my arms have become clumsy slabs. In my struggle with the shirt, panic detonates inside my head like a nail bomb, bits of anxiety shrapnel flinging this way and that, lacerating every nearby thought.

Something isn't right.

Hairs prickle on the back of my neck as Ricky's message swirls, echoes like a scream: HELP CONNOR. NIGHTLIGHT. Ricky gave me this message in his will. Not when he was alive. What did he think I could possibly help him with once he was dead? He died from an infected bedsore, nothing weird or suspicious. He had the Reverend, his mom, and a million other people who helped him with anything he wanted or needed. Why me? Why now? And what does *Nightlight* mean?

My chest suffocates with paranoia. I no longer feel alone in my empty room. I pivot around quickly to my bedroom door, expecting to find the sallow, pleading face of Ricky reaching for me, a ghost, the living dead. There's no one. Jumping, I pivot again toward my open window, expecting that sweet man's rotting, soil-matted corpse to be crawling inside. Nothing.

Yet the feeling of eyes surrounding me won't go away.

In a way, Ricky's ghost *is* here. His message is trying to reach me from beyond the grave.

A plea for help. Ricky's scrawled writing looks so pained.

I welcome in a clean breath of rationality to slow my heartbeat.

Ricky is dead, Connor. Whatever this is about, you can't help him anymore.

I need to get out of here.

The grip on my chest doesn't relax, but is instead buried under the heavy blanket of worry about what the hell I'm going to do about tonight. *I think she wants to kick me out,* I text Ario rapidly. Once again, I curl on the floor and wait thirty minutes for my phone to light up and teleport me out of this shit.

I fall asleep waiting.

"Connor, you need to wake up," says a tough British voice.

"Dad...?" I moan. My dreams have been a blizzard of footsteps and people whispering. I'm still sprawled across the floor, but my room is filled with strangers dressed in black. Two men stand over me, night shadows obscuring their faces. Not shadows—ski masks.

This isn't a dream. And that isn't my dad.

There are strangers in the house.

"Hello," another man says, dangling my backpack from his finger. "We have your bag."

"MOM, someone's in the house!" I scream, unable to stop myself trembling.

"We need you to come with us," the British man says. "We can do this the easy way or the hard way." I don't waste a moment. In the dark, I scramble upright, but my feet slip on the carpet and my hip collides with a rolling desk chair. "Easy way, then..."

My phone. It's still charging in the wall. I'm inches away from the glow...I lunge, but the men pounce viper-quick. My arms and shoulders hit the floor as lifelessly as wet bread. I can't even squirm as their powerful hands hold me flat. "MOM!" I shriek into the carpet.

Before I take another breath, I'm ripped from the room and hauled onto the upstairs landing. My feet leave the ground as one of the men hoists me—all 140 pounds—over his shoulder. We descend the stairs, and I clutch at the wall with numb, useless hands, dozens of family photos crashing down the steps as I slap them. A trio of crucifixes from Precious Moments fall, shattering into a pile of gold filigree and pink ceramic dust.

"Don't ruin your mum's nice things," the British man grunts as I flail.

Make more noise, Connor. Wake Mom up!

Finally, my mom's voice calls from the other room: "Buddy?" Upside-down, my head rolls around the intruder's sweat-dampened back until I glimpse my mother standing in the kitchen archway, still in her nursing scrubs from dinner. "I love you."

"Wait," I say, spittle sliding across my chin. "What's happening...?"

"He tried to run, Mrs. Major," the intruder says. "Sorry, but this is necessary. Apologies for the mess."

"I understand," Mom says. "Please be careful with him."

"Mom...?" I squeak.

"You'll be okay, Connor..." Her face cracks as a torrent of sobs sweeps over her. She's letting them take me. She *wants* them to take me.

"I'm not going anywhere!" But the massive Brit is already hauling me through the front door, held open by a shorter, heavier masked man. "Mom, what are they doing?!"

Outside in the cricketing night air, the British man hurls me off his shoulder like a sack of potatoes, and my back smacks onto the front lawn, my breath flying out of me. Four gloved hands wrap under my arms, and I'm weightless again as two men carry me down our sloping hill to the farm road. My bare feet glide over the dewy grass until we reach a parked van.

The black van.

The one that circled our house during dinner but is now idling along the Packard fields, engine running, waiting for me. *No way. No Goddamn way this is happening.* The British man slides open the van door, and a dark abyss smiles at me.

"MOMMAAAA!" I scream, air returning to my lungs far too late.

My cries echo over Reverend Packard's farm, but my mom does nothing except whimper into her hands at the top of the driveway as they shut me inside and peel away.

CHAPTER TWO
ALL ABOARD

*R*ibbit. Frogs keep ribbiting under my head while I'm trying to get some sleep. My eyes creak open to a set of blurry street-lights crashing through the night outside, and dozens of car horns blare as the ribbiting continues to shake the van's bench seats.

The van...

The only other sound is a low, industrial hum—a constant, unsettling tone.

Ribbit. When I was twelve, Mom and I escaped Florida for a quieter, churchier life in Ambrose. The expressway into Illinois vibrated our overly packed Hyundai...and the vibrations sounded like frogs ribbiting.

Ribbit.

We're on an expressway. My heart swishes through my ribcage as I fully emerge from my dream and remember with horrifying clarity that I have been kidnapped. I spring up from the vinyl bench—the skin of my arm unsticking painfully in the sweltering heat—and recognize my abductors.

"Connor, you're awake," the masked British man greets me from the front bench. Only my kidnapper isn't wearing his mask anymore. Whoever he is, he's shockingly boyish, like a boybander who got old; his dark, cropped hair runs silver along the sides. A desperate moan spills out of my mouth as I swing at him, but his rough, calloused hand closes around mine. "It's all right. My name is Ben Briggs."

My heart refuses to settle. *Breathe in through your nose, Connor. In through the nose, out through the mouth.*

"How long have I been out?" I ask. It can't have been long; I'm still in the cutoff hoodie and gym shorts I wore to bed.

"You've been drifting for an hour," Briggs says. "You fainted, sorry to say—"

Seizing what little opportunity I have, I lunge for the door, my fingers scrabbling in a terrible, frantic search for the handle in the dim light of the van. Once again, Briggs pulls me back into his snare with a gentle, unhurried strength.

"No, no, no," he whispers. "You don't want to do that."

I grunt, the back of my hand striking like a mallet against his temple, and he releases me to cup his stinging ear. I scramble again to the door as both the driver and the third kidnapper, who is in the front seat, yelp, "OI!" There's negative ten seconds to act, but with a final burst of adrenaline, my fingers slip around the vertical paddle handle and the door groans open onto a burst of electric streetlight. I wince. Beneath my bare feet, the expressway rushes past in a hypnotic, white-gray blur. I'm momentarily stunned, my hands trembling in front of me.

Do I jump? Can I jump?

Cars sail by too quickly to pinpoint someone to flag down for help. I gather a single, powerful breath and bellow "HEL—" before Briggs's paws close around my shoulders. I don't squirm because I'm terrified of overbalancing and tumbling out, getting walloped underneath a dozen tires in the process. I careen backward, falling flat on my back onto the bench. With one large mitt pressed against my chest, Briggs holds me in place. With his other, he struggles the whining van door shut again.

"Good way to get yourself killed, mate!" he roars as I attempt to catch my panicked, unsteady breath. His cheerfulness gone, Briggs wears the stunned, furious expression of a bully who wasn't expecting to be hit. *I hit him. I hit him; now he's gonna hit me.* I raise my forearms to shield my face from whatever's coming, but nothing does. Breathlessly, Briggs pants: "What were you gonna do? Run? Even if you jump out when we're dead stopped, you're not gonna get far on bare feet. That road is covered in rubbish, grit, glass, nails, car bits, drug needles, whatever, and look at you: soft as if you've been putting those toes up on a velvet pillow every night. DON'T. RUN. You're safe."

"Oh yeah." I laugh like a shotgun blast and crawl up to sitting. "Real safe."

Briggs's sternness finally breaks, and he brushes exhaustion from his face. "All right," he says, softening. "I know you're freaked. I would be too if someone grabbed me out of bed. If it was up to me, I'd do this another way...but I don't make the rules."

"Who *does* make the rules?"

"I promise, this'll all make sense soon. It's just part of the program."

"Program?"

"Aye," Briggs huffs, massaging his chest and taking in deliberately steady breaths, as if trying to calm himself out of a panic attack.

"Take me HOME."

"We actually are gonna take you home again real soon. Your mum just wants you to come with us first on a short trip."

"Trip?" I ask, almost offended at the idea. *He's* tripping. "Trip *where*?"

"Think of this as part boot camp, part tropical holiday." Briggs's pool-blue eyes flare in the strobing expressway lights, which the blacked-out windows have muted into a soft amber. He reaches over his seat to pat my shoulder, but I squirm backward. "You've been under a lot of stress, haven't you?"

"Stress? The kidnapping's been stressful, yeah."

My abductor throws back his head and unleashes a loud, obnoxious guffaw, his Adam's apple bouncing as his buddies join in. "How many times I gotta say it: you're not being kidnapped," he finally says. "Your mum said you need help sorting your life out—"

"Except for being thrown into this van by you, my life is fine!" Mom planned this. Whatever this is—kidnapping or not—it's something *she* arranged.

"We're a bit unusual, but we help scrappy lads like yourself get back in line." Briggs pats my arm with fatherly cheer. "Let's get you some fresh air, some physical routine, and your confidence will flow right back."

A fitness camp? Mom had me abducted for *exercise*? Is this like Tough Mudder or something, where grabbing you out of bed is all part of how "extreme" it is?

There *has* to be more to it than this.

I shrug. For now, it'll be best if Briggs thinks I believe him. He'll drop his guard, and when that happens, I won't hesitate to run.

Streetlights pass through the tinted backseat window, briefly re-illuminating Briggs. His gray shirt clings to perfect, bowling-ball-round biceps. "Your mum says your dad isn't with the family no more," he says, popping a stick of gum into his mouth. "He lives in the U.K.?"

"Um...yeah. A town called Tipwich."

"All right, I'm from Colchester, and that's a stone's damn throw! My family holidayed in Tipwich once. Seaside village. Aw, I miss the seaside..." Briggs's crinkled eyes drift, lost in some beautiful, watery memory, but then a memory of my own sweeps over me: Dad's Tipwich home lies along a rocky shoreline where waves chop against a massive lighthouse. A boardwalk overflows with a promenade of taffy shops and hundreds of different places to eat (Ambrose only has the one pizza joint). Before my dad screwed up our family, we'd constantly fly to Tipwich. Dad took me rowing and sailing; he taught me knot-tying and navigation. Life had variety then. Mom and Dad were already separated but didn't scream at each other as much—or at me—and for a few years, things were just...special. Then my grandma died, Dad ditched us, Mom went hyper-Jesus nuclear, and I've been staring at cornfields ever since.

"So, Connor, when's the last time you saw the water?" Briggs asks, as if he could hear my nostalgic thoughts. It's impossible, but...something in Briggs's voice relaxes me. He has Dad's accent.

"It's been a long time," I admit.

A warm, gum-chewing grin spreads across my kidnapper's face. "Well...you're in luck."

The moment I've been waiting for, the moment Briggs drops his tense, watchful guard over me, never arrives. After another hour, the van dumps us off at O'Hare Airport, just outside Chicago. A plane. They're planning on flying me somewhere. Briggs hums cheerfully, but always trots a few inches behind, his hands—as toughened as coils of shipping rope—never farther than a single grab away from my neck.

I can't get on a plane with these people.

At some point in the chaos of the airport, I'll duck away and scream my head off until security swarms all over this British bastard.

What'll happen then? I catch a ride home, back to my mom, the person who *planned* for Briggs to fly me somewhere? What if she just tries again?

Briggs, his team, and I wade through O'Hare's packed, early morning security line until finally reaching TSA. My nerve never shows up. I could run, but my brain is too agile at gazing into the future, a gift and burden belonging to all anxious people. Mom *would* try again. Or Briggs would inform the police that my mother asked him to bring me here, and a simple phone call would confirm this. Then there's the vague possibility that this really is nothing more than a bougie boot camp (one that's a bit overzealous), I make a big, gay, embarrassing federal case out of it, and the only one who ends up in trouble is me.

Now isn't the right time, and once again, I defeat myself.

Briggs approaches the TSA agent and flashes my passport—a picture of a ten-year-old with round, smiling cheeks, looking nothing like me now: shitty postured and frowning, with cheeks already scruffy from a day of no shaving. Briggs's coworkers—short, scowling men who keep tossing me sideways glares—load their bags onto the X-ray belt while Briggs empties his pockets. Once Briggs pours his wallet and change into a plastic basin, he carefully removes a stick that looks like an all-black Pez dispenser.

"What's that?" I ask.

"Good luck charm." He drops it into the bucket. "I don't fly without it."

I kick off the cheap, plastic flip-flops Briggs gave me and place them in my own plastic bin. Soon, it'll be my turn to step through the body scanner with its robot arm whirling inside a clear, plastic tomb. Ario's bamboo recorder bounces on its leather string underneath my hoodie. If I step through that gate, I'll be flying away from my boyfriend.

"This boot camp...how long will we be gone?" I ask.

"A few days," Briggs replies, slapping my back. "Come on, your mum bought you a vacation. Don't you want a break?"

The word "break" breaks me. Like a magic word, it loosens my shoulders and lifts my heart. *A Goddamn break. I need one so badly from this horrific summer.* I allow a glimmer of hope into my thoughts: Mom said she's tired of fighting. Is this really a vacation? Could this be a peace offering? Mom loves me. She hasn't shown it lately, but she does. So, either my mom hired men to kidnap and hurt me...or she hired them to get me out of her hair and toughen me up on a sandy beach somewhere.

Which one sounds more like Mom? The latter.

The image of a tropical beach worms its way into my brain's pleasure center, and in that moment, I choose to believe in my mom.

Briggs digs one final item from his pocket: my phone, boxed in its turquoise case. He must have taken it out of the wall charger after...*after he carried you screaming out of your home*, a nasty voice argues inside my head. "This phone is your reward for good work," he says. "All you have to do is put in the effort, and in a few days, I hand it back to you and send you home."

There isn't any time to reach for my phone before Briggs lobs it into the bucket already traveling away on a conveyor belt through security.

———

Briggs loads me up with trashy snacks and trashier celebrity magazines for the flight, which is a six-hour journey to San José. It isn't until we're seated for our flight that Briggs clarifies this isn't San Jose, California, but San José, Costa Rica.

Costa Rica? That's another country. That's Central America, like some Jurassic Park *shit.*

The urge to bolt out of the jet overwhelms me, but the flight attendants have already closed the cabin doors. I could scream, but every time I play that scenario in my head, it ends with the authorities confirming that, yes, my mom wants this to happen.

"My mom actually paid for me to fly to Costa Rica?" I ask shakily as I weigh whether to buckle my seatbelt.

"Costa Rican beaches, bright blue as a sapphire," Briggs says, the crinkles reforming around his young eyes. "You're gonna love our island, but I have to tell you: we're not cheap. And we've only been paid half. You're free to go home whenever you want, but if you break our contract, we still send you the full bill. And your mum's made it clear that if you break our contract early, you'll have to pay back everything yourself."

Pay for this entire trip myself? Whatever she's already paid, it has to at least be a few weeks of her pulling extra shifts in the ICU. She can't even afford to buy me new shoes.

"Why do we have to go to another country just for a boot camp?" I ask. "There's, like, a thousand of them in Illinois."

"Because Illinois isn't *gorgeous*," Briggs chuckles. "Why put

Disney World in Florida, why not in Illinois? Why go to Paris, there's paintings here in Illinois? Because Illinois sucks, mate. It's where people live; it's not where you holiday. We don't want our camp to be a bunch of hard work in some dreary bunghole of a strip mall. The unplugging and the beauty of nature are part of it all."

Unplug. After a century without my phone, I don't need any more unplugging. I need to be plugged in, I need my life back. I also need some beauty, it's true. I have had it with wall-to-wall soybean fields and nothing pretty in my life. Sometimes, a gay boy needs a little beauty, a little fanciness, a little *luxury*, or he'll starve.

This is a vacation away from the snake pit at home, Major. Try to enjoy yourself.

I buckle myself into my window seat. Around me, dozens of untroubled people leaf through magazines and nap against their shuttered windows. Satisfied that I've chosen to cooperate, Briggs grins, his salt-and-pepper scruff circling two bullet-hole-shaped dimples. He pulls out his black Pez dispenser and tucks it into the front pocket for takeoff.

As the flight crawls by hour after hour, Ricky Hannigan's note— *NIGHTLIGHT*—seeps back into my thoughts. He wrote it over and over. His dying words. *HELP CONNOR.*

I can't help you, Mr. Hannigan. I've got my own bag of crap to worry about.

By the time we land, it's daytime, but I don't know how many hours have passed because the sky is blistered with storm clouds. Guided by Briggs, I stagger through a large, sleek airport crammed with passengers in floral-print shirts and walls dotted with palm trees. This lifts my heart a bit; I haven't seen palms since Mom and I left Jacksonville. The possibility that this kidnapping is indeed a vacation continues to prove itself.

Briggs's two other men continue glaring at me as we navigate the emptying terminal. I'm dying to change out of these ratty clothes. I've had them on since...yesterday? It all feels like one day. It wouldn't take much to convince me I'm still in my bed in Ambrose—that there is no luxury boot camp, and I'm having one weird bastard of a dream.

WELCOME TO JUAN SANTAMARÍA INTERNATIONAL AIRPORT, a sign reads in English beneath a similar greeting in different languages. My mouth falls open as reality registers: Costa Rica. I'm not in America anymore...Pins and needles invade my head; being kidnapped was startling enough, but finding myself in a new country is a YIKES of a different color. I only have Briggs's word (and my mom's approval) that we're headed to a fitness camp.

Why is it so easy for me to trust scary, unpredictable men?

Oh, that's right, my dad.

All Briggs needed to do was speak confidently with a country English accent, and I let him smuggle me to another country without asking for so much as driver's license verification.

There's nowhere to run now. Even if I were coordinated enough to duck away from these men, I'm multiple countries away from anyone I know and I'm still in the clothes I fell asleep in, without money or a phone. Continuing with Briggs is the most sensible plan...for now. Then I'm going to need proof he's telling the truth—a pamphlet, at least.

The airport is refrigerator cold, but it's a sweet relief from the stinging, wet heat of the tarmac. Our caravan of exhausted bodies clomps toward the next gate, where a terrified girl waits for us.

Around my age and height, she shivers in a pale pink, spaghetti-strap dress. Dark brown, highlighted hair hangs in messy strands around her neck. Two other men, also dressed in black, surround her as she trembles in place like a frightened dog. But not her eyes—they're furious.

She's been taken, just like me.

The black-dressed men give Briggs a hard time about being kept waiting, but he charges ahead toward the girl and says, "Molly Partridge, I'm Ben Briggs. You're freezing. They keep it so nasty cold in here. Let's get you a coat."

"She won't wear a coat," says one of the men.

"No coat?" Briggs stares into Molly's steady, bloodshot eyes; she shakes her head quickly. "You don't have to wear one. Come on, we're late."

A gale wind kicks up as our endless journey continues with a Jeep ride through a lushly green Costa Rican party town. Store signs and posh hotels advertise the pleasures of Jacó to American tourists, who slurp booze out of coconuts as they stagger through the streets despite the worsening weather. Coconut palms spring out of every corner, their fronds beating frantically in this dangerous wind. The afternoon sky might as well be midnight. Rain hasn't fallen yet, but it absolutely has plans to do so.

I sneak my hand under my hoodie to hold Ario's recorder and try not to think of how we're thousands of miles apart.

The ominous weather has long since emptied the beach of its guests. Deck chairs are shuffled away by hotel workers, while out in the darkened ocean, catamarans bounce in the breaking waves against the pegs pinning them to shore. We arrive at a vacant dock with two massive, iron pylons tied to an open-shelled patrol boat, the kind they use in the Coast Guard. Molly and I turn to each other, neither of us able to open our eyes more than a slit.

A van, a plane, a Jeep, and now a boat? In this ocean? In THIS near-monsoon?

A heavy gale whips out from the gulf, tossing around my already unkempt hair. The pitch-black water...to say it scares me is an understatement. Anything could be out there—anything could be *down* there. Briggs scoots us along the dock as the other team members board their seacraft and secure our luggage with bungee cords. Time to climb aboard. I breathe steadily to psych myself into this, but as I grip the stern's ladder, Briggs tugs me back.

"Ladies first," he orders. I shrug at Molly, and she rolls her eyes before hoisting herself on board. I'm about to follow her when something stops me: a word stenciled in white along the boat's starboard side. A word I can't believe I didn't notice until now. A word that assaults every nerve in my body:

NIGHTLIGHT

NIGHTLIGHT, Ricky's Playbill message repeated. *NIGHTLIGHT. HELP CONNOR.*

It was a warning. Mr. Hannigan knew these men were coming.

My fog is gone. I blink my eyes clear and bellow, "MOLLY, GET OFF THE BOAT! GET OFF THE BOAT RIGHT NOW!" She spins on the deck, her hair and dress flapping like a flag in the wind. "Get back!" I shriek at Briggs, shoving the muscular statue with the last drops of power in my terrier-sized body. He doesn't budge. "MOLLY, THEY'RE NOT WHO THEY SAY THEY ARE!" Molly sprints back along the deck, but two of the men snatch her. She screams. Behind me, Briggs stands deathly still on the dock—a dock conveniently empty of all human beings except us—and his smiling eyes lock onto mine. "Who are you really?" I ask, close to hyperventilating.

Briggs digs into his pocket and removes the all-black Pez dispenser—his good luck charm—and touches it gently to my chest. I'm too curious to move. A smarter person would've moved. A crack of violet electricity punches my heart backward. As the force launches me off my feet, I slam against the dock, and once again, air vanishes from my lungs. Molly screams as I struggle to brush the dusting of stars from my vision.

Stay awake, Connor...Keep conscious...

Ben Briggs—my mother's hired goon—kneels beside me and whispers, "All aboard."

CHAPTER THREE

HELP CONNOR

TWO MONTHS AGO

Ario texts me at the worst possible times, I swear.

Mom and I are grabbing an early dinner at Sue's Diner before her night shift, and the hour before she goes to work is stressful enough without all these buzzing notifications. When I sneak a quick peek, they're exactly what I expect from my boyfriend: support. It's actually something closer to aggressive, hostile support, but it's hard to blame him. He's just trying to help me come out. The sooner I come out to my mom, the better. This "before moment" is like edging, but for anxiety attacks.

Let me know as soon as you do it! he texts, followed by emojis of crossed fingers. *I know it's hard,* he continues in rapid fire, *but omg you'll feel great on the other side! Here for you!*

I'm amazed I'm even able to hold my phone with this cold sweat pumping through my hands. He's right, I know I need to do this. Everybody who's gay does it. Nothing can happen in my life until I do it. I just, obviously, can't do it ten minutes before my mom has to go to work to nurse preemie babies for twelve hours. It's not fair to her, and it won't look good on me. Next week is finals, and I don't want this hanging over my head if it goes wrong. The week after that is my birthday, and I don't want that getting ruined either. So, it has to happen sometime after my birthday, and honestly, I never promised Ario I was having The Conversation today, so I don't know what these texts are supposed to be—a nudge? A mind game?

Realizing that I don't need to have this talk for at least another three weeks sends a cool prickling sensation up and down my arms, as if a strangler suddenly released his grip from my throat. I plop my phone onto the leather booth and return to my milkshake with a renewed zest for life.

Sue's Diner hasn't had a fresh coat of paint since the moon landing, but Ambrose doesn't care if things are old and busted, as long as they stay the same. These menus were printed eons before my birth, and there'd be riots if they changed a single item. The only menu modifications have been updated pricing stickers, which lay plastered and crooked over the yellowing laminate. Still, Sue herself has proudly never missed a day of work in sixty years. Well into her late eighties, she sports a Pepto Bismol-pink wig and totes around an oxygen tank as she observes her twenty-year-old busboy at work. He kneels on the countertop by the refrigerator-sized milkshake machine and fiddles behind it delicately with a wrench.

"You gotta slap the motor," Sue badgers him, huffing like she's frustrated that she can't hop up there and take care of the damn thing herself.

Sweating and fidgeting, the busboy says, "I'm gonna break it. It's fragile."

"That machine is gonna outlive you, Gabe. It'll bury us all. Slap it!"

Gabe winces and does as he's told. The moment his palm makes contact, the motor belches once and then shimmies to life with a satisfying thrum. The corners of Sue's lips upturn and she gives her iron monstrosity a grim, respectful nod. No one in Ambrose is happier than Sue at the cultural resurgence of old-timey nostalgia, or else someone would surely complain about this ancient beast. It probably spits flecks of lead paint into each milkshake. Nevertheless, Sue's shakes are famously brick thick and arctic cold, and I'll drink them until I die. I don't know how she does it, but her strawberry shakes taste like someone froze Fruity Pebbles in milk.

I shouldn't be freaking out so much about coming out. My sexual orientation isn't gay—it's milkshake.

I ignore Ario's next nudging text and scrape the final remains of my shake out of the galvanized tin sidecar. "You got your badge?" I ask my mom, and she jerks away from her Vanilla Pepsi to hunt through her purse. After a tense moment of searching, she pulls out her multitiered nursing badge: *Marcia Major, BSN, RN, St. Josephine's Medical Center*, and clips it to her scrub top. She forgot it last week and had to turn around and go all the way home to get it. Day shift nurses couldn't leave until she came back, people complained—it was a whole nightmare. Mom can't afford another write-up.

"Oh, thank you," she says on a relieved breath.

"Got your phone charger?"

"Yes."

"Wallet?"

"Yep."

"You got enough on Starbucks for a venti?"

"Who's the mom here? You or me?"

"Me, duh." I grin and chomp another fry as she giggles into her Pepsi. A surge of warmth surrounds me like a protective shield—almost visible, shimmering as gold and ultraviolet as sunrays. I will do anything to preserve the ecosystem between my mother and me.

If it means she goes on thinking I'm straight while I meet up with Ario during her night shifts, then that sounds like a pretty good life to me. "Do you got enough?"

Mom scrolls through her Starbucks app until she finds our card's amount. "Eh, maybe just a tall," she groans.

"Use the free drink reward."

"Oh, no—"

"You're gonna go through a whole shift with just that little wiener-sized tall coffee?"

"Connor!" Mom shrieks quietly, scandalized but delighted at my G-rated swearing. "I'll just use the Keurig in the break room."

"You said it's broke and they're in no rush fixing it, now come on, just take it, it's free."

"I said *no*; I'm saving the reward for your birthday."

"Well, I don't deserve all that."

It slipped out before I realized I meant it. Our eyes find each other as seriousness rapidly fills the space that moments ago had been nothing but lighthearted. Her dark-circled eyes soften; her head tilts as if to say, *My poor baby.* I don't mind her response—my mother's pity and empathy are all the stitches I currently need on my sliced-up heart.

"Don't ever say that," she whispers, taking my hand across the table. I almost gasp, it's been so long since she's done this. "You've had a tough time at school, and I see you trying. Everybody's got tough times. Lord knows I have. You've got a work ethic, Connor, and that counts for something. You're gonna make such a good da—"

My hand turns cold and limp inside hers as she stops herself.

A good dad.

She doesn't mean "a good dad" as in "someday," she means as

in next week when Vicky is due to have her baby. Mom slowly withdraws her hand from mine, as if loving me is a big-ticket purchase she's changed her mind about buying. She counts out cash for the tip and mutters, "I was reading an article saying it's good luck for dads and sons to have birthdays so close together..."

I turn as stony and quiet as a grave until a dreadful idea strikes me: *If I came out, that would kill this conspiracy theory that I'm Vicky's baby daddy good and quick.*

"Momma...?" I ask, my terrified throat clotted with a thick residue of milkshake.

"Yes...?" she asks, her voice engorging with hope.

Say it, Major. End this bullshit and say it.

"I forgot," I choke out as the door to the diner swings open on a ring-a-ling bell.

Every head in the room turns toward the enormous, bearded raven standing alone in the doorway, as if all the lights had gone out except in this one spot. For one startling moment, the Reverend Stanley Packard holds the diner's breath in his hands. His narrowed eyes appraise us through glasses perched above a beard so full it might be carved out of solid oak. As a short man myself, the Reverend's proportions never cease to stun me silent. He has to duck slightly to clear the top of the door and enter diagonally to accommodate the belly stretching the buttons of his black pastor's shirt. The white thumbprint of a clerical collar clamps around his reddening throat.

"He looks like a bear standing in attack mode," Vicky once said, but it felt weird to agree with her—*bear* tends to trigger a different response among gays, and my feelings about the Reverend are complicated enough. My mom is obviously in love with him; she'd

spend every waking moment volunteering at his church if she didn't have the hospital to think about.

"Oh no," Mom curses to herself as she spots the Reverend. "I gotta get going, but...oh..." Mom opens her front-facing camera to give herself a once-over, but her slumped shoulders tell me she hates her reflection. She can't wear any excessive makeup or scents in the NICU, so my mom is painfully limited in ways she can gussy herself up for the Reverend.

As she frantically brushes her long, frizzing hair, I distract myself from my embarrassment with Ario's texts: *So proud of u! This takes so much guts! Hope ur ok!*

The only guts I have at the moment are my intestines, tangled like a ball of rubber bands as the Reverend enters the diner. *God, please don't let him spot us.* He weaves through Sue's as a politician would: grinning wickedly, shaking hands, and cracking inside jokes with every customer—many of whom are donning John Deere or MAGA hats. So much red and green, it looks like Christmas. All of them flush to be blessed with the Reverend's attention as he greets them:

"I put in a word for your sister at Ben Sherman's."

"Have they fixed your transmission yet?"

"Let me see what I can do."

"You slipped out of my service eight minutes early last week. Hope everything's okay."

"Don't let him put too much hot sauce on it; pepper's not good for him, trust me."

It lasts for minutes. Person by person, Reverend Packard swoops through the crowd of diners—he's their preacher, their therapist, their mechanic, their doctor. If you've got a problem, he's on the case... And if you've got personal business, he's up to his nose in it. If I ever came out—*when, Major, when*—it won't be a conversation just between my mom and me. The Reverend *will* have his say.

Mom and I already paid our bill, but we remain in the booth, knowing we must wait our turn to be anointed by the Reverend. When our time comes, he looms like the Angel of Death for a moment and then plunks down beside my mom, kissing her cheek (*"Marcia!"*). I half-expect him to insist we stay and eat with him. Mom would totally blow off her shift if the Reverend asked her to, so I blurt, "Ah, Mom, you don't want to be late."

"Don't be rude," she snaps, instinctively leaping to the Reverend's defense, even though nobody asked her to take sides.

"Mr. Major," the Reverend says, booping my nose as if I were a puppy. "I'm not staying. I've got my own table. Ooh, I hope you're not drinking coffee? Too much, and you'll never get that growth spurt."

"Pretty sure I'm done with that," I say, slurping my second cup of the night. I haven't had a growing pain in over a year—it's officially going to be a teeny life. Honestly, I'm relieved I won't be cramming myself through doorways for the rest of my days like the Reverend.

"I—I wish I'd known you were coming," Mom says.

"Don't let me hold you up," he says. "You've got babies to save. The most important work there is." He tosses her a wink, and she blooms with an inner light. "And looking stunning doing it."

Mom can only laugh pitifully as she taps her flat, wilted hair. "This old smock." I battle a tidal wave of cringe as my mom falls prey to these warmed-over pickup lines.

"I only stopped by because I wanted to introduce Connor to a good friend,"—the Reverend only has *good friends*—"one of the ones he's going to be helping with Meals on Wheels."

Yesterday, my mom stunned me with the news that she's commandeered my entire summer by making me drive hot meals to the
elderly and indigent of Ambrose and Greater Noble County.

"Your friend's come here to the diner, but still needs me to
drive 'em meals?" I ask. Mom and the Reverend are momentarily
speechless by my attitude. "I'm just asking!"

"Ricky Hannigan is a very independent person," the Reverend
says with forced calm. "He likes being out and about, and he likes
being with people whenever possible. But the summer gets brutal
and tires him, and his health goes up and down like a yo-yo. Going
out is a treat for him, you understand."

"Yes, sir," I say as the Reverend watches me across the booth—
studying me, knocking his knuckles to the tabletop as he weighs
teaching me a lesson in manners.

"Ricky is a special person. To me and the town."

"Yes, sir."

Obediently, as if we didn't have any will of our own, the Reverend
leads Mom and me toward the exit. Vacillating as he does between
menace and jollity, the Reverend sets the tune and we all dance to
it. "Don't be late for those babies!" he cries, giving my mother a hug
she'll treasure for the rest of the night and then sending her outside
alone to our car. Before I can follow her out, the Reverend tugs me
through a crowd of smiling, gawping sycophants until we reach a
man in a motorized chair. He laughs at a table of three middle-aged
women I've never seen before—they must be from White Eagle or
somewhere farther outside of town.

"Ricky, I want you to meet a young friend of mine," the Reverend
says.

Ricky Hannigan lifts his large, round eyes and pivots his chair to me. His neck is bent slightly, pressed against the chair's headrest. A graying, sallow-faced man, Ricky is slender and, from what I can tell, immobile from the waist down: his slightly tremoring fingers operate a control toggle on his chair. Ricky smiles—a relaxed, warm smile, not the shark's grin the Reverend gives people. He glances me over before pivoting slowly to the Reverend and muttering, "C...cute."

Ricky's dining companions laugh, but the Reverend and I turn scarlet with unease. "It's nice to meet you," I say, charging ahead as if the man hadn't said anything, and I shake his hand, which he grips softly.

"G..." Ricky says, but each syllable requires concentration and determination. "Gentle...man."

"Good to see you out with your old theater gang," the Reverend simpers, dipping ever so slightly into contempt. Ricky's friends harden.

"Hi, Stanny," one of them says.

Before I can savor the delights of big ol' scary Reverend Packard being called "Stanny," he clears his throat and snaps back, "Reverend Packard works fine, thank you. You came all the way from the city to eat at our humble little greasy spoon?"

"For our friend," another one replies icily.

"Where would we be without friends?" The Reverend swallows hard and pushes me closer to Ricky with his hefty paw. "Anyway, Ricky, you'll be seeing a lot of Connor this summer. You and your mother will be on his Meals on Wheels route."

Smiling, Ricky moans appreciatively until a light switches off behind his eyes. His smile collapses. He glances at the Reverend with eyes frozen open in fright. We all stiffen as the mood darkens imperceptibly. "C...Con...?" Ricky asks.

"Connor Major, yes, I mentioned him—"

"No," he whines. In a blink, he's crying. Frustrated tears. Two of his friends scramble forward in their booth, reaching across the table to pat his shoulder, but none of us are sure what went wrong.

My name seems to have set him off.

"No *what*, Ricky?" the Reverend asks, glancing around the diner, petrified of being at the center of this growing tantrum. "You're all right?"

"NO," Ricky growls as he winces at the fussing hands of his friends. "Con...nor..."

"Maybe I should take off," I say, but no one is paying me the slightest attention. Ricky struggles in his chair as his friends and the Reverend fail to calm him. Weeping silently, Ricky finds me through the cluster of people surrounding him. Our eyes lock. A long, pleading glance. I want to run, but how would I explain myself to the Reverend?

"Conn...r...Y...you...can't..." Ricky pivots again to the Reverend, only this time, his eyes are red, wild, and pumping with fury. The Reverend jumps backward. "No...You kn...know..."

"I know what...?" the Reverend asks desperately.

"YOU...KN...KNOW." Ricky spins his fury to the other diners— not his friends, but the entirety of the restaurant. Accusing them. Grizzled, impassive faces stare back under the brims of mesh trucker hats. Even Sue has abandoned her watch at the struggling shake maker to approach Ricky. "YOU KN...KN...KNOW. ALL...KNOW."

"Ricky, you're frightening everyone—"

"Con—nor..." Energy abandons Ricky as swiftly as it came. He slumps an inch back into his chair, his eyes wandering back to me a final time. I can't be sure, but his next word sounds like *"help."*

CHAPTER FOUR
THE INK-BLACK DRINK

TODAY

For hours, Molly and I have been below deck in the Nightlight boat. My shoulders sway heavily in rhythm with the choppy water beneath our hull. Above us, floodlights pierce through the burlap canopy shielding our berth from a rainstorm that, in less than a minute, went from droplets to a downpour that is collecting under my feet in wider and wider puddles. We wait and worry on benches in the lampless lower berth where our kidnappers have stored the rest of their junk: shabbily folded tarps, coils of heavy rope, and open cans of paint. The boat's chilly iron bench unhinges the skin from my bones, and I have to tug down my gym shorts to better shield my thighs from the cold metal. As I do, my left wrist catches on something hard—*handcuffs*.

I'm so out of it from the taser, I forgot Briggs cuffed me to a pipe.

Seated across from me, handcuffed to her own bench, Molly stares through a jungle of wet hair. A tiny stream of rainwater overflows from the buckling canopy and drops down the back of her dress. She leaps, cursing wildly and dancing out of the way of the errant water. This is the second time she's gotten doused from above. Looks like I got the better bench.

"Where'd you come from?" she asks, her voice finally returning.

"Chicago," I generalize. Outside of Ambrose, no one knows

where Ambrose is, so I'm used to answering this question with "Chicago."

"I'm from Arizona. I was at a party...at my dad's club..."

"I hope these guys brought you a change of clothes. You're not dressed for running drills."

"Drills?"

"The boot camp."

"We're going to a boot camp?" Molly's lips tighten. Something in her tone drops my stomach. "They told me it was a retreat...to learn business management,"—her twitching eyes begin to water—"which was clearly bullshit." Molly whimpers into her raised arm and moans, "Clearly bullshit, clearly bullshit." I wish she'd stop because now my guts are swirling through my body like a Chinese dragon.

I'm one hundred percent sure this is a kidnapping, but I'm zero percent sure *why*. As I was abducted, Mom said "I love you" softly, reassuringly, the way she used to when carrying me to bed after I fell asleep in front of *Doctor Who*. Bubbling acid rises in my stomach with a panicked realization: Mom wanted this. Wanted me kidnapped. Wanted me handcuffed to a boat. The black van with its black windows—a PredatorMobile—lurked around my house all evening, so Mom must have arranged the abduction before dinner. Maybe even during her shift. Why? Because I needed toughening up? And what does any of this have to do with Ricky Hannigan? Mom and Ricky never met each other.

"You—you know R-R-Ricky Hannigan?" I ask, my jaw trembling from the cold.

"Who?" Molly asks, retaking her seat.

"Nothing." I bite the inside of my cheek to stop the tears already pooling. Crying would be easy—*so easy*—but it won't help me escape.

It was a long shot hoping Molly knew anything about the dead man I delivered meals to, but there has to be a connection between her situation and mine. One of the last things Ricky ever did was scribble the word *Nightlight* in messy, urgent letters. The name on this boat.

Overhead, a corner of the canopy flaps open in the wind, sending in more aggressive weather. I fold my legs together on the bench as seawater floods over Molly's feet. She whines—strained, like a dog left alone too long—and pulls against the handcuffs trapping her to the pipe. Except neither of us are going anywhere. Poor Molly—it's as if we're in one of those water rafting rides where there's always that one person in the group who gets the most drenched.

"Of course there's a storm," Molly mutters, wiping rain from her mouth, her arm tremoring inside the tightened bracelet. Molly's eyes are my eyes. *We're two trapped animals.* Heavy footsteps scatter back and forth above us on the deck. The storm must be stressing out our kidnappers because they haven't stopped scuttling around since we shoved off. "Who are they?"

"I don't know."

"You tried to warn me. Why all of a sudden? What happened?"

I blow out sharp breaths—*in through your nose, out through your mouth*—and tell the story of my deliveries to Ricky Hannigan, his death, his Nightlight warning, and how after traveling to Costa Rica...here Nightlight is, printed on the side of our boat. "But I live in Tucson and don't know any Ricky Hannigan," Molly says, her eyes narrowing with calculation. My story—and all of its disquieting incompleteness—has plucked her nerves. "My dad's the one who hired these people..." Her shoulders fall, defeated by her next thought: "Our families wanted us gone."

A thick ache moans in my chest. Mom and I have been fighting so much since my junior year ended, but I never thought she could do something like this to me. The whole idea is unbelievable—poor white trash Marcia Major, working night shifts and paying for her son's kidnapping with her overtime checks. "I dunno," I say. "Wherever we're going, it's not a boot camp."

"It might be a boot camp. Just a little extra *boot*—"

Rain floods our cabin as the canopy tears completely away from its hooks. A heaving splash ricochets off the floor, soaking my hoodie with tons of seawater. It was my turn to get drenched anyhow, but Molly didn't escape clean either: her pink party dress clings to every corner of her scrawny frame. I can almost hear her thinking, *Why did I turn down Briggs's coat?*

As the floodwaters settle above Molly's ankles, footsteps grow louder at the top of the stairs. Where the canopy used to be, Briggs looms overhead, floodlights silhouetting his dripping, body-built shadow. His blue eyes still shimmer, but they're darker—riskier—like ice over blacktop.

He descends the stairs shaking a key ring...

Once Briggs unshackles Molly and me, we're brought above deck to join the other kidnappers: blurry, faceless men in the storm-darkened afternoon. They hustle past us, their strained breathing like a whisper in my ears: *these men are freaking out about something*. My flip-flops squish through inch-deep water along the upper deck, and I crane my neck to the sky as the downpour hits my dry lips like nectar. I open wide to hydrate my even drier gullet, and although it does nothing to clear my mental fog, the rain does absorb the frustration that has grown around it.

As wave after wave spills over onto the deck, kidnappers grab plastic buckets and chuck the sea back into itself a gallon at a time. "Do not lose us out here," Briggs shouts at the captain—an older, stooping man gripping the boat's helm. "This'll only get worse as the night tears on!"

"I've done this before," the captain replies. "I kept the bearing."

Splashing thunderously, Briggs clomps across the deck, snatches a rounded handle at the base of the bow's floodlight, and scans it over the rollicking sea. In Ambrose, we use floodlights on winter nights to avoid colliding with deer. What is Briggs afraid we could collide with out here? A whale? A shark? A reef?

"They don't know where we are," Molly whispers, her whole body shaking. I wrap my arm around her shoulder to warm her, but she smacks me away with a stinging jolt. I mumble an apology as she throws me a jittery glare. It's not like I was trying to feel her up.

"Out there, do you see it?" Briggs hollers.

"I don't see a thing but open water," replies the captain.

Same, old man. There isn't even a horizon line. Endless black sea merges with a thunderhead-choked sky; we're in a rickety vessel flying through a void. I'm nowhere near home. Thousands of miles gone from my mom and Ario. He doesn't even know what happened to me. Or that I'm gone at all.

I have to get away from these people.

Then a greenish glob—only a speck at first—pierces the obsidian sea. A chorus of other kidnappers begin to speak up about how they've spotted land, and Briggs cries into the rain: "Do you see what happens when you BELIEVE?!"

Molly and I find each other's eyes at the same time. We don't need to say our fears out loud because we seem to instantly think the same thing: *that was quite a churchy outburst from the man abducting us.*

As we approach our unknown destination, white flashes of lightning play peek-a-boo with the newly visible horizon. *Flash! Peek-a-boo.* The outline of an island. Then darkness. Lightning comes again. *Flash! Peek-a-boo.* Dense jungle and a high rock cliff.

No lights. No life.

My stomach lurches as our boat slows into the island's mouth, a crescent-shaped bay eager to swallow us whole. "Look sharp, lads," Briggs orders. "Coming ashore." My soggy feet twitch on the edge of the dock as a shitty idea takes over me: *we aren't handcuffed anymore.* I hook Molly's spindly arm inside mine. There's no time for her to jerk away or even ask "What are you doing?" before I fling both of us into the water.

The sea is warm. Molly kicks toward the shore with vigor—she's latched instantly onto my idea; it's wild how you can sync up with a stranger during a crisis. Beneath the surface, everything blurs. One of my flip-flops disappears into a briar of brightly colored sea plants, but I have scarier concerns: as surge after surge rushes up my nostrils, my limbs struggle to swim or even kick against the surf breaks that fight powerfully to keep me away from shore. Energy evacuates my body like a stuck pig. A spike of fresh adrenaline forces my arms to paddle faster, but pins and needles fill my limbs and stiffen my fingers.

Atrophy. *You're panicking, and it's shutting down your body.*

I scream under the sea, vomiting a flurry of bubbles. The island's shoreline floats only a few feet away, but the fizzing continues to fill my skull. *My head weighs too much...*

I break the surface for a quick sip of air. Laughter booms in the distance. I kick my spasming, stiffening legs until, clutching at the sand, I crawl from the bay on atrophy-frozen hands and knees.

Already arrived, Molly limps over the shore to help me. I collapse onto my back, but that's when the real pain begins: a branch—as long as a wizard's staff—pokes into my windpipe. Molly's stringy hair and fierce eyes drill down as she pushes the staff into my throat.

"WHO ARE YOU?" she shrieks.

"What...?" I choke.

"What is Nightlight?!"

"I told you—everything—" I haven't caught my breath yet from the swim, and I'm already fighting for air.

"Tell me who they are!"

"I don't know!" A sob breaks from my throat. This must be enough to convince Molly I'm genuine because the branch loosens against my neck.

"Don't follow me." She chucks her branch into the bay and bolts toward a wall of midnight-dark jungle trees. I remain motionless on my back, my hands pumping open and closed with newfound freedom—at least Molly shook me out of my atrophy.

The Nightlight boat barrels across one final surf break and then collides with the beach. As the vessel shudders to a stop, four men leap into the shallow bay. Three sprint into the forest after Molly, while the remaining one—my good friend Benjamin Briggs—crunches closer over shards of driftwood. "Hope you're not too tired to walk," he says, kneeling fatherly by my side. "Bit of a trek from here, I'm afraid."

"Where are you taking us?" I whimper, thoroughly defeated. Couldn't I be dragged God-knows-where in the morning? Just let me sleep here, half-dead on the shore.

Struggling screams cut through the thunder. One of the kidnappers—nothing but a shadow—hoists Molly off her feet and carries her back. The rest of Briggs's team hauls their boat onto a wooden weigh station far from the tide, where it ascends a ramp before being fastened in place with bungee cords.

"Mr. Major, Miss Partridge," Briggs announces, rising, "as I said before, I'm Ben Briggs, and you're here to do as you're told. On your feet."

Standing sucks worse than I imagined. My legs are as limp and beaten as bread dough. Far ahead, a mile-high jungle looms while palm fronds flap like eagle wings in the storm. Briggs marches us to the jungle's edge, where the ghostly remnants of the dark-green sky illuminate a signpost. The sign—a crucifix carved from a broad chunk of wood—welcomes us:

NIGHTLIGHT MINISTRIES
SURRENDER YOUR SINS!

"The jungle gets darker from here," Briggs says. "Your families want you to have these, and they'll be proper light."

A bright, electronic blue illuminates the dark and burns my eyes as Briggs presents two phones, both displays lit with full battery charges (but no signal). One is encased in a turquoise shell—mine. The lock screen picture is different than usual: a gorgeous, shirtless boy with olive skin. Dark tufts of hair circle his nipples. He kisses at the screen. At me.

Ario texted this selfie weeks ago. Someone went into my phone and set this as my lock screen.

A chunky, black OtterBox protects Briggs's other phone; in this lock screen picture, Molly smiles like I've never seen her smile before. Her freckled arms wrap around a tall dark-skinned girl. A girlfriend.

Molly and I have something in common after all.

CHAPTER FIVE
ARIO'S RECORDER

ONE WEEK AGO

A man's dinner grows cold in the trunk of my car. But Mr. Hannigan won't have to wait long for his mashed potatoes and rice pudding—I'm ahead of schedule. I purposely delivered the other Meals on Wheels early so I would have time to make this side trip to Ario's. Both Ario and the Hannigans live one town over in White Eagle, which is still a fifteen-minute drive from my house. Illinois is made up of either Chicago, Chicago suburbs, or utter farmland desolation. Guess which section we live in? "My family is like the only Iranians for a hundred miles," Ario always complains. That's why after the summer, he's going to college in the city, so at least that isolation won't be a problem for him anymore. It's what I tell myself to feel better about the likelihood that in two months, I'm going to lose him.

Mom allows me to take her car for Meals on Wheels but *only* for this. If I'm not dropping off pureed dinners to sick folks, I can't drive. And if I'm not driving, I can't make it to White Eagle. And if I can't make it to White Eagle...I probably won't have a boyfriend anymore.

Which Mom would love.

Stay present in the moment, Major. For the moment, you have him.

Ario kisses me in the entryway of his bright, newly renovated house. He's nearly a foot taller than me, so I let myself be consumed in his furry arms, against his towering body. "How long do I have you?" he asks between loud, starving smacks.

"I have to be there by six," I huff into his mouth. Mr. Hannigan isn't expecting dinner until then, so I have an uninterrupted half hour with the spearmint of Ario's lips.

"How long do I have you?" I want to tell Ario "forever," but I'm not gonna risk admitting something that naïve. I have enough trouble as it is getting him to see me as someone other than a cute, inexperienced kid.

Ario strokes the bristling scruff on my cheeks (*I should have shaved first*). His fingers—nails painted glittery silver—slide beneath my knit cap and tug on my tangled hair (*I should have gotten a haircut*). I breathe in a rush of clean, ripened fruit (*He put on cologne for me, but I've been wearing the same nasty gym shorts for days*). Ario wouldn't know that though; we've been kept apart for a week. Mom confiscated my phone, so I haven't been able to text, call, send pics—nothing. If it weren't for these weekend Meals on Wheels, I'd never see him. I'd lose him to somebody he goes to school with; a boy he can actually see regularly; a boy whose family doesn't create nonstop bullshit.

I want to cry because I'm so relieved Ario wants to kiss me after all this time apart, but I don't cry because it'll spoil the mood (*but he'd be cool with it if I did, which makes me want to cry even more because I love him*).

Maybe I'll tell him that I love him...

"Hey, Connor," a tiny voice calls behind me. A nine-year-old girl, her dark braided hair fastened with a pink butterfly clip, trots past us into the Navissis' great room, her tininess emphasized by the room's chic, vaulted ceilings. A burning energy shoots through my neck, spasming the muscles and—against my will—forcing me to jump away from Ario.

Thanks to me, now our lips touch nothing but air.

"Relax, it's just my sister," Ario whispers, annoyed and rolling his Bambi-lashed eyes as he glides—*flip-flop, flip-flop*—toward his kitchen. "Come on."

The kissing is over. I ruined it.

Embarrassment scalds my skin. Thanks to my mom, I've been stuck at home all summer—no school, no friends, no Ario—with nothing to distract me from how *quiet* everything has become. It's her fault I'm so jumpy. Jumpy and nauseated. I've been out for over a month, and I still don't feel normal touching a guy. As exciting as it is to kiss Ario, there's a persistent...weirdness that comes packaged with each kiss. Sometimes it's an upset stomach, sometimes I get dizzy, sometimes my skin twitches, and sometimes I suddenly have to run off to use the bathroom.

Maybe that's how it's supposed to be. I tried Googling "gay kissing makes me nauseous," but all that came up was a LOT of homophobic tweets.

I follow Ario into yet another enormous room: a flawless kitchen that makes it clear just how cluttered, dark, and greasy my white trash home looks. Skylights pour intense sun beams across a kitchen island covered with trays of golden pastry pockets. Ario's mother wipes ghostly flour handprints onto her black yoga pants and greets us: "Connor, hold out your hand." Ario groans that we were on our way to his room, but his mother is already sliding a pastry into my open paw. "Turnovers. My first of the summer."

Sour cherries drip piping hot onto my tongue and boiling rage settles down to a simmer. "Mom, Connor only has, like, twenty minutes," Ario says, glaring at his mother's stubbornness.

"All right." Mrs. Navissi's lips tighten. "But your bedroom door stays open, got it?"

"YES, GOT IT." Ario yanks me away, with a turnover still half in my mouth.

Mrs. Navissi is cool with us just slipping off to his bedroom? It's unexpectedly lovely that I've stumbled into some different, kinder universe where no one lies to themselves about what goes on between certain teenage boys.

Nevertheless, my breath shortens as we climb his stairs. Are we going to have sex? I'm still dizzy from kissing, plus I suck at it—the blowjob I gave him in his car two weeks ago...ugh, I could tell he wasn't into it. My heart was beating too loudly, and Ario felt so heavy, so steaming hot in my mouth. It should've been this beautiful, passionate moment, and it was, but it was also awkward. I kept asking if he was liking it, but all he said was "Sure!" His voice went all high and fake, like he didn't have the heart to tell me I was giving him the Debbie Downer of blowjobs.

What a pathetic, churchy hick Connor Major turned out to be: all bark and no bite, eyes bigger than his stomach, with the emotional growth of a twelve-year-old. My best friend, Vicky, thought it was hilarious that I didn't know was 69-ing was. I'm seventeen, was looked dead in the eye, and got asked if I knew what this basic, ordinary, everyday sex thing was...and I blanked. My mom never told me anything, school certainly never told me anything, not even TV told me anything. And I was too wussy to look it up myself online.

Someone might as well have asked me to Google how to dismember a human body. I'm not putting that shit on my browser history.

In Ario's room, another guilty sting strikes me as I find the pictures smothering his baby blue walls. I'm in at least ten of them: our faces smooshed together outside Starbucks; us at the bookstore where we met; the Denny's where we stayed out way too late talking (*and doing other stuff in my car*). He's proud of us. He puts us on his wall like normal people do.

Ario deserves a boyfriend who doesn't jump away from him.

My second chance arrives right away. This time, I don't duck. This kiss is deeper than our one in the hallway; it's louder, more forceful, and on a mission. His fruity cologne mixes with something new: sweat. Grinning, Ario retreats to his desk to queue up what I've come to call a typical Ario playlist. I wait, marinating in my anxiety, as spooky electronica floats out of a Bluetooth speaker. He returns hungry-eyed, the crotch of his strawberry-pink shorts already swollen, and he guides me to his bed before lowering me onto the flannel sheets. *Maybe he'll just do everything himself, and all I have to do is let it happen.* With a large, toughened hand, he massages the bulge growing beneath my own shorts, and my breath quickens like a sweltering dog's. Pinned underneath his weight, I writhe as his hand travels down my bare thigh and then renavigates upward, inside my boxer briefs. The stinging sensation of his hand on my skin rests awkwardly somewhere between pleasure and pain. Ninety percent of my body craves this closeness, wants to guide Ario's hand further...

But that last ten percent is a whiny baby.

I pinch my boyfriend's wrist to stop his momentum, but immediately hate myself. "I'm starting to think you only come here for the turnovers," he whispers in my ear, making my erection come alive again. Part of me still doesn't want to do anything, but my heart's deepest wish is to get this boy buck naked. My head throbs with confusion—I have no clue what I want. Every thought contradicts the last one.

"I'm sorry," I moan. "It's just...if you don't stop, I'm gonna rip your clothes off and won't be able to help myself."

"Shred them, *beast*..." Ario plants a gentle kiss on my neck. If he knew how close I was to losing all control, he'd ease up. My breaths arrive more rapidly, tightening my throat and drenching my lips.

"Your door's open."

"Forget the door—"

I can't lose my head. Terror strikes my chest like a musical chord on a horror movie soundtrack and—for the second time today—I push Ario back. A tiny push, but that's all he needs to be done with me. In an agitated fit, he scrambles to the opposite end of his bed. We're only a foot apart, but it might as well be a football stadium. "So, what do you want to do instead?" Ario asks with a sigh that murders me.

But this *is* what I want to do. I just want to go slower. And if he keeps tempting me, I'm in danger of missing my delivery to Mr. Hannigan, getting fired, and then that'll be it for me and Ario. We only have a few months left before he moves to UIC, and the city is at least a two-hour drive away. There'll be plenty of boys there who would never reject the moves of a deadass fox like Ario. Boys who understand what he's talking about when he rants about politics. Boys who don't have to worry about what their Goddamn mothers think.

I can't lose any more time with him. I have to go for it.

Ario's box spring whines as I scoot closer in tiny hops. He remains rigid and motionless, even as I stroke the bits of fur peeking out from his sherbet-yellow tank top. He doesn't pull back, but he doesn't slide closer either. My unwelcome fingers—with their boring, alcohol-washed nails no longer electric purple—find the pendant slung around his neck, a bamboo recorder the size of a large Chapstick. My boyfriend avoids eye contact as he plucks the rainbow beads on his bracelet, his nails shimmering silver. We used to be silver and purple, but now we're just silver and nothing.

Please. Please don't ignore me.

"Connor—" cuts a voice from outside. With the speed of Olympic bobsledders, Ario and I drag pillows over our erect laps as a girl marches into the room. It's Ario's sister, but not the little one from downstairs; this one's older, about twelve, round faced with equally round glasses. "Gimme ten dollars," she orders.

"Hey, shitty," Ario snarls, "make some noise before you come in my room."

His sister rolls her eyes (a Navissi family trait) and shows off a sparkly, violet-cased phone. "You need to give me ten dollars to save this guy."

"Trini, no one's paying you—"

"Who are we saving?" I ask, taking Trini's phone, desperate for the interruption. I had no idea how much I missed the gentle weight of a phone in my hand. A fashion ad fills Trini's phone display; in the ad, a bare-chested god with blond surfer hair straddles a farmhouse fence. I scroll further. It's not an ad; it's a GoFundMe. A banner headline reads: *MISSING MODEL*.

"Drew Schreiber?" I read from the caption.

"He's a Calvin Klein model," Trini explains. "At least he *was*.

His aunt says his parents had him taken away. Some place where they do mind games to make you straight. Ten dollars goes to help finding him and you get on the aunt's email list. If you gimme the cash, I can set it up for you." Normally, I'd hold on to ten dollars like a life raft, but a chill sneaks up my sternum thinking about Drew, the Missing Model. His parents dragged him off to some awful place and ruined his career—a career at *Calvin Klein*! I dig two fives from my wallet and hand them to Trini before Ario can complain.

What do I need ten bucks for, anyway, when I'm stuck in my bedroom prison?

"Thanks for the breaking bad gay news, Trini," Ario says, "but Connor doesn't need to hear this right now, *as well you know*." He nabs her phone out of my hand and chucks it back. "You shouldn't be on queer sites, anyway. There's naked guys."

"Shirtless only," Trini groans, disappearing into the hallway with my cash. "Should I stay away from the underwear aisle at Target, too, or will that destroy meeeeeeee?"

Our laughter slices through the painful quiet. Ario's giggle is high and girlish—I want to jar up his honey-sweet laugh and spread it on toast. He squeezes my hand and I squeeze back, allowing a clean breath of relief into my lungs. He doesn't hate me.

"It's my fault," Ario whispers.

"What?"

"I promised you it'd be okay if you came out."

Ario is lucky his hand is so warm and calming. Because I'd never say it out loud, but it *is* his fault. And he did more than promise it would be fine; he made not coming out a dealbreaker for dating him. I tried to tell him that my mom is *not* his mom, but he wouldn't listen.

"Hey..." I pull his hand to my lips. "I'm really okay."

Ario doesn't smile; I can't sneak a lie past him. He rubs the back of my head in wide circles, softening the knotted pain in my neck. Finally, his touch feels the way it should feel—soothing. "I know it's hard to be stuck at home."

Damn it—tears. They drop hot and fast into my lap.

"I'm not allowed to talk about you." My voice comes out shaky and small, and I detest the sound of it. "I miss you so much...I don't want to go back there..." I kiss Ario's forehead, his ear, his dimples. A sudden, reckless urge to beg him to never leave me takes over. "I'm sorry I pulled away before. I want to have...sex with you, but I just can't right now." Ario shushes my crying and rests his curly head on my chest, which finally slows my panicked breathing. He's so beautiful. And I feel so crazy. This place—with Ario—has to be real. The place that's fake and wrong is waiting at home in Ambrose.

Anger. Silence. *That's* the fantasy bubble, not this.

Ario slides off his bamboo recorder pendant and drapes it over my head. The recorder has three note holes and actually plays. He fashioned it into a pendant after he got tired of it suffocating inside a shoebox. Ario's dad made it for his tenth birthday—two birthdays before he died. "A present to say 'sorry' for ruining your life," he says.

"I can't take your recorder."

"You have to." Ario kisses the scruff littering my cheek. "A little piece of me in case you get lonely."

"This was your dad's..." But he insists. I slip the recorder inside the neck of my hoodie, and the shellacked bamboo immediately cools my chest. He kisses me again. I want another minute with Ario, but Mr. Hannigan's dinner is waiting.

Thunder smashes through the sky as I trudge a death march down the Navissis' driveway toward my mom's Hyundai. My chest rattles from the Gatling gun of sobs that have overtaken me. I'm a boring boyfriend and a terrible gay. I firebombed my whole life by coming out for, like, zero rewards.

And this was my one Ario visit for the week—all I have left is this recorder. I gaze down at the lawn, trying to deep breathe myself out of this relentless pity party, when a wave of spicy cologne forces my head up.

"Mr. Major," announces the man standing in the cul-de-sac.

Reverend Packard leans, barrel-chested, against a dark green Taurus. My breath pauses at the sight of him, stopping me at the foot of Ario's driveway before we draw any closer. "What are you doing here?" I ask, trying not to sound as freaked out as I am. It's a strange violation—the Reverend doesn't belong anywhere near Ario's home. At my home or in church, sure; at Mr. Hannigan's, maybe, but not this sacred space.

"What are *you* doing here, is the question," the Reverend says, closing the distance between us. "Ricky Hannigan is waiting for his meal."

Thunder booms again as I rake fingers through my sweating flop of hair. "Well, Mr. Hannigan isn't until six—"

"It's called *responsibility*, Mr. Major."

A spear of pain twists through my chest. "Um...my friend Mackenzie lives here. I was just asking her about summer school—"

"No, this is where your boyfriend lives." The Reverend's darkened glare cuts deeper into me. "*Ario*...isn't it?" Pins and needles strangle my hands as I listen to the Reverend swirl my boyfriend's name in his mouth like it's something revolting.

"How do you know his name?"

"Ricky Hannigan happens to mean a lot to me." The Reverend tut-tuts his head. "He's suffered a great deal. That you would make him wait for a warm meal while you snuck off to...do things with this boy...It's not good."

Ricky's dinner might be less hot than it was half an hour ago, but it's not as if I'm running late. No excuse matters though. The Reverend caught me cutting corners on the one customer he ordered me to treat like royalty. It's over. He'll ax me from the program, and I'll never be able to sneak off to Ario again. I want to grab the bamboo recorder under my hoodie—"*A little piece of me in case you get lonely*"—but the Reverend would notice. He'd snatch it away...

"Please don't tell my mom," I beg like a two-year-old.

"Oh, Mr. Major," the Reverend sighs, "I'm no good at lying."

CHAPTER SIX
NIGHTLIGHT

TODAY

There's no beaten path on the island. Barefoot, I limp along in the daisy chain of kidnappers through the jungle, which is so crowded with palm trees that the storm can't break through. Rain sneaks in intermittently, but the bulk of it collects in a high forest canopy, which also stows away whatever illumination may have cut in from the last of the daylight.

Behind me, Ben Briggs marches at the rear of our chain. Ahead, Molly hikes up her knee-length party dress and stomps over wild underbrush, her path illuminated only by her phone's flashlight. I reaffirm my watery grip on my own phone as its flashlight cones outward, painting the jungle walls and the backs of kidnappers in bluish-white. A washed-out color. The color of dead things. But this jungle is *very* alive. Rain streams off palm fronds from shorter-growth trees as the shadows of tiny creatures scatter up the bark. To a calmer person, they might be harmless frogs or insects, but I've seen enough *Planet Earth* to know better. I'm convinced they're bizarre island spiders or some other poisonous assassin.

Don't touch anything, Connor.

With every squish of my bare feet through this wilderness, I promise myself it's just leaves and mud. The sharp pricks jutting into my toes are brambles or broken twigs—definitely not a family of scorpions angry that I'm carelessly stomping through their home.

Ario smiles back at me from my phone's lock screen—a cruel reminder of just how miserable turning seventeen has been: coming out, my grades tanking, my best friend having a baby and letting everyone think I'm the father, my boyfriend realizing I'm shitty at sex and wondering why he ever asked me out, my Meals on Wheels client dying, and my mom deciding having me kidnapped would be the cherry on top of this shit sundae.

Directly ahead, a kidnapper grunts as he slings one leg over a snarled tree root, followed by the other leg with more difficulty (and more grunting). I don't fare any easier. As I traverse the root, my foot slips in the unstable mud, sending my leg sharply right. A hand catches me by the shoulder—a large hand with a confident grip. "Take it slower, champ," Briggs whispers in his gravelly East Ender accent.

This man having my dad's voice shoots stabbing pains up my spine. Dad ditched me even worse than my mom is currently ditching me. Not long after their separation, Mom became uber-religious and didn't want anything to do with Dad after that. And he didn't fight her. Mom moved us to a town brimming with Jesus-y rednecks, and I never saw him in person again. Would Dad have let strangers pull me out of bed and fly me to an island for some unknown reason?

Maybe not, but the reason for Mom sending me away is less of an unknown than it was an hour ago. *Surrender your sins*, read the sign on the crucifix...

"Road!" shouts the kidnapper at the head of the chain. Our movement slows, but I stop too short. Briggs's taser—the Pez dispenser thing that fires a thousand-volt charge—pokes me in what might as well be my asshole.

"Sorry," I whisper. I actually *apologized* to my abductor. I'm the World's Silliest Dildo. After a long, marching beat, I ask, "How'd you get it on the plane? Your good luck charm."

"It's special," Briggs says with a chuckle. "We make them ourselves, designed to pass through any airport checkpoint. It looks like any old thing. The battery scans like a phone would. Same with the electrical wires. The gas propellant was the tricky part, but we got that sorted." The man draws closer, his hot breath steaming my neck as he whispers: "And you give 'em too much credit, airports. No one's looking too closely at what a chummy white bloke's taking through security, unless it's something obvious."

I'm sorry I asked.

Thunder rumbles as the seven of us stagger through curtains of stringy moss and long, sharp palm fronds to find a cleared trail. My feet sing as the ground suddenly becomes firm and free of the prickling underbrush. Greenish, dying light—and a torrent of warm rain—meets us at the path. "This is the Coral Road," Briggs announces. "It's the only beaten path on this island, so do not wander off, unless you want to die of thirst finding your way back to us. There may be more upraised roots along the way, so we'll keep taking it slow. Nearly there."

"Nearly where?" I mutter.

Before I can realize my mouthiness, Briggs raises his taser to my shoulder. My whole body spasms backward as the device makes contact...but no sparks come. Another shitty grin crosses his face. "Off you trot," he chortles. It was a fake-out, but he could've pulled the trigger and no one would've protested. It's not like there are cops around to call.

In the pale shine of my flashlight, Briggs's irises glow a sickly, bloodless white. Heebie-jeebies race down my arms, so I tap off my flashlight and stuff the phone inside my hoodie's pouch. The twisting path along the Coral Road could be magical if our destination wasn't so ominously unknown. Gargantuan tree roots snake along the ground, weaving in and out of the earth like the Loch Ness Monster emerging from its watery hideaway.

Around the next bend, a rusting generator—as enormous and cylindrical as the water tank in my basement—rattles beside a large cabin standing above the flooding road on a platform of raised stilts. I dash for the cabin's staircase to get the hell out of this rain, but Briggs seizes my shoulder. "Mr. Major, we go into the clinic when I say. Trouble, you are." The kidnappers snicker as I mumble another pathetic apology. "You and Miss Partridge follow me inside. The rest of you, let the director know we've arrived."

Not to sound like a scumbag, but Briggs was a lot prettier when he smiled.

Inside the clinic, lemony freshness surprises my nostrils. Outside, an Old Testament storm bashes through the raw jungle, but inside is pure modern civilization. Nothing like its shack exterior; old-fashioned, maybe (chrome-and-Formica countertops are very eighties), but the clinic remains untouched by this weather. As soon as Briggs shuts us in, Molly lets herself exhale. Under the harsh clinic lights, her pink dress reveals itself to be annihilated by splotches of brown and green. She scans the clinic, alert and ready to scrap, but when her eyes land on me, her head drops mournfully.

I don't blame Molly for choking me with a branch. My out-of-the-blue Nightlight warning scared her. *"Tell me who they are."* I have no idea, but the little voice in my head whispers: *Nobody good.*

"New recruits are here!" a woman's voice beckons from the lobby hallway.

New recruits? Recruited into what? Is this a cult?

"Quickly, Ramona," Briggs calls. "We've been traveling all day. The lodge beds are calling."

"I heard you come in," her voice returns, steadfastly gentle. Heels click closer as Ramona emerges lugging a leather doctor's bag, her smile bursting with capped white teeth. She sports a full face of makeup, and bouncy, fake hair tumbles to her shoulders; she could be the judge of a Lil' Miss beauty pageant—gorgeous but grotesque. Strangest of all, her butter-yellow sundress is patterned with rows of bright lemons...yet the hem is tattered and black with filth. Ramona doesn't mind wearing a ratty dress, but apparently, shabbiness in others bothers her: she stares disapprovingly at the dark mud caking my feet. "You didn't give this boy shoes?" she asks in her plantation lilt. Her attention darts toward Molly's similarly stained feet. "Ben, these children have no shoes. You marched them in the jungle half a mile."

Briggs snorts. "Oh, they had shoes, but they lost them in the bay. These two are runaways. Jumped ship a meter from shore."

"Most of them run. You have backup shoes." Ramona shakes her head as she turns to us. "Good evening. I'm Ramona Hayward, your nurse and sometimes-teacher during your stay at Nightlight. Before we send you into camp, there are a few tests I have to perform.

I wish I could let you scrub up and send y'all to bed"—her heavily lashed eyes linger again on my muddy clompers—"because you *really* need it, but I can't. Not yet. Let's start by refreshing my memory: tell me your names, ages, and where you hail from." She clicks open her pen and smiles me down first. Cotton mouth is all that comes to me. "All right, don't let Mr. Briggs's temper lead you on. No one's here to hurt you."

"...I'm Connor Major. Seventeen years old, from Ambrose, Illinois."

"Excellent, Connor. We'll be counting sheep before you know it."

Ramona pivots to Molly, but my new friend weighs giving out her name like it's a government secret. Finally, she sighs: "I'm Molly Partridge. Sixteen. From Tucson, Arizona."

"Give your phones to me." Ramona reaches an open palm to Molly, and she gives up hers without hesitation. *Ugh, we just got these back.* I wipe a finger across my phone's rainy display before begrudgingly handing it over. I've been through a lot to get that damn thing back in my hand, and now it's gone again. "This would go much faster if I could do it for you, but unfortunately, Nightlight insists you take this first step in the recovery process yourself." Ramona swipes to unlock both phones, holds them out to us, and Molly and I tap in our passwords. With a *tap-tap-tap,* Ramona opens my camera roll. "Connor, delete every picture you have of the shirtless boy from your lock screen."

My chest caves in with an inhuman pressure. *Delete...Ario?* I turn to Briggs as if he's somehow the voice of reason, but his sharp, ex-boybander cheekbones don't even twitch. With a tremoring hand, I scroll through my camera roll. There are six pictures of Ario—the lock screen selfie, two from our Denny's night, one in the bookstore where we met, and two kissing pictures.

Terror boils my neck as too many eyes—judgmental eyes—watch me open these intimate pictures. Pictures that I treasure, but are so, so private. Ario is only shirtless in some of them—maybe a little peek of treasure trail—but my brain is battering against my skull like I've been caught red-handed with the scummiest, vilest porn imaginable.

I hate that my first instinct is to delete them, even before this woman directed me to do it.

If I delete Ario's pictures, they're not gone. A Recently Deleted folder keeps a recoverable cache for thirty days. I'm here for a few days so as soon as I get my phone back, I'll just recover the pictures before Ario is deleted permanently. I vanish all his pictures and smile as I return my phone to the lemon-dressed nurse.

But she refuses to touch it.

"Go to Recently Deleted," Ramona says. My smile dies.

"Why?" I ask innocently.

"Ben."

At her command, Briggs unsheathes his taser and approaches with it drawn at my head, like a pistol. On instinct, my neck ducks into my shoulders. "This isn't *Glee*, mate," he purrs. "This isn't *Love, Simon*. You don't get to do what you feel like. When Ramona or me or the director tell you to do something, my darling little punk, you do it. Or my good luck charm will go clickity-click before you get time to argue. You won't be warned again."

Noiselessly, my neck still bent, I tap open my phone's Recently Deleted folder—there, everything having to do with Ario awaits my execution. Any evidence that he was ever part of my life. I tap Select All and each picture fills with check marks. On one side, Delete All.

On the other, Recover All. While Briggs and Ramona watch my thumb hover over the screen, Molly's lips tighten—she knows her turn is next.

"We made sure your mother got access to your social media accounts," Ramona adds, salting my wound. "She's already erased pictures there and on your cloud as well."

"Please," I say, my voice cracking like I'm thirteen again. If I delete these, that's it. I might as well delete every memory in my head. I don't know what would happen to me if Ario was truly, completely erased from my life. If all of this bullshit was for absolutely nothing. How could I get out of bed?

Briggs's taser tickles the little hairs on my ear.

"If you don't delete them yourself, you'll get a shock and I'll delete them anyway." Ramona's ruby-red smile stiffens. "And it will start your recovery on a bad note."

"What recovery?" I break. "What am I doing here?"

Molly's lip quivers as we await the nurse's answer. "You're joining Nightlight Ministries to be brought closer to God, and in doing so—embrace a straight life."

Molly's eyes squeeze shut, and the bottom drops out of my heart. *A Pray the Gay Away hellhole?* "Those"—the back of my hand wipes at my streaming nose—"those places don't exist anymore."

They don't happen. Queer boys make cheesy coming-out videos where their moms hug them, and dads are even starting to write blogs about taking the journey with their daughters as they transition. I know things are still bad for some queer people like me, but I thought it was getting better. *This* doesn't happen!

It can't happen...

Ramona strokes painted nails along her medical bag and says,

"If a family wants it enough, if they're desperate enough, they can find us." Her smile long gone, Ramona jabs the Recently Deleted folder of Ario's pictures. "He is distraction and temptation. Cleanse yourself of him. Now."

A low hiss of electricity rests inside Briggs's taser, waiting to assault me.

I'm not deleting Ario, I'm deleting his pictures. I'm not deleting him, it's just pictures.

Delete All.

———

Briggs and Molly wait outside while I strip to my waist in Ramona's office for a physical. As my blood travels through a needle into a vial, harsh fluorescents sting my eyes. The room blurs by the time she's finished; I haven't eaten since my last supper at home. Ramona scribbles notes, glancing up and down at me, the specimen. After all that's happened, I'm weirdly more self-conscious about being half-naked than about what she plans to do to me.

"What's this whistle about?" Ramona asks, feeling under my jaw for lymph nodes. Ario's bamboo recorder clings to the scant bits of matted hair on my chest as a chill snakes through my stomach. Once I deleted Ario's pictures, she made me delete our text history, his number, even the nineties playlist he made me. She won't take his recorder.

"It's a family thing," I blurt. Ramona tilts her blank, pink face at me. *Don't cry.* If I cry, she'll know what the recorder means and take it away.

"That's all you can tell me about it? Is it...secret?"

"It means *faith*." I seal the deal with a lie: "It's Celtic."

Ramona's smirk freezes into a sneer. She retreats to a stack of legal pads on her desk to find a gray, metallic rod—another Pez dispenser taser. "Working here as long as I have, you learn to spot a liar," she says, raising her weapon. My heart recoils inside my chest. "The breath shortens. The lips tense. The words come out short and choppy. Then there's that split-second delay before answering; you *really* see that in young liars."

"It's really nothing," I blurt. "It's my dad's; I haven't seen him in years."

"Sure it isn't from your boyfriend?"

"I'd tell you! You took away everything of my boyfriend's. I'd tell you. Why wouldn't I tell you? Please, I'm just so tired. I'm gonna have slow answers."

"Just be careful. We don't like secrets here..." One unbearable second later, Ramona lowers her taser and I unclench my spine. *You can't spot all the liars, asshole.* "Once I'm finished with Molly, Mr. Briggs will take both of you to meet the director." Without so much as a nod, I gather my sopping hoodie from a nearby chair and escape to the door. Ramona's hand—as leathery as an old belt—stops me. "While you're here, you're gonna start to think the world's forgotten about you. You come see me if that feeling ever gets real bad."

I wish everyone would forget about me. I'd enjoy the privacy.

In the next room, I comb beach sand out of my hair and rinse my scratched feet in a galvanized basin of filthy standing water. Ramona declares my clothes "riddled with travel" and junks them into a burlap laundry sack. Maybe she should change into something new, as well, and drop that horrible dress into the sack. Our delightful nurse summons Molly into her office, leaving me alone with Briggs while I dress in my new uniform, fresh out of summer camp: short athletic socks, white gym shoes, a powder-blue T-shirt with Nightlight's insignia (the middle "T" replaced with a crucifix—*love it*), and elastic-banded shorts (too short for my liking—*hope everyone here can handle thighs!*). I change as some frightening, roided-out man stands watch—it's my middle school sex nightmares all over again.

Exiting outside after acclimating to the clinic's fluorescent lights darkens the day. Briggs marches Molly and me back into the downpour of the Coral Road, and the privilege of being clean and dry comes to an abrupt end. Scurrying after us, Ramona switches off her generator and covers it with a blue tarp. Before returning inside, she smacks a tall tank hanging along the clinic wall: three cone-shaped gutters collect rainwater and guide it into the tank's reservoir.

That beauty queen nurse is a freaking sadist. Every memento of Ario is gone forever, except for his recorder. *A piece of him in case I get lonely.* Well, Ario, I'm sure as shit lonely now.

Molly changed out of her ruined party dress and into camper gear like mine. Both of us are faint with the exhaustion of our endless journey, and she wobbles against my arm to stop herself from falling. If I could just vomit, I'd be more comfortable. "Cheer up, you two," Briggs says. "You'll meet the director, get some food if you like, and then you can get to bed early."

Molly and I both groan, disgusted at the mention of food. She must be feeling the same inescapable nausea I am—a nasty byproduct of stress, erratic sleep, and having to banish all memories of our boyfriend and girlfriend. No food, thanks.

We don't talk back. We don't plot escape. We nod and keep trudging.

Around the next bend, flames dance between the raindrops. Kerosene torches surround a chapel three stories high, built from barn lumber. Like every other building on this island, the church stands on tiptoes above the flooding road.

"Ahoy!" hollers a man from the chapel doorway. "Hurry on out of that rain."

"Here's the director," Briggs says. The director strides down a steep staircase to meet us. Muddy rain douses his pants; his black pastor's shirt covers a prominent belly. The bearish man with round glasses reaches me with a smile, but the white thumbprint of his religious collar drops my jaw.

Him.

"Mr. Major, hello," says the director. "Welcome to my home away from home."

"Reverend Packard?"

I'm ready to throw up now.

CHAPTER SEVEN

THE WINNER'S WALL

*T*he director.

    The Reverend who organizes church fairs in Ambrose, runs the local Meals on Wheels, and owns the chicken farm across from my house...also orders men to abduct gay people to an island conversion camp. I didn't think anyone from Ambrose traveled as far as Chicago, much less a Costa Rican jungle, but this explains why the Reverend always leaves town for long chunks of time. Mom and I figured it was for charity missions.

But here he is. And here I am.

Reverend Packard—the director, or whatever he wants to be called—hustles us out of the storm and into the darkened chapel. *Ambrose Chapel*, reads the sign etched into the arched doorway. Ambrose Chapel is identical to my church back home, with a brass pipe organ sitting on a raised stage in the corner, rows of pews lining each side, and a pulpit commanding the center aisle—only instead of pale birch wood, this one is crafted from dark ash. Instead of whitewashed, cheerfully small-town walls, Nightlight's chapel is coated head to toe with a mahogany wood stain. Against the back wall, two cast-iron candelabras stand taller than me; their Haunted Mansion candles flicker, providing the chapel's only light.

"Briggs got told off by Ramona for not giving the kids shoes," whispers a kidnapper with thinning blond hair. Briggs's nostrils flare at his tattling coworker, but the Reverend is already spinning around with a red, veiny face. A face I've been on the receiving end of many times—when the Reverend gazes at you like this, he pierces *through you* until you can't think of anything but how screwed you are.

"Thank you, Archie," the Reverend tells the snitch before— *thwap*—bringing his fist across the back of Briggs's skull. My kidnapper winces like a battered dog. "You made them walk without shoes? I promised this boy's mother he'd come back without a scratch."

I wish I could enjoy a speck of relief that my mom is at least vaguely concerned for my well-being after everything I've been dragged through...but the Reverend is pulsing with too much barely restrained violence for me to relax.

"The kids jumped ship!" Briggs snaps, pressing a hand to his newfound lump. "The storm being what it was, I had to keep us moving—"

"Mr. Briggs,"—the Reverend snatches him by his soggy shirt collar, and I swallow my own gasp—"we will talk in the morning."

"Yes, sir." Briggs shuffles through the doorframe where Archie and the rest of the kidnappers congregate behind the pews. Archie glances away from Briggs, both of them racked with tension. Behind the men, a relentless shower continues to fall outside in sheets.

As raging as I've seen the Reverend get, he's never hit anyone before. Vicky said her older sister saw him slap a kid's neck with a ruler, but I never believed it. It was kind of cool to watch the Reverend coldcock Briggs, that thug who tased me in the chest...but I don't know; the attack was also weird, like something I shouldn't have seen. Like stumbling in on a family member naked.

As tough as Briggs acts, though, he *obeyed* the Reverend.

Beside me, Molly pokes my arm and whispers, "You know this guy?"

"He's a reverend in my hometown," I whisper. "My mom's friends with him."

"Find a seat," the Reverend booms, scooting us deeper inside the flickering light of the chapel. "Miss Culpepper has a pot of cocoa waiting. Hurry up." A wretched lurch wrings my stomach like a sponge at the thought of cocoa. Molly and I choose the front pew, mostly to stay as far from Briggs as possible. When I finally sit, enormous pressure releases from my feet and my vision spins in woozy circles.

On the raised stage, two teenagers—both dressed in Nightlight's camper uniform—emerge from a door behind a large crucifix. They march stiffly to the pulpit, as if they were in a grade school play and it's time for their big scene. The girl—Black with wide, catlike eyes—dons a short, bobbed wig (the kind you'd find in a yearbook from the sixties) and carries a tray of Dixie cups. *Is she Miss Culpepper with the cocoa?* The other teenager—a boy—leads her out, softly snapping his fingers—an absentminded tic he can't seem to help. He's tall and thick chested, with light brown skin and slicked hair that curls under his ears. With that hair and those black-rimmed glasses, he looks ready to sing "Greased Lightning." They've both stepped out of a time portal from the doo-wop era. *Or maybe it's me who's time traveled? Back to when people thought nothing of trying to switch kids from gay to straight.* When the campers settle beside the Reverend's pulpit, the candelabra flickers illuminate something else about the boy—he's beautiful. The eyes behind his retro glasses are large and glossy, as if in a perpetual state of hurt.

It's only for half a second, but his wounded eyes catch mine looking at him. I jerk away so quickly that my neck tremors with a near-painful spasm.

The Reverend mounts the chapel stage, and Miss Culpepper and Sad Puppy Boy flank him silently to await further instructions. "I'm Reverend Stanley Packard. You'll hear my staff call me 'director' or 'sir,' but you—my campers—don't need to be as formal as all that. You may call me Reverend Packard, which shouldn't be too hard for Connor to remember." He waves in my direction, and my hollow stomach lurches again. "Full disclosure, I've known Connor Major outside this island. He's a hometown Ambrose boy, and his mother often helps out at my church. One thing—and forgive me, Mr. Major, but I'm a stickler for details: you told Miss Partridge that your mother and I are friends. We're not. Your mother and I are *friendly*."

Ouch, Mom.

Honestly, I'm not shocked the Reverend overheard Molly and me whispering. The man knows all—things he should have no way of knowing. Like Ario's name. Where he *lives*.

"Welcome to my *real* church," the Reverend says with sweeping, carnival barker hand motions. "Nightlight Ministries has succeeded in conversion therapy for almost fifty years. You're in good hands. Please, take a cup, warm yourselves!" The young woman in the *Dreamgirls* wig summons a smile and begins doling out cups. "This is Darcy Culpepper, one of your fellow campers. She's made her famous cocoa for you, isn't that lovely?"

I take a cup for Molly and one for myself. We both stare into the sweet broth for long, suspicious seconds. *They wouldn't bring us all this way just to poison us...would they?* I bring myself to glance again at Sad Puppy Boy for some kind of signal that it's safe to drink. He must see this hesitation a lot because he nods knowingly, and my cocoa is history in a single gulp. The drink is nothing special, but it does stop my stomach from swimming. Molly, satisfied the cocoa isn't making me grip my throat in poisoned terror, tosses hers back.

"You change the recipe?" asks Archie, the tattling kidnapper, as he shakes the remaining drops into his open maw. Darcy and Sad Puppy Boy freeze, their legs rumbling like paint-can shakers.

"It tastes spicy, like Halloween," Briggs agrees, sniffing his empty cup.

The Reverend pivots to the two campers. Dreadful silence follows until Sad Puppy Boy, in a gentle Texan accent, says, "Darcy was sick of the old recipe. I gave her cinnamon to add. Kind of a spice blend...cinnamon and nutmeg, cardamom pods—"

"You were in the kitchen?" the Reverend asks, lunging forward. My heart squeezes for the petrified boy as his relentless finger-snapping quickens.

"Yes, sir...b-but she was having a hard time. The fire wasn't working right...she can't boil water, sir. And new folks coulda been in any minute—"

"Shut up, shut up, shut up," Darcy begs under her breath.

"Marcos, you are not allowed in the kitchen, unless it's to supervise," the Reverend interrupts, his tiger's eyes lingering on the Puppy-Eyed Chef. "You're her boss. She cooks; you're her boss. HOW DARE YOU cook for her, especially since you know how much she struggles with the program? Take the wall."

"Yes, sir," Marcos says, retreating. As ordered, he presses his nose to the chapel's back wall, so motionless in the shadows that he might be a sleeping bat. Both his hands ball into fists, probably to prevent any more nervous snapping. Molly squeezes my wrist with little signals of *What the hell; did you just catch that?*

Of course I caught that. *Take the wall?* The Reverend is a psycho.

The Reverend returns to us with a friendly grin, as if he didn't just punish a boy for stirring cinnamon into cocoa. "This is probably a shock for you, Connor," the Reverend says, but not directly at me—it's all part of his grand preacher performance. "Being here with me and the wonderful people of Nightlight, you may start to wonder, 'Why an island? Couldn't I operate Nightlight somewhere in America?' The answer is 'I wish it were so.' But the world has squeezed me out. They don't want me talking like this to you. The modern world has created a net of allowances—tolerances—that has, frankly, forced kids like yourself to fall through the cracks into a life that runs nowhere."

Behind me, Briggs and Archie grunt in approval. I squeeze Molly's hand, and she squeezes back—we're surrounded. Darcy, holding an empty tray, bows her head next to Marcos, who is still trapped against the wall.

"Why an island?" the Reverend repeats. "Because I must leech the modern world out of you, and it begins with culture shock. There are no phones allowed here. No phones will work." My stomach whines with the thought—*no calling for help.* "No internet. No TV. The only electricity we have comes from generators, and we monitor those carefully because fuel is a luxury. No plumbing! By now, you've seen the rainwater catchment systems I have in place around the camp. You have returned to nature, and soon I will return you to *your* true natures."

Marcos nods vigorously, his glasses scraping the wall. *NIGHTLIGHT*, Ricky Hannigan warned. What does any of this have to do with him? The Reverend had me deliver his meals, so they knew each other, but why would Ricky send me such an ominous final message? Did he know about the Reverend's secret side project? Did he know this is where I was headed?

"YOU KNOW," Ricky accused the Reverend when we first met. Hearing my name seemed to set him off. Ricky and the Reverend had been close. Did Ricky know I was headed for Nightlight; did his old friend tell him what he and my mom were planning for me? Was Ricky really trying to warn me? Something is missing from this. If that's true, why would Ricky care about me, a stranger?

"I want to ask you something," I blurt.

"No, you'll pay attention." The Reverend climbs beside me on the pew, his dank cologne an assault on my nostrils. This close, his sagging, black-bearded face reflecting the torchlight, I recognize him as the man who wasn't always such a prick. When I moved to Ambrose after sixth grade, the Reverend brought me souvenirs from his trips: snow globes, a boomerang...but he probably bought them on his way home from Nightlight Island. And now I'm being treated to a front row seat. "Connor, you've trained yourself not to trust people like the men on my staff. Men like me."

"Um...maybe."

The Reverend nods. He and I watch each other. The chapel watches us, and my shoulders ache from slumping. It takes inhuman energy not to beg him to take me home, to remember me as the boy he used to bring boomerangs to. "Men of God are still men, and men can't be trusted, can they? You're drawn to other boys because you're hoping you'll find the piece of you that's missing where your father has let you down."

Queasy goo roils in my stomach.

I never should have listened to Ario. I knew this wasn't safe.

"Don't worry," the Reverend says, patting my scruffy cheek, "you've come to the right place. Your mother was right about—"

"What was she right about?" I blurt. I've had enough. Enough rain, enough cocoa, enough bizarre tension, enough punishment. ENOUGH. "What did my mom tell you? You wanna know what Ricky Hannigan told me—?"

Something like an egg wallops the top of my skull, only this egg hits as hard as a fist. *Briggs's fist.* "Not your turn to speak, mate," he says before trotting back down the aisle. Molly grips my hand while I wince through a throb in my skull. Her breathing shudders audibly, a tsunami of rage barely kept back.

"Time for bed," the Reverend says, rising. Briggs was reprimanded for not giving us shoes, but a fist to a kid's skull doesn't move our glorious director to speak up—*good to note.* At Nightlight, mentioning Ricky is worth a smack. "Miss Culpepper, I want you to take Miss Partridge to her lodge and then you may go to dinner. Mr. Carrillo, do the same with Mr. Major. And I want you newcomers to follow their instructions to the letter or there will be punishment. Welcome to Nightlight. It might seem like you're giving up your freedom to be here, but we're actually *giving* you your freedom. Freedom to live the life you want. And you can achieve it. Whatever your hearts desire. Safety. Normalcy. *Children.*"

At the mention of children, the Reverend's laser gaze bores into me. He and Mom are Team Connor-and-Vicky, so I'm not surprised.

"Do good work," the Reverend says gently, "and before you know it, you'll be home again. I promise."

Marcos and Darcy emerge from the shadows and come for us. Molly stands, but I refuse. My mom is here—I *know* it. She's spying on me from some window, so eager to teach me a lesson that she got everyone we know together to scare me and trick me. Ricky's warning was just a forgery, that flight was fake, and this is all a movie set.

"Time for bed," the Reverend repeats, his shadow growing behind the candelabra flames.

"Is this for real?" I ask. Marcos's, Darcy's, and Molly's faces drop the same way at the same time. *We're really here. For real.*

"Marcos, before bed, show Connor the Winner's Wall," the Reverend orders, his face tightening into a blank death mask. "He'll know how serious I am." Whatever the Winner's Wall is exactly, the man who used to bring me boomerangs doesn't care about me anymore.

———

My head still throbs from Briggs's smack. I fight my vision's urge to spin as my kidnapper drives us in a banged-up Jeep Wrangler farther into camp. Black, endless jungle rushes past my open window, and floodwaters—dimly visible through our headlights—continue to overtake the Coral Road. Briggs swerves around fallen branches and roots, careening through the wilderness without once dropping speed. Marcos, Darcy, Molly, and I all cling to the "Oh, Shit" handles until we reach the next sign of civilization—a stilted, one-story lodge beside a vast lake. Two torches guard the building's entrance as our headlights shine across the road sign:

LAKE MONTEVERDE

Briggs pumps the Wrangler's brakes, and we hydroplane across the flooding road before coming to a rickety stop beside the lodge stairs. Adrenaline spikes my heart awake, but Briggs shrugs like he meant to do that. Over Briggs's shoulder, rain and moonlight dance together on the surface of a lake that stretches forever. If I have to be at Nightlight, at least this tropical view is less depressing than Reverend Packard's soybean fields.

This lodge is the boys' cabin; the girls have another drive ahead of them. It seems silly to room a bunch of horny, distraught queer boys in one confined place, but Briggs is way ahead of my thinking: "Behave yourself, Mr. Major. Mr. Carrillo is head of this cabin, and he'll report even the slightest hint of you boys acting on your...urges. And Mr. Carrillo is *very* loyal."

"Got it," I say, adding quietly to myself: *Don't bone anyone.* Briggs scowls at my snippy tone, seething under his duty to return me home "without a scratch." As the car falls into silence, Marcos devours his thumbnail and avoids my judgmental side-eye. *How many boys has Marcos ratted out?* It can't have been many—we're not supposed to stay that long. Still, a fidgety need to reconfirm this detail takes hold: "So, we're...leaving in a few days, right?"

"Your time here is up to you," Briggs says. "Put in the effort and go home." I blink and almost miss it, but as Briggs speaks, Marcos and Darcy turn away from each other in unison. Cool, that's suspicious.

As Marcos and I disembark, we land in two inches of rain and wave a drenched goodnight to Briggs and the girls. It's shitty to separate from Molly after everything we've been through. Before Marcos shuts the door, Molly mouths something that looks like, "It'll be okay."

Maybe that's what I wish she'd said. I wish I'd said that to her.

"Come on," Marcos says, and we splash through wide, unavoidable puddles before finally escaping underneath a wooden awning at the top of the stairs. Puppy Boy makes like a puppy and shakes the rain from his slick surf wave hair. "I—don't—like—being—wet."

"Spotty glasses." I point at his lenses smothered in raindrops. He slides them off, but his waterlogged shirt only smears around the rain.

"My shirt is soaked." He laughs, throaty and deep; not like Ario's honey-dipped giggle at all. A bracelet of wooden beads surrounds a small cross on his wrist; cruelly, I'm reminded of Ario plucking his rainbow bead bracelet after I pushed him away and ruined everything. "Like Briggs said, I'm Marcos Carrillo."

"Connor Major."

"Hey! M.C., C.M." I smirk at the coincidence of our palindrome initials, but this must not have been a strong enough reaction because Marcos drops his head in embarrassment. Avoiding my eyes, he tugs down the wet shirt hugging his cuddly torso. Pretty self-conscious for a guy trying to pull off the cool fifties thing. "Anyway, it's so kind of you to visit me in my loneliness."

"What?"

Marcos instantly switches back to his jovial laugh. "It's kind of you to visit me in my loneliness. It's my 'aloha.' I say it whenever I meet a new camper or say goodbye to one going home. The Wicked Witch says it to Dorothy in *Wizard of Oz*..." Off some hidden realization about himself, Marcos's eyes bulge behind his rain-smudged lenses. "Don't tell the Reverend I quoted *Wizard of Oz*. We're not allowed."

Don't tell him? The Reverend and I know each other, but I've never been a teacher's pet and—now that he's ruined my life for the second time—I'm not about to start.

"Wow, Marcos," I say, "mixing spices into hot cocoa and quoting *Wizard of Oz*...you're such a rebel." He laughs again, so powerfully that it echoes across the lake. I fake-laugh along with him until a darker thought pulls at me. "You quote this to campers when they leave too?"

"Mmhmm."

"So, how long have you been here?"

"Um...you look really tired. Let's go in."

Everyone at Nightlight speaks in creepy non-answers.

Marcos snaps his fingers as he extends a key ring from his shorts by a thin, retractable tether. He unlocks our cabin and holds the screen door open for me. As I stagger across the pitch-black threshold, Marcos opens a Zippo lighter and its little flame guides us inside the barracks. Six rows of bunk beds fill the boys' lodge, but all of the blankets are tucked in, unoccupied. Everyone is at dinner, which is where I'd love to be, but the power of sleep is taking precedence. I crave the horizontal softness of one of these empty bunks.

"You'll meet everyone else in the morning," Marcos whispers as his smooth, cool hand grazes my elbow. I jerk away and am reminded again of Ario. "Sorry, I'm not supposed to touch the other boy campers except for handshakes, but you're all worn out and, um, I don't want you to, like, fall over in the dark." Using the faintest possible touch, he pilots me toward my assigned lower bunk. But before I'm able to crash into this gorgeous bed, dozens of miniature faces smile from the wall. Pictures of teenagers—*many, many pictures*—stack together in neat rows from floor to ceiling. "I totally forgot! The Winner's Wall."

My shoes squish closer to the wall, and Marcos catches up with his lighter. Through the weak flame, a blur of signatures appears next to the photos. It's too dark to read, but what is clear are the banners of encouragement hanging above:

YOU CAN DO IT!
REACH HIGHER!
VICTORY IS CLOSE!

Each photo is pasted onto a corkboard, which hooks onto the cabin walls themselves. *Walls. Plural.* The Winner's Wall of faces wraps this wall, continues around the corner, and ends at the front door. 2017 jumps out from the blur. 2016. 2015. 2014. Each picture has a date and a signature, and as I move left, the dates get older. 2011. 2010. I step backward in time, Marcos following dutifully with his lighter. When we reach the two thousands and then the nineties, the pictures become larger, glossier prints. Frozen in the past, teenage boys in blue Nightlight shirts greet me: some smiling, some sad, and some even twinkle with a sinister glint in their eyes.

Repulsed, I advance. The pictures don't just have one date—they have two. One reads *1997 to 1998.* A year. Some of these boys spent an entire *year* at Nightlight? I want to claw the flesh off my face. I want to steal Marcos's lighter and burn this cabin and the chapel and the jungle until everything is fire. Name follows name until the flame reaches the door. The pictures continue on the other side of the doorway, but my attention remains fixed on one in particular: a Polaroid, its colors bleached from decades of humidity and sun. In this picture, a handsome, sandy-haired young man smiles with apple cheeks. Yet the creases under his eyes display a severely depleted child older than his years.

Autographed in neat cursive below: *RICKY HANNIGAN. 1990 to 1991.*

Ricky—the man who warned me about this island before he died—was a Nightlight camper thirty years ago.

"Someday," Marcos whispers, "we'll be on this wall."

CHAPTER EIGHT

RICKY'S DEAD

ONE WEEK AGO

A rio's recorder rests between my lips as I follow the Reverend up the farmhouse driveway with two stacked dinner trays—one for Mr. Hannigan and one for his mother. *"A little piece of me in case you get lonely."* I'd be less lonely if I had my phone to talk to Ario. My saliva soaks in the instrument's musky, woodsy flavor, but I don't mind—it's the closest I'll get to kissing him for at least another week. Yesterday, the Reverend busted me while I was sneaking off my route to see my boyfriend, so now my Meals on Wheels has to be chaperoned—and who better to tag along than the snitch himself? All day, the Reverend has driven me from delivery to delivery, and as soon as the Hannigans get their meals, he's returning me straight home like a convict.

This is how it's gonna be. All because my mom fell into the Reverend's flock. I'm not angry, I'm just...embarrassed. I'm embarrassed she's my mother.

"What are all these cars doing here?" the Reverend shouts. Three vehicles crowd the Hannigans' sloping, asphalt driveway, which is three cars more than usual—Mr. Hannigan and his mother live alone and very rarely leave, hence the meals. The Reverend squeezes between the brick home and a pickup truck parked at an obnoxious slant. When he emerges on the other side, a smear of corn-yellow road dust decorates his neat black shirt. As his growl-ing obscenities litter the air, the sight of the Reverend covered in off-roading trucker shit has magically made my day worthwhile. I hoist the dinner trays over my head and maneuver through the same squeeze without difficulty.

When I reach the broken slab of concrete propping open the Hannigans' front door, a collection of cheerful window placards greets me: *No solicitors. Curb your dog. Hillary for Prison.* The stickers may have sun-faded in color, but each one holds steadfastly beneath a wind chime of wood blocks that have been whittled into cardinals and American flags.

Inside the kitchen, the Reverend grumbles as he dabs at his stain with a wet paper towel. The place is empty except for us. All those cars and nobody home. Normally, Ricky's mother keeps a cinnamon-vanilla candle burning at the kitchen table, but today, the house stinks of too many flowers. Something pungent, an awful overload of sweetness, dominates in a way I will never not associate with my grandmother's wake. Floral bouquets of death.

"Where is everybody?" the Reverend hollers as he stalks away from the sink, the ghost of his stain refusing to be exorcised. As he disappears around the corner, I set the meal trays on a crusted stovetop burner and twist the creaking oven dial to 350. While it preheats, I follow the Reverend—and the distant drone of a vacuum cleaner—inside Ricky's dark-carpeted living room. Same as always, an adjustable hospital bed sits in front of the TV like an altar.

Except there's no Mr. Hannigan in it. The Reverend and I stare at an empty bed.

No big smile. No enormous, bug-eyed glasses. No skinny body under the bed sheets. As my stomach cartwheels, a young Black woman rolls a PowerVac around the room while wearing earbuds. A second, very old woman—white and obese—slumps in her recliner. Ricky's mother's permed hair is pearly white to the point of being see-through. She digs into a bag of pretzel Goldfish while she and the Reverend exchange a pregnant, wordless moment.

"I tried calling you," she finally says, her voice as heavy as her eyes. "I left a message."

"Where is he...?" the Reverend asks, his voice cracking.

"Ricky passed away last night."

The empty bed...I knew it. My stomach somersaults again, but the Reverend's heaving breaths stop completely. The cleaning woman's vacuum barges through the tense space between the Reverend, Mrs. Hannigan, and me, as if we were furniture or potted plants to be navigated around.

Goodbye, Mr. Hannigan. He was my favorite appointment. Everyone else on my route either sent me away with a nasty look or warned me not to steal anything. *"I know the family, and the kid's got no father. All this trash moving into town; we're gonna have to lock up everything we own!"* Ambrose thinks of Mom and me as one step up from the trailer park, but Ricky never treated me that way. He knew the real me, and better yet, he liked what he knew.

Garlands of multicolored blooms hang from rows of fishing wire above the bed like a magical fairytale canopy. The flowers are new, but what they're draped over is not—yellow Broadway Playbills. Dozens of show programs hang off the lines, some still visible under the onslaught of bouquets. Older musicals—nothing recent—probably from a time before Mr. Hannigan ended up in this bed.

This empty bed.

"He was fine yesterday," the Reverend whispers.

"He was not fine yesterday," Mrs. Hannigan says, nibbling another goldfish. "He had an infected bedsore we didn't notice—"

"That useless medical aide!" The Reverend juts the entire heft of his body forward on a wounded scream. I didn't think he knew Ricky *that* personally. He ordered me to treat Ricky as higher priority than the others, but he never specified why. I assumed the Hannigans were once big givers to his church.

"Should I wait outside?" I ask, wishing I could be as laid-back about this unfolding drama as the woman vacuum-dancing around the room.

"I'll drive you home," the Reverend moans into his hands.

"You can't," Mrs. Hannigan says. "Those two detectives came by looking for you."

The Reverend widens the gaps between his fingers to better glare at Ricky's mother. Before I can get excited about how visibly nervous this news has made the Reverend, footsteps descend the stairs. The home's entire structure whines with each step until two women emerge from the staircase behind Mrs. Hannigan's recliner. A faint powder plumes into the air as the detectives snap off their latex gloves—but not a speck falls onto their perfect, ironed pantsuits.

"Reverend Packard, we were hoping that was you," says the woman with short, severely parted hair. The Reverend hacks his throat clear as Mrs. Hannigan blindly devours pretzel fish. I resist the urge to thrust my hands into the air.

"I'm Special Agent Rhodes," the longer-haired woman says, gesturing first to herself, then to the woman beside her. "My partner, Special Agent Elms. You remember us, don't you?" They wave badges that chill my blood like I've been injected with IcyHot menthol: FBI. They're not detectives; they're FBI agents.

"You're searching the place again?" the Reverend asks, keeping a wary distance. "Ricky's body isn't even cold. We're still grieving—"

"I invited them," Mrs. Hannigan chimes in.

"You're *upset*."

"I don't care about anything anymore." Mrs. Hannigan gobbles another Goldfish while the Reverend tries (and fails) to deep breathe himself into a lighter shade of beet red.

"We just want to ask you some more questions about Ricky," Agent Elms says, pocketing her badge.

Holy shit, holy shit. They want to ask the Reverend about Ricky. Is it about him dying? If Ricky died from an infection, why are they here, acting like they're looking for a murderer? Did his medical aide mess up? They wouldn't call the FBI in for that. The Reverend said the agents had been here before to search Ricky's home, and the agents wanted to ask him some *more* questions. More. They're grilling him.

"The night Ricky was injured—" Agent Rhodes begins, but the Reverend bounds forward, outstretching his arms the way he greets local truckers at Sue's Diner. His smile is supposed to be jovial and winning, but with his size, Agent Rhodes takes an instinctive, retreating step back.

"Whatever I can do to help, agents," the Reverend says before ticking his head in my direction. "But this is a talk we better have in private, don't you think?"

All eyes float toward me. In a single breath, I blurt, "I'm just Meals on Wheels; I don't know anything."

The pressure crushing my neck releases once everyone agrees that I'm an invisible nobody who can be no help whatsoever to this investigation. On his way upstairs with the agents, the Reverend squeezes Mrs. Hannigan's shoulder; a gesture either to comfort her for her loss or to communicate *We'll talk later about how pissed I am that you called the FBI.*

Both, probably.

"The night Ricky was injured..."

This isn't about his infection at all; it's about his original injury.

My feet turn to ice inside my flip-flops as I'm left alone with Ricky's mother and his empty, haunted bed. The first time I met Ricky, he called me "cute." He was never vague about being happy to see me. Maybe he was into me, but I don't care—he was never creepy about it. The Reverend explained that Ricky had good days and bad; that he had limited use of his body below the neck; that it was difficult for him to communicate verbally or even through writing, but his thoughts were still there. Nobody *ever* explained how Ricky got into this situation, but I never thought it was for a reason that would require the Oh-My-God FBI. Now I wish I'd Googled him when I had the chance. Good luck doing that at the moment, with no phone or laptop.

"I'm real sorry..." I tell Ricky's mom, suddenly hyper-aware of my empty hands and shabby clothes. "Um...I put the oven on. You want me to heat you up his meal too?"

A-plus comforting, Connor. "Your son's dead. Want his food?"

"I can't eat that caca," Mrs. Hannigan says, munching another Goldfish. "All I can stomach right now are my little fishies." Her hand jitters as she nips the corner off another pretzel. "I should have called you, too, but I..." She taps her forehead and winces back a headache.

"It's cool. I don't actually have a phone."

Mrs. Hannigan's lips upturn in a surprised half smile. "You're the first kid I ever heard of who doesn't got his nose buried in a phone."

My nose would be buried in a phone if it could, BELIEVE ME.

"No," I admit, "I...actually got punished."

Ricky's mother scrunches her brow as her round face begins to collapse. *God, she's going to start bawling and I'll be the absolute worst supportive stranger ever.* "Come here," she says weakly. I step deeper inside the room, and somehow, the flower stench gets worse. A rank, deathly smell. "Connor, you and my son talked a little, and you're a good boy... Ricky told me you've been having trouble at home."

Disorientation tilts the room again. I *had* brought Ario up to Ricky—maybe unwisely, given how things turned out—but I assumed Ricky couldn't speak well enough to repeat much. Was he the one who told the Reverend about Ario?

"What's this trouble you got going with your mom?" Mrs. Hannigan asks, her recliner's springs plunging down as she scoots closer. I really don't want to hear any religious crap from this lady because then I'll have to tell her to mind her business and she just lost her son.

But, hey, she asked.

"I got a boyfriend," I say. Mrs. Hannigan doesn't blink, so I elaborate: "My mom didn't like it, and uh...she took my phone away. It's getting impossible to see him or even talk to him, and um...he's leaving for college soon. We're running out of time."

My heart liquefies as the truth rises in me—*I might never see Ario again.*

My confession doesn't sit well with Mrs. Hannigan, either. She swallows a quick, gasping breath, dusts her fingers free of pretzel salt, and reaches for me. Gently, she traces her fingertips in a circle around my face and simply watches me. I watch her. In this moment, she reminds me so much of my grandma, seeing me clearly and with perfect understanding. The only one in my family who could make me feel okay again. The only one who could talk sense into my mom.

"—I told you I don't know!" the Reverend shouts from upstairs.

Neither of us blink. The spell doesn't break, even as Mrs. Hannigan's serene expression buckles like a cloud ready to storm. She's so vulnerable—this is my only chance. "Mrs. Hannigan?" I ask. "What happened to Ricky? Why was he in this bed?"

She turns away, and I follow her attention to a silver-framed picture of a teenage boy beside the TV. Time has bleached the photo's colors into a single, reddish hue, but the boy's apple-cheeked smile remains instantly recognizable. *Ricky*.

Mrs. Hannigan's lips tighten, but nevertheless, tears escape her. "Whatever happened," she says, "whatever the Reverend tells you...it wasn't an accident."

CHAPTER NINE
THE MISSING

TODAY

The other boys in the cabin are still asleep under their thin bed sheets. I push back the wavy hair swooping low over my forehead and I stare horizontally into space. Dim morning light creeps inside the mesh-covered windows, shining like a beacon onto the Winner's Wall. Onto Ricky Hannigan's teenage face. The boy's eyes flare open helplessly, reaching out of the past and begging me to get out of this place before whatever happened to him happens to me.

"Whatever the Reverend tells you...it wasn't an accident."

I wish I could un-hear Mrs. Hannigan's ominous words about her son, but it was all I dreamt about. Luckily, the generator outside was kind enough to spring on five minutes ago and wake me from my nightmare: *I was in Ricky's hospital bed and couldn't move. I screamed for my mom and Mrs. Hannigan in the next room. They wandered in to see what was wrong, only they weren't exactly themselves—they had on the pantsuits worn by those FBI agents. Mom took one look at me in Ricky's bed, and then disappeared into a pillar of smoke and fog.*

Dreams can be evil like that.

My drying lips cling to Ario's recorder, still slung around my neck on its delicate leather string. I need to play it—I need the connection to him. I don't care about waking anyone else up. If the clattering generator outside weren't enough to shake these boys awake, some soft music wouldn't either. I cover two of the recorder's holes and blow out a hollow, arrhythmic tune. As the bitter taste of the instrument settles onto my tongue, a memory rises of Ario resting his curly head on my chest...

I stop playing. My chest hurts too much, and this recorder sucks. At the foot of the bunk bed, my backpack slumps against the floor. Somewhere inside it is a Playbill bearing a warning—*HELP CONNOR*—written by an ex-Nightlight camper. And his story didn't turn out so well.

Seeing my backpack in the light of day only makes me angrier with Ario. This wasn't supposed to happen. This isn't the world he promised me. He promised it would be fine if I came out, and now, where am I? A camp with Ramona, the fifties housewife; Marcos, the fifties bebopper; and Darcy, the sixties dreamgirl. It's permanently the past on this island, a relic untouched by any of the progress Ario insisted was waiting for me.

All I had to do was come out.

This is your fault, I curse silently at the pendant. *Lying to my mom was safer.*

While jungle birds chatter in a grove of trees outside our lodge, I slide one foot onto the cool stone floor, so gently I couldn't crush an ant. Now, the other foot. I collect my shirt and shoes from under the bunk, pull them on, and edge toward the door. *I forgot my backpack.* I turn, and Marcos—pretty, nervous, pretty nervous Marcos—is already stirring in his lower bunk. Long, brown feet stick out the end of his blanket as he stretches and yawns at the morning, exactly how I imagine waking up next to Ario could've been like.

I can still wake up next to him.

I'll find my way out of here, and Ario's family will take me in until I can smooth things over with my mom. I need to hurry though—like I told Mrs. Hannigan, Ario and I are running out of time before he disappears off to college. On the other hand, once he finds out what happened to me—what forcing me to come out too soon did—he'll feel so bad, he'll never glance at another boy when he gets to school.

Maybe I can turn this into a win, after all.

Marcos's eyes remain closed, his glasses still draped over the bedrail. If I leave now, without my backpack, he definitely won't spot me.

I pull back the cabin door's rusting handle...and meet a firm deadbolt.

"*Rise and shine, Nightlight,*" the Reverend's voice crackles from a speaker above the door. I yelp and topple backward in clumsy jumps. "*The time is six-thirty. Breakfast is in one hour.*"

Horn music drifts out of a decrepit, gunmetal-gray speaker as five boys leap from their beds and tuck their sheets with energetic, military precision. Before I can summon the will to trudge back to my bunk, my stomach explodes with an electrified thought: *they're children.* Marcos is around my age, as is a handsome boy with long, blond surfer hair and obnoxiously clear skin, but the three others are tiny—thirteen at the oldest. Like a prison warden, Marcos addresses each of the young boys by name as he inspects their bed-making. The first boy, Owen Regis, is so dainty he has trouble opening his sheet wide enough to fold it. The next boy, Alan Gardner, is taller, but not by much. His freckled wrist hangs limply, absentmindedly, in midair until Marcos taps the telltale wrist with a rubber-tipped pointer.

"Oh my gosh," Alan gasps, straightening his wrist, curling it over and over to make sure he shook all the gay out of it.

"It's okay, you got it," Marcos says, genuinely supportive. He brushes back his own sleep-mussed hair and pops a retainer out of his mouth and into a green, plastic snap case. *Adorable.* Marcos Carrillo may be the cabin snitch, but there's just something about a big, tall cutie with correctional dentistry. I glance away, and only just in time—he turns, alert as a cat, as if he could feel the weight of my attention.

Ario never mentioned being gay would literally be as exhausting as Olympic swimming.

The last boy, Vance Olmos, is small, round, and copper skinned. He whistles along with the speaker's jaunty classical music as he straightens his sheets, but Marcos crinkles his brow as if smelling something diseased. "Vance, you're whistling," he says.

Whistling over. Vance nods, grateful to be corrected.

Behind me, the cabin door unlatches and, once again, I jump. The screen swings open onto Ben Briggs, looking well rested in his black tank top with a plunging neckline that accentuates his impressive chest. "Everyone up and out," Briggs orders. "Mr. Carrillo?"

"The Beginners are ready," Marcos says, waving Alan, Vance, and Owen out to meet Briggs. The boys (*Beginners?*) haul gray knapsacks over their shoulders on their way out into the sunshine. Before vanishing around the corner, Alan—the tall Beginner with the dangling wrist—leans back to sneak one more peek at me. *Cool—I've been cruised by a tween.* This cabin is full of kids with eyes in constant states of looking and not looking, like roving prison lights. I've only been here half a day and I'm already so self-conscious, I don't even know where to put my attention anymore.

Still looming in the doorframe, Briggs cocks his eyebrow. "Hop to it, Mr. Major. You don't get a lie-in, even on your first day. Twenty minutes 'til departure." With that, he stomps down the stairs, leaving the screen door drifting open in the lakeside breeze.

Completely open.

My heart boils to even consider such an immediate, simple escape, but I force myself to remember the facts: it's not smart to run. *What if Ricky tried to run?*

"You're new?" a nasally voice asks behind me. I turn, coming face-to-face with the final camper my age—the annoyingly handsome surfer.

"Connor Major," I say, shaking his hand, which is muscular but somehow soft as cotton. His Nightlight tee fits snugly across his lean, defined chest. Hot boys—like, Instagram hot—make me nervous to death. How can they stand themselves?

"Drew Schreiber." He slings his own knapsack carelessly over his shoulder. "I'd chat more, but I'm always the first shower of the day."

Drew Schreiber...the missing Calvin Klein model. Ario's sister pops into my head with her amazing, four-eyed face. *"He was taken. Some place where they do mind games to make you straight."* A woman was raising money through GoFundMe to find her nephew, this missing model right in front of me. Ario's sister is looking for Nightlight. I want to gush about everything: his aunt's website; the money I donated; the whole *internet*—from LA to Illinois—searching for him. They're going to find him. They'll find us both.

"Drew Schreiber?" I repeat.

"Yeah...?" he asks, likely unsettled by my silent grinning.

"Uh, good to meet you."

Drew rolls his blue slushy-colored eyes. "Look, don't try to sit with me at breakfast, okay? I really can't make that clear enough."

Once Drew leaves (slinks away is a better phrase), Marcos rushes up, carrying two knapsacks. "Morning," he chirps as the toothbrush sticking out of his mouth falls to his hand. "New boys always want to sit next to Drew."

Oh, so Drew doesn't want anyone sitting with him because he gets flirted with too much—*Oh no, I don't get to kiss his perfect peach of supermodel ass over toast and eggs?* All I was gonna do is let him know that someone loves him and is trying to find him.

"I gotta watch you make your bed," Marcos says in a Sorry-for-Being-a-Nudge tone.

"Sure, fine," I groan.

I pout all the way to my bunk—I couldn't care less about a well-made bed right now. I shake out the rumpled twin sheet, lay it on the mattress, and smooth it out in one long stroke of my wingspan. *There, done.* Marcos nudges his glasses as he inspects my bed's uneven lumps, its untucked ends, and the pillow with its case half yanked off. "You're such a guy," he giggles, dropping his knapsack. In under thirty seconds, he redoes my bed properly using sharp, precise tugs.

"Well...shouldn't being a guy, whatever, be a good thing here? Isn't that the point?"

"The point"—Marcos finishes and stands—"is control."

Control. Interesting word choice.

While Marcos retrieves his knapsack, I unzip my JanSport and right away find Ricky's Playbill for *South Pacific*. NIGHTLIGHT, it says. *Well, here I am at Nightlight, Ricky—Home, Sweet, Home.* I fold the thing in half and pocket it for later; maybe there's something else written inside, some other nasty surprise he needed to warn me about. I scan the Winner's Wall one last time before departing with Marcos. In the daylight, the number of faces is overwhelming. An endless missing persons wall. How many of these kids were just as "missing" as Drew Schreiber, only not famous enough to warrant a GoFundMe? Through the chaos of names and photos, a pair of cold eyes stands out in a teenager with black, glue-spiked hair:

BEN BRIGGS. 2001 to 2002.

"It's him!" I shout. "It's Briggs. He was a camper."

"I don't think he ever wanted to leave," Marcos says from the door. "Come on, we're gonna miss our shower."

A year. That angry dickhead spent a year of his life at Nightlight and then asked for more? *"Put in the work and go home,"* Briggs said. How much work did he put in? The boy in this picture is so pasty and nerdy, such a long way from the gymrat thug who hauled me down a flight of stairs, I can't even do the mental geometry.

I hoist my knapsack and pay another nod of respect to Ricky at the doorway's break in the wall. Near the very top, a scrap of corkboard hangs loose in the gap between the ceiling and Ricky's picture. A strand of congealed yellow glue dangles off the cork like a live wire.

It's a missing picture. Someone's been removed from this wall.

CHAPTER TEN

TROPICAL TRIP

"**S**hower's good today, boys," Briggs announces to the row of campers queued behind Drew Schreiber. Around the rear of our cabin, an open-roofed, concrete beach shower surrounds a raised water tank. Just beyond it, Lake Monteverde lies as still as a mirror, as if there had never been a storm at all. As of last night, the wild beach grass lining the road had been drowned under inches of rain, but this morning, the land is as arid as a Texas backroad. "Damn equator sun," Briggs grumbles as he mops his forehead with a hanky. "When it hits high noon, you'll be fever-dreaming of winter." My tongue is already the texture of crisp sandpaper—how much more merciless can it get?

"You each get one minute in the shower stall," Briggs says, marching up the line. "And lather yourself up before you pull down the water. It saves you trouble." As he passes, Briggs claps the model on his shoulder. "All right, Drew?" The boy blushes like he scored a gold star from Teacher, and the two of them exchange long stares before Briggs continues on toward the shower block.

Oh my God, those two are hooking up. My jaw drops so low it almost unhinges, but no one else in line pays them any attention. In fact, Marcos and the Beginners seem to be purposely turned the other direction. My muscle memory wants to text Vicky all the dirt: *Sksksjsksl hot counselor is banging one of the campers, and he's like 40!!!!*

"In you go," Briggs orders, and Drew dashes into the private shower. Inside, a gigantic splash erupts like the world's biggest water balloon just exploded.

"WOOOO!" Drew cackles. "Thank you, Jesus!"

After Marcos, Owen, Alan, and Vance each run inside the shower for their squeals, it's my turn. There's no showerhead: a lime-rotted pipe leads from the floor to one of their hanging water catchment cones, except this tank is three times larger than the ones at the clinic. A metal triangle attaches to a chain at the tip of the cone. "Right, pretty basic, really," Briggs says, following me into the enclosure. "Stand under the cone here, pull that chain there, and water comes out. Got it? Hang your shirt on them hooks. And I'll warn you: your fellow campers are still at-risk little gay boys, so you better put your shirt back on before stepping outside. Even though you're not much to look at."

"Excuse me?" I ask, my arms shielding my chest in an "X" as he scans me.

"Your pale and...mehhhh...patchy chest hair. It's not exactly appetizing. We're all about to eat."

Briggs departs on that zinger. Once his footsteps fade away, I gather the courage to whisper: "Maybe if I looked more like Drew, you wouldn't mind me strolling out shirtless. *Fag*!"

The word falls out of my mouth like a loose tooth. *Fag*. The forbidden word. It's been hurled at me online more times than I can count, but looking at this smug dude who's had his sweaty paws all over a twinky camper...it made the hate rise in my throat as naturally as a wolf cub's first howl.

Fag. Act like one and you get called one. It felt almost...cleansing to say it at someone else.

Speaking of cleansing, I eagerly undress and finally step into the shower basin. Inside my knapsack is a towel, toothbrush, tube of SPF-55 sunblock, and a bottle of hot pink body wash labeled *Tropical Trip* in funky letters surrounding a cartoon bird of paradise. Reverend Packard droned on about no plumbing or electricity at Nightlight because we've returned to nature. Good to know returning to nature includes Herbal Essences. I squirt pink ooze into my left palm and yank the cone's chain with my right.

Come on, shower, I need you. I need you bad.

The shower spray is like a bucket of cold water dumped on my head. Chilly rainwater surges down my back, and I release a long, pained moan as every hair on my ass stands at attention. Despite this drenching, my front barely gets wet and I forget to lather on the Tropical Trip. I spread the banana-coconut-scented wash around my pits and pale/mehhhh/patchy-haired chest and pull the chain a second time. Before I can chicken out. My teeth clench, but nothing falls from the pipe except a few dribbles. I pull again. A drop.

"Um, hey!" I shout. "This tank's empty."

"That's it for you, then," Briggs replies. Already, there's a bunch of Goddamn snickering.

"But I got all this soap on me."

"Wait for the next storm." More laughing. More gay laughing.

After the shower, I beg my way into a dip in the lake to wash off my Tropical Trip, which Briggs agrees to only because my muddy feet incident from last night got him in trouble with the Reverend. When I finally emerge bare-chested from the lake, he and Drew make hilarious retching noises.

Hot gays are so funny. They're such a good crop of human beings.

I dress while Briggs alerts the campers that our morning drills will be run double-time because I put us behind schedule. Luckily for me, I'm still pulling on my shirt so I'm unable to catch what are most assuredly five aggravated scowls.

My damp, wavy curls aren't lying the way I want them to, so I roll up my sleeves to better display my arms. I like my arms, I've got good arms, and I need to feel better about my body ASAP. Twenty minutes into our double-time drill, I remember why it is I despise running: I get hot and cranky easily, and I hate the noodley way my limbs fly everywhere. At school, when guys kick a ball my way, I refuse to kick it back; that's another rule. I'm not running or kicking balls, making myself look gay so they can laugh their asses off.

At least we're running toward breakfast.

At the head of our drill, Briggs jogs backward, hopping raised roots along the Coral Road like a show-off. The Beginners run behind me, panting, while Marcos jogs at the rear to make sure the boys keep to the path. Drew's pace stays lively at the head of the pack, a dark stripe of sweat lovingly staining his shirt from his neck to the small of his back. Meanwhile, Tropical Storm Connor has soaked me from head to toe since our first lap along the lakeshore. Tropical Storm Marcos has also struck pretty hard—his blue shirt runs black with sweat. As Briggs hollers for more hustle, he dodges the sharp palm fronds jutting out from the dense green surrounding the road. His smiling eyes never break from Drew. The two of them are locked in a strange dance, Drew charging forward and Briggs skipping backward—the gap between them never closing.

Sure, I'll be a captive audience to this awful thing. Is this just hardcore flirting or do they actually do it? *Where* would they do it? And Briggs is old enough to be his dad.

Briggs orders us to slow as we approach a signpost for *PURA VIDA*. The village of Pura Vida is little more than a cul-de-sac of stilted cabins surrounding a gravel courtyard. I never thought I'd be this happy to see a bunch of crummy old shacks, but my chest is on fire and this running bullshit needs to be over yesterday. Around the bend into the village, an arrow points onward for Ambrose Chapel. The way out.

Above us, horn music flies from a bird's nest watchtower so high it climbs above the jungle canopy. A woman's voice on a record warbles an old, crackling song. Just as the singer belts out a rousing finish, an old man leans out of the nest, his sagging, yet muscled arm gripping a wooden gutter for support. Burly and gray whiskered, like an orangutan stuffed into safari khakis, he bellows the song lyrics a half-step behind the recording.

"Good morning, Bill," Briggs calls up to Safari Grandpa.

"Welcome back, sissies," Bill hollers, clucking his tongue disapprovingly. "Breakfast is on, but the girls beat you by three minutes."

Briggs waves us—the melting, staggering sissies—over the courtyard connecting Bill's watchtower to the cul-de-sac of cabins. Drew mutters bitchily about me making everyone late, but I don't care; I'm too busy massaging the heart attack out of my chest. Two of the Beginners hurry ahead into the cafeteria, but it takes all my remaining strength not to collapse and drag myself over the gravel toward food. I lace my fingers behind my head, frantic to steady my breathing, but I'm not alone in my desperation. A third Beginner—the whistling Vance—drops to his hands and begins weeping in large sheets.

"Mr. Carrillo, deal with it," Briggs sighs, jogging in place with Drew.

"Yes, sir," Marcos says. Marcos is wearing his own sweat for a coat, but he is a natural runner and barely needs to catch his breath before approaching the blubbering child. He casts an enormous shadow over Vance, choosing to loom overhead rather than help him up. "Vance, don't cry. The Reverend will hear you."

But Vance refuses to be consoled. "My stomach hurts!" he wails, rolling onto his back.

"Stop crying, Vance," Marcos repeats urgently. "You know you gotta."

Up above, Safari Bill dances along to his brass band music, oblivious to the boy's fit. The kid is totally losing it. My heartbeat finally settled, I take a knee next to Vance. "My stomach hurts too," I say. "Running really sucks. Let's get you up—" I slide my hand behind Vance's back to scoop him to his feet, but he slaps my arm with a scorpion's sting.

"You can't," he hisses. "You're not supposed to touch me with your hands." I jump back to standing, rubbing the welt above my thumb where the little bugger got me.

Fine, have your meltdown.

First Drew, now Vance. Nightlight campers don't want a lick of help.

"Vance..." Marcos says, commanding the boy's attention again. His voice rolls out as smoothly as warm maple syrup. "I'm hugging you. I'm comforting you now." Except he isn't. Marcos stands two feet apart from Vance, but the kid's whimpering is already dying off into faint squeaks. "That's good, Vance. I'm putting you in a big mama bear hug. When I pat the back of your head, you feel so

118

much better. You feel together, you're on top of the world, and you know you got a friend."

At last, Vance exhales. He sits, his eyes clearing. "Thank you so much," he whispers. *Wow, that even made me feel better.* Marcos smiles softly as the Beginner shuffles toward the cafeteria. He's ten yards ahead before he spins around. "Are you gonna write about me that I cried?"

A nervous twitch interrupts Marcos's smile like static. "I have to," he says.

Vance's shoulders collapse, and he mopes away to his devastated breakfast. *Write about him crying?* Marcos comes off as this sweet, gooey-pie kind of guy, but he's ready to report this (admittedly annoying) kid for...what? Crying? Everyone at Nightlight is competing to gross me out the most, and so far, everyone is winning.

"Enjoy your breakfast, campers," Bill's voice reverberates from the watchtower's speakers. Marcos and I turn to the old man and shield our eyes against the sun rising over the jungle canopy beyond. "I'm Karaoke Bill," he coos into a microphone, "and this has been your morning Karaoke Bill's Opening Number."

"Let's go, I'm starving," Marcos says, tapping my shoulder.

"Not supposed to touch me with your hands," I whisper.

"You're right! I'm so sorry." His hand curls away, fingers snapping in an anxious loop.

"No, I was just messing with you—" But Marcos is already scuttling across the courtyard, his long runner's legs making incredible strides away from me. I don't think I've ever seen anyone look like such a frightened puppy as Marcos Carrillo.

I make it three steps across the courtyard before Karaoke Bill's voice stops me: "Today's Opening Number was 'I'm Gonna Wash That Man Right Outta My Hair' from *South Pacific*."

South Pacific.

Sailors dance around a tropical island...

Karaoke Bill played a selection from the musical on Ricky's Playbill. Memories flash, as quick and vicious as bacon grease spitting from a pan: *Ricky's watery eyes try to warn me, but his mouth won't let him. A hospital bed lies empty. Playbills hang off fishing wire. The room stinks of too many flowers...death bouquets.*

"Whatever the Reverend tells you...it wasn't an accident."

CHAPTER ELEVEN

THE SOUTH PACIFIC GULCH

The cafeteria is a hive of activity. Swinging saloon doors separate the main dining hall from the kitchen, where a trio of darkly sunburnt lunch ladies scurry around each other. One scrubs cast-iron pans while the others deliver fresh breakfast plates onto an "Order up!" windowsill. Next to the ordering window, a magnetic board displays the day's menu and declares, *Let's have a good summer!*—except one of the o's in *good* fell down, so now it just reads, *Let's have a god summer!*

Basically.

Above the double screen door entrance, a draping banner reads, **THE SOUTH PACIFIC GULCH**—*South Pacific* again. Ricky's Playbill won't stop telling my future.

The Gulch's country-western theming is reinforced by upbeat string band music from Karaoke Bill's watchtower outside. Strangely, it reminds me of home—a shithole, but a familiar shithole. Familiarity is what I crave most. These other campers aren't fellow queers, they're aliens—cold, remote life-forms of a hostile planet where I've found myself marooned. Molly and I spot each other at the breakfast line. She's also an alien, but a more familiar alien than the rest. We were shackled together in a boat, we escaped into the ocean, and we watched as we were forced to delete the most special people in the world from our phones. A witness to the worst moment in your life can't help but generate some level of intimacy. With no better options, Molly and I wordlessly, instinctively, gravitate to the same table.

We don't know what to say to each other, except to share the same petrified expressions that scream, *I didn't dream it, I'm still here.*

A minute later, breakfast arrives. Darcy Culpepper, the rail-thin girl in the bob wig we met last night, busses plates of sausage and piping hot scrambled eggs to each table. Another Black female camper I don't recognize trots after Darcy with an enormous percolator pot. Coffee Girl—a large, beaming young woman with her hair barrette-pinned into a poodle-puff bun—introduces herself as Lacrishia Sims. She pours steaming coffee into our tin cups and then tosses me a bashful smile before moving on to other tables.

Nightlight turned two of its Black campers into waitresses—I shouldn't be surprised. This camp has a boner for freezing us inside a snow globe of detestable, old-timey America. *Just how things are, here in the South Pacific Gulch!*

Finally, Darcy and Lacrishia sit to enjoy their breakfasts, and I no longer feel rude digging in. The fork is in my hand, about to dive into savory delights, when the room stands and places their hands over their hearts. Molly and I frown at the realization: prayer time. We pray before we eat, no matter how starved we might be. Ten campers and a dozen staff members sing heartily together:

"*Oh, the Lord is good to me,*
And so I thank the Lord
For giving me the things I need,
The sun and the rain and the apple seed.

The Lord is good to me!"

A second doesn't pass before Briggs downs his coffee in a single, greedy swig, and the Gulch fills with a cacophony of scraping silverware. As Molly and I attack our eggs, we investigate Ricky's Playbill cover to cover, which offers no further clues or warnings other than *NIGHTLIGHT* and *HELP CONNOR*. On the page listing *South Pacific*'s musical numbers, I point out one of them to Molly—"I'm Gonna Wash that Man Right Outta My Hair"—the song Karaoke Bill played a few minutes ago. We aren't shocked by this discovery so much as consumed with dread by it. I can't pry the tune out of my head now that I know where it's from. I inhale a heap of crispy, seasoned home fries, and my thoughts begin to flow more easily: the likeliest explanation for Ricky giving me this Playbill is that he wanted to put me on my guard. Briggs's friendliness in the airport manipulated me into obedience. If I hadn't recognized *NIGHTLIGHT* on their boat, hadn't been forewarned of the omen by Ricky, how deep into the program would I have gone before I smelled a rat?

How long did you know your mom before you smelled a rat with her? the nasty voice in my head whispers.

The South Pacific Gulch is the loveliest of all the shacks so far at Nightlight. Picture windows run floor to ceiling, allowing us an unspoiled view of the tropical jungle beyond the Coral Road. Rust-colored benches line a dozen tables; far more than they need, even with all campers and staff accounted for. Nightlight's popularity must be shrinking to only a few remaining wealthy fanatics. Back in Ricky's day, these benches were probably overflowing with "troubled" teens.

Across rows of empty tables, Marcos giggles with Darcy and Lacrishia. They sang the breakfast blessing loudest, prompting a telling-off from Karaoke Bill: "A little less *gospel*, thank you!"

Three Beginner boys eat with three just-as-shockingly young Beginners from the girls' cabin: two of them white and husky, the third taller and dark skinned. Bill dines with Briggs, Archie, and five other men—all in gray staff T-shirts. Ramona, still in her hideous, lemon-print dress from last night, eats politely by herself and dabs her lips with a napkin after each bite. After the Reverend, I hate Ramona the most. Her smug smile when she forced me to delete Ario is tattooed onto my brain.

The remaining table is for Drew Schreiber—all alone, as requested. He digs into a parfait with strawberries and blueberries, the rest of us with our oily eggs and sausage. I didn't notice any parfait on the breakfast menu. What makes him so special?

"Molly," I whisper, "look who's staring at Calvin Klein." My zombified friend stabs eggs around on her plate until she finally looks up, her head tilted like a confused puppy. "Follow my thumb." I make an air gun. My index finger points at nothing, but my thumb points at Drew—a trick my dad taught me when you want to point at someone without them noticing. The supermodel sends a smoldering look toward the staff table, and Briggs returns a panther-like stare. It's impossible, but Molly and I are the only ones who notice or care that these two are eye-banging each other in front of the entire Gulch. Does the Reverend really allow one of his ex-gay employees to openly flirt with boys half his age?

But the Reverend isn't at breakfast. When the cat's away, Briggs will play.

Briggs and Drew aren't the only ones caught in a mating ritual. Marcos can't peel his wounded animal eyes off me. Across the room, he spies me through the gap between Lacrishia and Darcy. Marcos slowly munches his sausage link and stares, entranced, not realizing what he's doing. Marcos's attention feels like a sweater on a hot day, a warm, comforting sensation that grows stifling and more cumbersome the longer I sit with it.

He's really sweet and a professional dimple operator, but the last thing I'm here to do is flirt.

So far I've only been stealing glances at Marcos, but once I turn my full attention on him, he leaps backward in his bench as if I'd lit his eyeballs on fire. His sausage drops to his plate as a coughing fit overtakes him. Darcy and Lacrishia lunge forward to help, but he waves them off, gulping down an entire glass of water. As if psychically linked, his humiliation fills my thoughts—*people caught me staring at another boy. They know. Everyone saw.*

Marcos slaps his broad chest to clear it and doesn't glance up from his plate again. I don't want him to be embarrassed; he probably hates himself enough already.

"Hey," Molly says, interrupting my guilt spiral, "I need to say sorry."

"For what?" I ask.

"Uh, you know...choking you with a stick on the beach."

"Oh my God, don't worry about it," I laugh with a mouthful of home fries. Our dramatic arrival on the shores of Nightlight Island feels like ten lifetimes ago.

Over Molly's shoulder, Karaoke Bill shambles between our tables, each step of his mud-stained combat boots leaving a filthy trail. Through tangles of white-gray hair, he has foam-padded headphones shoved over his ears and hums along to a selection of his own private music. I can't make out the song, but I miss my earbuds like I'm missing a limb.

As Bill closes in on our table, I return Ricky's Playbill to my pocket. "You two didn't sing along with the breakfast hymn," Bill admonishes, wagging a blistered finger toward a placard on the cafeteria wall: in block letters are the lyrics to the "Johnny Appleseed" hymn. "You get one free pass, but tomorrow, I want to hear those pipes of yours loud and flawless." He leans close, the full blast of his sour body odor threatening to turn us all off our breakfasts. His crinkled skin runs deeply red, almost purple; there's a looseness to it, as if the top layer could peel off as easily as baked chicken skin. What exact function does Bill serve at Nightlight? He plays showtunes, cracks jokes, and shuffles around like the town drunk in a western.

"Make believe you're at a Pride parade if it helps you sing better," Karaoke Bill chuckles before moseying along to unsettle other campers.

"I've sung a churchy song before," Molly whispers, rolling her eyes.

"Right?" I laugh. "Like our tongues are gonna roll back in our throats if we have to say the word *Jesus*."

"So, Darcy and Lacrishia told me we're here for a weeklong probation"—Molly nods silently for a moment—"then we get reviewed."

"A week?" I pluck Molly's last sausage link from her plate—she's been ignoring it too long, and eating is my only medicine. "So, what, we just play along, pass the review, and go home?"

"Uh-huh, that's one plan." Her chest rises and falls on a shuddering breath. "But if we don't pass the review, our one-week stay is automatically extended to three months."

Three months?

Nightlight's dirt-bitter coffee scalds my insides as I remember the Winner's Wall—so many campers left in a different *year* than the one they arrived in. Like Briggs. And Ricky. I'd have to delay my senior year. I'll miss college application dates. Ario will move away, find someone new, and forget I ever meant anything to him. Mom won't let this happen. She couldn't pay for three months, anyway, even if the Reverend gave her a "friendly" discount.

"We better pass our review, then," I chuckle, dropping Molly's half-eaten sausage back to her plate. It's grossing me out.

"Or..."—Molly lowers her whisper further—"*or* you and I run to the beach. We steal their boat and get the hell out of here *right now*."

"How?"

"We'll find the right moment."

"Do you know how to drive that kind of boat?"

"I've driven speedboats before."

"Listen...I can make it through a week."

"And then what?"

"I'll pass their stupid review and go home."

"What if you can't?"

"I can fake it."

"Everyone thinks that—"

"I CAN FAKE IT." I grind my teeth so hard, my neck cramp escalates into a headache. "You don't know what this month has been like for me. The last person who gave me advice on coming out and never hiding and fighting back and blah, blah, blah was my boyfriend, and it screwed me over. As for your 'wing it' escape plan, an ex-camper I know somehow got an injury that made him nearly quadriplegic, and every staff member here has a mega-charged taser and isn't afraid to stick me with it. So, I'm sorry, but I'm leaving in a week, and I'm leaving safely."

"All right." Molly struggles through another sip of dark, medicinal coffee. "But you ought to know my cabinmates over there sound like they've been waiting a long time for their ship to come in. Ask your boys how successful *they've* been at faking it—"

"More coffee, dumplings?" Lacrishia asks, startling us and shaking an almost-empty percolator.

"No, um, thanks," I say, slurping my half-drunk brew. "I'm awake."

Lacrishia giggles through her nose while Molly thrusts her cup forward: "Fill 'er up."

"Sorry," Lacrishia says, wincing. "Girls are only allowed one coffee per day." She floats away with her percolator as Molly's face collapses into a mask of fury. We've stumbled onto another one of Nightlight's arbitrary, hypocritical rules: *"Return to nature! But here's some supermarket shower gel. Boys don't belong in the kitchen! But here's a jaunty musical number to start your morning!"*

I offer Molly the rest of my cup, but she waves me off, preferring to drink her own disgust instead. Hot on Lacrishia's heels, Darcy bops over and reaches for our plates. "All done with these?" she asks in a light New Yawk accent. Molly and I nod, both full and vaguely nauseated. As Darcy plunks forks and knives onto our greasy plates, her smile never wanes. "Limiting our coffee intake keeps us calm and agreeable." My stomach tightens as Darcy burns with a strange intensity. "You two shouldn't whisper. When you whisper, people lean in to hear. Talk in a normal voice; that's when people tune out." Darcy reports this nugget of information in a normal volume as she piles our coffee cups onto the stack of plates. "You were whispering, and I was right over there. Now I know Molly is planning to run for the boat, like nobody's ever thought of that. And Connor is planning to fake it through a week and go home, like nobody's thought of that, either." She lifts her head, smile frozen. "Welcome to our crisis, already in progress."

I am literal goo. My intestines clench painfully at the idea that we might've been overheard by someone other than Darcy. Molly, meanwhile, is only toughening. "So, what are you, on our side?" she asks, in compliance to speak at a regular volume. "You weren't talking this bluntly in the cabin this morning."

"Well, that's 'cuz there might be snitches in our cabin."

"So, are we supposed to just stay here forever?" I ask, forcing myself to speak above a whisper. In my paranoia, I imagine Briggs, Ramona, and the Reverend all hovering behind my shoulder, ready to bop me with a rolled-up newspaper.

"Connor!" Darcy giggles, shoving me like I've said something hilarious. Gray-shirted staff members sneer in our direction as they dump their trays with the lunch ladies and exit the Gulch. Darcy has put me so on edge, I want to crawl up the ceiling like Spider-Man and hide in the rafters. "You arrived ready to stir the pot, didn't you? I couldn't believe my ears last night when you started mouthing back to the Reverend about Ricky Hannigan, of all people."

Noise and oxygen leave the Gulch, and my attention narrows to a pinhole—it's only Darcy and me left in the whole universe. "What do you know about Ricky?"

"You could probably tell me a lot more than I could tell you." Darcy pulls a folded wad of paper from her pocket. "Nightlight is just like school, only you're watched more closely. Question is: In school, you ever get into trouble? Like, if you were passed a note,"— she slides the folded paper across the table, her fingers pressed on top—"would you unfold it out in the open for people to see, or would you find a way to read it later, nice and private?"

My heart whams against my ribcage. I knew the answer to her

question halfway through the asking. Vicky and I are masters of texting during class. I could text under my desk without once looking away from the teacher—never made a single autocorrect error and my phone was never confiscated. The only person to ever successfully separate me from my phone was Mom, and that was only because I decided to stop keeping secrets about myself. A mistake I won't repeat. With unblemished confidence, I say, "I don't get caught."

Darcy lifts her fingers from the folded note. Immediately, I drop Ricky's Playbill on top of it and slide both items back to the safety of my lap. She scoops our piled-high plates into her arms, and we nod to each other. Molly doesn't know what to make of either of us.

"Any of this gets back to me, I'll deny it," Darcy says. Archie and another gray-shirt stalk past us on their way out, but Darcy gives them a Gulch-friendly smile. "Church is up next," she says once the men are gone. "Then a class called Home Life Behavior. We'll talk again, but not until class. Do not approach me before I approach you."

Darcy vanishes our plates through the saloon doors into the kitchen, and pleasurable anxiety whirls through my skull. She knows something about Ricky.

"Well, what's it say?" Molly asks, back to whispering. Underneath the table, I unfurl Darcy's note and hide it in the middle of the Playbill's pages like I'm shuffling a deck of cards. If anyone catches me with the Playbill, who gives a shit? It was in my backpack, so they've already seen it and determined it's nothing. Briggs walks past, and my arm trembles with the memory of his taser shock. When my kidnapper finally departs, I open the Playbill—deep-breathing until my hands stop shaking—and find Darcy's secret message:

WHEN THEY ASK YOU TO BE MY HUSBAND, SAY YES.

CHAPTER TWELVE
LEPERS

After breakfast, the Costa Rican sun rises over the jungle canopy and cooks us on our walk to church. The sweltering, dusty march of campers and counselors comes to an end at the familiar torchlights of Ambrose Chapel flickering through the daylight. Darcy leads the head of the pack, with Molly and me tutting along at the rear with whatever is the opposite of a spring in our steps. We're both indescribably bummed: Darcy's note had nothing to do with Ricky Hannigan, and if anything, its mysteriousness has only freaked us out more.

"What does she mean, 'be my husband'?" I hiss. "I don't want to marry anybody..."

"Obviously, I don't know and don't care," Molly says with an agitated huff. "I'm not trying to solve a puzzle. Everyone here is a secret-keeping snake!"

"Agreed."

Hellfire-winged butterflies swarm my stomach at the mere possibility—*they can't just force me to marry somebody*. But something in Darcy's catlike intensity won't let me shrug this off; she doesn't seem the type to invent something ridiculous. She *meant* something by this. While Darcy's note has unsettled me, Molly has only further steeled herself to commandeer an escape boat. "As soon as I see my chance, I'm taking it," she says. "And I'm not waiting around for you to think it over."

After a morning of bed-making, sing-alongs, and secret letters, Molly reminds me Nightlight is a place not to be settled into but to be done with as soon as possible. I want to know what happened to Ricky, but the FBI is involved and the Reverend could be hiding something legit serious. I can't snoop around *and* appear to be a solid, flag-saluting citizen of Nightlight.

For now, I have to let go of Ricky.

My heart plummets like an elevator at the idea of living here another three months if I fail their review. When I make it back home, I'll find Ario's social media flooded with pictures of him and some new college boyfriend—someone with a dynamic, alliterative name like Ash (*Ario and Ash! Ariash!*), and their Instas packed with hashtags and sponsored by Crest Whitestrips.

Nightlight will have to be the performance of my closeted career.

Inside the chapel, two standing candelabras remain lit because even the harsh sun can't crack through these filthy inches-thick windows. Each pane of glass is stained with an amber sheen, dousing the chapel in a warm, yet ugly hue—as if gold could rot. Two battery-powered air conditioners the size of lunchboxes blow a merciful breeze onto the congregation, while a third aims directly at the Reverend.

All in black, the Reverend puffs his chest like a massive, ominous raven. The man thundering scripture before me is the same red-throated preacher I've known since seventh grade, but the familiarity is oddly comforting. The pews are the same pews back home—my mom could be sitting right behind me. Church wasn't always a storm cloud in my life. When I was twelve and we'd recently moved to town, Mom and I helped out at every church function. The others in Ambrose clocked us for southern trailer trash cluttering up their "you betcha" little farming village, but we managed to carve a little place for ourselves in the Reverend's congregation where we were something close to wanted. Perhaps more like needed. Mom thrives when she feels needed, and at church, she's indispensable. Back then, Christmas was my favorite time to help; Mom would bake her gingerbread cupcakes, the air smelled strongly of the Reverend's sugar plum tea, and the chapel would be warmly lit—making the snow-covered fields outside shimmer violet in the dusk. Last but not least, I got to perform in and run the Nativity play. *At twelve years old, finally, my chance to direct!* Mom cheered my curtain call and took me to get any video game I wanted. She didn't just love me back then, she *liked* me. So did the Reverend. Ambrose looked at me and saw a mouthy, scuffed-up rat, but to Mom and the Reverend, I was their darling boy, a gleeful little chatterbox, ecstatic to find myself the center of attention.

I don't know when it happened, but one day, I woke up and wasn't their BFF anymore.

Now I'm the enemy.

"Ten lepers with nowhere to go," the Reverend chants behind his pulpit at Nightlight. "Ten lepers cleansed as pure as snow. One came back to give thanks to God, but nine never returned."

"We talk a lot about healing at Nightlight." The Reverend raises his hands to a literally captive audience and continues: "In Luke, Jesus met ten men with leprosy. They yelled out, 'Jesus, hello, Jesus, take pity on us!' Jesus told them to drag themselves over to the priests, and as they went, they were healed." The Reverend makes ten plucking gestures in the air, as if he's removing each invisible leper's affliction. "One came back to Jesus, one of the healed lepers, and praised God for returning him to good health. Jesus, in one of his *moods*,"—a jittery chuckle rises from the pews—"Jesus said, 'Wait, but there's only one of you. Didn't we heal all ten lepers? Where are the other nine?'

"Where are the others?" The Reverend descends his stage, meeting Lacrishia's eyes and then Drew's; their heads drop in unison, lowered by the weight of his attention. The Reverend stalks his pews like a blackbird surveying its choice of roadkill. "Nightlight has healed many people. But where are they?" He glances at Briggs, who huddles in the open doorframe next to Archie, the tattling guard. "You came back. Where are *your* fellow campers?" Briggs's eyes drop and glisten as if his heart was suddenly stung. "When you current campers are healed, which of *you* will come back to thank God?" One by one, the campers turn away as the Reverend approaches as a deathly shadow. The Beginner boys crumple in their seats, a trio of shoulders wilting like flowers in a cold snap. The Reverend's presence is *thrumming* with wicked electricity.

But I was raised in the Reverend's hellfire. This is nothing to me but another Sunday morning. When the Reverend's Rolex-clad grip lands on my shoulder, Marcos jumps an inch off his pew, but I hold the man's gaze as well as my breath. "Which of you will *not* return?" the Reverend asks, peering over his glasses.

The memory of his sugar plum tea wafts back to me.

I can't go it alone forever, away from my family. I can't pretend to be straight, but I can't just say "peace, y'all" and leave my mom for good. She and I are going to be close again—this is temporary. Which means I can't escape; I need to leave here on good terms. I'll fake whatever I have to. I'm going to be the best camper Nightlight has ever seen.

CHAPTER THIRTEEN
THE BIRTHDAY BOY

After service, the Reverend stays in the chapel while Briggs, Ramona, and the gray-shirts return us to the South Pacific Gulch. No one speaks. The world has become so *silent*—this is the most walking I've ever done without earbuds. Ninety percent of Nightlight's program is nothing but mind-numbing routine; they're going to shuffle me from one hotbox to the next until I finally shout, "I give up! I'm straight!"

Without stopping, Marcos and Darcy lead the campers back inside the Gulch, but Molly and I are blocked by a pair of friendly faces: Ramona and Briggs. "Hey, newcomers," Ramona says, swishing the filthy hem of her frock. "Y'all ready to jump into the nitty-gritty of your first day?"

"Yes, ma'am," I report cheerfully. Molly tosses me a flash of scorn before she, too, agrees to accept whatever is coming next.

"We appreciate your new attitudes," Briggs says.

"I am tickled pink to present you with the most important belonging you'll ever hold in your hand," Ramona squeaks, thrusting a brand new composition book at each of us. *EXPULSION DIARY* is written across the top. "It's your new best friend!"

"Before your first class with Ramona," Briggs says, "there's a very important—and private—conversation we need to have. Mr. Major, you're with me. Miss Partridge, follow Ramona."

There isn't a moment to ask questions before Ramona disappears with Molly into a grove of trees disguising the cafeteria's eastern wall. Greenery brushes against Molly's hair like a beaded curtain as she anxiously follows Ramona into the unknown. At the opposite end of the courtyard, Briggs and I arrive at the base of an enormous treehouse—a cabin, standing sentry at the edge of Pura Vida's cul-de-sac and raised three stories off the ground on taller versions of the floodwater stilts protecting every structure in Nightlight. A zigzagging staircase ascends through the jungle ferns, not much higher than Karaoke Bill's watchtower; and the two structures are so close, I could hang a clothesline between them.

Briggs's furry, Clydesdale legs make short work of the climb, while I'm sweating off five pounds. The worst part about Nightlight so far is how my damn eyes won't stop roving and thirsting at every single adult male I see. *Can I stop being such a gay monster for two seconds?* The higher we climb, the deeper the island's floor sinks beneath us. *A long way to fall, Major.* A rebellious urge to run back to Molly and hop aboard her boat-hijacking plan seizes me. But I wait and remember my own strategy.

At the top of the stairs is a door, already floating open on its hinges in the breeze. A placard above the frame repeats the welcoming phrase I recognize from the beach signpost: *Surrender your sins.* This demand, edging on low-key threat, grows poisonously sweeter every time I see it. *Surrender your sins*—what we're all here to do. The inside of the treehouse office is a rustic, vacant space except for a whiteboard bolted to the far wall and a dozen half-moon school desks. Briggs weaves between the desks on his way to a chair with a stuffed red folder lying on top. "Take one of the closer seats," he orders.

Before I can oblige, my heart stops at a magnificent view.

Natural light cascades through a window, open-aired but shielded with a net of iron bars. The air up here is sweet: honeysuckle and mist, wet wood, river rocks; a soothing, summer smell. The trees are even different at this height. Below, the bases are wide and sturdy; here at the top, thin branches curl their crooked fingers toward the sky, which hangs like mounds of dark clay over Lake Monteverde. From this vantage, the edge of the island finally comes into view with a mossy-green clifftop and a waterfall dropping onto the rim of the lake. My awe lasts only another moment before the creature arrives: spindly legs creep over the windowsill, and a tarantula the size of my fist crawls inside.

I can't even gasp; I leap backward (almost into Briggs's arms, Satan help me), and my jaw hangs open as the many-legged spider rests on the ledge between two of the bars. Except it's not a tarantula; its limbs are encased in a spiny shell. "It's a coconut crab," Briggs says, glancing up from his notes. "It'll go away." Almost at his command, the enormous crab scuttles across the window and out of sight.

"*It's a coconut crab.*" Last week, the most exotic thing I'd ever seen was a white-tailed deer.

As soon as I catch my breath, I tap the bars barricading the window and ask, "These to stop me from jumping?"

"The bars have always been there," Briggs says, arching his eyebrow. "Homosexuals are more likely to off themselves than their normal friends, and poofs with unaccepting families...well, they're twice more likely than them, aren't they? So, everyone here is at risk, and bars on my window make sense. Sit!"

"I was kidding..." A grave new weight lying on my shoulders, I take the closest half-moon desk. Somebody threw themselves out the window? *Was it Ricky? Or did someone push him?* No matter how many times I make up my mind to shut out this mystery, my thoughts flow back like a raging river toward theories about Ricky Hannigan's injury. Ricky was probably well-acquainted with this room...those tarantula crabs...and a man sitting across from him with a folder full of notes.

Discarded on the floor next to Briggs is a torn-open envelope housing a neon blue and orange greeting card, which reads: *Today Is a Big Deal—and So Are You!*

"It's your birthday?" I ask.

Briggs stares, baffled for a moment, before remembering the card. His lips harden as he replies, "Something like that. Grab your diary."

Never mind the chitchat then. I tap the unbroken spine of my Expulsion Diary until, finally, Briggs closes his folder and retrieves a small tape recorder. He clicks a red button and two spindles begin to turn. "This is Ben Briggs," he dictates. "Day one of the Expulsion of Connor Major."

"Expulsion? Sounds like an exorcism," I say, doing a superb job of sounding casual, even though my heart is rattling against Ario's recorder. Briggs places the running tape recorder under his chair and grins disarmingly, the way he fooled me into trusting that he wasn't *really* kidnapping me. *No, no, no, not kidnapping. We're taking a relaxing, tropical holiday.*

This is a man who knows the power of his own smile.

"Mr. Major," Briggs says, "I want you to know that even though you're family friends with Reverend Packard, you're receiving the exact same care as everyone else."

"Even the kids?" I ask. "Those ten-year-olds?"

"They're around thirteen, actually."

"How come you call them 'Beginners'?"

"Beginners are campers, ages twelve to fourteen. Middle school, basically. You are an Under: our high schoolers fifteen to eighteen. Then there are the Overs: post-grads. Any age, really, but the director gets nervous about...older men, so we cap the age limit at twenty-two."

"Twelve to twenty-two?" Off Briggs's nod, I continue: "So, is Drew an Over or an Under?"

If he's an Under, you're in deep shit, Mr. Briggs.

Briggs's smile falters and his gnarled fist moves to slap off the recording. But instead of stopping it, his fingers hover an inch above the spinning tape. He controlled himself—*the point is control*—and once more, he calls upon his smile. "An oddly specific question," he says. "Mr. Schreiber is twenty. He's an Over."

"That's good news," I say, not blinking. A thunderclap of scarlet rage passes through Briggs's eyes. *So, it's true about him and Drew.* Briggs knows I know, and now he has a small taste of the panic I've been living with since my mom ordered him to abduct me.

I'll stop poking now. It's been fun, but I need to be a good camper to pass my review.

"So, how are you getting on here?" Briggs says, returning to business.

"How are you getting on?" When Dad bothered himself to call the house, that's how he'd ask about school: *"How are you getting on?" Not well, bitch.* Anxiety spills slowly out of my heart like air from a pricked balloon. Somehow, I manage a shrug. "It's the first day. I ran drills with you...whatever..."

"You think this is horseshit, don't you?"

"No!...But is my mom really paying you guys—?"

"Your mum will pay anything if the Reverend can return a straight son to her."

Scalding heat spreads down my back. *Breathe, Major.* I want to scream that she'll never have a straight son and she's taken money we can't afford and flushed it down the toilet.

But I scream nothing. I smile. I'm faking my way home.

"I hope we succeed," I say, wiping heat from my eyes.

"This is part one of a class I consider to be the most important section of treatment. It's called 'Expulsion.' You'll write in your diary every day,"—he reaches across the gap between us and pokes my notebook—"and later, you'll read what you've written out loud to the class."

When Marcos helped Vance through his crying fit, the boy was terrified he would write about him. Is Marcos going to tell the entire class that Vance cried because Briggs ran him too hard? "So, eh..." I mumble, "we just journal about what we did during the day?"

"No. You'll write about the past. Sins—sexual encounters; sexual thoughts; sins of your family members. Create an emotional map of all the different factors that brought you to Nightlight." Briggs flips to another page. "Like this story: as a boy, you frequently played *Alice in Wonderland* with your cousins. You played...the Queen?"

Briggs looks up, waiting for me to confirm the story like he doesn't have the answer right there in his folder. My throat burns with this girlish—but accurate—memory. "My mom told you that...? Yeah, I played the Queen, but it was *Alice in Wonderland*—"

"Your girl cousin should have been the Queen and you could've played the Mad Hatter."

"My cousin Mick was older. He had to be the Hatter or he

wouldn't play. And my cousin Maddie wanted to be Alice, so I *had* to be the Queen."

Briggs drags his finger further down his notes: "No...there were frequent disagreements—*childish fits*—when Madeline didn't want to be Alice. You insisted on being the Queen."

My mouth hangs open in space. My mom has been taking notes on my gayness from when I was seven years old. She knew this whole time. She knew what was happening to me, even though I had no help figuring it out for myself. Somewhere inside me, a fuse blows. "I didn't fall in love with a boy because I played the Queen of Hearts! Okay?!"

I shouldn't have yelled; it just sprang out of me. My hand floats to the knotted bamboo of Ario's recorder. I miss him so much. He's not a sin to be Expulsion-ed. The Reverend is why I'm at Nightlight, not Ario.

"You don't have to use that specific story," Briggs sighs, dropping his folder of homosexual evidence beside the recorder. "You could lead with something more serious, like your dad leaving."

"Why?"

"Your dad left you with a giant hole in your heart. I understand drinking played a role—that's another Expulsion detail. Alcoholism— any addiction, really—is vulnerability to sin. A vulnerability you inherited."

My brain clangs inside my skull like a wind chime. I'm not gay because my dad left our family. My mom was *happier* without him. The years after they separated—and before she fell into the Reverend's flock—were the happiest of my life.

"He's nothing to me," I scoff.

"Rejection of reality. Your father, out there running around with other women while his son runs around with boys. An obvious pattern. A weakness that's part of your emotional map, and it should be the first thing you tackle during Expulsion."

Mom refused to admit to her own mother about Dad's girlfriends and drinking, but she told Briggs? She is so desperate for me not to be me—desperate for any explanation other than the truth—that she has drawn this absolute stranger into our family's most painful, *private* moments. I don't even know what to say back to him other than *"NOPE."*

"Expulsion is about recognizing patterns so you can break them," Briggs adds. "Which is why, in the end, you'll need to take responsibility for your son."

"My...what?"

"Avery Woodbine. You've let him go, haven't you?"

The baby. The Goddamn baby again.

I drop the Expulsion Diary to the floor with a *thwap*. Briggs glances at the notebook, then at me before withdrawing a piece of crisply folded paper from his Evidence Folder of the Damned. He unfurls it in front of me like a magician would present the Ace of Spades—*nothing up my sleeves!*—and when I recognize the paper, my hands shake with rage.

Ink-dark baby footprints adorn the official document: a birth certificate.

Avery Woodbine's birth certificate. His name is clearly visible beneath the footprints.

My head throbs, as Briggs's next instruction confirms my worst, plummeting, odious fear: "Before this is over," he says, "you will sign this as Avery's father."

"Vicky gave this to you...?" I gasp, choking on the very thought that my best friend in the world is in on this relentless conspiracy against me. Who else is left to betray me—is Ario next?

"No, this is a copy. Your mum got the original from Vicky's mum, who is equally eager to see her grandson have a father. This won't be an official record of your paternity of the child; that'll come later once you're home. But consider this a symbolic gesture of your commitment."

"So, does Vicky know anything about this…? Me coming here?"

"No, but your mum is positive that when you return with the signed copy, Vicky's relief and gratitude will have made this whole ordeal worth it."

A sip of breath returns to my lungs. Vicky isn't part of my kidnapping. Thank God for small favors. "The baby's already born," I say. "Isn't it late to be signing that? Don't you have to kinda do it, I don't know…on the day?"

"Mums don't sign. Obviously, they gave birth, the hospital saw it for themselves. But when the couple isn't married, signing a birth certificate is how they establish who the dad is. The sooner the better, but it can be signed any time. One signature from you, and the deal is done."

Briggs waves Avery's birth certificate like some enticing coupon. A white-hot headache grips my skull. I can almost hear it thudding in my ears. Mom literally snuck a picture of a little boy's birth certificate, copied it at FedEx, and then handed it to a man whom she'd just paid a fortune to kidnap her own son to a Costa Rican island. She has finally crossed the line—the lengths she'll go to support this idiotic conspiracy theory have officially surpassed my ability to understand. How *long* am I going to be arguing this?

"He's not mine," I growl through gritted teeth.

"No judgment from me, Mr. Major," Briggs adds, putting *mea culpa* hands in the air. He bends to retrieve the birthday card from the floor and presents it alongside the birth certificate copy. "It's not my birthday. My son Phillip, he just turned eighteen. I was wishing him well at UNI."

"The envelope's torn," I say. "You opened your own card?"

Briggs's crinkled expression sinks into shadow. "Right, well... see, like I said, no judgment from me. I'm, um...not in the boy's life no more. He sent back the card without opening it. His mum's turned him against me. Doesn't like me working here. She doesn't have good memories of this camp."

The math clicks into place: Briggs was listed on the Winner's Wall as having left in 2002. Eighteen years ago. When his baby was born.

"His mom was a camper too?" I ask to a stony glare. "Well... their loss, I guess."

"Mr. Major, I rejected my responsibility, and I hate myself for it. I'd hate to think someday you'll send Avery a birthday card, pour your heart and soul into it, everything you ever wanted to tell him, every apology, and he'll just send it back. Never opened."

Briggs flings the card over his shoulder and it collapses open on the warped, knotted floor: *Today Is a Big Deal—and So Are You!* "You of all people should know the pain of a father's rejection," he says, leaning closer. "I won't let this happen to you too. We've got work to do."

In the midst of humid, sweltering tropical air, my skin becomes ice. *This is it. This is my mother's endgame with Nightlight—to force me to claim Avery as mine.* Nightlight won't let me leave until I confirm he's my son.

Did Mom get this idea herself...or was it the Reverend whispering to her during all those lonely, heartfelt phone calls? The terrible thought climbs inside my mind like a coconut crab—hideous and unwanted.

My eyes fall on Briggs's son's birthday card, and I suppress a dull laugh.

Well done, Mom. Checkmate.

CHAPTER FOURTEEN
MISS MANNERS

Briggs returns me down the zigzagging stairs and departs with some words about fatherhood and responsibility that I refuse to pay attention to—all sounds drown in my rage. Mom has trapped me at Nightlight, and my only way out is through Vicky and Avery. It doesn't seem real. It doesn't seem *possible* that my mother could be calculating enough to do this alone. This ploy reeks of the Reverend.

I'm only one class in, and already my plan to fake my way through Nightlight has met a grotesque wrinkle: they're going to force me to lie and say I'm Avery's dad. Or worse, the pressure will get too intense and I'll blurt the truth: Vicky had sex with her adult boss and has been protecting him. She'd never speak to me again.

But what if I did lie and say I was the dad?

A white lie to save myself. Vicky would understand. I could come home and help her out until we graduated, and then we'd quietly go our separate ways. Later on, we could admit we'd been lying. Before Avery gets old enough. Whatever I decide, that's the line I can't cross—Avery can never think of me as his dad. I can't break a kid's heart.

Like Briggs did.

Briggs has a son older than me! He got some girl camper pregnant. Here. How? On purpose, or did the Reverend mate them at some point? I mouth a quick, silent prayer that Nightlight's program doesn't include forcing us to have sex. *When they ask you to be my husband, say yes.* Darcy's note reverberates in my head. I can't stop picturing nightmare scenarios:

Darcy and me, in bed together while Briggs and the Reverend watch with notepads in hand.

Darcy, pregnant.

Me, a deadbeat gay dad, with one official child and one unofficial one.

My mom, jubilant that her son is a trailer trash teen dad through multiple women, but at least he's not getting sexed in the butt.

How do I begin to write about Avery, a boy who isn't mine, in my Expulsion notebook, never mind read it aloud to a room? And what *sins* did Ricky Hannigan surrender in that office? He collected too many Playbills?

On autopilot, I follow Briggs's orders and step through the draping palms that had earlier engulfed Ramona and Molly. The brutal, wet heat dissipates, and I emerge into a blissfully shaded hollow where a mobile home crouches like a hermit. This home is larger than any trailer I've ever seen; a creature made of iron and plywood squats among waist-high underbrush, as massive as a shipping container.

Inside the home, everyone waits for me—and for a moment, I forget I'm on an island. A comfortable, suburban living room has been constructed within the mobile home, complete with a solid oak coffee table, a sofa smothered with throw pillows, and a circular rug to tie the whole visual together. I gravitate to Molly's side with the pull of a magnet. She offers me a paper cup of water and a weary smile. The water evaporates the moment it reaches my tongue, and

I return Molly's glum expression. Her eyelids have drooped heavier since I left her; Ramona's introduction to Expulsion wasn't any more pleasant than Briggs's. What was Molly's Expulsion story, anyway? What was her version of "You Can't Come Home Until You Support Your Mom's Life-Destroying Conspiracy Theory"?

In front of the coffee table, Ramona clasps her hands and greets us: "Now that we're all here, welcome to my two newcomers. This will be your first course of Home Life Behavior."

"'Miss Manners,' they call her," Molly whispers. Miss Manners is definitely a more fitting name than Ramona, but all I need to know is where she keeps her taser. It must be in a garter belt. Where else could she keep one inside that hideous dress?

As campers go, the gang's all here: Molly, Marcos, Drew, Lacrishia, Darcy, and me. The Beginners aren't here, so it's Unders and Overs only. When I meet Darcy's placid, calculating eyes across the huddle of campers, her secret message to me returns with a slapping jolt: *When they ask you to be my husband, say yes.*

"Ramona, I'm sad you won't be giving sermons anymore," Drew whines from the back. He pouts next to a frightening painting of a squid strangling a clipper ship, his face framed by a mane of golden hair—rope thick from months of weak island showers.

Miss Manners pivots to him: "Thanks, dumpling. Just glad to have the whole family back."

While our teacher jumps into an introduction about "finding straightness by learning your place in the home," Molly whispers: "Miss Manners was in charge until the night we arrived. When the Reverend isn't here, Briggs is in charge. When they're both gone, she is."

"Your cabin just told you everything, huh?" I whisper with more than a little bitterness. Apparently, Darcy handed Molly the whole inside scoop on Nightlight the moment she woke up, while all I got was some stuck-up supermodel, a kid having a fit, and Marcos. Marcos could've easily caught me up on what to expect, who is who, any tips at all. Nope. He just tut-tutted the way I made my bed and left me to puzzle it all out myself.

Marcos: *"Here's a camp, figure it out."*

Darcy: *"Here's a note, figure it out."*

Ricky: *"Here's a warning, figure it out."*

I'm going to figure it all out, no thanks to Marcos, who is currently listening to Miss Manners with rapt attention. A strand of his slicked hair tumbles over his glasses, and my legs shiver at how painfully cute he is with his smooth, almost chubby cheeks.

Ever since my coming out flopped, it depresses me to find guys cute—it's not a pleasurable feeling, I know that. Not the kind straight people get. They can check each other out and don't have to think of ten thousand other annoying things at once: *What's it gonna do to my mom? Is it gonna get me cut off? If I'm cut off, will I be able to afford college on my own? Is some guy gonna punch me for looking at him? Will I be sent to some dangerous jungle camp?*

Can a cute guy be worth all this trouble? Ario pushed me out of the gay nest too soon, and I've fallen *splat* onto the sidewalk. Maybe I need to just spend a year raising Avery with Vicky, give myself time to figure myself out, away from Mom and the Reverend.

Finally finished with her introductory spiel, Miss Manners arranges the girls in a row alongside the coffee table, then asks the boys to take a seat on either the sofa or a set of cushy lounge chairs huddled under the window; even though the blinds are closed and our building is shaded, heat pushes inside with a bullying intensity.

Drew nabs one of the chairs right away. Marcos motions me to take the other, and as I sit, a smile spills over me. I have no idea if I smiled to be polite or because he genuinely struck me as sweet (attention I am starved for). Either way, Marcos didn't miss my smile, and his grin blossoms before he realizes what he's doing and stomps it out. Head bent and fingers snapping, Marcos seats himself at the end of the couch farthest from me.

Nice one, Major. Way to totally flirt with a guy mere seconds after swearing it off.

"All right," Miss Manners says, interrupting my spiral. "Molly, you're exempt from the first exercise, so just observe. Lacrishia? Darcy? Which of you wants to be Connor's wife?"

My spiral resumes. *This is it—Darcy's note. Say yes.*

But it isn't Darcy. Lacrishia is already cautiously jutting her arm into the air. "I could be Connor's wife, please," she says in a hopeful voice, barely above a whisper.

"You like Connor, Lacrishia?" Miss Manners asks.

"Yes, ma'am. He's handsome, even for a little guy, that scrappy black hair, I don't know." Lacrishia ends with a nervous laugh on the crest of a moan I know all too well: it's the sound anxiety makes as it escapes the body. I've made a few involuntary moans like this in my time, mostly when talking to a cute guy making me self-conscious.

"Damn it, girl," Marcos groans, humiliated, into a decorative pillow.

As Lacrishia throws another sweet, pathetic simper my way, I seriously contemplate grabbing Molly and running for the escape boat. *Jesus flipping Christ, they wouldn't marry me for real to one of these girls, would they? First Vicky, now this? How many wives does Nightlight want me to get before I turn eighteen?!*

Darcy won't even meet my frantic eyes. If I'm going to be force-fed a wedding (*oh my god oh my god oh my god*), can I at least find out what Darcy wanted to tell me? Maybe I should refuse Lacrishia and ask for Darcy instead...

There won't be a need for that, though. Miss Manners groans, visibly put off by Lacrishia's performance. "Darcy, you should be Connor's wife." Darcy straightens her tilted bob wig, shrugs, and agrees to be my wife as if someone asked her to run a quick errand. "Connor, will you be Darcy's husband?"

Ramona lowers a dead-eyed stare my way, an indifferent gaze, the kind a sea creature wears just before it devours you.

Be a good Nightlight camper, Connor. Say yes.

"Yes," I blurt.

"I messed up?" Lacrishia asks, overflowing with sorrow for herself as she fiddles with the bottom of her shirt.

"Can anyone point out Lacrishia's mistake?" Miss Manners asks the room. *Um, besides making me so uncomfortable I want to crawl inside my own nutsack?*

"She was forcing it," Marcos says, raising his arm. "It sounded fake. Sorry, girl."

"I'm not, though," Lacrishia replies desperately. "Honest. Connor's a cutie. I said this before class, even. Ask anyone. I did the right thing. Finding a man cute is the whole point, ain't it?"

"The point is control," I catch myself whispering. Marcos's cheeks flush as he battles another smile at me remembering his lesson.

"It's not that it sounded fake," Miss Manners corrects. "Anyone else?"

"Too forward," Molly's voice comes from behind Lacrishia.

The room is now pin-drop silent; I laugh to myself that anyone could think a gentle cat like Lacrishia, scared of her own shadow just to admit a boy is cute, could be too forward. Nevertheless, Molly's insight has struck a chord. A shimmering light explodes in our teacher's eyes. "Molly, that's incredibly sharp for someone new to the program," Ramona says. Her heels click closer. Molly inches backward, but the woman lands her painted claws gently under her elbow. Hairs stand rigidly upright on my friend's arm. "Yes, Lacrishia was too forward. But my exact reasoning is more specific. Darcy, please expand on Molly's wonderful insight."

"Uh, women," Darcy says, "natural, godly women, we don't talk about men that way, all descriptive talking about his hair and him being a cute shorty. Lacrishia was talking up a boy, sure, but her behavior still screamed, 'I know what I like,' which screams, 'I'm an in-your-face lesbian.' She would've done better to, like, bat her eyes and smile. Say nothing."

Lacrishia's defeated shoulders drop, and Miss Manners erupts into furious clapping as she twirls away, back behind the coffee table. "Darcy, *that* is why you are Connor's wife!"

Tension crashes upward through my body like an avalanche in reverse. I roll my neck in circles to release the building pressure. *Darcy is my wife for fakes, right?* If I weren't so distracted by my own panic, I would've noticed the veins in Molly's neck turning bright scarlet over the last twenty seconds.

"What a crock of shit," Molly spits.

Marcos gasps. Terror contorts every expression in the room as Miss Manners faces Molly with a single pivot of her stiletto. "Molly, you have some constructive criticism?"

"Don't—" Lacrishia warns.

"Let her finish her thought, Lacrishia," our teacher snaps. Lacrishia, Marcos, and Darcy exchange frightened winces while Drew tsk-tsks his head in the lounge chair, totally unconcerned. I'd like to smash his teeth in for being so blasé, but I can't look away from Molly, her chest heaving with each breath. Her fury with the program cannot be dampened, not even by her growing realization at how badly she's stepped out of line.

"I used to fight dogs in my darker days," Miss Manners says, fiddling with the ruby-encrusted ring on her finger. She spins the gems so they face inward. "A baby pit-terrier couldn't hurt a lamb. Sweetest puddings on planet Earth. They gotta be *taught* to attack you or another animal. They must be taught, and it's best teaching them young."

Her fingers bend into a fist...

Pins and needles flood my chest as she lunges for Molly. Before anyone can move, Ramona vaults over the coffee table and snares my friend's cheek between red-painted talons. Frozen solid, Molly can't make a sound. "I will teach you girls how to be a wife, and I'm gonna teach you young." When Miss Manners finally releases Molly's cheek, her claws leave behind a long, crimson gash. "Your lesbian trouble...is not knowing when you're wrong."

"You cut my face," Molly says, slapping a hand to her wound.

"Say you were wrong."

"You're craz—"

"You were wrong. Say it."

No one moves as Ramona stalks away, past the coffee table, her sinewy arms tensing with barely caged rage. Her gnarled fists open and close, as if calculating who to snatch next. I'm trapped in this lounge chair, my feet filled with numbing concrete.

GET. UP. CONNOR.

At last, she closes her claws around a potted ficus and with one single grunt, yanks the plant out at the root, cascading soil across the floor. Blood returns to my legs, and I beeline out of my chair toward Molly, where the other campers are rapidly congregating away from our wild teacher. Drew presses himself flat to the wall, while Marcos and Lacrishia hold their arms over their heads like threatened armadillos.

"You okay?" I ask Molly, but her eyes stare past me, transfixed by our teacher.

Miss Manners drags the small tree across the rug—its dirt-caked base crumbling as she swishes it around like a filthy broom. This bizarre act is performed casually, purposefully, like she suddenly remembered that she'd been meaning to take care of this all day. A second later, apparently satisfied, she drops the tree, and hope seeps back into the room that the storm might be over. After a clarifying moment, Miss Manners walks to us calmly.

"Don't," I say, but she pushes past me to Molly.

"Young ladies," Miss Manners huffs, "*women*...admit when they're wrong. And they're wrong a lot. So, you best get used to saying it: I. Was. Wron-*guh*."

"...I was wrong," Molly whispers.

Miss Manners unleashes her pageant smile and reaches again for Molly's cheek. Molly flinches, but our teacher shushes her, softly tapping the wound now blooming with blood. "The rest of you will pair off, but Molly, I want you to treat this classroom as if it were your own home." Molly nods, swallowing a large chunk of fear. "Good. There's supplies in the cupboard. Clean your home."

Nobody argues. I lend a brave smile to Molly, even though I

don't know why. Maybe to leave her with a small glimmer of kindness in such an ugly moment. Either way, she doesn't return the smile. I want to help her clean, but she can handle this. Molly can handle more than I ever could.

CHAPTER FIFTEEN
CONNOR'S WIFE

O n her hands and knees, Molly scrapes a horsehair brush over the piles of planter soil littering the rug. Sweat beads down her forehead, meeting fresh blood bubbling from a cheek wound that won't stop gushing—Ramona's talons cut deep. A ceiling fan does its best to mobilize the home's stagnant, muggy air, but it's a losing battle. While Molly labors, Miss Manners relaxes on the sofa and sips from a thermos; chunks of ice slosh around inside the plastic.

We all hear it. We all want it. No one more than Molly.

At the other end of the classroom, the rest of us pair off into husband-and-wife teams. *Which, blessedly, turns out is just for fakes.* I'm with Darcy, and Lacrishia is with Marcos. Since Molly is otherwise occupied, Drew is allowed an absence from today's exercise. He skips outside to see Briggs about "camp business," and it takes every ounce of patience not to wave my finger at him and bellow, "Dirty, dirty, DIRTY!"

I'm at conversion camp for only a day and already my gut instinct is "gay sex is bad!" *Way to chameleon to your surroundings, Major.*

The rear of the mobile home is cordoned off from the living room with a black curtain, but once Marcos draws it aside, the lesson becomes obvious: we're having a date night. Three cocktail tables line the back room, each separated from the others by a partition wall. Lacrishia and Marcos disappear into the privacy of their sectioned-off table, and Darcy and I claim ours. A small lamp casts an intimate glow on our hideaway. *Finally alone.* Beyond Darcy's shoulder, Molly and Miss Manners are still visible in the living room, but the dark partition wall has effectively quarantined us. Lush, Italian restaurant music waltzes out of a radio, strong enough to muffle Marcos and Lacrishia's conversation down to a murmur.

"Can anyone hear us?" I whisper.

Darcy's lips curl into a grin. "No," she says, sliding her cold hand inside mine, "and let me do the talking. We got a stroke of good luck with Molly having to clean that living room. It'll keep Miss Manners out of here for now."

"Her face is bleeding—"

"It's only her cheek. I'm gonna talk fast and not repeat myself, so keep your eyes on me and off of Molly."

"This is why you asked me to be your husband."

Giggling, Darcy brings my hand to her lips. The kiss clamps my throat as tightly as a blast door, but I understand—Miss Manners can't hear us, but if she happens to look over, she needs to see two happy, opposite sex people on a date. "Yes, it's why I asked you. If you partnered with Molly, you'd just be rehashing your same, pathetic opening day escape strategies, and if you went with Lacrishia, she'd probably spend the hour staring at you with heart eyes."

"Yeah, she really faked it up."

"That wasn't fake; Lacrishia is bi." Darcy nudges her Retro Yearbook Wig back into place and continues at top speed. "Nightlight doesn't want Lacrishia to *want* a boyfriend, they want her to *have* a boyfriend. But she doesn't have a boyfriend; she has a girlfriend. So, she stays and doesn't correct them when they tell her she's here for being gay. Saying you're bi is a little too complicated for the Noah's Ark Gang here at Nightlight."

Hypnotized as I am by Darcy's whirring lips, I still spot Miss Manners rising from the sofa to direct Molly toward a spot on the floor she missed. If Darcy has anything important to say—other than the intricacies of Lacrishia Sims's sexual orientation—she'd better spit it out. "Briggs gave you your Expulsion Diary already," Darcy says, nodding to the notebook at the foot of my chair. An hour ago, it was as crisp as a new dollar, but I have since worried it into a curled tube. "He's got a file on you, right? A red folder?" At my silent nodding, Darcy's expression finally softens. "He dredged up something bad?"

"He...he said it was my fault..." My throat denies exit to the rest of my sentence. I don't know how to begin to describe my situation with Vicky. If I'm going to lie and pretend to be her baby's father, should I let Darcy in on the truth?

"Did I lose you?" Darcy asks, squeezing my hand across our candlelit table. The Italian restaurant accordion returns me to reality, followed by a swirl of lemons on a dress in the next room. Miss Manners has retaken her seat while Molly attacks the floor with Lysol wipes.

"Huh?" I ask airily. "No, I'm here, I—"

"The Expulsion Briggs gave you was a nasty one, I can tell."

"I guess so..."

"You don't gotta tell me what it was. Just know that it's a lie. And you have to take responsibility for telling yourself it's a lie every single day."

"I know—"

"It might seem obvious now. 'Oh, my mom did this, my daddy

did that, and now I like dick.' But spend a couple of weeks, a couple months at Nightlight…" Darcy taps two fingers to her forehead, her tone deepening. "That lie won't go away. Won't let you sleep. And that idea, that easy excuse, for why you're still stuck here, starts to look real friendly."

"I'm leaving after a week," I blurt without energy.

Those words have never sounded like such a fraud as they do just now. Darcy cups her hands over mine; she notices the pins and needles tremoring my fingers. "Connor, believe me when I tell you… nobody has left Nightlight after one week. Ever."

My breath evaporates. We hold each other's eyes like trapeze artists holding hands, petrified but utterly responsible not to let the other one go. "You know that for a fact?"

"It's why I wanted to talk to you." Nauseated as I am, I don't look away. I need to know what she knows. "Campers are all given jobs. In my first few months, mine was organizing the Reverend's paperwork. Secretary shit. I found a room that stores camper files, and these files are filled with Expulsion Diaries and tape recordings of our sessions. Bit by bit, I referenced the names on the files with the names on both Winner's Walls. The files covered every person who's ever been a camper, and no one left camp until at least the three-month mark. Now…imagine what kind of information might be inside Ricky Hannigan's camper file."

Breath drops back into my lungs, hot and clear. Of course— over his year-long stay, Ricky must have filled dozens of Expulsion Diaries. "Do you know what happened to him?"

"I don't. Because Ricky Hannigan is the only camper to *not* have a file." My face deflates over yet another dead end, but Darcy remains steeled. "But his file has to exist because there was a big, empty space where it should've been."

"Somebody stole it?"

Darcy nods. "And when I asked about who Ricky was, the Reverend terminated my job at his office and I was shuffled to waitressing. And I didn't hear Ricky's name again until the night you showed up, talking about how you've actually *met* him."

This confirms every hunch that's been kneeling on my gut for a week—the Reverend is covering up whatever happened to Ricky... and the FBI wants to find out. "So, what else do you know?"

"Nuh-uh. It's your turn to tell me something I don't know."

Past Darcy's shoulder, Miss Manners joins Molly on her hands and knees and presses a tissue to my friend's cheek wound. When the cotton comes back soaked with fresh crimson, Ramona mutters, annoyed that her assault isn't healing fast enough.

Molly's cleaning time might be over soon, so I confess quickly: "Ricky's dead. A long time ago, he was in some kind of accident, and it left him almost quadriplegic. Only his mom says it wasn't an accident, which makes me think he was attacked. I delivered him meals until a week ago when he died from a bedsore, which means that if he was attacked, whoever attacked him is now responsible for his death. Which is probably what made the FBI come to his house and question the Reverend about what happened to Ricky. Then Ricky left me a message in his will warning me about something called Nightlight. Then I was taken to Nightlight, a place where everyone seems to know who Ricky is, but nobody will talk about him. Which makes me suspicious that this mysterious attack might've happened when he was a camper here. The end."

"The FBI...?" Darcy asks, her lower lip shuddering. "Congrats. It takes a lot to scare me."

I only glanced away from the living room for a second, but a second was all it took. The lemon-dressed woman charges past the drawn curtain into our dining area, and danger drops on us too swiftly for me to get out the full warning: "Lemons—"

"Listen to me carrying on!" Darcy cackles, switching instantly to flirty date-speak. "You have the manliest speaking voice."

"First time I've heard that." I chuckle through sweat as Miss Manners reaches us, stopping in a clean one-two halt like a military officer.

"Everyone, into the living room for the rest of the hour," she spits, glaring back at Molly. My friend presses a napkin to her wound, her head drawn down and inward. "I'm taking the cry-baby to the clinic." Ramona's eyes flare demonically under the electric candle-light. Darcy and I don't regard each other as we oblige the teacher and leave our table.

Enough has already been said.

CHAPTER SIXTEEN

TAKE THE WALL

A fter Ramona hauls Molly off to the clinic, Marcos happily assumes the task of keeping us engaged in Husband and Wife roleplay. His "wife," Lacrishia, pouts in my direction as if I were the One Who Got Away. I can't even focus on this conversion crap; in the span of an hour, my hope of leaving Nightlight has shattered, my paranoia over the Reverend has tripled, and my feisty friend Molly has been terrorized into a silent, bow-headed child. What happens if Molly decides that now, on the way to the clinic, is the right time to follow through on her plan of running for the boat? Miss Manners will tase her—or worse. A fantasy slithers through my mind of Molly lying in Ricky's hospital bed, her back broken...

And I just stood here playing house.

"I'll be back," I say, cutting off Marcos mid-instruction.

"Oh, there's a bathroom behind the fake restaurant," he says, jutting his thumb over his shoulder. "But the bathroom is real."

"I'm actually gonna see if Molly's okay."

The three remaining campers freeze before I can navigate another step toward the door. "Um, you can't..." Marcos snaps his fingers at his side. "You gotta stay put. Sorry. Molly's fine."

"She didn't look fine."

"It's just a cut. We all got—"

"You all got what?" From his toes to his shoulders, Marcos

clenches like a fist. Darcy and Lacrishia exchange glances. "You've all been cut up by Miss Manners before, that what you were gonna say?"

"It's not as bad as you think—"

"Look, I'm gonna be careful. I just need to make sure Molly's okay."

"You're already learning Nightlight's gender roles," Darcy interrupts snidely from the sofa. "The woman can't take care of herself, so the *man's* gotta follow and make sure."

Hairs ignite on my neck. Darcy hasn't done a thing except put me on edge, but she wants me to chill on a couch while Molly gets hurt? I don't have to explain myself, even if I had time. Molly might run, and at least one camper got his ass beaten so badly he never walked again. If that makes me a Problematic Dude, so be it. "Whatever," I snap, smacking open the front door. "You want to snitch me out, call the Reverend."

When I emerge from the mobile home's shaded hollow into the open courtyard, cloud cover has already masked the sun. My heart shakes as thunder smashes through a darkening sky. The courtyard is empty. The gray-shirts are still in whatever ramshackle cabins they haunt while the rest of us play house, and none of the other campers follow me—the first useful thing any of them have done. At the end of the courtyard, the *plunk-plunk-plunk* of a ukulele drifts from the bird's nest watchtower. Karaoke Bill rests his mud-caked boots on the tower ledge, a bent-brim cowboy hat pushed low over his eyes as he reclines and strums. He won't be able to spot me through his siesta.

Christ, I wish I had my phone and some earbuds right now. Bill's ukulele reminds me of how brutally quiet this camp has been. In the real world, I wouldn't step outside without some kind of soundtrack for the day—music sets the pace for my heartbeat like a metronome, and without it, I'm adrift. Unfocused. Every peep of nature digs under my fingernails.

Beneath the village sign for Pura Vida, an arrow points further down the road toward *Ambrose Chapel* and *Clinic*. I depart as noiselessly as possible, sidestepping the crunchy gravel by stomping through mounds of underbrush surrounding Bill's tower. I already walked this path to church this morning; it should be less than ten minutes to the chapel and another five to the clinic. Molly and Miss Manners can't have much of a head start, but they don't have to sneak around.

Molly, don't do anything nuts.

The brambly underbrush makes a full sprint impossible. Wild roots curl along the dirt road as wide as river snakes. As carefully as I tread, my doofus foot still catches the edge of a raised root, so I sling my arm around a palm tree to avoid eating total shit. My grip on the bark falters under my sweat-slicked palms, but I manage to stay upright. Blood surges to my head, giving me the push I need to launch onward. *Breathe in through the nose and out through the mouth.* On my next breath, a pleasing whiff of hibiscus floats from the pink blooms dotting the jungle's edge. Don't these flowers know better than to be so flamingly colorful in a place with such a gray mission statement? On that topic, the sky is more cooperative—it's lost almost all of its blue. Bill's ukulele fades into the distance on another rumble of thunder.

I reach the chapel, and my heartbeat slows—two Beginners, one with dark, ponytailed hair and the other silvery-blond, press their faces to the support stilts raising the structure. *"Take the wall,"* the Reverend ordered Marcos, and Marcos obliged. *Sick.* The punished

Beginners have been left alone, but they remain dutifully motionless. They might as well be scarecrows.

I pass unnoticed.

One chest-thumping eternity later, the clinic welcomes me. My heart finally breathes at the familiar sight of the rattling generator and water catchment cones stacked against the back of the building. Inside, the clinic lobby is bright and empty. There's no one at the counter desk or at the large filing cabinet, nobody standing next to the Sparkletts water cooler, and nobody in the hallway of doors stretching from the lobby to its farthest room in back.

Voices murmur behind one of the doors, and blood rockets through my neck. Nevertheless, I refuse to stop moving, one foot in front of the other, deeper inside the clinic. If I stop, I'll lose my courage. If nothing bad is happening to Molly, I'll go back to the mobile home and finish my conversation with Darcy.

A brittle, yellowing poster peels off the lobby wall. *NIGHTLIGHT. Your path through the dark*, it reads in the sort of curvy, decades-old font from the first-edition Stephen King books my mom takes from the library. I pull Ario's recorder from the depths of my humidity-dampened shirt and place it between my teeth. The woodsy, bitter flavor calms my drumbeat heart as I remember him...*his meaty, confident fingers sliding up my thigh*...Unfortunately, the recorder also resurrects memories of showing up to the Hannigan home with a meal for someone who was already dead.

"—remember that instead of interrupting next time," Miss Manners's syrupy voice floats through the door.

"I won't," Molly whispers. "I'm just new. Sorry."

"'Sorry' is a step in the right direction." The blood in my neck comes to a full boil. "There—all better. It won't scar."

Molly's okay—okay enough. *Now go, Connor. That was the deal. Piss off before you get your face cut.* I'm creeping, heel-toe, back toward the door, when my attention snags on a plaque hanging above the open filing cabinet. Framed with carved, pastel flowers, the cozy décor is irritatingly out of place in such a cold, official space. The hand-stitched blessing on the plaque reads:

> *If tears could build a stairway,*
> *and memory a lane,*
> *I'd walk right up to Heaven*
> *and bring you home again.*

Pitifully, my first instinct is to take it because it's exactly the kind of sentimental, Christian gobbledygook my mom would love for her birthday. I'm not really in the gift-giving mood this year on this day, but maybe once I'm out of here, if I gave her a present, Mom would feel *extra* guilty about what she's put me through.

Ah, Major, it's cute you think your mom feels the human emotion known as guilt.

On a boom of thunder, rain finally breaks and smashes against the clinic's corrugated metal roof. Its tinny racket makes me nervous to just be standing here; someone might come out to investigate. Beyond the counter, a slatted closet door creaks open on its own. I almost leap out of my clothes, but there's nothing inside but a row of white lab coats. Still, a paralyzing thought grips my chest that I might not be alone.

Blood leaves my feet as the room begins to tilt. Someone is behind me.

The front door shuts softly, and I inhale a gasp as I spin...

Marcos. Doused in rain, the sweet-eyed boy trembles a foot above me. "You have to come back right now," he hisses, petrified. "I followed you."

"Yeah, no shit," I whisper, my heart slowing a beat. I want to be pissed off that the snitching, cutie-pie nerd followed me, but I'm just so relieved it wasn't the Reverend.

"Let's go." Marcos clicks his fingers like castanets. "It's totally not worth what'll happen to you if Miss Manners catches you. What she did to Molly is NOTH—" Before Marcos's tightening throat can form the "ing" in "nothing," a door unlatches at the end of the hall. Marcos launches himself onto his tiptoes and gasps, "She's coming!"

"In here!" I hiss.

I don't waste a hummingbird's heartbeat. I pull Marcos by his wrist toward the closet of lab coats. He mumbles about how I'm not supposed to touch him, but his heart isn't in it. His fight/flight instinct has kicked in, which is a relief because if he was dead weight, I wouldn't have a prayer of budging him. As I push Marcos through the hanging jumble of lab coats, his broad, surprisingly muscular back contours perfectly to my hand. The feel of his back spins my stomach with excitement bordering on electricity and, as usual, the touch of a man dissolves into nausea. I pull back my hand, resettling my stomach, and we vanish into the closet.

And no, the irony of us hiding in a closet to escape from violent zealots isn't lost on me.

The closet reeks of stale, rotting cedar, and Marcos's skin emanates wave after wave of heat, which sucks even more fresh air out of our hideaway. At the sound of footsteps, Marcos holds his breath, and I press my nose to the closet's thin, slatted openings and observe.

"Stay in the room," Miss Manners orders Molly as she stomps into the lobby. A half second later, Molly's door shuts again, and

Miss Manners surveys the lobby in tight circles like a roving security camera.

She smells a rat.

CLOSET BOYS

I should've listened to Marcos.

The clinic door opens from the outside, and everything gets worse. Through the slats in the closet, I catch the Reverend entering, almost floating like a vampire, his bearish face and raven's body a perfect, genetically engineered machine of intimidation. "How long has Connor been missing?" Miss Manners asks without greeting the director.

"Fifteen minutes," the Reverend reports. "You haven't seen or heard anything?"

How does he know? How does the Reverend always know?!

"Did you tell on me?" I mouth to Marcos, who returns a silent, horrified, "NO."

I have to believe him. He wouldn't snitch me out, only to come running after me and end up in the same hot-closet situation. These people need to get lost before I faint from heatstroke. I'd check on how Marcos is holding up, but I can't afford to miss anything from my peephole. Luckily, the tittering of rain on the metal roof muffles our breathing.

"Connor's making a run for the beach, then," the Reverend surmises.

"He can work the boat on his own?" asks Miss Manners.

"Don't ask me what that hillbilly is capable of. He's delinquent trash. No parenting whatsoever. He does whatever he feels like, and"—the Reverend pivots a suspicious scowl around the lobby—"and thanks to Ricky, now he's scared and acting recklessly."

Oh, I'm the hillbilly? The Reverend's chicken farm stinks up the whole town for miles.

"What does Connor know about Ricky?" Miss Manners asks.

"Nothing," the Reverend answers. "We need to find him before he gets himself hurt. And where the hell is Briggs? He's not answering his walkie."

"You know where he is." Ramona and the Reverend exchange long, narrowed looks as if the same unpleasant thought is occurring to both of them. And to me. *Drew—they know he's with Drew.* "Keeping Briggs on the team is a mistake—"

"Really not the time for office gossip, Ramona."

"It's not gossip."

"ENOUGH. What did I say? Focus on the kid. I need him back here." Miss Manners nods, while Marcos and I struggle not to exhale. "Connor Major does not leave this island."

With that grim directive, the Reverend thrusts open the clinic door and swoops out like the mammoth blackbird that he is. But Miss Manners doesn't follow. She scans the lobby another round...*There's no way she doesn't feel our presence in the room. Our furnace-like heat.* Something brushes against my arm. Next to me, Marcos's fingers twitch. *His nerves. He's going to snap his fingers, and she'll hear us.* Marcos and I move slowly as if in a nightmare. His thumb and middle finger push together, preparing to snap. My hand lunges for his like I'm catching him in a skydive. Just before he can snap, I lace my small, thin fingers into his thick, balmy ones and squeeze. Marcos's pale brown eyes watch me through the curtain of lab coats, and—reluctantly—he squeezes back. He doesn't pull away.

Marcos's hand is smooth, soft, and, with a tuft of dark hair, tickling me just lightly enough to make my entire spine tremble. Marcos stares at our clasped hands, hypnotized at what I've done. The thrill of merely holding this boy's hand—so dangerous that we're both begging for this moment to end...and not end. Right on schedule, the trouble activates—every pleasure must give way to pain. Horrible images assault me, one after the other: *Ario horrified, my hometown congregation scowling over their pews at me, and my mother...brutally, purposely silent.*

Nausea grips my belly, tilting my already uneasy balance in our sweltering closet, but it isn't safe to let go of Marcos. He'll snap and give us away. I wince through the pain and rush back to the door slats, praying I won't see Ramona's dolled-up eyes staring back from the other side. Apparently satisfied, the lemon-dressed woman clip-clops out of the clinic to join the Reverend...and locks the door from the outside.

I'm halfway out of the closet when I realize I'm still clutching Marcos's hand. He reemerges with me, and our overheating fingers unstick from each other, finally relieving my stomach. "Sorry," I say. "I had to stop your snapping."

"You had to do it," he says, searching our surroundings to make sure Miss Manners isn't crouching behind some chair. He pushes his ear to the front door and listens, bug-eyed and breathless. "She creeps me out. You have to keep away from her."

"Thanks for the hot tip," I say, caressing Ario's recorder until my heart finally rests.

"You know, you've got a little attitude on you."

"Well, I'm in trouble! You heard the Reverend. He's not gonna let me leave the island."

"He just means for the week that you're here."

"Yeah, that sounds exactly like what he meant." *Nobody leaves camp after a week.* As I lock eyes with Marcos, with those permanently wounded eyes, the knot of pain tying together my neck and shoulders begins to loosen. He was just trying to help. I've been an asshole. "I'm sorry...I don't know what's going on, and nobody will give me a clear answer. Are you okay?"

Marcos stares in disbelief, as if this is the first time someone has ever asked about him. "I'm...cool. We just need—"

He is cut off by the sound of keys jamming into a lock. Not the front door, but down the hall. It can't be Molly—she doesn't have keys. Someone else is here.

Nearing his eleventh heart attack of the day, Marcos squishes his eyes shut and accepts my hand again as I yank him, swan diving both of us back into the stifling hell of the closet. Our door shuts at the precise moment the mystery room down the hall unlocks. Braving seasickness once again, I hold on to Marcos's hand for safekeeping (safe from *snapping*), and he's too frightened to resist.

It isn't Molly.

Two men run into the lobby, giggling. One of them, wearing nothing but his camper shorts, spins around the older man and peels the black tank top from his torso. They kiss hungrily as Briggs's large, rough hands travel over Drew's bare thighs.

"I thought they'd never leave," Drew purrs.

Grinning, Briggs quietly appraises the room before snarling, "All right, baby, get on the counter." Drew obliges his man, his long, hairless fawn legs spread apart on the countertop next to jars of cotton balls and tongue depressors. Marcos and I can only stare—beyond helpless, beyond screwed—as the oxygen flees our bodies and Briggs gets to work on his boy.

I turn my head the moment Calvin Klein's shorts hit the floor, with nothing between him and the countertop but blond ass hairs. Marcos and I face each other—overheated, terrified, and in full, psychic agreement that this is a private show not for our eyes. I only wish I weren't still clutching his hand as the muffled *oohs* and *unhhhs* float through the wafer-thin closet door. It feels like we're part of a very bizarre foursome.

We have two choices: stay put or barge out of the closet and get destroyed by Briggs. So, for the next four minutes (give or take seventy hours), Marcos and I *quietly* deep breathe ourselves out of lightheadedness. Drew and Briggs keep making a fair amount of noise, so whenever a loud moan comes, I seize the opportunity to gulp a fuller breath. Eventually, I release Marcos's hand, and he fans himself in a futile attempt to coax a breeze onto his parched skin.

Finally, stillness arrives. Neither man speaks. Only indistinct shuffling.

Can't these dudes just mop themselves up and beat it?

Ario and I never took this long. Our few times together involved a lot of starting and stopping so I could get comfortable—a moment which never really came. *Gosh, Ario is so lucky he met a gem like me. All my bad sex and constant crying must be totally worth the trouble of dealing with my asshole mother.* I wish being gay was more fun. Everyone else looks like they're having so much fun, but as soon as I enter Queer Land, it's all danger camps and punishment and being too tightly wound to enjoy the little sex I was getting.

God, do I want to be straight?

Ask again later, you mess, when this closet isn't cooking your brain.

A burst of radio feedback interrupts my hellish spiral, and a breathless voice comes: "This is Briggs." A muffled response returns from his walkie—anger. The Reverend, most likely. He's been trying to reach him, but for some reason, Briggs wasn't answering. "I know," Briggs responds testily. "I've been trying to reach you, too, but something's interrupting the signal. Weird. I'll be there in a minute."

They're leaving!

This news is the next best thing to a cool drink of water. Marcos wipes his sweat- (and possible stress crying) dampened face, and I peek out of the slatted opening just in time to catch Briggs yanking up his shorts. "Fun's over," he says, chucking Drew his camper shirt from the floor. "I gotta round up Mr. Major."

"What's so special about this new kid?" Drew pouts as they both pull on their tops.

"Eh, the Reverend knows his mum." Briggs slides behind Drew, both of their fair skins still rashy pink from their workout. "And apparently...the kid knew Ricky Hannigan."

"No shit!" Drew spins around at full attention. I press against the slats, not daring to blink. "Does he know about—?"

"Absolutely not. And he can't find out."

Find out what? Does Drew know what happened to Ricky?

Marcos tenses next to me as Drew rolls his eyes and carelessly brushes a knot out of his golden mane. As quick as a cobra, Briggs clamps a hand to his boyfriend's cheeks: "HEY. I'm not joking. The Reverend's been wigging out ever since Ricky died, and the topic needs to GO AWAY. You don't want to see what'll happen if the Reverend thinks we've been talking about Ricky—"

"Jesus, fine!" Drew slaps Briggs's hand away, and to my astonishment, there is no trademark flash of anger. Satisfied, Drew smirks and puts another inch of distance between them. "I didn't know you were so scared of the Reverend. It's kind of a turnoff..."

"Is that right...?" Briggs closes the distance that Drew opened, and his hand disappears somewhere south. Whatever he's doing, it forces a gasp out of Drew, momentarily suspending the boy on his tiptoes, until ecstatic smiles spill over both of them. *Oh my God, these two.* "Just stay on the Reverend's good side, Blondie."

"If I don't?" Drew whispers, his lips hovering a centimeter from Briggs's.

"Then I'd have to choose between you and the Reverend."

"Who would you pick?"

Their bodies tense and clasped, neither moves except for Briggs's slowly rising hand. *Flick!* A switchblade opens next to their near-kiss. Drew doesn't flinch; he pets a slender finger across the edge of the blade. "It'll be a bad day for the Reverend," Briggs whispers. They engulf each other's mouths, and I'm about to look away again when the kiss ends abruptly. "Wait five minutes, baby. Then head back to class."

"'kay," Drew says from the countertop, hugging his knees to his chin. Briggs shuffles backward, grinning like a wolf, until he reaches the front door, unlocks it, and kicks it open. Drew settles back onto the countertop. As the rain dissipates and a thick silence finally drops over the clinic, a familiar disturbance brews among the lab coats. *Guuuurrrg.* Marcos and I turn to each other. *Gurlllggglgle.* It comes again. Marcos's eyes shut in horrified embarrassment, and he cups his stomach as it groans again. *Guurrrg.*

The countertop creaks as Drew bolts upright, newly alert.

Marcos covers his mouth as he seems to silently berate himself for having a functional digestive system at a time like this. I'm on my way to check the slatted door again when it batters open. A rush of fresh air washes down my cheeks and frees my lungs. Terror and fury kaleidoscope over Drew's expression as he clocks what exactly is going on here. Marcos's mouth hangs open as he debates running for the front door with or without me.

"You," Drew stammers, "you—you're sick! You watched—?"

"I'm sorry," I confess at a mad clip. "We had nowhere to go. We turned our heads away, I promise." Purple-necked and spittle flying, Drew struggles to find the next words he wants to hurl at us, but I'm certain they're going to be, "I'm calling my boyfriend right now to come beat you up."

Those words never come, though, as a second creaking noise behind Drew forces him to whip around again. *Molly*—creeping toward the door, now caught just like the rest of us. Puffy medical gauze lies taped across her cheek where Miss Manners sliced her.

"I didn't hear anything," she whispers, frozen mid-sneak.

Drew wheels around at the three of us, drowning in the awful reality that we heard *EV-ERY-THING*. On a final spin toward me, the model explodes into a trillion wilting flower petals as vulnerability consumes him:

"OH MY GOD, YOU GUYS, HE CAN'T FIND OUT YOU WERE HERE, PLEASE DON'T SAY ANYTHING!"

CHAPTER EIGHTEEN

MODEL MOUTH

I t took five minutes to reassure Drew that Molly, Marcos, and I would also prefer Ben Briggs live his whole life never knowing that three teenagers were eavesdropping on him screwing a fourth teenager. Well, Drew is twenty, but still. Marcos and I consume our body weights in icy water from the Sparkletts dispenser. I'm less muggy than I was in the closet, but a stifling, sticky inner heat refuses to vacate my body. Similarly flush, Marcos drinks and avoids looking at me. I don't blame him after the series of humiliations I put him through by holding his hand—but nevertheless, the avoidance stings. Having his attention was nicer than this put-off, ignoring energy.

Once we've hydrated, the four of us sneak out of the clinic. We opt to avoid the open exposure of the Coral Road, instead choosing to climb through the heavy green cover of its be-jungled edges. The rain comes and goes so quickly here. What was a storming onslaught only five minutes ago has dried up entirely; overcast skies break apart like ice floes, flecks of baby blue peeking around their edges in a promise of good times ahead. But I may be the lone optimist—each of my traveling companions has grown jumpier during our return to camp. Every snapped twig, every rustle of underbrush could be a gray-shirt—or worse, Miss Manners.

"We need to escape RIGHT NOW," Molly whispers.

"Not until I find out what the Reverend's been hiding about Ricky," I respond, gentlemanly pulling aside a swath of bracken to let Molly and Drew pass. Marcos stalks a path far ahead, his tree-trunk legs and hyperactive energy achieving much longer strides than the rest of us. Swampy sweat traps Marcos's shirt and shorts to the robust curves of his body, and to be honest, the view is doing a lot to mellow my skyrocketing anxiety. I'm being a perv, but it's impossible to fix my attention anywhere else because everywhere else lies the truth: that we're bunny rabbits, lost in a wilderness teeming with predators.

And some of the rabbits are cozying up with the predators.

"Look, I'm really sorry again, but we didn't have a choice," I tell Drew, who has spent the entirety of our walk engulfed in a self-conscious implosion. "We were already hiding, and then you two ran out. If we showed ourselves, Briggs would've gone apeshit."

"It's fine," he hisses. "Literally don't talk about it again."

"You know, no judgment, but you're handcuffing yourself to some seriously bad people—"

"And you keep getting in their way." Drew spins, his sweat-stained face reddening. He shivers with rage as the rest of us stand in the jungle, catching our breath and falling obediently silent.

"Hey, honey," I sneer, straightening. "If you want to hook up with Evil Hagrid who kidnaps kids to Homophobic Hogwarts, that's your business—"

"*This* is how things work at Nightlight," Drew snaps back, swooping his supermodel height downward to me like some elegant, furious bird. "You find a friend and stick together. You're less of a target if you're together." Like the passing storm clouds, Drew softens again. "It's none of my business if you want to get yourself killed, but you should stop trying to dig up stuff on Ricky Hannigan."

Marcos pinches back a headache while Molly and I draw closer.

"Yeah," I say, "I couldn't help overhear...sounds like your man told you the whole Ricky story." Over Drew's shoulder, Marcos nervously tugs at the hair curling under his ears. Adorable as Marcos is, I hold Drew's crumbling attention. "Here's the thing: I wouldn't need to go poking around anymore and causing all this trouble...if I knew what you knew about what happened to Ricky."

"You mean, you don't know *anything*?" Drew asks, scrunching his nose like I said something rude. "You know it's, like, a famous hate crime, right?"

Hate crime.

The words plunge the temperature in the jungle by forty degrees. Whatever happened, the news wasn't famous enough to make it out to Ambrose, Illinois. "I haven't heard, but you're a lot more worldly than us, I guess," I tell Drew, who isn't immune to flattery. "If it's so famous, why hasn't anybody ever heard of Nightlight?"

"Because it didn't happen here."

"Where did it happen?"

Until now, Drew has been grinning with the pleasure that he knows infinitely more about what's going on than the rest of us. But that grin is fading. It seems Briggs's warning to shut up about Ricky is starting to echo back to him. "Never mind..."

"Remember how Briggs told you I actually met Ricky?" *How could Drew forget? Briggs was basically inside him when he told him.* "Well, he was a friendly guy. But he got put through hell. Then I delivered him meals because it was difficult for him to get them himself anymore. Then he died, and I don't know who did this to him. He meant something to me..."

I hadn't realized it until this moment, but it's absolutely true: Ricky looked out for me in a way my parents flat-out didn't and couldn't. Drew's Grecian statue of a face doesn't crack, except for a miniscule eye twitch. He's thinking about Ricky—and the weight of his story is crushing him. "It happened in California," he whispers. "My aunt lives there, so I heard about it from her."

Oh, I know of your aunt, girl. But now isn't the time for that slice of information.

"Ricky got hate-crimed in California?" I ask. "Doesn't seem like the kind of place where that happens…"

"What are you, twelve years old talking?" Drew asks. "It can happen anywhere. Besides, it was, like, twenty years ago or something. Ricky left Nightlight fine. He moved to LA, ran into some bad people, and that's where it happened."

Drew can't hold my unblinking gaze. *He's holding something back.* The closer I step, the more his resolve crumbles. "Then why is it such a big secret?" I ask. "If Ricky got attacked after moving to sinful California, and Nightlight had nothing to do with it, the Reverend *I know* wouldn't shut up about that story. He'd open every sermon with it."

Marcos shrinks beside a nut tree and pretends not to listen. Meanwhile, Molly's focus narrows as she scratches the edges of her cheek bandage. I'm only inches from Drew, jabbing upward at him like a chipmunk bossing around a flamingo. But Drew's ready—he *wants* to tell me what happened.

"Ricky got attacked in California…" Drew turns his whisper so low he's practically mouthing the next words. "But nobody ever caught the one who did it. That's because they escaped to the island. They're hiding here. They're here right now."

"And Nightlight knows about it?"

Drew nods.

HELP CONNOR.

The truth. At least part of it.

Now I know why Ricky left me such a baffling message in his will: it's very likely the Reverend told Ricky I was headed to Nightlight, no ifs, ands, or buts, and I'm Ricky's last hope of making sure his attacker is caught. Making sure *the Reverend* is caught, whether the Reverend is the attacker himself or merely hiding them. The FBI couldn't find proof about the Reverend, but that's only because the proof is here, just like Darcy said.

Arrest a hate-crimer. So, that's all I have to do, huh?

With one last plea to not breathe a word of this, Drew decides he's had enough of us beasts and bolts toward the Coral Road to finish the journey back to camp on his own. Marcos, Molly, and I appraise each other queasily as we digest Drew's *"The devil is among us!"* warning, but we know we're running out of time to avoid being found. We press on into the forest. "Darcy told me Ricky has a camper file that's gone missing," I whisper, pulling back more draping moss for Molly to pass underneath. "We're gonna find it."

I'd still prefer to leave Nightlight the old-fashioned way, even if it means lying about being Avery's father—but something switched in me when the Reverend said he wouldn't *let* me leave. However I make it home, I'd feel safer doing it with some evidence in tow. Something I could shut down Nightlight with, or at least prove the Reverend did something—*anything*—illegal. When I leave Nightlight, I need this to be the last time I ever have to deal with him.

"How do you know Ricky's file is still here?" Molly asks. "If it's missing, they probably got rid of it."

"Maybe they did, but we don't have anything else to go on."

Then Marcos, that lovely tall boy with the slicked-back hair, swirls 180 degrees, halting us in our tracks. Sweat rains down Marcos's cheeks under his black-rimmed glasses as he growls, "BE QUIET. And I don't mean talk quieter, I mean zip it. Darcy got herself a week in the bunker for poking around in old camper files, and the bunker *sucks*—believe me. Y'all want to escape or snoop or whatever, fine. I can't stop you and I'm done trying. Just let me get back to class without you getting us caught first."

Marcos could beat me up if he had it in him. I've had a few bullies in my time who were nowhere near as big as Marcos, but they could still pummel the shit out of me. One of them—Jason—used to be my best friend in second grade. I didn't realize it then, but Jason was the first boy I fell in love with. Years later, he called me a fag for looking at him too long during P.E.

Goddamn, is that why I feel like puking whenever I get close to Ario or Marcos?

I haven't thought about Jason in years, not until this exact minute staring at Marcos Carrillo's terrified, furious face in the jungle. And how easily his smiling could turn violent for me. "No more talking," he whispers. "Got it?"

"Whatever you say, Buddy Holly," I say, desperate to lighten this tension between us.

"You making fun of me?" His tone steps unexpectedly into a puddle of hurt. Self-consciously, he fiddles with his fifties-style rimmed glasses and continues, lunge after lunge, away from me into the forest.

"No, I wasn't making fun! I'm just trying to be cute—"

Behind me, Molly smacks my arm like she spotted a wasp. "What are you *doing*?" she demands. "We're in a ton of trouble here, and you're trying to hook up with this guy?"

"I have a boyfriend," I say, shaking Ario's recorder defensively, as if that was even her point, as if I wasn't blatantly flirting with Marcos.

"You're gonna have a whole lot of nothing if you don't start taking Nightlight seriously." Molly taps the anthill of gauze taped across her cheek. "This was just me getting a little mouthy. You're talking about collecting evidence to send someone to jail, maybe all of them if they knew who they were hiding. They're gonna make you disappear, Mr. Cute. Mr. Flirty, Cute, Jokey-Joke, Flute Around the Neck."

The jungle becomes arctic cold as Molly's wham-bang truth trickles down my skin like egg yolk, chilly and unpleasant. "You're right."

"It's my life you're messing with too."

"I wasn't flirting." The only response I could think of was also the weakest. Of course I was flirting with Marcos. He's hunky and it took my mind off how overwhelmed I am with the job ahead of me—and about how crummy and alone I've felt for weeks. Regardless, Molly is right: my head needs to wrap around the seriousness of this situation before I run off trying to be Connor Major, Island Detective.

Ricky is dead and nothing I do will bring him back. Finding his missing file is only doable if I can do so safely—for me, for Molly, for Marcos, for anybody.

"So, who was that girl in your lock screen picture yesterday?" I ask. The one she had her arms wrapped around on her phone's lock screen. One of Nightlight's people changed my lock screen picture to Ario to embarrass me, but maybe Molly was prouder than I was and put hers there herself. Maybe every day before yesterday, she got to unlock her phone and show the whole world whom she was with.

I asked because I'm tired of being the only one on the defensive. I risked my ass trying to make sure Molly was all right, and suddenly, I'm getting attacked for some harmless flirting.

Molly crunches through leaves in silence before admitting, "Girlfriend."

"I figured that much," I say. "What's her name?"

"I don't want to talk about her."

"Why not?"

"Because I don't feel like crying right now." Molly stops cold on top of a fallen palm branch, which snaps underneath her as she spins to me. Fire dances behind the water in her eyes. "I'm leaving ASAP, I'm grabbing her, and...we're never going back to Tucson. My brain can't comprehend spending the rest of the *day* on this island, much less a week, three months, or however long my dad plans on draining my trust fund to keep me away from her. I'm also in a bit of a hurry because, apparently, there's a gay-bashing maniac on the loose."

With that, Molly passes me. Rude, correct Molly; now I'm awash in anxiety *and* guilt. I have to get home to Ario. If I stay here too long, I'll lose him to the city. I need to put the Vicky plan into action and get out of this place. Then I can find the Reverend's FBI agents and let them catch Ricky's killer themselves. It's their job, not mine.

We need to catch up with Marcos, but I can't make him out through the trees. Molly and I hurdle snaking cable roots and jagged tree stumps until a low-pitched yelp stops us. A scream of surprise—*Marcos*—echoes through the forest, scattering birds from their roosts.

Someone has found him.

CHAPTER NINETEEN

THE WATCHTOWER

Molly hesitates, but I run in wide, confident bounds toward Marcos's shouting. *The bunny hops toward the predators.* Marcos left class to protect me, and I'm not going to let him get his cheek sliced open for his trouble. I whip past curtain after curtain of tangled green until I can't hear Molly behind me anymore. The next curtain parts, and the claustrophobic forest opens into a serene clearing. A ring of low, secondary growth trees encircle an extinguished fire pit as the sweet hit of barbecue lingers in the air.

Beyond the pit, Karaoke Bill holds a Pez dispenser taser to Marcos's chest—the ancient bastard in grubby safari clothes is only an inch shorter than Marcos is. Bill lays eyes on me, and his onion skin lips crack open into a wide grin. "You said you didn't know where the new kid was," he accuses Marcos, who is speechless.

"What are you doing here?" I ask Marcos without thinking twice, my brain formulating a plan one step ahead of my lips. "I told you not to follow me."

"What?" Bill asks, his smile collapsing like a brick pile.

"I had a migraine and needed aspirin from the clinic, and I didn't want to wait for Ramona to come back. Marcos said he wouldn't *let* me leave—can you believe that?—and it looks like he followed me to come drag me back."

Humidity hangs thickly among us as Marcos and Bill are both silenced. I'm a gunslinger of a liar. *You're a liar and a cover-upper,* my mom always said. It started with sticking a thermometer to a light bulb to fake a fever and eventually grew into hiding my browser history. We queers are a devious breed. Quick storytellers.

"I told you not to run off," Marcos says, joining my lie, breath coming easier to him now that Bill's taser is lowering. "They think you escaped."

"No, they don't!" I guffaw. Squinting, Bill pivots his taser to me. "You thought I was escaping?"

"*They* did," Bill grunts with a stammering, uncertain laugh. "I told 'em there was nowhere for you to run. The boat isn't even docked right now; it's gone to the mainland for mail and supplies. But the Reverend had to whip everyone into a great, big fuss."

"Well, that sounds like Reverend Packard," I chuckle along with Bill.

The lie works—Bill's taser drops to his side. "Let's get you back, then!" Vaguely agitated, he leads us to the clearing's edge that routes back to the Coral Road. I don't regard Marcos, and he knows not to regard me. We're just two strangers, up to nothing. Wherever Molly went, she'll have to invent her own excuse.

—

"Where is everybody?" Molly asks from the gravel courtyard as we return with Bill. She's alone, signaling to us like she's spotted friends at a party. Drew must already be back inside the mobile home. The closer we approach, the more visibly Molly's shoulders pump with exhaustion. She sprinted back, probably arriving only a moment before. "Ramona—Miss Hayward—she told me to hustle back to class, but now I can't find anyone. I was getting worried."

"Don't stress your head, girlie," Bill says, but his chuckling narrows into suspicion as he scans the cul-de-sac—from the South Pacific Gulch and mobile home to Briggs's vaulted office and his own watchtower. Marcos, Molly, and I exchange rapid glances but keep our lying smiles about us.

But for Karaoke Bill, things aren't adding up: "You people…I can't turn my back on you for a second. I don't know what it is. All of you, even the little ones. I never hear you coming; you're always popping out of nowhere. Y'all move like cats, the bunch of you."

"Don't like cats?" I ask.

"It's not about 'like'…Can't drop your guard around cats." Bill shakes the creeps out of his arms, then tips a bent-brimmed hat to Molly. "Get back to class and stay there."

"You heard the man," I say, waving Marcos and Molly toward the shaded hollow, but no one needs to be told twice.

We're already yards ahead when Bill's dusty voice calls again: "Except you, new kid." Marcos and Molly face him, but I don't move. My concrete feet won't allow it. "I gotta radio the Reverend, let him know I found you."

"I was just getting…pills for my migraine," I stammer, finally turning around.

"You'll explain everything nicely to the Reverend, but I can't let you out of my sight until he's got you." Karaoke Bill stands at the foot of his watchtower, his legs wide apart like a cowboy in a show-down. It wouldn't be smart to run when I'm so close to convincing everyone this was all a misunderstanding. I nod to my friends, and they excuse themselves—Molly most tentatively—behind the tropical veil leading to the mobile home. "We'll wait in the shade. Come on." Bill jabs upward at the slant-roofed bird's nest of his watchtower.

Just say "yes" to everything. Be Mr. Agreeable.

The climb is arduous, but breathtaking. With each subsequent, splintering rung of the watchtower's attached ladder, the vastness above the forest canopy comes into focus: an ocean of camouflage green surrounding the camp all the way to the lakeside cabins. From there, overgrown hills climb to the island's highest point—a clifftop overlooking the sea.

Being in Bill's bird's nest is like being in the basket of a hot-air balloon. Other than his rocking chair and ukulele, Bill's micro-apartment is littered with technological fossils, bric-a-brac, and just straight-up trash: a vinyl-record player; stacks of beat-up thrift store records piled inside a fruit crate; a boxy CB radio on a desk beside a microphone and subwoofer; an assortment of apples and mangoes hanging in a fishing net; a hunting knife jammed blade-down into the railing; and lastly—and most bizarrely—a dozen bottles of mouthwash, some spearmint green, some electric violet, lined side by side on the floor.

"I'm always stocked with mouthwash," Bill says, twisting the cap off a half-drunk bottle. "Mouthwash was my best friend in Vietnam. When they train you, they say to only take one personal item. Most men pick a knife or some all-purpose tool, and that's fine enough. I pick mouthwash. Gotta get the kind with alcohol." Bill swigs the scalding liquid straight from the bottle; he swishes, gurgles, and then hocks neon foam over the railing and into the trees. He replaces the bottle as a sympathetic, phantom burning stings my gums. "You got mouthwash with you, it'll keep you fresh, bring down inflammation, clean your wounds, soothe razor bumps; it'll sterilize a knife—there's dozens of other uses I'm forgetting."

"I'll Google it when I'm back," I say.

"You'll giggle it?"

"Uh...Google, I said."

"What's that, slang?" Bill flips a red switch on the radio, and it beeps to life.

"No, um, Google. You know, the thing. It's been around my whole life. The internet thing?"

"Internet..." Bill laughs as if that mouthwash he swigged was filled with broken glass. "Does it look like I'm an internet wizard to you?" The bird's-nest speakers crackle with harsh, tinny feedback, and Bill slaps a button on the base of his microphone. *"Attention, Reverend Packard and Nightlight staff,"* Bill's voice sails across the canopy and toward the sea. *"This is Karaoke Bill telling you to stop your searching. I've found the new, eh..."*

He squints in my direction for a clue. "Connor Major," I whisper.

"Connor Major, he's here. He's not going anywhere. Come collect him."

The radio switches off with a dying squeak. The Reverend won't be long.

Karaoke Bill unspools a Walkman cassette player from the depths of his cargo pants and tosses it and a pair of foam headphones onto his desk. A Walkman—he really is pre-Google. Bill settles into his rocking chair and awaits the Reverend...but my attention remains locked on the cassette player. Music would hit the spot right now, even whatever dirt farmer country crap Bill enjoys. Music is the only surefire way to banish the pins and needles from my blood.

Less than a minute later, Reverend Packard arrives—alone, no gray-shirts—in a fabric-topped Jeep Wrangler and skids it into park under the watchtower. Bill vaults himself out of his rocker to greet the Reverend, but I steal another glance at the Walkman.

I've earned some music.

My thieving, Aladdin monkey hands swipe the Walkman, which fits snugly into my pocket. The rigid headphones won't fit alongside Ricky's Playbill, so I hook them in my waistband and join Bill at the ladder. I do all of this without losing more than five seconds—I'm a born pro at mischief. Down below, the Reverend scowls from his window and hollers, "Happy to see you're safe and sound, Mr. Major."

"Guess I screwed up," I shout, shrugging. "I had a bad headache and nobody was around. I'm not used to this heat—"

"It's okay, it's okay. Pop down here. You and I are taking a field trip."

Panic floods my nervous system. Marcos and Molly have long since disappeared back to the mobile home—there's no one else around except Bill. While the old man remains in his perch, content with his Listerine, I descend into the courtyard—each step like a blade rammed into my chest. When I reach the Wrangler, I smile at my old family friend and he smiles back. "You shouldn't have left class," the Reverend says, his cheeks rashy from the midday swelter.

"I messed up," I agree, my standard *mea culpa*.

I goofed. I'm a silly gay baby. Certainly not a spy you need to get rid of.

"It's all right." The Reverend waves me inside his car, forgiving my mistake like the cheerful, vaguely sinister stepdad he's always been to me. No choice left, I climb into the passenger seat and allow myself to be alone with the Reverend—Ricky's possible attacker.

"Stick together," Drew warned. *"You're less of a target if you're together."*

And now I'm alone.

CHAPTER TWENTY

ONE CAME BACK

We speed out of camp, and I buckle into the Wrangler's leather seat, which is severely cracked from years of merciless island sun. My brief survey for blunt objects with which I can batter the Reverend's skull comes up empty. This Jeep isn't functional for anything but camper transport: no tools or gear, only rows of empty bench seats and a yellow poncho slung over the headrest. The Reverend keeps his space immaculate, as usual.

Deeper down the forest road, we reach the shower by the boys' cabin...except the Reverend keeps driving. Our hacked-clear trail banks right, away from the untamed grass along the lakeshore, and Nightlight as I know it vanishes into the rearview. Two more cabins zoom past, one of them most likely where the girls sleep. The view from my passenger-side window is obscured as the trail ascends a steep hill, sinking the lakeside cabins beneath us. The silence infecting our road trip has to be deliberate—*the Reverend is messing with my nerves.* His bulldog grin spreads beneath his sculpted beard as he increases speed, and our vehicle climbs the rest of the way up the incline to a grassy cliff—the island's highest point I recognized from Briggs's classroom. Beneath the clifftop, a narrow jungle river coils through a moss-strewn gully and ends at a grand waterfall that spills onto Lake Monteverde. Far below, the river crashes and mists onto a bed of black-green stones, each the size of a car. The drop would be enough to break anyone's back...

But according to Drew, Ricky was attacked in California, not at Nightlight.

It still doesn't mean I'm in the clear. A few days ago, I was staring at a soybean field, and now I'm about to be thrown off an island cliff by my reverend. It's so ludicrous, my panic might turn into laughter.

At the summit, there are no trees. We're bare to the sun and the vast, churning sea, now visible and stretching for miles toward the horizon. I truly am on an isolated island; the sudden tangibility of this reality strikes my chest like I've been walloped with a dodgeball.

I have to get away from the Reverend.

I can outrun him. I'm little, and he's too out of shape. I'll hide in the jungle for a few hours, steal their boat, grab Molly, make it to the mainland, and call Ario—then I'll find a way to call those FBI agents...

Good plan, Major. Awesome plan. That's the plan.

As the incline levels out, the Reverend throws the Wrangler into park. I'm unable to take another breath before he stabs a meaty finger down on the automatic locks. Unblinking, he pulls out a taser. My back stiffens, but I don't drop my smile. I nurse some vague, absurd hope that maybe he hasn't brought me here to kill me. That his loyalty to my mom is too much to consider what he's probably already considering:

Murder. Permanent injury.

"Tell the truth, Mr. Major," he says. His glasses reflect the noon sun, his eyes disappearing behind a flash of blinding white. The effect is monstrous.

"Truth about what?" I ask, shrugging. In the ensuing silence, I shrug again. If I shrug one more time, I might collapse into tears.

"You went into the clinic, didn't you?"

My heart caterwauls, begging for escape from my body. The Reverend knows. Somehow...*somehow*...he always knows. "I had a migraine and I needed—"

"You found out something about Ricky, didn't you?" Sweat weeps down my ears, but I'm too frightened to wipe it off. Beads roll under my chin and inside my shirt for long, brutal seconds before I finally nod and the real tears come. I can't stop them—nor do I want to. It's about time I cried. "It's okay, Connor. You're not in trouble."

I'm in nothing but trouble.

I want my mom. But my real mom—the woman she was before the Reverend sank his talons into her. Before I came out and permanently changed the look on her face whenever I walk into a room. The "I like guys" talk was horrific—it reminded me of the only other time I'd been in this much trouble. In seventh grade. It was winter. I'd thrown a snowball at this girl during recess. It must've accidentally hit her eye wrong because she wouldn't stop crying. The principal let me finish out my day, but I had to bring a note home saying what I'd done and that I was getting detention. I walked the ten minutes home, trudging through sidewalks overtaken by dunes of hard, compacted snow. The brutal tundra separating me from my home was punishment enough...but when I walked in the door, my mom was so happy to see me. She had baked Christmas tree cookies with almond paste—the smell still triggers the memory of what came next. She sat me on the couch, humming carols as she pulled off my socks and warmed my frigid feet.

Her love for me was murder. Guilt tore through my lungs.

Any minute—it was my choice when—but soon, I'd have to tell her the bad news. An awful truth about something I'd done, and I knew—*like I would know years later when I came out*—that as soon as I said what I needed to say, her face would change forever. I'd batter away her cheerful mood with a sledgehammer, and there'd be no preventing it. She would slowly remove her hands from my feet and stop comforting me. She'd give the almond paste cookies to our neighbor instead. She'd remove her love, closed for business, and I'd never get back to that warm place on the couch.

I told the truth, and I lost her.

In this moment, seated across from the Reverend, a similar truth pulls at my chest. The truth that I know Ricky's attacker is with us—maybe even in this very car. If I speak it aloud, something terrible will happen.

"Who talked to you?" the Reverend asks, drifting his taser closer. "Briggs was acting strange when I saw him. Was it Briggs?" In the seconds it takes me to weigh framing Briggs over snitching on Drew, the Reverend makes up his mind. "It was someone else."

"No one told me nothing," I sputter, my hand creeping toward my door's manual lock—but I might as well be a football field away. I'll never make it out before getting grilled with that taser.

The Reverend strokes the edge of his weapon and thinks hard about his next words. "Sharon—Ricky's mother—didn't handle his death well. Those FBI agents she called finished with our case years ago. You must be so curious what that was all about."

I swallow a reservoir of tears, my neck frozen with tension. "...her name's Sharon?"

The Reverend never once drops his taser. "Her mental health isn't great. She was wrong to call those agents. It was all settled with Ricky. Ancient history, and we need to let him rest in peace. Don't you agree?"

I'll bet that's what you want. No more prying.

"Like I said, I don't know anything," I sniff, blood returning to my fingers. "Other than that Ricky was a camper. That's all."

Does he believe me? If he doesn't, I'm dead.

The muggy air stiffens. Neither of us blink.

Click. The door locks open, and my heart gulps a gigantic breath like it's been trapped underwater. "Come on," the Reverend says, alight with excitement. He slides out onto the bed of grass covering the cliff's lookout point—taking the keys with him so I can't commandeer the Wrangler. As I step outside, I pat my waist and right pocket to double-check that the Walkman and headphones are secure. Don't need them falling out and making things worse.

A brief relaxation spills down my back and cools my skin: the lookout point boasts an unimaginable view of the ocean. Not the ink-black drink from my arrival, but a picture-perfect, sapphire-blue ocean of serenity. Even the rollicking surf breaks are insignificant up here. *Up here.* My relaxation dissolves: there's nothing "up here" but a long way down. Where the cliff meets the long drop into the ocean, a fire hydrant-red bench has been installed—four rivets fuse the seat into solid rock. In two strokes, the Reverend wipes the previous day's rain from the bench. When he stands again, he's holding handcuffs.

Run. Run now.

I jerk backward quickly, straining a muscle in my lower back. "Am I going to need these, Mr. Major?" the Reverend asks, circling the bench.

"I didn't do anything," I insist, staggering backward, but already out of room. Behind me is another cliff's edge—the waterfall. A few slimy, moss-eaten stones are all that stand between me and a very, *very* rocky landing.

"I'm going to do this"—the Reverend closes one of the metal bracelets over his own wrist—"so you can trust me."

"I didn't do anything!"

The clifftop isn't wide. A few steps back and it's a hospital bed for me. *If I survive the fall.* The river rushes through a muddy embankment to my left; to my right, the Wrangler blocks my path back down the incline; and straight ahead, the Reverend marches closer with an open handcuff. "I know how paranoid you must feel," he says. "I would be too. But trust me—you won't be hurt."

I bet you said that to Ricky.

The gap closes between us. I've retreated too far. I can't go forward, left, or right without the Reverend getting in a good shove. One shove is all he'll need. "My mom'll find out..." I whisper. The Reverend snatches my arm. "NO—!" My legs become weightless noodles as I lose my footing...but the Reverend has my arm. He yanks me forward, nearly tossing the Walkman out of my pocket, but the ground solidifies. The other end of the Reverend's handcuff swallows my wrist with a rattling click.

We're linked together. More importantly, I'm not falling.

"There," the Reverend says. "Now, we can talk." I struggle not to bawl my eyes out as my ribcage vibrates with alternating terror and relief. The Reverend, still clasping my arm, walks me back to the little red bench. My body is overflowing with so many endorphins that I follow him as willingly as a toddler. "These handcuffs mean I can trust you not to run. And you can trust me not to do anything crazy like push you."

"It's true...?" I ask. "You pushed Ricky?"

"No. I didn't. But you're scared, and your brain is clearly pulsing with hundreds of overwhelming theories, and I need you to relax." The Reverend squats on his bench, and the three-inch chain connecting us tugs me down with him. When my ass finds the seat, the vertigo coursing through my skull finally balances and dissipates.

I'm not falling. I'm sitting. I'm safe.

In these handcuffs, if I fell, he'd tumble with me. The Reverend *is* making sense, but the truth would relax me a lot more than these handcuffs. Ricky's Polaroid, smiling and wide-eyed, floats through my memory. "You probably already knew," I say, "you know *every-thing*—I found Ricky on the Winner's Wall."

"Surprise," the Reverend says.

"Does Nightlight take such good care of all their old campers? Or just ones who've had accidents?" I don't say *accidents* shadily; I'm as innocent as apple pie. Nevertheless, my blow lands. The Reverend anxiously adjusts his glasses.

"My father installed this bench twenty-seven years ago." He squints as the high sun reemerges with a vengeance from behind its cloud cover. "Dad and I would watch the ocean and discuss our vision for the camp. When he died, he left me in charge. I became the new Reverend Packard." He snorts as if it's the most ridiculous thing he's ever heard. "Nobody cared what I had to say until I became the Reverend."

So, it's a family business. The Packards run a chicken farm in Ambrose and an island cult in Costa Rica. "How much does an island even cost?" I ask, bewildered. The Reverend's family is rich, but small-town rich, nothing like this.

"We don't own the land, Connor," the Reverend says blankly. "Nightlight is part of a management company that leases the island from the government of Costa Rica. Long time ago, management poached Dad for the job. And I became his successor..." He stares, not at the rollicking water, but at some point beyond the sea, as if he's trying to find our little town out there.

Poached for the job, I think with a shudder. By whom? This mysterious management company that wanted to start a radical brand of conversion therapy on a paradise island? I can't help picturing some kind of Hydra Organization—a room of shadowy men and women, scanning the globe for the perfect fire-and-brimstone preacher before landing on the Reverend's father and making their dark decision.

As the Reverend watches the horizon, warm understanding fills my head. If the truth always costs me, then a lie must set me free. If there was ever time to play this card, it's now, before it's too late.

"I'm the father," I blurt. But the Reverend doesn't glance away from the horizon. "My girlfriend Vicky. Her baby Avery. I'm the dad...it's true. I didn't want the responsibility...I wanted a boyfriend, not a baby. It was wrong."

The Reverend has pushed this theory almost as hard as my mother. He should be throwing confetti into the air right now that I've finally told him what he's been dying to hear...but he doesn't turn from the horizon. Like he hasn't even heard me.

"Mr. Major, I'm offering a trade," he says. "Be honest with me, and I'll be honest with you."

"I was being honest..."

How does he always KNOW?

"Your mother and I had plans for you to join Nightlight for a long time, but I accelerated the timeline when you and Ricky became close. I needed to know what you knew, and I needed to find out far away from any investigations."

"I don't know anything," I say automatically. "Ricky could barely talk."

Why is he purposely ignoring what I said about Vicky and Avery? This is everything he and Mom have been screaming about for months!

"Ricky left you a Playbill in his will. I've let you keep it as a memento because I respect Ricky's wishes for you to have it."

"You read it?"

"I did. He scribbled a note inside. *NIGHTLIGHT. HELP CONNOR.*" Like the sun intermittently slicing through clouds, the Reverend smiles, but it's gone in a flash. "No wonder you're so jumpy. Did he...tell you anything else?"

I don't even have to lie. "If he had, why send me the Playbill with those vague little nothing clues? I *don't* know what he's talking about. I just want to get back to my son—"

"All right, my turn," the Reverend interrupts brusquely. "What do you want to know from me?" *Is he really going to pretend I didn't just confess to being this baby's father? Give me the ridiculous birth certificate, I'm ready to sign!* "You want to know what really happened to Ricky?"

He's going to confess. He'll admit he attacked Ricky in California, then unlock my handcuffs and throw me into the ocean—*me! The father of a newborn baby for all he knows!*

"Ricky lived happily ever after," the Reverend sighs.

"No, he didn't." The lie is almost offensive.

Just say you attacked him. Say what I already know in my gut is the truth.

"You don't understand...Did Ricky seem unhappy to you?" the Reverend asks.

I mean, technically no. The Hannigan home was filled with showtunes and smiles. Ricky always smiled, but that doesn't mean he wasn't scared. Those scribbled warnings weren't cheerful. A grin spreads across the Reverend's feverish face. "Ricky lived many years after his attack—happy years. Years that had nothing to do with this place. He married a man. His name was Rigo. It didn't last, but what can you expect? When his mother's health was better, she took Ricky wherever he wanted. They did everything. That Playbill you say you've got, that was from after his accident."

I would have kept better care of the Playbill if I'd known how much it meant to Ricky, how difficult it was for him to get all the way from White Eagle to Broadway just to see the show. It's lovely to know Ricky had a husband named Rigo and that he was happy, but rage nevertheless rises like a hot-air balloon, filling every corner of my brain, my organs, down to my skeleton. Rage for the Reverend. Rage for Mrs. Hannigan, who refused to tell me what really happened. I suppose staying quiet about the Reverend's misdeeds meant he'd pay for Ricky's health care, Meals on Wheels, and Broadway tickets. That was worth more than justice. In a depressing way, I understand. The Reverend would've been carted off to jail, and Ricky's care would've been left to the state or whatever measly money Mrs. Hannigan could scratch up working at Denny's or whatever.

It's worse that it makes sense.

"Mr. Major, I'm happy to finally share this vista with you," the Reverend says, nibbling the nails on his uncuffed hand. "It helps to appreciate the view with someone who has fresh eyes. I've lived in Ambrose my whole life, and believe me, I'm as sick of those fields as you are. But then...after a while, this ocean becomes its own field." I spin my wrist inside the tightened cuff. There aren't any loose rocks anywhere near the bench, nothing big enough to pummel him. "Don't dream of escape. Focus on your therapy. Take this first week—"

"*First* week?" I snap, pulling his arm with me as I jump to standing. "I have to get back to my son. I can't—"

"You *can't*?" The Reverend stands taller, his stomach bumping the top of my chest. "You can't? You can't *what*? Stay here? Mr. Major, you'll be surprised what you can do. What this place brings out in you." The Reverend digs into his pocket with his uncuffed arm and—after a struggle—presents a crumpled ball of plastic. Bits of corkboard crumble off into the wind. "You're such an excellent student of the Winner's Wall. You probably noticed some damage above Ricky's picture."

Something *had* been torn off the wall in my cabin—only jagged corkboard and bits of glue were left behind.

A Polaroid blossoms open in my hand, and I pinch the plastic so the wind won't catch it. In the picture, a teenage boy smiles with baggy, tired eyes. Despite that, he's gorgeous—long, wavy black hair frames an oval face and pouty lips. My first thought is, *I want to hold him.* My second thought is, *Oh shit.*

STANLEY PACKARD. 1990 to 1991.

The Reverend. He was a camper at the same time as Ricky.

Reverend Packard glowers over me, his long hair decades gone, his pouty lips now pursed into a thin, angry line almost vanished behind his beard. "You were a camper," I whisper.

"I took down my picture because I was...I didn't want you thinking of me as some ex-camper. But telling the truth can be addictive, once you get a taste for it."

The Reverend's father was the perfect man for the job...because his son would be first on the chopping block. I can't combine the boy in the picture with the man handcuffed to me. The idea is so repulsive, it refuses to take root.

"So, don't say you can't, Mr. Major," he sneers. "Because I did."

The Reverend is gay too. I *know* I can reach him. I can make him understand about Vicky, and he'll send me home. Maybe he isn't even the one who hurt Ricky. Maybe he's just covering for someone. Gays can still commit anti-gay attacks, but...maybe I've been thinking about this all wrong? Sea wind blows in, fast and cold. The Reverend pushes a miniature key into the lock on my wrist, and my hand breathes free air.

He won't hurt me. He won't push me.

"Talking to you, I'm relieved." The Reverend sighs. "I brought you here to find out what you know, and what you know is...nothing." The Reverend staggers toward the Wrangler. "Ricky wrote you a goodbye note. He left me one too."

"What did yours say?"

"*There is still time.*" He smiles, almost cruel. "You tell me you're this boy's father, but you're just a kid. You refused to admit it after months of people asking, months of Vicky struggling on her own. You finally confessed when you thought you were in danger—a convenient moment for you. Your mom told me if you did confess, to send you home immediately. But I have got to be satisfied. Let go of Ricky, and I'll think about it."

Another smile rises on the Reverend's face. This one isn't sinister—it shaves thirty years from his face. He becomes the beautiful boy in the photograph again. Overhead, clouds re-form, darkening as they merge like one shitty thought attracting another. Thunder ricochets through my heart as it splits the air, echoing over the endless fields of water trapping us on this island.

CHAPTER TWENTY-ONE

THE RIDDLE OF
THE FOG

FIVE YEARS AGO

I can't find the Reverend anywhere, so I might as well check the school. It's a public school, but Ambrose doesn't care about separating out the local church. Seems like every time I bike past Heather Street, the Reverend is toting boxes of God-knows-what in and out of this school. Probably food and clothing drives, or maybe he just isn't satisfied until he's butted into every single corner of this town.

Yeesh. When I need to find this son of a bitch, he's nowhere.

As soon as I burst in through the double doors, a forgiving blast of arctic air hits me. The August heat has been brutal—Mom was right to rag on me for the double layers I'm wearing: camo pants and a black Strokes tee underneath ripped, sleeveless flannel. *"I don't need you looking like Jacksonville trash when we're trying to make a good impression,"* she huffed, but I don't give a shit about impressing anyone in a town that doesn't even got a decent mall.

Ambrose Middle School is as dark and cool as a cave, its halls empty and still. A hibernating animal about to welcome new students in a few weeks and become restless once again. It's weird being in a school I don't attend yet—we moved here from Florida in June, and while I already know the church like the back of my hand, school is a totally different beast. A small, warmly lit office in an alcove just inside the entrance is the only sign of life I can make out. Inside, two secretaries laugh behind a counter as they cool themselves with miniature battery-operated fans.

"I'm looking for the Reverend," I say without introducing myself, my overgrown, mulleted hair plastered to my forehead. "Y'all know where he's at?"

The women, no older than my mom, stare at me like a muddy dog just got loose inside. They have to know where the Reverend is—what is a one-horse town good for except to be up in everybody's business?

"What's that blood on your cheek?" asks the first secretary, a pole-thin Black woman I recognize from the library.

I dab at the rough, healing wound on my cheekbone and roll my eyes. "Just a scuff from my go-kart."

"Well, you got dirt in it. You gotta clean that out, it's bad for you."

"I'm looking for the Reverend. Is he here or not?"

My cheeky response causes both women's eyebrows to leap off their faces, but I'm hot and want to get back to Hometown Days before they shut down all the cool rides. Ambrose celebrates Hometown Days in the run-up to the new school year, sort of a low-rent county fair. Corn dogs, carnival games, and a raffle at the church bake sale. Every one of Ambrose's 3,300 residents come out to hurl a softball at a target to see if they can dunk the Reverend in a giant tank. All I want is to attack a funnel cake and ride the Chaos Casino, a rickety tilt-a-whirl painted to look like a deck of cards, but I can't do any of that until my mom delivers her damn peach cobbler muffins directly to the Reverend himself. She's obsessed. She won't just set her basket on the bake sale table like everybody else. She needs him to accept it right out of her hands, like he's got nothing better to do. She got all glammed up for him too—the good pearl earrings, coral lipstick, butterfly hair clip, the works.

Thinking about my mom hustling the Reverend to turn him into my new stepdad makes me want to hurl, and if I'm gonna hurl, I'd rather it be via the toxic combination of funnel cakes and Chaos Casino.

"Last time I checked, reverends are in churches, not schools," says the second secretary, a scowling, red-headed woman.

"Well, I already looked there, duh," I say. "And last time I checked, school ain't started yet, so I don't know what y'all are doing here."

"We're getting ready for the new year," the first secretary says. "If that's all right with you, little man."

"How old are you?" asks the second.

"Twelve," I huff, "but I—"

"Connor Major, then. We just finished your paperwork."

"How'd you know...?"

"Got a seventh grader slot for a new kid coming from down south. Your little sassburger country accent tipped me."

I broil at her clocking my accent as she scans me imperiously, from my ripped-up Keds to my unkempt hair. Mom warned me to talk normal around these Midwesterners, but when I'm worked up, the accent busts out. Ambrose, Illinois—this dump is countrier than I am. Nothing but cornfields and Christian billboards all the way into town. Which is exactly why Mom moved us in the first place.

"Connor, where's your mom at?" the first secretary asks kindly. But I'm too annoyed to return her kindness.

"Where's YOUR mom at?"

"All right, little man," she replies, stiffening. "Why don't you get on back to Hometown Days and—"

"What do you think I'm trying to do? JESUS!"

They don't know anything. Already overheating, even in this air conditioning, I storm out as the red-headed woman calls out, "You better fix that attitude before school starts!"

With that, I slam the office door and slide down to the cool linoleum. I can't shake this heat, like it's under my skin. What's the big deal about the Reverend anyway? Everyone acts like he's this big celebrity, and I've never seen my mom get so girly about someone before. *I know what it is.* The Reverend is tall, bearded, and strong looking. Just like Dad. It doesn't matter that he's losing his hair or has glasses—he's got authority. A leader. People like him.

That is very unlike Dad.

It bugs me that Mom is being so obvious. It bugs me that the Reverend reminds me of Dad, but a "better Dad," although that's not a high bar to jump.

There's something else. Something about him...I can't put my finger on.

A fog hovers constantly over my thoughts about the Reverend. As if there's something about him, just beyond my brain fog, that I'm supposed to understand. The fog feels like amnesia, or a dream—a secret I'm trying to tell myself. My brain knows what it is, but it can only tell me in riddles. What is this secret? There's something the Reverend and I have in common. Something embarrassing. Something bad. Something neither of us *want*. My entire being senses our connection, but my brain is being stubborn and won't tell me the answer.

It's just on the tip of my tongue.

The frustration is too much sometimes, and I want to cry or yell at somebody, even if they don't deserve it.

"You see that boy's face?" I can hear the first secretary talking inside the office. "That cut's gonna get infected if his mom doesn't wash it."

"Trash," the second woman says, and I press my ear to the door without making a sound. "We're gonna have no end of trouble with that kid, you wait. And he stank like tuna."

"Maryann—!" the first woman shrieks, but in a fit of delighted giggles.

"I'm serious, she probably puts a tin of cat giblets on a plate for him and the little monster gobbles it up." Humiliation finds me as I crouch beside the door. Maryann is more right than she knows: we've had the same stinking StarKist dinner every night for over a week. My ribs have grown gills by now.

"That's not right," the first woman says. "The father ran off, they don't have anything—"

"Don't give me that. How cheap is a jar of peanut butter? I know the type, she just doesn't give a damn. You said it yourself with that kid's scab."

"Oh, kids fall down all the time. She probably can't keep up with that one."

"I saw that mother in church. Wanna know what I saw...?"

Beyond the door, the room stiffens with silence. Secrets are catnip to me, so I flatten my sweat-dampened ear to the door and forget my agitation with these women for gossiping about my family.

The red-headed secretary—Maryann—must've whispered because I can't hear anything. A second later, the other woman gasps, "NO."

"YES," Maryann replies.

"Oh, so she's looking to marry rich then?"

"I saw it all. She's angling to be a preacher's wife by Christmas."

WHAT. THE. HELL? What did this rude-ass Maryann see? Was my mom with the Reverend? I debate scramming out of here before any more upsetting details come spilling out of this office, but the thrall of gossip can't be denied.

"I've got two words for her," the first woman says, "*good* and *luck.*"

The second woman moans in agreement. "Barking up the wrong tree; it's sad. Someone ought to tell her."

Wrong tree...?

My chest shrinks and pinches inward as the fog thickens in my head over the repeating words: *wrong tree, wrong tree, someone ought to tell her.*

"You know what else," the first secretary says, "that poor boy needs the Reverend in his life like a hole in the head." Except this time, Maryann doesn't understand. The previously kinder secretary lowers her voice to a conspiratorial hush and adds: "You know, you saw him. The boy. Came in here all sassy and hands on his hips, giving us the business."

"Clair..." Maryann says warily, as if fearful of the turn her toxic gab session has taken. I don't like it either. I don't know why. I don't know what me putting my hands on my hips is supposed to mean, but I know one thing: the fog is clouding my brain. I press closer to the door—no longer to catch their gossip, but out of a burning need to understand what it is they know about me that I don't.

"You know, he had those bracelets on," Clair says. Like a homing beacon, my eyes lock on to my wrist and the series of bracelets I put on today: a thick leather strap and two colorful ones made of yarn. It's how my dad always wore them, and there's nothing wrong with them.

It doesn't mean anything.

"*Someone ought to tell her...*" a voice echoes.

"I'm not saying anything you're not thinking, Maryann," Clair hisses. "You watch: if that boy's mother gets her way and gets in with the Reverend...it's gonna go down. I know stories about the Packards, that whole family, that'd keep you awake for days."

The fog grows too enormous to contain. It swallows every thought, not just the ones about the Reverend. Maybe it's the heat, maybe I've been crouching too long and am losing circulation. Pins and needles flood my whole body like a leg that fell asleep.

I don't remember fainting.

All I remember is cracking my head on the cold linoleum...the darkened school corridor filling with a crackling light...my eyes blurring...people running...Maryann frantically jumping on the phone as Clair tips a cup of water across my lips...the two women, thick as thieves five minutes ago, now spitting blame at each other...

The rest of my memories of that day remain smothered in fog, all except one detail: I wasn't the first person to solve the riddle of my fog. They were.

CHAPTER TWENTY-TWO

THE WOLF
AND THE CALF

TODAY

Being in the closet is like being stuck in some highly realistic dream. The dream has its own logic and makes perfect sense. To people outside the closet, outside the dream, things are simple and straightforward—but to us, they aren't. And once we're out, once we wake, thoughts that used to make sense now seem impossible.

How could I *not* have known about the Reverend?

Stanley Packard was a Nightlight camper for over a year. So was Ricky. So was Briggs. *"No one has left Nightlight after only a week."* Darcy's words are a stale cracker I keep chewing but can never swallow. Leaving behind the open expanse of the cliffs, the Reverend returns us to the claustrophobia of our inland jungle camp. He stares blankly at the twisting road, saying nothing. Ricky's Playbill jostles in my pocket next to Bill's Walkman and the Reverend's teenage picture.

I should have known he was a camper.

Maybe I did. I didn't know *exactly*, but seeing the young Reverend wear a camper's uniform cleared the fog that has been squatting on my brain for five years. The thing I couldn't figure out about myself, I also couldn't figure out about the Reverend. Before I had any premonition the Reverend could be gay—before I even wondered it about myself—something inside me whispered, *I don't want to be him.* I knew it on a subconscious, subatomic level. Whenever the Reverend argued with his mother in that farmhouse (when she was alive), whenever they snapped at each other in Sue's Diner like an old married couple, whenever he preached hot hell about people like us in church...something tugged at my heart. Something that refused to fit. It was like I was the only one with good enough radar to sense the disturbance. I was twelve when I met the Reverend, and back then, the emotion I'd eventually call "gay" was just a nameless, gray fog in the back of my mind. Gay didn't mean boyfriends yet or even fantasizing about other boys' bodies. Gay meant loneliness. Omnipresent loneliness. It meant no future, no family, except you and your mother in your same Goddamn house until you both went old and crazy together.

Nothing would ever be new again. Just...gray.

I thought I came out because Ario demanded it, but now I'm not so sure. Maybe I did it because the thought of staying closeted and becoming the Reverend someday scared the fingernails off me. The more I learn about Stanley and Ricky, the less I know. Ricky was out and the Reverend wasn't. Did Stanley attack Ricky because he was jealous that Ricky escaped Nightlight's mind cult, but he couldn't?

Whatever happened to Ricky, he spent his dying day writing two messages—one to me (*HELP CONNOR*) and one to the Reverend (*There is still time*) that have set the two of us on a collision course with each other.

"Did you ever guess about me?" the Reverend whispers, almost croaking, as our Wrangler hurtles through a tunnel of green.

"Of course," I reply, never taking my eyes off the twisting path.

"How?" He almost sounds offended, like an expert thief desperate to know how he could've been caught with all his genius, careful planning.

"*Planet Earth*. It's this really cool nature show. All about how animals behave. People are basically the same."

"You have my curiosity...*how*?"

"The wolf and the calf. It's kind of a sad episode, but really important if you like understanding how people work. The wolf runs at this herd of animals. I can't remember what kind they are. They get scared and scatter, start running. But the wolf's not trying to get 'em all...just one. Everything's so crazy, everybody running, that the calf gets split up from his mother. It's alone. It runs, but it's never fast enough. Wolf eats the calf."

"Ah," the Reverend says, maneuvering each wild bend in the road with confidence and grace. "So, I'm the wolf and you're the calf. You think I plan to eat you?"

"No," I reply. "You're the calf."

"Then who's the wolf?"

"The world."

"Really?" The Reverend's breath catches in his throat, as if surprised by an unexpected knot of emotion. I've spent the past hour so tense, the truth falls out of my lips faster than I realize I'm thinking it. The Reverend's response proves my hunch is correct—he has always seen things as him against the world. Him against me, him against Ricky, him against whoever brought him here as a camper. There's only one good guy in the Reverend's story. "Very interesting, Mr. Major, but that doesn't answer how you guessed about me."

"You're this big man in town. Always helping everybody. Not just with spiritual stuff—their Meals on Wheels, their car repairs, their jobs, their little dumbass problems, my mom's damn love life even. I know you. If you make yourself invaluable, get people depending on you for every tiny thing...makes it harder for them to cut you out if they find out you're queer."

The Reverend makes no sounds. Harsh coral soil crunches beneath our wheels as the Wrangler climbs in speed, sending us faster and faster through the blurring, tightening walls of jungle green.

I got him. Hell, I got myself.

I was my mom's best buddy, taking care of everything for her. Cleaning up her messes, getting her to work on time. She needed me. I thought I had her love locked in. She needed me, but I still ended up on the island.

Whew. Turns out, Nightlight really is therapy.

"No straight guy cares that much about what people are up to," I say, shrugging bitterly. "You can act like the butchest lumberjack; nothing takes that stink away. I guessed about you because we're doing the same thing—running like hell, like that calf. Never fast enough."

That pretty much guarantees the Reverend won't ask me another invasive question for the rest of our drive. When we reach Pura Vida, the Reverend whips the Wrangler in a tight U-turn around Karaoke Bill's watchtower before settling in the middle of the courtyard. Being back in camp with other people is a small relief. I'm ready to lay some serious distance between me and the Reverend. "Howdy, Bill," the Reverend calls from his window.

Bill watches us from his bird's nest, his crinkled eyes smiling like a dog whose owner has finally returned. "The boat came while you were out," he hollers, waving a piece of paper like a winning lottery ticket. "There's mail! And...Stanley, I got a letter!"

"You did?"

"I got a letter from my family!" Bill's rust-colored skin cracks underneath all his smiling. "They said they're coming tonight. Tonight! I—I can't believe it!"

"Aw, good for you. Are you happy, Bill?"

"I'm happy!" Those two words—*I'm happy*—bring Bill to the edge of tears, and a few tears of my own rise to the surface. It sounds nice to be visited after an eternity of isolation. "I never thought it would happen...Hey, you,"—Bill shakes his letter at me—"kid, you gotta know what a special person you have in that car with you. A good man. A *great* man!"

"I'm happy I could make you happy, Bill," the Reverend says, beaming. "All you needed was a little faith." But like every other word that comes out of the Reverend's mouth, it rings empty—poisonous, as if his tongue has been laced with cyanide.

"I have faith," Bill mutters, nodding as he returns to his letter.

"See?" the Reverend asks, turning to me with a twinkle like Santa Claus. "It's not all frowns here at Nightlight."

"What's the deal with his family?" I ask. "Is he another old camper?"

The Reverend's hollow chuckle fills the car. "Actually, very few who work here are former campers. All kinds of different circumstances pull people to Nightlight." When his smile fades, a chilling shadow falls along with it. "Mr. Major, you're here to learn, not be a detective. Ricky Hannigan was a wild boy who came to Nightlight, lived a relatively long life, and died. Do you understand?"

I nod, praying the Reverend can't hear my rapid, tin-drum heartbeat. "I'm done with Ricky. He was just a guy I delivered meals to. He's gone, and...what happened to him doesn't matter."

"Good boy." The Reverend drops my Expulsion Diary into my lap. Until now, I didn't realize I hadn't had it with me. I must've left it in the mobile home when I went to look for Molly. "Expulsion class is next. Write about your sexuality's most powerful root. Begin with the full story of how you got your girlfriend pregnant, and we'll see—if there's no more talk of Ricky Hannigan, maybe I'll choose to believe you."

He exits the Wrangler without another word and jumps down to the gravel.

CHAPTER TWENTY-THREE

EXPULSION

On my journey up the zigzagging stairs to Briggs's treehouse office, my pockets sink under a growing weight: Bill's headphones in my waistband; his Walkman in my right pocket; Ricky's Playbill in my left, alongside the Reverend's Polaroid. If I collect anything more, I'm going to need cargo shorts or something.

At least I'm safe among campers in the office. Saf-*er*. Each of the dozen campers—Overs, Unders, and Beginners—gathers in the half-moon desks and awaits the reading of our Expulsion Diaries. Molly, Marcos, and Darcy crane their heads toward me. I don't know how to begin catching them up on all the breaking news that's happened since I set off for the clifftop, so I dodge everyone's eyes and rush to an open desk in the back. Only a few hours ago, Briggs assigned me to write about my queerness's "root cause," but that request was immediately followed by Miss Manners attacking Molly, Darcy roping me into her spy games, having to hide from Briggs and Drew while they went at it like dogs, and the Reverend practically dangling me off a cliff.

When was I supposed to have time to write anything?

The chill smothering my arms runs deeper, into my skin, into my blood. I thought supporting the Vicky Lie would be my ticket out of this snake pit, but somehow it's only brought the walls in closer. Already, it doesn't seem like the Reverend is buying my lie. But what if he *does* believe me, and my mom won't relent until I ask my best friend to become Mrs. Vicky Major? Added to that, I've been assuming Vicky is desperate for help, but I've never once entertained the *wild* notion that perhaps Vicky doesn't want to co-parent with me. That this is all something the Reverend, my Terminator of a mother, and I have been considering without any input from Vicky herself. So, now I've committed to a lie, and it's going to force Vicky into this situation where she has to back up my story or else my life is ruined. She'd do whatever she could to help me, but then what? Once I'm in the clear, what do I do—become Avery's dad and then ditch him? I could never do that.

But I've already said, "I'm Avery's father." The words are out there, even if my signature isn't on the birth certificate...yet.

Before I have a chance to write down my Expulsion story, Bill collects our diaries. His whiskered, sunburnt jowls sag a little less under the buoyancy of his good news. Grunting, he drops my diary on top of the stack he's carrying. Then Bill delivers the stack to Drew, who lingers by the front whiteboard, his golden lion's mane turning sherbet orange in the glow of the afternoon sun. Drew managed to use the last half hour to stitch his smarmy old self back together. I was actually starting to like him. "Thank you, Bill," he says with smug authority.

"Anything, your *majesty*," Bill mutters.

"No more of that, you," Briggs snaps, leaning against his window's suicide-prevention bars. Bill waves "sorry" as he shuffles closer on mud-caked boots. The men whisper briefly, but the only word I can make out is *headphones.* My hand closes over the Walkman in my pocket like the spring on a mousetrap; Bill is looking for his tunes. *Why the hell did I take this thinking he wouldn't notice?*

Fortunately, Briggs just rolls his eyes. "How should I know where you left 'em? I'm not your nanny, Bill."

I hold my breath as Karaoke Bill trudges from the room with his remaining scrap of dignity. I have to abandon this Walkman somewhere; no matter how badly I need music, I can't be caught with this thing. The door shuts behind Bill, and Briggs whistles, focusing the room's attention into an immediate, pin-drop silence.

Drew sets our diaries on an empty desk and begins: "Connor and Molly, welcome. You should've already been introduced to the idea behind this class's therapy: locating the roots of your condition and then expelling them. If you're wondering why I'm here, I am an Over. I've been at Nightlight for more than a year, and it's my desire to pursue teaching, so Ben"—he points to a suddenly cheery Briggs—"let me take over."

Molly rolls her eyes as Drew blathers on about the "great honor" of becoming a Nightlight teacher. Drew's aunt is in for a rude surprise when she sees him again. I hope I can get back my GoFundMe donation. Once he finishes, Drew calls on a Beginner—the stout, ponytailed thirteen-year-old from Molly's cabin I found "taking the wall" at the chapel: "You went last yesterday, so start us off today."

The Beginner clomps miserably down the aisle to meet Drew and accepts their Expulsion Diary with a bent head. Mr. Calvin Klein steps aside to give them the floor, but when they open their lips, they're already on an exhausted, labored breath: "I used to love going to comic cons, gamer cons, or whatever I could get to by bus from Minneapolis. I'd spend weeks making my cosplay costumes. I loved going as Solid Snake from *Metal Gear Solid*, but my best look was Sheik from *Legend of Zelda*. I had the bodysuit and the bandage mask,"—they take a giant, pausing breath—"and I bought a chest binder to hold back my boobs."

The young Beginner breathes out in a deliberately steady stream. My insides twist with a painful understanding: *this is private.*

"It relaxed me to bind my chest," they say, their focus never straying from the diary. "My girlfriend—the one I used to have—sh-she tricked m-me. She put an idea in my head that I'm still getting rid of. She'd been noticing things about me...and said maybe I wasn't a gay girl. Maybe I was a straight...boy. On the inside." They wipe a trembling hand against an oncoming storm of tears. "She did this to me. She made me think, she opened a door, and I couldn't stop thinking. That's why my mom made me..."

"Keep going, you're doing wonderfully," Drew urges.

Shut up, Calvin Klein! This isn't your moment to be a smug prick, and it isn't right for me to sit here like everybody else, tsk-tsking my head at this Poor, Confused Soul.

"The body is true and immovable," the Beginner reads from their diary as they sniff back an emotional avalanche. "The mind is soft. Only the mind can transform. God made the body and the Devil made the mind."

Finished at last, the Beginner faces the room with blinking, pink-kissed eyes and is soon met by a whirlwind of applause. Drew's biceps ripple as he pounds his hands together, but an electric shock of pins and needles barrels through my chest. By the time Molly and I realize we need to join in the applause, the child is already hurrying back to their half-moon desk. A fire roars in me imagining the gamer cons and wildly creative cosplaying they've missed out on since coming to Nightlight.

Without warning, with no one paying attention except me, the young Beginner does something that sucks the air from my lungs: they look me straight in the eye...and contort their face in an expression of wiseass, mock anguish. Then they smile, wink, and discreetly make a jerking off gesture that neither Briggs nor Drew spot.

The Beginner's story was all for show. At least, the misery of it was.

The kid is fine—at least, they seem fine? Cocky, even. I flash the ponytailed little dude a thumbs-up as they take their seat, and relief returns to me with cold comfort: I'm not the only one faking my way through Nightlight.

My inferno doesn't stay away long, however. It erupts again as the Expulsion entries continue for minutes that stretch like hours: Lacrishia confesses her early childhood crush on Harley Quinn and Molly reveals her brother's schizophrenia—both of which Drew gives equal weight in laying the groundwork for their sinful, queer destinies.

Molly's mother ran off a few years ago, leaving her to become the mother to her dependent older brother...and a maid to her useless father. "My dad's right—it's my mom's fault I'm like this," Molly reads from her diary, clearly lying but nevertheless carrying on. "She left and I found a girlfriend 'cuz I've been looking for another woman to replace her." Rage bends Molly's fingers deeper into her notebook paper, but she knows to stay in line. *Just get through the reading, Molly. It's all bullshit.* "I got a girlfriend because I wanted to be like my mom and avoid my responsibilities. It's my responsibility to look after my brother...no matter how he treats me. It's my responsibility to be the Woman of the House, at least until my dad can find a new wife. A girlfriend is only going to make trouble for me..."

No wonder Molly wants to grab her girlfriend and disappear

from Tucson. Her animal of a father has been using her. More responsibility talk—*Molly, be responsible for your brother. Connor, be responsible for this baby that's not even yours.*

This isn't responsibility, it's control.

Molly sits to a round of applause, her pursed lips swirling in a courageous attempt to hold back the forest fire laying waste to her soul. Not only did she have to stand there and lie—she had to share this vulnerability with the class. And Molly doesn't share.

By the time my name is called, I'm emotionally wrung from these brutal stories. Even if the storytellers are playing up their shame for the room, the details are real enough. The pins and needles are so close to my brain, I might faint. *Breathe in through the nose and out through the mouth.* Slowly, I step to the front and summon a winning, Briggs-like smile as Drew hands me my diary. By the time I face the room so eager for my Expulsion, I've already made up my mind not to talk about my mom. Or my dad.

I'm improvising.

"I gave money to a website," I begin with a clear voice. Drew moans with an understanding *mmmm.* "It wasn't for porn or anything. It was fundraising: this woman was trying to find her nephew who'd gone missing. She was convinced his parents sent him away someplace...a camp." Everyone in the room freezes at once—from Molly to Marcos to Darcy—and I hold their breaths in my hand. "This camp she's looking for is a place where they do mind games to change you...make you straight." Darcy leans forward, eyes sharpened. Marcos can only click his fingers under his desk. "I was wrong to give this woman money because those camps are good. But even if the website doesn't end up working for her, I got the feeling this woman would never stop searching for her nephew."

Behind me, Drew's breath clatters through his nose in an agitated, staccato rhythm.

"She could probably go on searching forever because she has lots of money," I say, allowing myself a brief glance at Drew. His perfect skin has drained of color. "Her nephew is a famous model."

Drew's shoulders buckle, and his soulful lips shrivel like a raisin.

Who's vulnerable now, asshole?

"CLASS. IS. OVER," Briggs growls, cutting through the intense silence crushing the room.

"But most of us haven't gone—" Marcos begins to argue, but stops at first sight of Briggs's death glare.

Briggs scans the classroom, his muscular torso pulsating under his tank top like an angry boiler room of machinery. "Everyone except Connor...get out," he hisses, and Marcos is the first to his feet. He shepherds the stampede of campers out of the treehouse and away from almost certain murder. Finally, Briggs spins toward Drew. "You too."

Speechless, the model flees, accidentally ramming into Molly. They collide into the stack of Expulsion Diaries, sending the notebooks spilling across the wood-planked floor.

"LEAVE THEM!" Briggs screeches desperately.

Molly sends me a final, helpless look before Drew rushes her out and abandons me alone with the monster. My intestines run cold. What has my mouth done this time? *Learn to shut up—that's today's lesson.* Another lesson is that if I *am* going to run my mouth, I need to leave myself plenty of room to escape. My only way out is blocked by a dozen half-moon desks and one pissed-off psycho.

Briggs catches my arm with a cold, chapped hand and walks me until I hit the whiteboard ledge. Pain rushes to the soft patch of exposed skin below my shirt, which grinds into the base of the whiteboard. A terrified pitch of blood fills my head, freezing me to the spot under Briggs's power. He's a centimeter from me, close enough for his musky stench to invade my nostrils. A slimy sheen of sweat covers the salt-and-pepper bristles on his cheeks.

No one is here but us. I can't think of anything else except this horrible fact.

"Not much fight in you," Briggs snorts like a bull about to strike, and I let out a mousy squeak. He withdraws his taser from a hip holster and slides the entire device inside my gaping mouth. Instinctively, I bite down. Saliva floods my tongue as my heart scuttles to the back of my ribcage. The weapon's dull tang soaks my taste buds, reminding me of the rotting metal of a water fountain nozzle.

Please don't shock my mouth, please don't shock my mouth.

"The story you just told the class," Briggs asks, "it's not the one you wrote in your Expulsion Diary, is it?" I shake my head, but it does nothing to loosen the device from my tongue. "Good. Smart not to write it down. Now...I want you to take that story, put it between two halves of a roll, slather on some mustard, AND EAT IT. I want you to really chow down and then shit that story out and flush it because if I ever hear you tell it again—to Drew, to anyone—you and me will have a problem."

I don't struggle anymore. I stare at the handsome man who looked so young this morning but whose face is now gouged with deep, mean crevasses.

This man is threatening me with my dad's voice.

Spittle flies off my lips as he continues to press the taser down like a tongue depressor. "If Drew asks you any follow-up questions," he says, "about his aunt or her website or any attempts to find this camp, you go stupid. You don't know what he's talking about, the stress of your first day is getting to you, blah blah, that sort of thing." His scowl contorts with a sudden, enormous fear. "Drew stays HERE—you do anything to change that, and I'll make sure you never leave. Your one week will turn into six months, a year, two years. You'll be a teacher by the time I'm done with you. I don't care if your son never sees you again—mine hasn't, and look how I turned out. We'll be two deadbeat dads working the Nightlight grind. Is this clear?"

Gagging on his taser, I nod shakily. Finally, Briggs slides the weapon from my mouth, pulling out a string of saliva with it, and I choke on a fresh intake of air. He holsters the weapon—without wiping it clean—as I groan deep, grateful breaths. "Don't be clever," he whispers, his boyish cheer returning. "Ricky Hannigan was clever, and look where that got him. Ricky *suffered*."

"You didn't know Ricky. He was happy," I say, regathering strength. Why I choose now, in this deadly moment, to defend the quality of Ricky Hannigan's life is beyond me. Maybe I'm just tired of being threatened today. "Ricky was free. The Reverend told me he even married a man."

Briggs's dark glare brightens at this information, but it isn't comforting. "So, the Reverend told you about Rigo?" he asks, his smile twisting with sadistic glee.

"Yeah..."

"Did he tell you how Rigo died?"

"Wh...? Rigo's dead?" Wind blows into the office, brisk and unpleasant, from between the anti-suicide bars. *"It didn't last long,"* the Reverend remarked about Ricky's marriage.

Someone killed Ricky's husband...and then tried to kill him too.

Briggs hops out of the classroom with a kick in his step, pausing long enough to order me to pick up the fallen notebooks on my way out. Then, he's gone. Silently, numbly, I stagger across the office's filthy barn floor until I reach the diary pile. As I bend down, my back screams where it hit the whiteboard railing. In spite of the pain, I collect the diaries into a neat stack...but my weakened fingers open with a will of their own, dropping them all again.

Alone on my knees, I cry. I don't care who hears.

My chest thumps with each sob. I cry for myself, for Ricky and Rigo, for Drew's aunt, for that trans Beginner, for Vicky, for Avery, for Briggs's son, and for every day my mother has stolen from me. Every day that was supposed to be mine with Ario. Drew was right: violence surrounds us, and if I'm alone, I'm a target. The Reverend, Briggs, Miss Manners—they all could have injured Ricky with the same ferocity I've seen them use on other campers. Anyone here could become another Ricky.

Even me.

The dull, steely flavor from Briggs's taser lingers on the back of my tongue, and a desire to not be alone overwhelms me. I grip Ario's recorder, but it does nothing to subside the hurricane building in my head. The knotted, shellacked bamboo has turned cold; there's no more warmth to it. Ario can't help me. Pins and needles gather in my hands, which grow heavier and more numb by the second. My fingers bend inward like lobster claws and won't pry apart—*atrophy*. I need to calm down, but my throat is shrinking to a pinhole.

Music.

I need Ariana or Kim Petras or even the Mormon Tabernacle Choir, I don't care. Music is the only thing that gives me power over my rebellious body. I search my pockets until my tingling fingers clamp around Bill's Walkman. Weakly, checking quickly that no one is around, I pry the puffy headphones from my waistband and struggle them into the headphone jack. *Breathe in through the nose and out through the mouth.* Foam slides over my ears, soft and bristling, and I slam down the play button before my appendages can become dead hammers. The cassette spindles turn, and a peaceful, artificial crackle of audio fills my head.

All right, Karaoke Bill, what are we listening to?

Except no music comes. Only a man's voice: "*Beginning of tape two.*"

Ugh, is this a book? An audiobook wouldn't be the worst thing in the world, but I expected something more pop from a guy named Karaoke Bill. The cassette's voice comes again, deep and grim, as if he were narrating a ghost story: "*This is the Reverend Gary Packard, and this is day seventy-one of the Expulsion of Ricky Hannigan.*"

CHAPTER TWENTY-FOUR

THE EXPULSION OF RICKY HANNIGAN

THIRTY YEARS AGO

GARY: This is the Reverend Gary Packard, and this is day seventy-one of the Expulsion of Ricky Hannigan. The date is September fifteenth, 1990. Also present is another camper—my son, Stanley. I've allowed him here today to help Ricky with his...uncooperative behavior.

            <long silence>

RICKY: What are you looking at? You can't just always sit there, not talking, and expect me to talk first.

STANLEY: It's better if you start—

RICKY: Zip it, Stanley! Okay? Blow it out your ass!

STANLEY: It's going to be worse for you if you—

RICKY: I'm done talking to you, bitch!

STANLEY: Dad, I'm sorry—

GARY: Stanley.

            <silence>

RICKY: You control him like a dog. You think you're gonna do that to me? NEVER.

GARY: Ricky, give me time. As you know, we have nothing but time on the island.

RICKY: I'm nineteen, and you have no right—

GARY: What your parents want—

RICKY: They have no right!

GARY: You've been on our island for over two months. Isn't it time you gave that line a rest?

           <heavy exhaling>

           Ricky, YOU have no rights. You gave them up the second you brought my son into that...place. I'm going to ask you one more time, and you had better believe me when I tell you you won't enjoy the consequences of lying...

RICKY: Jesus, just shut up and ask already.

GARY: Did you seduce my son?

RICKY: Stanley can't even touch himself. What makes you think I'd let him touch me?

           <loud clatter of a chair violently shoving backward>

GARY: ANSWER ME.

RICKY: He's my cousin! The answer is no. I didn't screw my own cousin.

           <silence>

GARY: I'm going to move on, assuming that's true. Your Expulsion today will be a full, honest confession. If I think you're lying, I'll dump you in the bunker for a week. Tell me EXACTLY what possessed you to bring Stanley into that bar.

           <soft laughter>

           Is something funny?

RICKY: Nope, nothing.

GARY: Looks like you're laughing at me.

RICKY: Uncle Gary...all right, hang on to your wig.

STANLEY: It's okay, Ricky. You can tell him.

RICKY: Oh, good, as long as I have your permission. Goddamn two-face...The first thing you gotta know is that I took Stanley to that gay bar twice, not once. You didn't hear about the first time because Stanley actually had a good time the first go-around.

STANLEY: Ricky!

RICKY: Whoops, I'm sorry. Did I tell your dad something that was supposed to be a secret?

STANLEY: I'm gonna choke your neck off, you—!

<silence>

Sorry, Dad. I'll be quiet.

GARY: When did it happen, this first time you went to the bar?

RICKY: After I came home for Christmas break. I was poking around Stanley's room—don't ask me why because I don't remember—and I found some nudie dude magazine I thought I'd lost...I found it wedged between Stanley's mattress and the box spring. Like it was his first time hiding something.

GARY: And you gave this filth to him?

RICKY: You know, this is gonna take forever, you being such a bad listener. I said I *thought* I'd lost it, but clearly, at some point, Stanley went through my shit and took it. I would never give him something like that. Little blabbermouth Stanley? He'd freak out and tell you. I'd be screwed.

<brief laughter>

And I was right.

STANLEY: You didn't seem so worried about me tattling when you dragged me into the city.

RICKY: Twice. I dragged you twice.

<brief pause>

I knew about you, Stanley. I didn't know, but...I knew. You know? When I realized you took my magazine, I knew I had to get you out. Show you someplace different.

STANLEY: Yeah, well…you did. Thanks for nothing.

RICKY: You had fun. I watched you dance. It was the best night of your whole life, remember? You said that. You begged me to go again. You couldn't wait for Christmas to be over so I could take you! I got you your first kiss—tell him!

<silence>

Tell him the truth! Please. What difference is it gonna make now?

GARY: Stanley, this kiss, who was this person? Did he get you sick?

RICKY: Stanley isn't sick. Neither of us are sick. This was nine months ago, and we're fine.

GARY: I was talking to my son.

STANLEY: The man didn't tell me his name…

GARY: Oh, my Lord…

STANLEY: We only kissed, I promise. I stopped right away. He was a Marine or…an Army guy, I don't know. A soldier.

GARY: You are seventeen…I want that man's name. Tell me right now.

STANLEY: I promise I don't know or I'd tell you. He told me to call him "B."

RICKY: I was looking out for Stanley the entire time. They just kissed. That was it. It was like a PG movie.

GARY: You've talked enough!

STANLEY: I pushed B away, and I said, "No." I said, "No, I don't like that." I said, "No." Dad, I promise.

RICKY: He's lying.

GARY: Enough—

RICKY: You're such a tool if you believe him—

STANLEY: When I told B that I was only seventeen, he got angry

231

and said, "I don't give a shi—you know, I don't care about that. I've had younger boys—"

RICKY: This was totally NEVER SAID.

STANLEY: B got so mad at me, he pointed across the bar at Ricky and his friends—

RICKY: I was at the exact next table. I was not "across the bar." He never left my sight!

STANLEY: B pointed at Ricky's friend and told me to watch out. His friend was all skinny. B said, "watch out for that man"—Ricky's friend—"he has AIDS."

<silence>

Then B left. I went home right away and told Mom everything.

GARY: You brought my son to a bar where somebody had AIDS?

RICKY: He was my friend's friend. We barely interacted—

GARY: And you're all sharing drinks?!

RICKY: We didn't share any...AIDS doesn't even work like that—

GARY: Underage drinks, I might add.

<knocking, door opening>

UNIDEN-
TIFIED
VOICE: Sorry, Reverend, I wouldn't interrupt an Expulsion but—

GARY: What, what is it?

VOICE: That Scottish lez—Anderson—she broke her wrist.

GARY: Take her to the clinic.

VOICE: She broke it slugging it out with Ellis. She's blown a fuse, sir. She's still swinging her good arm.

GARY: Boys, we aren't finished. Stay here until I deal with this.

          <murmuring, door closing>

VOICE: She slugged it out with Ellis! ELLIS.

          <voices fade, silence>

STANLEY: I'm sorry, Ricky.

RICKY: Sorry doesn't begin to cover it. You snitched me out so badly, I lost all my college money. You don't even know the scrounging I had to do, for months, just to stay enrolled...because of YOU.

STANLEY: You want to hit me, don't you?

RICKY: Trying to help you out cost me everything...I can't even explain...And then you tricked me. You got me to come home...so my dad could jump me in the dark...and take me here. Yeah, I've really wanted to hurt you.

STANLEY: If your friend got me sick, I could've been hurt a lot worse—

          <loud clatter of a chair falling, followed by the loud thud of a body slamming>

STANLEY: No touching me with your hands—

RICKY: You baby! Stupid, dumb, weak baby. You were never going to get sick and you know that, and you let them take me!

          <soft crying>

STANLEY: I don't wanna get sick...I see them on the news, Ricky. I watch them...their bodies. They're so sick. I can't...

          <harder crying>

RICKY: You don't even know what you're talking about.

STANLEY: Ow...

RICKY: You kissed that guy all on your own. I watched you do it. I saw LIGHT in your eyes.

STANLEY: He made me—

RICKY: You wanted him to be your boyfriend, didn't you? There
           was a moment—I saw it, you can't lie to me—you took
           his hand and...you wanted him...

           <whimpering>

           How could you ever be anyone's boyfriend? You're just
           an idiot kid.

STANLEY: We'll see how stupid I am...You're going into the bunker.

RICKY: You ruined my life—

STANLEY: You ruined MY life—

RICKY: I HAD a life! I got out, I had somebody who loved me.
           A whole lot more than you had in Ambrose, living in
           your mom's pocket!

STANLEY: You're hurting my neck...

RICKY: GOOD.

STANLEY: Ricky...

           <crying>

RICKY: I could do it. I'm on the island now. I'm on the island.
           There's no good, no bad on the island. I should do it.
           You deserve it—

           <struggling, gagging>

STANLEY: I deserve it...

RICKY: Don't say that!

           <soft clatter, shuffling>

           <For the next one minute and thirty-nine seconds, there
           are no sounds except crying and indistinct muttering.
           Reverend Gary Packard does not return, and the tape
           abruptly ends.>

CHAPTER TWENTY-FIVE
THE CUT

TODAY

It happened here.

Thirty years ago, Ricky almost strangled his cousin on the slightly warped barn floor of Briggs's treehouse office. The same floor I'm collapsed across now. Am I a Ricky or a Stanley? Am I the boy who had his life stolen away or am I the "idiot kid who could never be anyone's boyfriend"? It could be either: Ricky's rage pulsates through my neck, but Stanley's helpless terror lays heavily on my chest.

If I stand, the whiteboard cut on my back will start screaming again, so I remain trembling on my knees. It gives me a front-row view to the bumps and knots in the wood where Reverend Packard almost died—but Ricky couldn't let himself go through with it. Ricky was nineteen and the Reverend was seventeen. My age. Cousins. As close as brothers, it sounds like. Ricky was an out college student; he was only trying to help his scared, closeted cousin...but the Reverend snitched him out, giving them both a one-way ticket to Nightlight Island.

"I got out, I had somebody who loved me!" Ricky screamed, his throat ragged from crying. He lost everything because of Stanley, but Stanley—*the Reverend*—was just a kid afraid of his dad. He looked

up to Ricky, and—according to this Expulsion—experienced at least one truly happy night in his life thanks to Ricky.

My hands no longer atrophied, I slap off the foam headphones; the rigid headband slides around my neck and settles. The pain in both boys' voices is impossible to shake. On the tape, the young Reverend wasn't authoritative; he was a tulip—a high-pitched, gentle lilt that months and years of Nightlight therapy ground into the guttural purr it is today. Ricky's voice was equally bizarre; I'd never heard him speak so fully before. I wish I knew both of them back then. I would've helped them get along. Helped them understand the real culprit behind all of this: the Reverend's father. That monster tore apart his son's life, his nephew's life, and the life of any other Nightlight camper in the nineties. The Reverend's dad died before we moved to Ambrose—I don't know when—but after listening to this, it seems possible that he was the one who attacked Ricky and killed his husband.

My hand floats over the empty floor where Ricky pinned Stanley, as if by magic I could summon them from the past and comfort them. I was also attacked in this room—Briggs's unwashed jungle scent won't leave my nostrils. The Reverend's father ignited a chain reaction that has mutated gay boys into violent, unstable hyenas when we should be helping each other. A brutal cycle—*'round and 'round and 'round*. I don't know who attacked Ricky—Briggs, the Reverend, his dad—but I'm going to break the cycle.

"I'll fix it," I whisper to the empty office.

My brain processes a thousand different shifts in reality at once: *the Reverend is Ricky's cousin; Nightlight turned Ricky into a wild animal; I actually feel bad for the Reverend*. My body moves automatically, without thought. I gather the dozen Expulsion Diaries back into a stack on one of the half-moon desks—the one Molly bumped into, which now crooks at an odd angle to the others. I lick moisture back into my lips, resurfacing the metallic tang of Briggs's taser as my newfound courage sinks down a drain.

It seems I'm all talk—Briggs grabbed my arm and I froze. I was as useless as Stanley trapped underneath his justifiably unhinged cousin.

"*Ricky suffered,*" Briggs said. So did Stanley.

I'm alone with the porcelain-feathered birds gathering between the iron bars on the windowsill. Alone, except Briggs is still every-where. He *could* be anywhere. Nightlight staff members have a habit of popping out of doorways and around corners like performers in a haunted maze. The campers do this too—I don't realize anyone else is in the room until a soft voice carries through the air: "Connor?"

The birds scatter, and one heart attack later, I lift my heavy neck to Marcos weaving through the desks to reach me. He totes a clear plastic box, and the sunlight streaming through the barred window forms a broken halo behind his head. Humidity has fluffed his slicked-back hair, which now resembles licorice-colored soft serve. He smiles, but something behind his glasses communicates: "*I know. I'm sorry.*"

I'm so grateful to see him, I cry again. Gobs of tears rush to the brim of my face, but stop as soon as Marcos puts a finger to his lips. "Stop that," he hushes, "and answer something for me."

Marcos's tone seizes command while somehow never losing its gentleness. Holding back a dam of emotion, I concede, "All right."

"Did he hurt you?"

"Marcos...he put the taser in m-my mouth—"

"He what?" An unusual fire ignites behind Marcos's eyes, yet he continues standing like a soldier at attention—the way he did when Vance freaked out. The world is a swirling mess, but Marcos remains unshaken. It's comforting to have this anchor.

"Briggs said things," I confess from the floor. "The shit he said to me…" The memory of Briggs's threats return, overwhelming all other thoughts of Ricky or his Expulsion. My face buckles as the dam restraining my emotional monsoon gives way. Marcos, intent on stifling my meltdown, extends a "stop" hand. Once again, he's astonishingly easy to obey.

"If you can, I need you to take everything you're feeling and hide it in a little bottle inside your heart."

"What…? I'm serious, I'm like *not* okay—"

"I know you're not. But I need you to listen because they're coming. And if they find you how I did, looking a mess, they're gonna find out Briggs did something, which won't do you any good except get you in deeper trouble with him."

"I'm listening," I sniff.

"Everything you're feeling, stuff it in a little bottle in your heart. Just long enough to make it through lunch."

"I…I'll put it in a little bottle in my heart."

"And screw the lid on tight. You gotta act totally normal or we're both gonna get questions."

"I shouldn't have run my mouth," I break, choking on air. The enormity of how far I've crossed the line with these dangerous people engulfs me. "I think I'm being so smart, but I'm stupid—"

"You're not stupid," Marcos says with a finality that shuts me up.

I collect a deep breath and dry my eyes with the bottom of my shirt like an apron. My fingers and toes twiddle until the pins and needles vanish and I can move again. "Can you help me up?" I ask, coughing through post-crying phlegm. Sexy.

"You have to get up on your own," Marcos whispers with a twinge of impatience. "I can't touch you."

Lord Almighty! A Nightlight boy couldn't touch another Nightlight boy even to save him from drowning. This place sucks so much dick (and not in the way Drew and Briggs do to each other). Nevertheless, I follow his instructions and stuff every complicated, terrified, awful feeling into an invisible Mason jar. My frantic emotions resist this act like a cat being crammed into a Halloween costume, but into the jar they go. A corked bottle of pain—an SOS—shut away in my heart while I eat lunch.

Preferably half a cow.

I psych myself into facing the pain of standing and clamber upright. As expected, a long, searing pain awakens in my back. "You're hurt bad?" Marcos asks, his all-business demeanor dropping a peg.

"I hit the whiteboard. Can you see it?" My shirt doesn't rise halfway up before Marcos gasps. "What, is it bleeding?" I spin twice to spot the wound like I'm trying to catch my own tail.

"I gotta work fast. Turn around." Marcos scuttles closer and snaps open the latches on his plastic box—a first-aid kit. Inside are Band-Aids, two spray cans (antibacterial and bug repellent), a roll of gauze, medical tape, a tube of Neosporin, and a bite-sized Hershey bar.

Marcos anticipated Briggs injuring me, and he came prepared. Violence is not only allowed at Nightlight, it's expected.

I can't blame Marcos. Having someone at Nightlight actually give a shit about me is too much to handle, as if I'm embarrassed to have such an extravagant luxury as someone else's concern. Marcos risked serious punishment leaving class to get me from the clinic, and after that narrow escape, he risks it again to patch up my sliced-and-diced torso.

"Should I take off my shirt—?" I ask.

"NO." Marcos's answer comes as quick as a switchblade. "Just, um, hike it up a bit."

Slowly, I peel my shirt like a Fruit Roll-Up, and Marcos's presence—warm and enveloping—closes in behind me. My flesh ripples with goose bumps—the wound on the small of my back is strangely intimate. As soon as it's exposed, Marcos's breath quickens, landing in soft huffs on my neck. "You sure you can do this without touching me?" I ask.

"You don't gotta be a smart-ass." Marcos pops the top off the antibacterial spray. Without warning, the hiss of the spray covers my sore, and I yelp like an underfoot dog. Alternating between chilling and burning, I jog in place until Marcos orders me to simmer down. I do as I'm told, but the tingling spreads up my entire back.

"Sorry I act like a dick," I whine through my burn, "...but I'm a cute dick."

Silence drops on the office as Marcos smears cool goop over my cut. *Why did I have to say "cute dick"?* If Molly were here, she'd scream at me again about flirting with Marcos given all the danger we're in. Before I can change the subject to something other than how close his finger is to my butthole, Marcos finally whispers, "Nah, you're not a dick. You're just a doofus."

He unpeels a Band-Aid and places it gently over my cut. He presses it flush, and his finger traces the small of my back, doing nothing to slow my racing heartbeat. As he does, a thousand eyes surround me—judgmental, doom-filled glares. *My mom, the Reverend,*

Ario, and countless other sneering faces. All of them sickened that I'd let another boy this close to me—all the vile things I must be thinking. *The glaring eyes know what I want. They see the blueprints of my heart better than I do.* Marcos applies a second Band-Aid in an "X" over the first one to hold it in place, and I face him. We're close—closer than I expected. He's a foot taller. *Ario's height.* My recorder suddenly weighs a trillion pounds, but the boy in front of me is so much like Ario: big-bodied, black hair, soft skin.

"Thanks for the patch," I say, a swoop of hair collapsing over my forehead.

"Sorry I couldn't help you off the floor," he says, chewing his lower lip.

The longer no one says anything—the longer Marcos's candy-brown eyes stay with mine—the queasier I feel. My dick grows warmer and heavier underneath my shorts as panic crashes over me. A *"not here, not now"* panic, the kind a werewolf gets when he's in public and realizes he forgot about the moon. But my pre-*dick*-ament is as inescapable as the Wolf Man's. I'm one bold move away from Marcos's lips, as pink as a rare steak. I'm terrified to glance down at the rise in my shorts that is probably as obvious as the cut on my back. The dreadful, glaring faces in my mind's eye burn hotter. *Gross,* they whisper. *So, so, so gross.*

Kiss him, echoes a distant, friendlier voice. *Ario will understand...*

"Where'd you get those headphones?" Marcos asks, shattering the spell.

"What?" I ask, my hand absentmindedly jumping first to Ario's recorder and then to the headset wrapped around my neck. My erection drops like a switched-off faucet as the blood rushes back to my brain on a revelation: in all the excitement and drama of the

Expulsion tape, I overlooked one big surprise I learned. "Bill was listening to Ricky's Expulsion," I blurt at the exact moment Marcos arrives at a similar, more horrified understanding:

"You stole Bill's Walkman?"

"I have to tell you something," I whisper, railroading over Marcos's baffled "*Huh?*" Breaking the land speed record for confessions, I bring Marcos up to date on the Reverend's time as a camper and his relationship to Ricky. I open Bill's Walkman to display the proof, and his puppy eyes flare open.

"What are you *DOING?* It's only your first day, and you're gonna get yourself killed."

"Do you have any idea why Bill would be listening to Ricky's tapes?"

"No! I don't poke around like this."

"I mean, it's possible he wasn't listening to it. Maybe the Reverend needed to hide the tapes, and Bill's stash was just the safest place?"

"Yeah, that sounds like the answer. Case closed; time for lunch." Marcos clicks his fingers and retreats to the doorway. But I can't follow him out yet.

"That means Bill has the other tapes in his bird's nest..." I limp to the window, my lips moving independently of my brain. Through the suicide prevention bars, Bill's watchtower stands, completely vacant, across the courtyard. An itchy tingling bullets up my spine. *Bill isn't there.* I could scurry up and nab another tape before lunch.

"Please," Marcos says, testier than ever. "I helped you, now you help me. Just take a breather and come to lunch. No more crazy detective stuff, okay?"

The sore on my back whines in agreement. I need to eat. And I don't want to piss off Marcos or get him in trouble. I'll take Drew's advice: *stick together*. Darcy and Molly can help with what has to come next, and they need to know what I know—that Ricky Hannigan's missing files were in the watchtower all along.

CHAPTER TWENTY-SIX
LUNCH IN THE GULCH

Molly, Marcos, and I get the worst part of lunch over with first—seeing Briggs again. After Lacrishia delivers plates of peppered fish and instant vanilla pudding to us, my attacker stalks toward us on the way to his staff table. The hairs on my shoulders frizz and fly up, drawn to his presence like static electricity. It could be my imagination, but as soon as Briggs notices me, his boots slap harder against the cement floor.

I was prepared for this moment—Marcos insisted we rehearse.

"Watermelon, cantaloupe, watermelon, cantaloupe," he and I murmur to each other. On the outside, we're laughing, full of smiles, miming a lively conversation—"Watermelon, cantaloupe!" But inside, Briggs's dread-soaked presence crushes every sound in the room into a muted, underwater silence like in war movies when a mortar goes off. "Watermelon, cantaloupe," we repeat until Briggs passes. Marcos was right: jabbering nonsense kept my mind task-focused and unemotional. If we hadn't, my attacker's presence could've sunk me into a fugue—maybe I would've passed out or started sobbing without even realizing.

The world refocuses as soon as Briggs reaches the Reverend's table at the farthest end of the South Pacific Gulch. Stanley Packard is in a fabulous mood. With his sleeves casually rolled above his meaty forearms, he cackles—mouth crammed with pudding—over some joke to Briggs, who isn't up for a laugh at the moment. The

Present Day Reverend still refuses to merge with the Boy Stanley I met on Ricky's Expulsion tape.

How could that wounded, Pretty Young Thing become such a domineering creep? And potential murderer?

"What happened after class?" Molly asks, her stunned expression reminding me I forgot to explain why Marcos and I would suddenly be saying *"watermelon, cantaloupe"* over and over.

"Just a talking-to from Briggs," I reassure her. "I just got scared, you know. Just a tiny scratch on my back and a little scare, that's all. Ricky Hannigan got worse."

"A scratch? Are you okay?"

"I'm laughing, aren't I?" But her uncertain gaze loosens the cork on the little bottle of emotions in my heart. She heard my voice crack—everyone heard it—a crack as small and ominous as a pebble striking a windshield.

"Hey, um, no more questions, okay?" Marcos asks. "Let's let him eat." Telling Molly what to do traditionally never ends well, but given the circumstances, she nods and strokes the puffy bandage on her cheek—her own memento from stepping out of line. Marcos pivots to me with soft, mother hen-like seriousness. "Eating helps."

How come he has so much firsthand knowledge of how to make it through an assault from a staff member? I can't consider that right now; that sort of thinking might burst open the little bottle. Instead, I gulp my pudding, and the cold, vanilla-sweet treat instantly erases the filthy taser metal from my tongue. If only eating could erase the throbbing gash on my back. Or the memory of Briggs's stale breath...

"Lemonade?" asks the girl in the bob wig. Darcy doesn't wait for my answer before refilling my plastic glass with life-giving nectar. She pours with her left arm; with her right, she drops Karaoke Bill's

Walkman onto my lap, and I cover it with my napkin. She'd been bussing dishes in the back long enough to listen to it for herself.

"Thoughts?" I ask. It took Darcy three rounds of serving coffee and lemonade before she, Molly, and Marcos were finally caught up on the events of the clinic, the clifftop, and this Ricky Hannigan's Walkman surprise.

"We need to talk to Drew again," Darcy says, reaching past me to top off Marcos's lemonade. "And we'll get the truth this time."

"I think he's done talking—" I say.

"And I think he can help us find more Ricky tapes."

Clueless about how to respond, I swallow my entire glass. A slurry of radioactive-yellow Country Time powder collects at the bottom, and if nobody was watching, I would gulp that too. Marcos doesn't look up from his tray, apparently too exhausted to ask us again to please, *please* stop plotting. Darcy's frown tightens as she stomps away through the swinging kitchen doors, where overworked lunch ladies remain stuck in a loop of scrubbing pans and prepping new hot dishes. Darcy hasn't eaten yet, but I need her to come back so we can formulate some ghost of a plan before we're split up for our next class. However, before anyone tries to get blood from a stone prying more information out of Drew, we need to search Bill's watchtower for other tapes. Across the table, Molly wrestles with a stubborn, double-tied knot of a thought.

"Do you want to listen to the tape?" I ask.

"Thanks, but no," she says, lost in her thousand-yard stare. "I've heard enough Expulsions." When Molly's attention lands on me, my Little Bottle of Emotions unscrews another quarter-turn. It's shocking to see her so vulnerable. Her bandage makes her look severely wounded, more than if she just had some badass exposed cut.

Outside, Karaoke Bill's watchtower pipes out a slow country jamboree tune. After setting the record on repeat, Bill made his way into the Gulch with a skip in his step. We thought he might start flipping cartwheels. "Make room," Bill laughs as he wedges between Briggs and the Reverend. Briggs rolls his eyes as he's forced to scoot his chair, but the Reverend eagerly welcomes another upbeat person to the table. The men talk across Briggs—who only wants to eat his meal in peace—but Bill is undeterred. He proudly shows off the letter he received like it's a diploma: "My family is coming tonight!"

The rest is unintelligible, but it's obvious Briggs couldn't care less about Bill's good news. His discomfort is more scrumptious than this blackened fish. I can't think of any better punishment for Briggs right now than a shitty, irritating lunch break.

"The Reverend seems happy," Darcy reports, sliding beside Molly with her own tray at last. She swallows half her fish in two forkfuls.

"I noticed," I say.

"Happy is good. He'll be less suspicious of what I'm about to do." Once again, Darcy commands the table's attention. Molly and Marcos exchange nauseated glances. "We've got two more joining our group."

"Joining us in what?"

"Scavenger hunt. We have Ricky tapes to find and no time to find them." Next to me, Marcos curls further inward until he's basically a man-sized Cinnabon. He's shutting down. I promised Marcos no scheming during lunch, but Darcy is leading this train, not me.

"Coffee, miss?" Lacrishia asks, descending on Darcy with a percolator.

"Gracias."

"I spoke to your little birdies," the larger girl whispers while Darcy gulps down her coffee. "They're on their way."

"Gracias mucho." Darcy slaps the empty tin cup to the table. Before Lacrishia can top anyone else off, two Beginners trot over from their respective tables and slide into ours. Vance, the Beginner who melted down during this morning's run, sandwiches himself between Molly and the swaggering trans boy from Expulsion. Lacrishia casts me another warm, bashful smile before floating back to the kitchen with her coffee pot.

"What is this, your secret *Mission: Impossible* team?" Molly asks, frowning as Vance nudges closer.

"Well, Miss Comments," Darcy says, "actually yes."

"Hi, Marcos," Vance greets my seatmate, who's grown even more sullen since they sat down. Vance stares, smiling, his eyes glistening like he's a kitten who's decided it's finally time for his attention. *Is he flirting?* This jellybean might be just some eighth grader, but nevertheless, noxious chemicals flood my brain as it enters Jealous Attack Mode.

Am I really jealous of a middle schooler flirting with a guy who isn't my boyfriend? I'm truly in a great place mentally right now.

Darcy knocks the table, and we snap to attention. "This is Vance Olmos, and next to him is Jack Singer." Darcy waits a pregnant moment before Jack smirks and leans in to clarify:

"You've heard me called a different name in class. If you want to use that name, Nightlight certainly would love that. But if you do, you're not with us. Call me Jack and you are." The dare doesn't rest on the table long. Molly, Marcos, and I smile and whisper, "Hey, Jack" in unison. "Yay," Jack says with a grin as he wiggles a toothpick between his incisors, every inch of him a rascal. Another strong gust of relief blows into my head knowing that Jack, like Darcy and Lacrishia, is putting on an act for Nightlight and isn't as conflicted as his Expulsion story had Briggs believe.

"Connor, let our birdies know what you need them to find and where they can find it," Darcy instructs as if this is some business meeting.

"Uh, not sure what you're asking," I say, "but I'm not putting these, like, twelve-year-olds in harm's way—"

The Beginners flinch at the insinuation that they're anything as common or tawdry as *twelve*, but Darcy speaks for them: "They're thirteen and fourteen, and you can't be the spy, new guy. Everyone's watching you."

"I'm with Connor," Molly says. "If we all work together, we can easily just steal the boat—"

"Hey there, People On Your First Day," Darcy interrupts, ramming her spoon into her half-eaten pudding. She scans the table like a cobra ready to strike. "Jack, Vance, me, and Marcos have been Nightlight residents for over half a year. We LIVE here. So, while you two got your asses cut up on your first day, Jack and Vance have been stealing evidence for months and haven't been caught a single time. They're capable. And Molly, we haven't commandeered the boat yet from a lack of desire. If some of us take the boat and leave, the rest will be stuck here. And your escape will taste like shit whenever you think of who got left behind. If that matters to you."

Molly's scowl hardens at the implication. "So, you want to shut down Nightlight?"

Darcy returns to her pudding. "I want to present a story against them, backed by evidence."

"You have evidence?" I ask, pins and needles collecting in my toes.

"Maybe. We've been making copies of camper injury reports."

"You can't use mine," Marcos pipes up from the end of the bench. "I'll help y'all in other ways, but...if this gets out, I don't want to have to go on record. Y'know, talk about stuff in public..." He retreats into silence, sipping lemonade and looking thoroughly anguished. Nightmarish fantasies of what injuries Marcos may have suffered arrive in my mind: *Cuts from Miss Manners's jagged nails... the Reverend smacking his neck...Briggs causing any number of bruises or shattered bones...*

"Don't worry," Darcy sneers. "There's plenty of other reports."

"Are these injury reports enough to, you know, shut Nightlight down?" I ask, the depressing answer already forming in everyone's eyes.

"Of course, people love believing gay people over youth ministers," Molly says. "It's their favorite pastime."

"We're going to *try*," Darcy says. "And we're gonna sprinkle some positivity on top." She straightens her wig like it is a painting knocked askew. "What *would* be a slam dunk is if we had a really vicious attack to pin on them. An attack where the victim eventually died. You could even call it a murder." *Did he tell you how Rigo died?* Briggs's taunt echoes, and I wince back a crack in the little bottle in my heart. *Had there been an outright murder when Ricky was attacked?* As we stare at Darcy, ominously transfixed, she continues: "Up 'til yesterday, I could only dream of such a crime falling in my lap." A multitude of eyes land on me, but I don't break from Darcy. She and I understand: she has evidence against Nightlight to put a permanent *For Sale* sign on this island, and me solving the Ricky Hannigan attack would be the closer.

There's only the small issue of catching a killer and somehow escaping alive.

"Um...a murder?" Jack asks through a veil of midnight-dark bangs.

"Long time ago," I say, marveling at how carefree I'm able to sound. "Don't worry."

While Darcy licks her pudding cup clean and Marcos signals Lacrishia for another lemonade, I clue Jack and Vance in on the *barest minimum* of what Darcy and I need: Ricky Hannigan's Expulsion tapes from the watchtower. Jack is keenest on the task—he moves quickly and softly, and a litheness is essential for this operation. But it's Vance who adds the wrinkle: "What if the Reverend made Bill hide the rest of those tapes in the bunker instead?"

"Damn..." Darcy whispers.

"The bunker?" I ask, alive with the memory of Ricky's Expulsion. Stanley mentioned—*all too happily*—that Ricky was headed for the bunker as some kind of extra dose of Nightlight punishment. It was the only time during the tape when the Reverend's sadistic future tendencies peeked out.

"It's jail, and you don't want to go there," Marcos whispers.

"The bunker is an outpost, one of the cabins by the lake," Darcy says, folding her hands to her mouth, her mind racing through possible solutions to this complication. "Bill sleeps there, but there are jail cells too—animal cages. It's secluded and far from camp. You can't sneak off there without someone noticing you're gone—"

"So, one of us needs to get sent to jail," I blurt, on the edge of either a happy dance or a nervous breakdown. I'm one nasty remark away from a night in the bunker anyway, and I'd have tons of time alone to look through Bill's room for tapes. And I'd have the Walkman to listen to them. "Am I suddenly useful again as one of your spies?"

"Mayhaps," Darcy says slowly. "Before we do that, we should search the watchtower. It's easier. Then if we do your bunker plan, you'll need keys to let yourself out of the cage to snoop..."

This time, accusatory eyes fall on Marcos, one of the trusted keepers of Nightlight's key rings. "You can't use my keys," he says, fingers snapping. "They'll know I helped you and—"

"You know, I've fully had it with you," Darcy hisses at Marcos, half-lunging across the table. Molly and the Beginners glance behind at the Reverend, who is still guffawing with Bill and Briggs. No one noticed Darcy's outburst. "You can't have it both ways. You can't help us and these kids without snitching on these Goddamn people. You're nervous to get involved, nervous what'll happen if we get home and rat out Nightlight, nervous what your daddy'll say, nervous kids at school will know you're a big, snitching homo and you won't be welcome back at your la-dee-da church. Sorry, but stay nervous. I've been busting my ass for months and so have these kids, doing things that could get our necks broke. You're *going* to help us."

"I'm sorry..." Marcos moans, unable to look up. "I just can't."

Darcy retrieves her lemonade, but she's too shaking with rage to drink. "Connor, like I said before, Marcos has been at Nightlight for over half a year. Got here in January when I was on month two. His daddy is a preacher at some Texas megachurch, some widow-swindling—"

"—that's *not true*—"

"—I ain't finished. Some robbing, gangster, hypocrite preacher, and he's going to Hell for it, saying nothing about being damned for what he's done to his son. Marcos, you came here first week of January. That means the Carrillo clan had one last Christmas together, and then *Happy New Year!*—off to the island with you. Probably decided the whole thing over presents and ham."

A bitter chill falls on the Gulch. We are stricken silent, both by what Marcos has been through with his family and the serious in-fighting going down just three tables away from the Reverend. Furious, exhausted tears pool in both Marcos's and Darcy's eyes, but it's Marcos who speaks first: "You know nothing about my family."

"I've been listening to your Expulsion horseshit since you got here. I know everything about your family."

"I take this program seriously. It means something to me."

"You deserve this place—"

"Don't say that to him," I interrupt.

"Marcos," Molly interrupts with greater calm. "Whatever Christmas you had with your family, if things don't change, you'll be spending *this* Christmas with Briggs and Miss Manners."

"And so, what, Nightlight closes?" Marcos asks, glowing with rage. "I leave before I'm ready and...my family just lets me back? I have Christmas with them again, no trouble? I am on this island helping people or I'm nowhere. I don't have some fun aunt with a website like Drew Schreiber who could take me in. Every person I got in the world is wrapped up in the church. I was supposed to be valedictorian, but I dropped out to come here. You want to make me homeless? I'm a *valedictorian*..."

Boiling over with tears, Marcos abandons his tray and races for the double-doored exit and vanishes into the courtyard outside. "Oh, baby girl," Vance mutters, pressing an anguished hand to his heart.

I'd be annoyed with Vance's theatrics if they weren't my exact same sentiments. We're forcing Marcos into the same predicament with his family that Ario put me in with mine. *Do it, it's the right thing! So what if you get thrown out?* I should've known better, even though Darcy is also correct—she, Jack, and Vance have risked a lot more than Marcos and I have for the greater good.

What a complete mess.

I didn't think it was possible to be any more desperately sorry for Marcos—*maybe even desperate to kiss the sadness out of him*—but here I am, spinning around on the bench to run after him. Darcy's sinewy hand lands on my wrist. "Don't," she says. "You'll make it worse."

"Ah, you just know what everyone needs, don't you?" I accuse. One of my weaker barbs, but still effective. Darcy briefly turns into a quivering bowl of Jell-O.

"Good going, Darcy," Jack moans. "You didn't have to punch low on Marcos like that."

"Listen to me," Darcy says. "Marcos isn't the only smarty-pants here who got his hopes and dreams vampired out of him by Nightlight." Discreetly, she pushes a tear back with the edge of her thumb. "I'm just trying to get us home, is all."

While I crawl inside my own belly button, Molly cautiously waits to speak until everyone has finished lobbing poison darts at each other. "Our emotions are high, and that's okay," she says. "Marcos will be fine. We're all looking out for each other. So, what's next? Actionables!" She swirls a finger at Jack and Vance. "One of you chipmunks is heading up that watchtower,"—she swings over to me—"and Connor gets himself thrown in the bunker. Is that right?"

"We still need keys for the bunker plan to work," Darcy says.

"I can get Marcos to give me the keys," I say as if it's a fact. Marcos is the sort of puppy you have to approach carefully—but if you do, he's all yours. What you don't do is bark, *"Help us because it's the right thing, asshole,"* as honest as that may be.

The tone in the room changes in a blink.

Outside, Bill's country music halts as searing radio feedback cuts through the watchtower speakers. At the harsh sound, Bill and the Reverend leap from their table. Almost immediately, a new song begins—a woman's silken voice croons over a lush, old-fashioned piano recording.

"What the hell...?" Bill asks, his happy-fool face crumpling like paper.

"This is the same record as your lunch music?" the Reverend asks.

"No, it's Vera Lynn. It's a different record..." Bill's jaw tremors as a realization consumes him. "Someone's in my watchtower."

As the ghostly woman sings, the temperature in the room plummets.

Briggs vaults himself from behind the table, and Molly, Darcy, and I face each other with a panicked jolt. Someone else is looking for Ricky's tapes. Someone other than us is in Bill's watchtower—but they changed the record that's playing?

Something's wrong. Very wrong.

In under five seconds, the South Pacific Gulch becomes a maelstrom of running. Briggs leads Archie and a half-dozen gray-shirts in a charge toward the courtyard. The Reverend and Bill follow at a slower clip.

"BENNNNNNNN!!!" someone cries outside. The voice like a lion's roar blows through the Gulch with a gale-force wind, shaking my ribcage and sending me into a sprint. My mind switches off; all my body understands now is running toward the mystery. "BENNNNNN!!!" the voice shrieks again. Already having weaved past the Reverend and Bill, I close in on Briggs at the double doors. The sound of Briggs's name forces him to run double time.

"Who is that?" Bill demands, frightened into a hush.

"I don't know," the Reverend says. "Ben, get out there!"

Briggs batters open the double doors with a linebacker's shoulder. The flimsy wood strikes the sides of the building with a shocking *clang*, and a herd of Nightlight staffers hustle into the open courtyard. Molly, Darcy, and the others follow, but I have to reach the watchtower first. My terrier-sized body zigzags between the towering men, none of whom can be bothered to stop me. We all have the same urgent mission.

A low, internal whisper rings through my head: *Where is Drew? He isn't at lunch.*

The music grows disquietingly louder as we hit fresh air. The next sound isn't Briggs's name again, but a piercing scream. The watchtower comes into view, and a boy falls. The following sound is like a car crash, a collision of wood and weight. The ledge of the bird's nest buckles under the pull of a long rope, and Drew Schreiber's body strikes the ladder on his first plunge, pulverizing two of the slats.

A chorus of screams erupts—*I can't tell one from the other*—but we are united in instant grief. Drew, the Missing Model, swings by his neck from the watchtower as gentle, soulful music dances out of Karaoke Bill's radio station. I'm the only one to approach close enough to notice: the golden boy gazes down, his eyes half-open like someone who is just a bit sleepy—a child saying goodnight before he can't stay awake another second.

The initial screams soon silence, and his body metronomes through the air.

CHAPTER TWENTY-SEVEN

UNDER THE NOOSE

D rew Schreiber swings hypnotically like the pendulum on a grandfather clock as the record ends on a dreamy note that echoes over the high-canopied trees. When his body pulled against the noose, it battered the watchtower ladder, catapulting a flurry of nesting birds from their roosts. Beneath the body, people are sobbing—guttural, animal moans. I can't tell if they're campers or staff, but I'm not among the screams. I'm as silent as a void.

I don't turn my head. I refuse to make eye contact with Briggs. I can't fathom the wrath about to explode from him.

Beside me, Lacrishia clutches two Beginners to her chest: Owen, the tiny one, and Alan, the taller, strawberry blond kid who checked me out in the cabin. Both boys shiver against her, ten levels deep into an anxiety attack. Lacrishia brushes their hair and lets them wail, Nightlight's no-crying rules be damned. I don't think they're crying because they particularly loved Drew—his suicide is simply one wretched thing too many.

Regardless, despair emanates from Drew's body. A great sadness hits the air like a siren, into the ground like rain, and into my lungs like smoke. His death is a gas bomb of pain that, within seconds of detonating, fills every available inch of space.

I didn't mean to make you feel bad about your aunt, Drew.

Everything unfolds like a movie, floating separately— two-dimensionally—apart from me. When Drew slammed into the ladder, he left stress cracks so big that the wood gives way under Briggs as he attempts to climb. Briggs yelps, dropping ten feet back to the Coral Road, but he cannot be stopped. Muttering "no, no, no, no, no," he scurries up the ladder and around the broken rungs like a muscular cat. Inside the bird's nest in under a minute, he maneuvers around the speakers that played that haunting song only a moment ago; now, only a low hiss rumbles out, spitting dissonant, deeply bad vibes into the air. After slapping the needle off the record, Briggs leans from the nest and pulls the boy's rope closer, a switchblade outstretched in his other arm. "Come on, come on," Briggs hyperventilates as he slices. "Keep breathing, Blondie, just breathe, big deep breaths, baby, please, come on, come ON!"

Of course, no breaths come. We all heard his neck snap. *I'll be hearing his neck snap for the rest of my life.* Drew's half-open eyes stare downward, our last conversation running on a loop in my head:

"Your aunt will never stop searching for you."

My jaw locks as it holds back a maelstrom. Drew's aunt will never get the chance to make him feel okay and loved again. She'll always worry if she tried hard enough. And it's my fault. My mouth has finally *killed* someone.

Outside the rim of a panicking circle of people, Karaoke Bill lingers beside the Reverend, who looks more than ever like a death-scavenging raven. *An omen of doom.* Bill can't tear his bloodshot eyes away from the boy as he and the Reverend mutter angry, rapid sentences at each other. But they're too far—and there's too much loud grief—to make out any details.

"This changes things," Darcy says, arriving with Jack. Where Jack and Darcy are steely eyed and collected about this newest tragedy, the other campers shrink away by the entrance to the South

Pacific Gulch: two Beginner girls hide inside the double-wide door frame, while Molly and Vance clutch each other on the porch, wide-eyed like actresses in an old horror movie. As for Marcos, after his emotional exit from lunch, he must have sought solitude near the mobile home. He was the only one already outside when Drew screamed for Briggs. Emerging from his hiding place in the jungle hollow, Marcos approaches like a passive observer. Like me, he numbly watches Drew sway gently in the air, as if this were happening on the news to somebody else.

"Y'all okay?" Marcos asks. Darcy and Jack shake their heads. "Dumb question."

"No, you might as well ask how people are doing," Darcy says, flicking her head toward Drew. "Can't ask him any more questions."

"I think I've bothered Drew enough," I whisper, summoning the energy to speak. Grisly reality seeps in drop by drop, and with it, a tsunami of pins and needles invades my arms. I wish I could hold on to one of Marcos's warm, soft-baked cookie hands—it might stop mine from shaking.

At the sound of a brittle branch snapping, Briggs successfully separates the rope and Drew plummets. The impact of his body against the Coral Road sends plumes of well-tread dirt toward the crowd, causing everyone to gasp and leap backward. Karaoke Bill covers his mouth with papery hands as the Reverend pats his back. Briggs descends the high perch; when he reaches the ladder's broken mid-section, he jumps, landing nimbly on both feet.

"Drew..." Briggs repeats frantically as he rushes to the body. He opens the noose, unravels it from Drew's neck, and sends it flying across the courtyard. "Get this thing off!" What follows is the most brutally quiet CPR I've ever witnessed. Briggs pumps Drew's hollow chest for a heartbeat that won't come. He blows stale, terrified breath through the boy's cold lips.

Can't he see Drew's blank eyes? How long is the Reverend going to let this go on?

"What is WRONG with you?" Briggs shrieks at the body like some irritated spouse. "You're supposed to breathe when I do this!"

While the rest of us avert our eyes from Briggs's futile efforts, Archie and the other gray-shirts surround the Reverend and Bill in a quiet, businesslike huddle. They whisper among themselves for another moment until the huddle breaks and four gray-shirts swoop down on Drew. The Reverend approaches Briggs grimly as Briggs, my once-intimidating kidnapper, frantically pushes the gray-shirts away from the dead boy.

"Ben, he's dead," the Reverend says as gently as he knows how. But Briggs writhes under his touch and pumps Drew's chest with heavier and heavier thrusts. "Stop it, you're upsetting everyone!"

Briggs whips his head to the crowd like an animal caught mid-feast: red-eyed, teeth bared, and dripping saliva. Like a homing beacon, his gaze falls immediately on me. "You..." he snarls and launches toward me before I can process the danger on its way. Luckily, Marcos and Darcy are a step ahead. Marcos's strong hands pull me defensively backward as Darcy throws herself between me and the grieving monster. "YOU DID THIS!"

But Briggs never reaches us. The Reverend, taller than his staff member, wraps bearish arms around Briggs's chest and hurtles him backward as if he weighs little more than a Chihuahua. Briggs's musculature may be showier, but the Reverend's mass is functional as hell. Briggs can only squeal desperately and claw at his boss's unshakable grip.

"YOU DID THIS TO ME," Briggs wails as the crowd backs away slowly. It's only after his tears come that I realize Briggs is speaking to the Reverend, not me. "GET OFF ME! GET OFF ME! YOU DID THIS!"

The Reverend releases Briggs, only to spin him violently around to find his eyes. "What do you mean, I did this?"

Like air flying out of a balloon, Briggs's rage empties, leaving the Reverend face-to-face with nothing but a husk. "We're going to leave you," Briggs says, defeated. "We're gonna get away from here."

Present tense.

It pulverizes my heart, but nothing will loosen the director's grip. "Yes, I know," he says. "I heard a rumor you were thinking of leaving us. Your home. Me. Everything I've done for you. To run off with a child—"

"Drew's an Over, an adult—"

"SHUT UP." The Reverend's fist arrives at Briggs's stomach like a wrecking ball. Marcos and I gasp as the body-built man is laid low with a single strike. Whimpering and clutching his aching belly, Briggs crawls over the gravel bed to Drew but collapses in agony after a few inches.

"Tell me something," the Reverend continues, flexing his fist open and closed as he collects his rage into something more sensible. "I've given you the longest leash out of any staff member here. You could've taken this boy whenever you wanted. But you denied his review eight times. All you had to do was approve him, get on the boat, and we'd never see either of you again. But you denied him over and over. You denied him last week! You must've fed him some real promises. Were you EVER going to take him home?"

Wheezing and trapped on the ground, Briggs can't speak the

answer. But he doesn't have to. He wanted Drew as his secret island boyfriend, with all the strings of a jailer and his prisoner attached. Maybe he worried that out in the real world, without his leverage, he would lose such a beautiful young model's attention to scores of other hungry men. Ricky Hannigan's voice from the Expulsion tape echoes in my memory: *"How could you ever be anyone's boyfriend? You're just an idiot kid."* But in this scenario, Briggs is the kid.

"I think Drew realized you were trapping him here," the Reverend says, tutting his head. "So...YOU did this, Ben."

Briggs and me both. We pushed Drew to the edge, to a place where his thoughts had nowhere left to run.

Briggs, ignoring this harshest of truths, resumes his crawl toward Drew. "I love you," he tells the body. "Can you hear me? If you can hear me, I love you. I'm ready to say it now..."

As Briggs dissolves in front of us like the Wicked Witch—*my beautiful wickedness*—no one can look at each other. We can't believe we're finally seeing Briggs broken and humiliated and no one can even enjoy it.

"Take. The. Wall," the Reverend growls.

"W-w-where?" Briggs asks between shuddering breaths.

"The bunker." Darcy and I turn briefly to each other. *With Briggs there, what semblance of a bunker plan do we have now?*

"I can't leave him," Briggs whines, clambering to his knees, bits of gravel clinging to his forearms.

"Mr. Briggs, I'm not asking."

Back on his feet, Briggs's muscled back hunches like a shamed dog. He can't lift his eyes to anyone, not even the Reverend. "Don't leave him alone. He doesn't like being alone."

Without another sound, without another glance back at Drew,

Briggs retreats one painful step at a time down the Coral Road—toward the lake, the cabins, the clifftop, and Karaoke Bill's infamous bunker—to take the wall.

Unbothered by this catastrophic drama, Archie the Tattletale smacks one of the gray-shirts on his shoulder and regards the others with a scrap of paper. "All right, gang," he says. "We got our shopping list. We're going to the clinic for supplies to wrap up the kid, and we're not coming back 'til we've got it all." *Guess there's a new Briggs in town.* Archie and the quartet of sour-faced gray-shirts nod to each other and vanish in the opposite direction toward the clinic.

For something to wrap up Drew's body.

Nightlight has no TV, no running water, no basic necessities... but they've got body bags.

Karaoke Bill squats to shut Drew's eyes like they do in movies. The only other staff member left in the courtyard, the Reverend approaches the (surviving) campers, and on the end of a sigh, says, "I'm devastated you all had to witness this horrific thing. It's a sin, one of the worst. Drew was a very disturbed boy—and he broke a very serious rule. I hope you see now where that life leads you."

"I thought it was supposed to be Briggs's fault," I ask, exploding out of my calm. I can't believe the Reverend is standing in front of a dozen (minus one) traumatized, vulnerable, at-risk children and laying the blame on Drew having sex with a man.

Huddled next to me, Marcos sucks in a sharp breath at my outburst, but I truly don't care anymore. I refuse to be quiet while the Reverend leads more children to their own gallows.

"Yes," the Reverend says, shrugging—a *mea culpa*. "Mr. Briggs is...a pathetic soul."

"He's an idiot kid," I say. "How could he ever be anyone's boyfriend?"

Ricky's words emerge from the past like a poltergeist, and the Reverend—that grizzly, indomitable ogre—becomes a child again. I don't know what compelled me to say it or what I hoped to gain, other than the juicy terror currently spread over the Reverend's face. Maybe I'm just not good at letting assholes get the final word.

"How did you...?" the Reverend begins, but then trails off. His cold, dead eyes find me as his wheels turn rapidly. "It doesn't matter. What you heard happened a long time ago. I'm not that boy, not anymore. I'm something else now. I am the Goddamn director of this camp, and you all Goddamn answer to me." The crowd's whimpering tears silence as the Reverend searches for anyone not paying him the strictest attention. He finds no one. His hands, however, find my jaw. Two purple, pulsating clamps fit snugly around my entire face. No one breathes. His perfumed wrists suffocate my nostrils. He could pop my head clean off my shoulders like a dandelion or one of his chickens, but just as easily as he slid his hands into place, the Reverend removes them. "Such a little one. You never did get that growth spurt."

The Reverend leaves us in petrified, mouth-agape awe as he clomps away after Briggs, now a speck in the distance, still slouching toward his punishment. "Mr. Major, I think I've had enough interruptions," the Reverend barks over his shoulder. "I've decided to cut my losses...and believe you."

Before my chowder-filled brain can process what he means, he turns again, producing a piece of folded paper from his pocket. As he approaches, tiny, inky footprints appear on the outstretched paper—Avery's birth certificate.

Now? With Drew lying plastered to the ground ten feet away, he wants to do this?

"Sign," the Reverend orders, clicking open a pen. He hands it and the certificate to me like he's the Devil Himself collecting a soul. He pretty much is. Either way, my vibrating fingers accept the contract. *Avery Woodbine,* it reads. *Mother: Victoria Woodbine.* Next to *father*, there's a vacant space just for me. "You know what to do. Sign your name as the father, commit to your family and a straight life...and I will put you on a boat home within the hour."

Gasps rise from the crowd, but I can't look at them. In one accidental glance left, I catch Marcos's saucer eyes widen behind his chunky frames and then crumple. There isn't time to explain. Everyone in camp is watching, processing a million new realities: I fathered a baby, I ran away from my baby, and worst of all...I'm ditching them in this snake pit to go home.

Home.

I'll be in my bed tonight. After all my waking nightmares considering the possibility of spending years on this island, I'll only have stayed a day. I'll be able to text Ario. I'll be able to see love come back into my mom's face for the first time in months. Briggs and Miss Manners will fade into nothing but a bad dream.

But so will Marcos. And Molly. And Darcy.

And Drew...his face...his scream...that snap of his neck...

Death hunts children on this island. Whether it was the Reverend or someone else, all clues point to there being someone among us who permanently injured Ricky...and may have killed his husband, Rigo. The faces of the Beginners peek out at me. Owen, the little boy pressed against Lacrishia's chest, waits to watch me write my name to save myself from a fate he can't escape.

Write your name, Major, and you'll be with Ario tonight.

Will I? I'm agreeing to father this baby, assuming Vicky will let me, assuming Vicky is even aware of this deranged plan, and for how long? At least until I'm out of high school. When will I ever have the time to sneak off to Ario, when I barely had any before?

An hour ago you were begging to sign this!

An hour ago, Drew was alive. Things change.

"Can I sign it later?" I ask, my eyes flitting from side to side so I don't have to catch the utterly betrayed glares of my friends. "I'm a little upset from—"

"This isn't a negotiation," the Reverend growls, "and your window is closing. You either are this baby's father, or you're not, and you lied to avoid your obligations to this program."

My friends are about to witness me lie to save myself from Ricky's killer, from Nightlight, and from the chaos that's infested this courtyard since we watched Drew fall. Jack, that brave boy who's collected evidence for months, will watch me peace-out after half a day. Molly, my boat buddy, will be ditched to fend for herself. Marcos, the boy with the soft hands and warm smile, will never smile at me again.

And they'll all know the truth: surrender to the Reverend—debase yourself—sink to your lowest point—and that's how you'll survive.

The faces in my mind's eye are worst of all. Faces of people I'm betraying, or will betray. Vicky. Avery. Ario. Their judgment looms in my mind like stone monoliths. Just to make my mother happy... just to make the pain stop...I'll make this one compromise.

Drew Schreiber lies dead, his golden mane ground into the filth where he dropped. His utter lifelessness warns me—*it won't just be this one compromise.* I can lie and sneak my way out of parenting Avery, sure. But there will be other compromises, other lies I'll be asked to tell. One after another, I'll make them, thinking I'm in control of the situation. But each compromise will turn me more into Briggs, and before I realize it, I'll be back where I started: the island. Crying over a boy I thought I was saving but was only manipulating.

Like Marcos.

He risked the bunker to save me from the clinic. He bandaged my back after Briggs attacked me. And without a thought about what will happen to him when I'm gone, I'm going to leave.

Sign. And you'll wake up in your bed. Nightlight will be just a bad dream.

As Dorothy Gale says, *"Some of it was terrible and some of it was wonderful,"*—okay, maybe only Marcos was wonderful—*"but the whole time, I kept saying I want to go home. And they sent me home."*

I'm out of time.

It's home...or the island.

"Now!" the Reverend barks.

"No!" I shriek and my frantic hands tear the copied birth certificate into ribbons. The little bottle of emotions in my heart shatters, releasing tears and sounds from my chest I've never heard before—but that I've felt my entire life. "No, no! It's not true! It's not my responsibility! He's not mine, none of this is mine! Leave me alone! DON'T EVER ASK ME THIS AGAIN!"

I chuck the pen and the remains of the certificate into the wind, and the scraps whip around me like autumn leaves. My trembling knees strike the earth and I clutch fistfuls of soil. I have no idea why, but my little hands scrape against the ground like a dog digging a hole. Another delirious moment later, and I stop, sense returning to me in waves.

The Reverend kneels, lowering his bulldog snarl to mine. I don't cower—I bare my teeth defiantly and hiss, "No."

"You're a stupid boy," he mutters. "I gave you an out. Remember that in the end."

With that warning, the raven orders us to stay with Bill until Archie and the gray-shirts return with the body bag for Drew, and he flies away to the bunker. In less than a minute, the campers are alone with Bill and the body. I clamber upright and dab my shoulder against my furious tears.

Everyone is stunned silent at exactly how much has happened in the last fifteen minutes. Some avert their eyes, some are crying, and some (like Marcos) are gobsmacked. Strangely, an urge to smile comes over me. I finally did the right thing. I didn't leave them. I stayed. Whatever comes next, we're on the same team.

But somewhere, in the dark of my mind, Ario drifts further away.

CHAPTER TWENTY-EIGHT

THE UPPER HAND

The sun begins to dip beneath encroaching cloud cover, but that does nothing to guard us from its merciless heat. In the court-yard of human wreckage underneath Karaoke Bill's watchtower, Darcy sidles next to me and mutters, "Okay, what was that about?"

"I couldn't do it," I say, dumbfounded at myself. It probably wasn't the best strategy to finally take my stand against the Reverend while one camper is dead, and we're trying to snoop around for Ricky's killer. But the right time is the right time. The crushing feeling in my chest is already dissipating. Tiny specks of freedom seep into my swamp-filled mind.

I don't have to keep some ludicrous story straight anymore, I don't have to get drawn into the twisted reality of my mother's conspiracy theory—I am actually, literally, for real NOT Avery Woodbine's father. His father is some dirtbag who had sex with his underage employee and then dumped her. And I'm not going to spend the rest of my life covering for a statutory rapist, even if it benefits me in the short term.

"You're gonna get yourself dead," Darcy whispers. She and Jack shake their heads in dismay, apparently not at all grateful I didn't abandon them and take the Reverend's Devil's bargain. I realize my mistake: I blurted out *"He's an idiot kid"* and the Reverend knows I found at least one of Ricky's tapes. He knows I'm still trying to piece together Ricky's story.

"I gave you an out. Remember that in the end."

The Reverend wanted me to sign this hideous birth certificate, not because he wants to help Vicky and Avery but because he's desperate to stop me from finding out the truth about what he did to Ricky. He knows we're after him.

As Darcy and Jack stalk a few paces away to whisper, I'm left alone with Marcos. He's not necessarily smiling, but an awed hush fills his voice: "You didn't leave."

Marcos forgot to add the last word of that sentence. He meant to say, "You didn't leave me."

I fight the familiar, fidgety nausea that comes whenever I'm this close—and this alone—with Marcos. "I've got more to do here," I whisper. And it's true. The real work begins because I've firebombed my path home.

Escape is rapidly becoming my only option, or Nightlight is going to be home for a while.

"Bill...sir?" Lacrishia asks, lugging over two Beginner boys—both pale to the point of being transparent. "May I take Alan and Owen to the cabins? The other Beginners too?"

"What for?" Karaoke Bill grunts, hunched over Drew's body like a wary crow.

Lacrishia clears her throat, summoning the courage to continue: "Well, they don't need to be seeing this."

"What, are they too *fragile*?"

"You sit in on Expulsions sometimes...You're obviously aware of the suicidal thoughts several of them live with. They don't need to see any more of this than they already have. So, may I take them to their cabins, please, sir?"

Suicidal thoughts? This nightmare is traumatic enough without realizing some of these sweetie-pies have thought about actual suicide. Karaoke Bill scans the crowd, and his drooping eyes soften—briefly—before rolling. "All right," he says, "get 'em out of here. But Beginners only. The others stay."

My heavy heart warms for Lacrishia, who bothered to focus on the kids in this moment rather than on murder mystery clues. She mutters thanks to Bill for being a human being and then waves over the remaining Beginners. Two girls—Anke and Christina, she calls them—dart to her side like bullets. Vance unclenches from Molly, whispering, "Oh, thank God, thank God, thank God" as he joins them. Jack nods to Darcy before completing the Beginner squad. The tiny boy, Owen, refuses to move or even pry himself from Lacrishia's chest. "Owen, come on," Jack says, patting the boy's head. "Let's go to the lake." Owen peeks open his eyes before letting himself nod.

Without looking back, Lacrishia leads six children down the road, leaving the remaining four of us with Bill, Drew's body, and a chorus of screeching insects and birds of paradise. Molly abandons the safe distance of the Gulch's doorway to complete our group, and Darcy snatches my wrist. "You really think there's Expulsion tapes up in that tower?" she whispers. I make it through half a nod before she powers through: "When I leave, you won't have a lot of time. Five minutes, maybe ten. No dicking around. Find the tapes."

"When you leave?" I ask. "What?"

"What are y'all whispering about…?" Marcos asks.

"This is our only chance," Darcy says, gathering short, quick breaths like she's prepping for a marathon. She studies Bill, hovering over Drew's body as he coils the hangman's rope around his elbow. In one fluid move, Darcy tears off her poofy bob wig, flinging rainbow-colored barrettes into the air. Her natural, cropped hair hits the wind, and she runs her fingers through the tight curls. "Good luck," she says, winking. "And don't fuck it up."

She breaks into a sprint toward Bill. "Wait—!" I yelp, but it's too late.

"SONS OF BITCHES!" Darcy roars as her lithe body leaps, clears Drew, and crash-lands into the old goat's chest. Marcos, Molly, and I scream as Darcy slaughters him: scratching, kicking, flailing, cursing. Darcy pummels Bill, who is too startled to fight back properly; he can only shield his face. "You're crazy? Well, *I'm* crazy too!"

"Darcy!" Molly and Marcos holler, but my hungry eyes turn red. *Get him. Terrify him. Make him bleed.* Darcy's fury is real and *highly* relatable.

"What the f—?" Bill whines, finally using his elderly-but-hearty weight to scoop Darcy off her feet. Still shrieking and clawing, Darcy hits the dirt ass-first. By the time she's back on her feet, the taser is in Bill's fist—she absorbs a crack of violet lightning to her ribs and drops limply next to Drew.

"No..." Molly says, itching to join the fracas, but I stop her with a gentle nudge. Whatever this is, it's part of Darcy's plan.

Bill's chest heaves, his cheeks lined with bleeding, angry cat scratches. "You got something to do with this?" he demands, waving his taser at me.

At the sight of the weapon, my stomach retracts and hides behind my lower intestine. "She's totally losing it," I say, shaking my head.

"Goddamn lunatic is right. That really hurt!" Bill sheaths his taser and hoists Darcy over his shoulder like a sack of laundry. Our friend is awake, but powerless and moaning. "She's going into the bunker. Mr. Carrillo, watch these two and wait for Archie."

"Sure," Marcos says.

"If Mr. Major runs or touches anything or breathes funny, it's on you. Yes?"

"We're staying put. Promise."

Karaoke Bill groans again, pissed and lobbing F-bombs the entire journey down the Coral Road to the lake: where the Reverend and Briggs went; where Lacrishia and the Beginners went. It'll be at least ten minutes before news reaches the Reverend. At least five minutes before the gray-shirts come back. Darcy has ensured that Molly, Marcos, and I have our time alone with the watchtower after all.

The clock is ticking.

CHAPTER TWENTY-NINE
ALONE TIME

Darcy and Bill disappear noiselessly around the bend in the Coral Road leading to the lake, and from there, Darcy will be thrown into the bunker—*animal cages*, she called them. She leapt headfirst into severe punishment (and gave Bill the beating of his life) to secure this opportunity for us, so I'm not going to waste a moment. Two minutes ago, the courtyard was packed with every soul on this island, but now there's only Molly, Marcos, me, and the body.

Drew's body.

A sudden, intense need for the bathroom kinks my stomach as I close the final few steps separating me from Drew. He looks younger dead. His long, hairless legs no longer remind me of some Olympian Instagram god, but a child who will never grow older than twenty. Trembling, I reassemble the shattered remains of the Little Bottle In My Heart and stuff all my fears inside: grief over the pain Drew must've felt, self-pity that my goading about his aunt may have triggered him, anguish that his aunt will never see her nephew alive, frustration that Drew took the secret of Ricky and Rigo's killer to his grave, and finally...terror at coming face-to-face with my first non-funeral dead body.

He isn't dead. He's just sleeping.

"What did Darcy say to you?" Molly asks, mildly hyperventilating as she joins me under the watchtower. "What the hell did she do that for?"

"Darcy bought us time to look for Ricky's Expulsion tapes," I say.

"We're *still* doing that?"

"What do you want to do? Run for the boat and leave the kids here? I already made my choice: I'm not leaving Nightlight until I can get us off the island—all of us. Nobody gets left behind. Nobody else gets hurt."

Molly deflates, the heaviness of Drew's death weighing strangely on her. It's sitting strangely on me, as well. The only one of us who actually knew Drew well is Marcos, and he's withdrawn into a blank shell, his wet, saucer eyes focusing on everything and nothing at once.

"I can't believe he hung himself," Molly whispers.

"Hanged," Marcos corrects, joining us with rapid, anxious steps. "Drapes are hung, people are ha—"

"I understand!" On an exhale of agitation, Molly peels the bandage from her cheek, exposing a pink, glistening gash to the sticky air, and drops it to the road as carelessly as Darcy's wig.

"One of us needs to climb the tower and look for those tapes," I say, "and one of us should look over Drew's body for...anything. A note, anything. Drew knew who killed Ricky, and maybe he has something on him that'll point us in the right direction. And I don't want any of you slowing us down with questions or nervous bullshit." I swerve first to Molly, then to Marcos—neither of whom are thrilled about my tyrannical tone.

"Go nuts with Drew!" Molly sneers, craning toward the hacked-off nub of Drew's rope, which still dangles off the bird's nest. Her eyes narrow. "I'll do the more useful thing and find those tapes."

"Amazing idea, teammate!" I snipe as Molly mounts the ladder. "Careful with the middle rungs. Drew hit them when he fell."

"Oh, should I? Should I be careful climbing a ladder that's obviously broken?"

Marcos quickens his finger snapping, and Molly begins her climb—clammy hand after clammy hand—up twenty-eight good rungs and two bad ones. With this grubby, tropical heat and the rungs spaced so far apart, her ascent is slow. As I consider the lifeless camper at my feet—a camper I badgered right before he died—a cold guilt grazes my shoulder.

"Molly?" I call softly.

"What?"

"Sorry about...my 'tude."

Only four rungs high, Molly presses her forehead against the wood to catch her breath. "I'm sorry too. Whatever that baby stuff was about...thanks for not ditching us."

I pivot to Marcos, his shellacked hair starting to wilt. "And I didn't mean to be mean about your nervousness, I'm—"

"I thought we didn't have any time," he says, waving his hands like windshield wipers. My rudeness is the last thing on his mind, apparently. We get to work; Molly continuing her climb, and Marcos and I kneeling beside the camper who warned us—however reluctantly—that there was danger in our midst. Now he's dead. I saw him jump with my own eyes, but something intangible won't stop dragging my mind into a dark pit whenever I replay the moment:

He leapt. He swung. But first, he screamed for Briggs.

My hands float over Drew's body like a planchette over a Ouija board, hoping his ghost will guide me toward whatever it is I believe I'm supposed to find—something that points to Ricky's killer. Marcos hovers over Drew's face and does something the Reverend should have: with a lightly tremoring hand, he marks a blessing of the cross and then quietly whispers an unintelligible prayer to his lost friend. I'm breathless watching Marcos perform this kindness, the first churchy thing on this island that hasn't given me the creeps. Once finished, he whispers to the body, voice shaking from tears: "It was so kind of you to visit me in my loneliness."

His aloha. Both a greeting and parting words. Drew really feels gone now.

When my fingertips make contact with Drew's arm, I shudder. You could chill a pop can on him, even in this swelter. This vaguely refreshing coolness curdles as another inconvenient thought tugs at me: "He's *really* cold."

"Well, he's dead," Marcos says, a worry line permanently etched into his brow.

"Yeah..." I stuff away the nagging thought for later, and Marcos searches Drew's body, charging ahead into the icky job at hand like the biology lab partner everyone wants. He rifles through Drew's pockets, finding nothing in the first; but in the second, he retrieves a small, folded magazine. Its splashy, school-bus yellow cover instantly registers with me: "Another Playbill."

Absolutely no way.

"Like your first message." Marcos nods, handing it over. The pages are crisp and brittle under my fingers, so I keep a light touch. Drew's Playbill is less vibrant than the one for *South Pacific*—this cover design is faded black-and-white, with curling tree branches forming the show's title: *Into the Woods*. A memory of warm, familiar music dances between my chaotic thoughts:

The Witch, singing to her daughter Rapunzel, begging her to stay with her and be afraid of the world outside their little home.

I was eleven. Mom brought me to the Into the Woods *movie after Grandma's wake. Grandma was leaving the mall after buying some last-minute Christmas presents when another woman T-boned her car. She died waiting for the ambulance. The driver hadn't been paying attention. At Grandma's wake, my stomach turned at the stench of all the flowers*—like the death bouquets draped over the Playbills above Ricky's bed. *In her coffin, Grandma didn't look like herself. Skinnier, maybe? Just...different. I grabbed her hand to make sure it was her, to prove that a terrible mistake had been made and she was actually still alive somewhere. She was so cold*—just as Drew's body is already freezing to the touch. *Dad yanked me back from the coffin. He hurt my arm. In the corner, Mom gasped and cussed him out in the funeral parlor. She could smell "it" on him. We went to the movie because she hoped it would heal the pain still slicing through my arm. The songs in* Into the Woods *were beautiful and made me cry. Mom cried too. Later that night, Dad never said goodbye; he went right back home to England. Mom put me to bed, singing and crying the Witch's song. The song where she pleads to her daughter to stay and, once her pleas don't work, turns to threats.*

I sing the tune under my breath to Drew's body. Temporarily, I had left the island. I was in a place much more familiar, but no less chaotic: home. A few months after Grandma's funeral, Mom moved us to Ambrose and into the Reverend's flock. She and Dad were already separated, but after this, he never visited us again. She protected me, but in doing so, led herself directly into the Reverend's mind cult. She was prime for the picking—naïve, fleeing a bad man, unable to handle losing her mother and her marriage all at once, and desperate for normalcy for her son. Yet with each passing year, she became more devout, more rigid and disagreeable...and ultimately, drifted further and further away from me.

But she did it to protect me. She loved me. She *loves* me. She'd protect me again if she knew what was really happening.

I press Ario's recorder against my chest as a searing pain cuts through it. *I'm too young to have a heart attack.* My eyes blur, double-visioning the Playbill and Drew's body. *It's panic. Breathe in through your nose and out through your mouth, Major.* After a few controlled breaths, my lungs and throat reopen, and my vision snaps back into focus. I don't have time to dive into the great mystery of my mother. I drop these thorny memories into the Little Bottle In My Heart. I'll deal with it—and *her*—when I get home.

Back at the ladder, Molly keeps adjusting and readjusting her grip on the rungs. She stares at the shattered planks ahead of her as if studying how she's going to surmount them.

"This is from the original Broadway run," Marcos whispers as my panic attack putters to a final stop. He taps the swirl of trees on Drew's Playbill cover. The boy knows his theater. For the briefest moment, we lock eyes without any anxiety. *Into the Woods* is a show we both know, and he freely admitted it, without worrying about what it might "say" about him.

"How do you know it's the original?" I ask.

"I just know..." he replies bashfully. "Look inside. Is there a message?"

As predicted, at the top of the inside page is a handwritten date: July 29, 1989. Beneath it, a note in faded blue ink:

Stanley, what a totally perfect night. I know you're worried I'm gonna go to college and become this stuck-up prick who doesn't have time for his cousin, but I promise to never leave you alone too long with those nutjobs. I've always got your back. Thanks for turning out so cool.

    —Ricky

    P.S. If there's anything you ever want to talk about, something you can't tell your dad about (and DEFINITELY not my dad), I'm a phone call away. I'll drop everything.

"Shit," I whisper as Marcos and I finish Ricky's inscription to the teenaged Reverend, amused but shaken down to our dampened socks. Ricky's sendoff to his cousin, the young Reverend, lingers in the air, sharp and dissonant like a final piano note.

"Thanks for turning out so cool." Spoken too soon, Ricky.

If I'm putting the timeline together correctly, the summer of '89 was the last time the Reverend and his cousin hung out before Ricky left for college. A few months later, at Christmas, Ricky found the magazine the Reverend stole from him, took him to a gay bar, and launched both of them down the nightmarish rabbit hole to Nightlight.

"If there's anything you ever want to talk about..." Ricky sensed the truth about his cousin and told him he could call him any time. I'm pretty sure that call never came.

The *Into the Woods* Playbill is such a mysterious relic of the past that I almost forgot the ghoulish present in front of us: Drew Schreiber, stone-cold dead, a trail of plum-colored bruises circling the ligature marks on his throat where the noose caught him. In his pocket was a Playbill with a message from Ricky to the Reverend— *what was he doing with this?*

"Why would he do this to himself?" Marcos asks, transfixed by the body. "He seemed okay..."

Clouds of noxious, pitch-black smoke snuff out every fair or empathetic thought in my head as my mother's memory returns. Mom sang the Witch's song. Mom wanted me to delete Ario—and my entire identity—off social media, but I wouldn't do it. The Witch's song meant do as I say or I'll make you pay, and Mom is no different. Puppet strings meant more to her than her son. She ordered Briggs to kidnap me. Briggs—the man who kidnaps kids. The man Drew Schreiber thought it would be fun to kiss and mess around with. Drew allowed Briggs to torture these kids and did nothing to stop him.

"Good," I growl. Marcos turns, confused. Drew's eyes stay peacefully shut, but his throat is ragged and charred with dark violet. The clouds in my head won't break apart, and I can't think of anything except: "GOOD!"

"Hey," Marcos says, and his soft hand cups my cheek. My stinging eyes dart from Marcos's relaxed, open face to his hand. He's touching me...not pulling back or twitching. His touch still brings the topsy-turvy carnival of pleasure and nausea to my stomach, but I don't flinch—I want his hand there. His empathetic touch Pied Pipers the cruel, bilious thoughts out of my mind, and the pain my anger had been blocking returns like a backdraft. "Connor...?"

"I'm okay," I sniff, my chin trembling in his touch. "I'm not happy Drew's dead. I didn't mean to say it."

"I know..." Marcos releases me, but a nagging inconsistency remains: *What was Drew doing with this Playbill?* Along with this unanswerable question comes the mounting concern over how long we've been here, kneeling alone at Drew's body with no Reverend or gray-shirt in sight.

Stalled halfway up the ladder, Molly considers her next move. She's arrived at the two splintered rungs. The rung above the damage is within her reach, but when she pokes it, it wobbles against the flimsy nails pinning it to the structure.

"Is it safe?" I call up, my question echoing through the jungle's stillness.

"I don't Goddamn know," Molly groans, poking the semi-loose rung again. "What if I fall?"

"I'm not gonna let you fall," Marcos says. His assurance makes me swoon and imagine tumbling into his beefy, waiting arms, but Molly returns his gallantry with an eye roll.

"My hero. Save your showing off for Miss Manners." Molly stretches her trembling fingers over the unsteady rung, but before she lets her feet leave the safety of her perch, she turns back to Marcos. "Actually, I would like to take you up on your offer of not letting me fall, please."

At Marcos's generous nod, Molly sucks in a breath and swings for the next rung.

The plank whines even under her birdlike weight, and her legs dangle in midair until she secures her hold. "Oh shit, oh shit, oh shit, shit, shiiiiit," Molly mutters, steadying herself on the wobbling rung. Marcos launches off his knees, like a track runner, toward the ladder and throws out his arms.

"I got you!" he hisses in a carrying whisper.

Yet Molly slams her foot against the shattered lower rung for momentum, alley-ooping herself onto the next one, which thankfully remains solid. The three of us breathe, and Marcos cautiously retreats back to Drew and me, leaving Molly to her remaining climb. While Marcos resumes his hunt through Drew's back pockets, my attention returns to the Playbill. I flip each aging page carefully, like a paleontologist exhuming a brittle fossil. I need this memento to remain as intact as possible. Four pages later, across the cast bios for Joanna Gleason and Bernadette Peters, Ricky's second message appears. Unlike his handwritten note from 1989, this message is written in black Sharpie and is enormous, jagged, and fresh:

THERE IS STILL TIME.

There is still time. The words bring me off my knees and into a panicked, shuffling circle around the body. I'm no longer sweltering from the island sun...I'm as cold as Drew. Just like me, the Reverend received a final message from Ricky in his will. Mine was *HELP CONNOR.* His was *THERE IS STILL TIME.*

This Playbill belonged to the Reverend—and *recently*—so what is Drew doing with it? The deluge of nagging thoughts circles back a third time, stronger and clearer than ever: *Drew is freezing cold; his complexion is already blue; his neck is purple from bruising.*

He was bringing this Playbill to show me, but something stopped him.

Someone.

"Marcos, let me see something," I say, tapping him away. Without question, he scoots backward. I don't hesitate—I touch Drew's bruised neck, tracing the ring around his slim, elegant throat where the noose's toughened bristles gripped him. A halo of peeling skin covers a row of long, dark purple splotches. But these bruises don't appear anywhere else on his neck, except for these two spots. They extend upward to his jaw...in the shape of fingers.

Carefully, I grip Drew's neck as if I were choking him...My fingers align perfectly with the bruises. "Oh my God," Marcos whispers, witnessing the same horror I am.

"He didn't kill himself," I say, my hands still clasped around his neck. "He was already dead. Somebody strangled him and pushed him off the tower." They would've had plenty of time. We only heard *someone* scream for Briggs, and then a body falling. Everyone was at lunch; it was the perfect time to have everyone witness it happen and swear the boy jumped.

Above us, Molly grunts as she ascends another rung closer to the bird's nest.

"Someone else played that music and screamed for Briggs?" Marcos asks. Between the two of us, the puzzle pieces are locking together faster and faster. Too fast. The momentum can't be stopped.

"The Reverend did this."

"No, he was with us at lunch the whole time. So were Bill and Briggs and everybody."

"Drew was bringing me this Playbill, I know it. He wanted to help. It has to be the Reverend!"

"Connor, I watched Drew fall. It couldn't have been the Reverend. It has to be someone who wasn't at lunch."

"Someone who was in the watchtower during lunch? We've been here since Drew fell. How could they have had time to sneak away?"

"Maybe they're still up there." The words escape Marcos so quickly, he doesn't immediately realize the implications of what he's said. But realization does come—crashing as loudly as silverware clattering onto a kitchen floor.

Molly clears the ladder's final rung, and we move in slow motion. Gripping the slats, she looks down at me, her face twisted in fear. "Connor..." she whispers. "Someone's up here—"

The killer stands, throws off the tarp that's been concealing her, and emerges from her hiding place like a great white shark out of the ocean depths. Miss Manners straightens the filthy hem of her lemon-print dress and smiles at her new company. Molly's hands jolt off the ladder rungs like they've transformed into snakes, and—shrieking—she plummets back to earth.

CHAPTER THIRTY

NOBODY MOVES, NOBODY GETS HURT

"Molly!" I shriek.

Pins and needles trap me on my knees next to Drew's body. Molly hurtles downward so quickly—and the shock of discovering Miss Manners has stunned us so completely—that Marcos is only able to reach her in a photo finish. Molly's screams continue until she crashes into his arms, the impact slamming both of them into the dirt in a tangle of limbs. If the grayshirts had placed Drew's body a foot to the left, we'd be scraping Molly off the Coral Road with a shovel. Luckily for her, Marcos is practically made of pillows. Pillow arms, pillow thighs, pillow chest, and a pillow...well, let's just say when Molly struck him, he landed on his ass and seems fine.

Molly rolls off Pillow Man like a concussed person staggering out of a car wreck. Dazed and silent, she crawls toward the dense jungle wall beyond the watchtower. Still on his back, Marcos stares catatonically upward, but I don't need to follow his gaze to know who's holding his attention.

Miss Manners.

She heard everything we said. She knows what we're up to. And she hanged Drew, already dead, to make it look like he did it himself.

You're next, whispers the voice in my head.

Adrenaline flushes the pins and needles out of my feet and launches me toward my friends. The next few seconds are critical—I don't waste any time gawping at Miss Manners or even asking my friends if they're all right. I know in my heart that we're dead. The danger at Nightlight is no longer some nameless, opaque anxiety; it's an unhinged woman who's caught us with proof that she's a murderer.

Hiding in the jungle is our only option.

"Run away," I gasp. Marcos clutches my hand willingly, rolling first to his knees, then his feet. Despite her head start, Molly hasn't made much progress scrambling across the dirt. Marcos and I hook our arms underneath hers to hoist her up, but she squeals in protest until a loud click stops us. The metallic click echoes through the forest, stopping my heart.

We all heard it—*the cocking of a gun.*

"Nobody moves, nobody gets hurt," Miss Manners orders from her bird's nest perch. "Stand where you are and face me." The three of us do as we're told as obediently as programmed robots. In a way, I'm overwhelmed with gratitude; I expected a shot to ring out and to watch the back of Molly's head explode—or for Molly to watch it happen to me. *Click, bang, darkness.* That's how fast it would happen. No time for last words or even a final, reflective thought. It would be chaos, then nothing forever.

A single-action rifle points downward, but it's impossible to tell which of us Miss Manners has in her sights. She could take out anyone in a heartbeat; the watchtower is the perfect vantage point for a sniper. Exhausted with worry, Molly raises her arms, and Marcos and I follow.

"It was her," I whisper. "She wasn't with us at lunch."

The Reverend had an alibi for not murdering Drew: he was at lunch with Briggs, Karaoke Bill, and the gray-shirts. I was so distracted by Bill's Walkman and plotting our next moves, I failed to notice that Miss Manners skipped lunch entirely. While I ate peppered fish, she crouched inside the bird's nest with Drew's body and waited for the right moment to turn on the music, scream for Briggs, and shove the model overboard. And Briggs was too consumed by freeing Drew from the rope to notice somebody hiding underneath the tarp.

But why would Miss Manners want to kill Drew? And in such a grotesque, dramatic way to disguise it as suicide? Obviously, Drew knew more about Ricky's death than he admitted, so he had to go. On our drive to the cliff, the Reverend sensed that I'd found out something I shouldn't have about Ricky—he knew someone talked. Did he put the pieces together that it was Drew? Did Miss Manners act alone or on the Reverend's orders? Who wrapped their hands around the boy's throat so tightly, they left dark purple prints?

An aching thought wallops me: *It's my fault.* I forced Drew to talk, and he paid the price.

"Lunchtime's over," Miss Manners says flatly, not a scrap remaining of her quaint, southern charm. Calm tumbles over me like I'm in the eye of a hurricane as we wait for the riflewoman to squeeze her trigger. Beside me, Molly's horrified expression hardens into fury as Marcos drowns in his own confusion.

"You've had a busy lunch break," I speak carefully, ordering my mouth not to get us all shot. "Must be starving."

"You little gays." Miss Manners laughs behind the cold, black eye of her rifle barrel. "So witty. I've worked here for years, and you know what? I am *sick* of witty."

"Sorry, miss." I chomp down on my tongue as ten thousand gallons of fear hormones flood my cerebral cortex.

"Mr. Major, empty your pockets. Miss Partridge, call out what you find."

It's all useless paper to me now. Slowly, without sudden movements, I lighten my pockets one item at a time. "A Playbill for...*Into the Woods*," Molly shouts.

"We found it on his body," I confess. "It's a memento from Ricky Hannigan to the Reverend when they were kids. Why would he be carrying that?"

Behind her rifle, Miss Manners studies me for a long, grinning moment before admitting, "Because the Reverend was right about Drew. Briggs was weak and told his little girlfriend everything...and he was about to tell you."

The hideous truth I already know in my gut is rapidly approaching the surface of my thoughts. "Those are some big-ass handprints on his throat. Wasn't you, was it?"

"Nope," she replies coldly. "An hour ago, the Reverend comes to me holding a body. Unlike Briggs, I do as I'm told without questions. I'll be a much more reliable second-in-command than he was. Now, drop the Playbill."

I lob Ricky's final message to his cousin over my shoulder, and it joins Darcy's wig and the shredded birth certificate on the Coral Road. My head sways under the heat of the truth: the Reverend killed a kid. Snuffed him out with his bare hands.

Mom's hero. My pastor. The wounded boy on that tape.

But the Reverend isn't that boy anymore. *"I'm something else now,"* he warned. It's becoming even likelier that he's the one who attacked Ricky and killed his husband. This entire week has been about the Reverend covering his tracks because the FBI reopened Ricky's case.

You're next, Major...you had your chance to get out of Nightlight, and you blew it.

"Miss Hayward...why are you telling us this?" Marcos asks, hands in the air and anxiety at a fever pitch.

"Because we're not leaving this courtyard alive," I say, keeping my eyes on the rifle. I don't have to turn my head to know my icy reality check has fallen over Molly and Marcos. The barrel of Miss Manners's gun is giving me nothing but clarity, as awful as that clarity might be. "How are you gonna do it? Make it look like we all hanged ourselves—*goodbye, cruel world*—when we've clearly been shot? I mean, my mom will believe anything the Reverend says, with or without a bullet hole in my skull. But what about Molly and Marcos? Their families might want a closer peek at the details of their dead kids. So, what's the plan?"

"I'm not sure yet..." Miss Manners purrs behind her weapon. A hot wind rustles through the palms, and in a flash of inspiration, her eyes light with excitement. "Maybe...Drew snapped. Killed you three. And the guilt made him do himself in."

"Nah. Won't work." I battle a rising lump in my throat, but I refuse to spend my last moments begging this cretin.

"And why's that?"

"Everyone's already seen Drew dead and us three alive. The stories won't match."

"Interesting...I'm sure we'll think of something."

"Yeah," Molly scoffs. "More murders. That'll solve everything."

"Not too worried about it, to be honest," Miss Manners replies, her plucky southern lilt slowed to a dull, lifeless drawl.

"You just like hurting us," Marcos accuses, glowering at Miss Manners. His voice is newly deep and dripping with scorn. "Y'all could've handled Drew or any of us without having to...but you won't. You're just looking for any reason to do what you've always wanted. To kill us." The bottom drops out of my stomach as Marcos's accusation brings a deeper reality to light: these people live to inflict pain on queers, and they barely need a logical reason to do so.

"I never thought of it like that," Miss Manners says, impressed. She steels herself against her rifle and pivots it one degree my direction. "What else is in your pockets?"

"Why don't you just take it off my corpse?" I ask, sampling a taste of Marcos's fury. "Seems like your brand."

"I'm looking for something you took, and if you don't got it on you, I need you alive to show me where it went."

Bill's Walkman. The Ricky tape. They lie heavily in my left pocket. Once she has the tape, I'm dead.

Numbly, I withdraw the next item from my pocket: "A Polaroid," Molly calls out. "A picture of a boy...looks like it's from the Winner's Wall."

"Toss it," Miss Manners orders. I ditch the teenage picture of the Reverend, the last-known proof that he was ever sweet, saucer-eyed Stanley Packard.

The next item is sentimental for me: "Another Playbill. *South Pacific.*"

"We've seen it already. Toss it." Down it goes, my gift from Ricky—one of the last totems tying me to my old life, back when my only worry was Ario leaving me to go to college.

The only thing remaining in my pocket is the Walkman.

Miss Manners's rifle lowers to a more relaxed (*for her*) position.

The millimeter's difference between having a gun pointed directly at you and not having a gun pointed directly at you stretches as wide as the ocean trapping me here. "Mr. Major, anything else in your pockets? Turn 'em out."

There's no room left for fear. Another emotion takes its place: the will to survive.

Hell with it, I'm dead anyway.

I pull the smooth jersey material of my pockets inside out. As they invert, I grip the Walkman and unplug the headphone jack with my thumb. It's as dense and hand-shaped as a grenade, so I throw it like one. The tower is too high for me to have a hope of beaning Miss Manners with the device, so I chuck it to my left.

It flies up and begins to descend…enough to draw her eye…

"GO!" I holler. A moment later, the gun fires.

But Marcos, Molly, and I are already leaping for our lives toward the base of the watchtower. The Coral Road erupts with the ping of a bullet. It missed everyone. Pressed flat against the base of the tower, the three of us can't be seen from above, much less shot. The jungle wall—our dense, camouflaged sanctuary—lies only a scant few feet away. Above us, the pageant queen cocks her rifle for the next shot with a grinding, metallic scrape.

She won't stay in her blind spot for long.

An inferno renewed in Molly, she loses no time in scooping a handful of dirt and pebbles before lobbing them down the road. The soil scatters noisily. A half-second behind it, Miss Manners's rifle barks with another reply. The sound tears through my heart like it's made of construction paper, but Molly's distraction worked. "Now!" she hollers, faith-jumping from our blind spot into the shrouded labyrinth of green ahead. Marcos follows, achieving miraculous distance in a single leap as the scraping of the rifle bolt sounds again.

What are you waiting for, Major?!

I have no awareness of jumping. My eyes blur, my shoes depart from the ground, and I collide with a curtain of draping moss in an actual somersault. Not the graceful, Lady-Spy-in-a-Black-Catsuit movie somersault. This somersault is a series of brutal tumbles where the sky is up one minute and down the next; each time I roll, my jaw slams against something wet but hard.

Inside my fear-addled brain, the chittering of birds and insects morphs into a chorus of pained, humanlike screams, soon joined by another, more artificial noise: the crackle of Bill's radio speakers. A voice follows, its fearsome power reaching into every corner of the woods:

"CONNOR MAJOR IS ESCAPING!"

CHAPTER THIRTY-ONE
THE SANCTUM

I have to have been wandering in the jungle for at least an hour. The dense canopy of palm fronds overhead spreads as wide as tarps, so I can't even use the sun to track how long I've been lost. I always kept time by my phone, anyway.

All of this started because of my phone.

For the first twenty minutes after my escape from the watchtower, Miss Manners hollered over Bill's loudspeaker for my immediate capture, but then suddenly, she stopped. That was ages ago, and her voice hasn't returned. Not that I'm complaining; her booming orders rattled my spine, even as I fled deeper into Nightlight's island wilderness. No matter how far I ran, her voice remained just over my shoulder: *"CONNOR MAJOR IS ESCAPING. HE'S IN THE WOODS."*

The island's woods are a lightless cocoon of massive palm stalks, underbrush nearly five feet tall, and coil after coil of twisting, moss-eaten roots. It's impossible to run through nature this untouched—what I'm attempting is more like frantic, messy walking. I've traversed God knows how many upraised roots, and I keep rolling my ankles on pockets of the uneven ground hiding beneath the jungle floor's bracken.

Molly and Marcos are nowhere in sight, but they have to be just as lost as I am.

Lost is good. It'll be worse if we're found.

My tongue, dry and spongy, scrapes against the roof of my

mouth in the hopes of finding some moisture to suckle on. No luck. The afternoon heat has dug itself under my skin and sapped me as dry as an autumn leaf. If I really need water, I could peel off my shirt and wring out my own sweat, but I think I'll wait until I'm a bit more desperate. The night we arrived—*last night; God, it's only been a day*—Briggs warned us not to wander off the Coral Road. He said we'd die of thirst.

The Reverend might get his wish after all. Unlike Drew, it wouldn't even be murder.

The longer I spend in these woods, the less I care about who killed Ricky or how to shut down Nightlight. Those concerns evaporate with each passing, thirsty second, leaving behind only my most immediate concerns about surviving the night. Thunderstorms have been building for a while, but every rumble of thunder is nothing but a tease that fresh water might descend and rescue me. Although, I doubt any rain could penetrate this thick canopy, even if it did fall.

"ARIO!" a voice echoes faintly through the jungle. At the sound of my boyfriend's name, I grasp the recorder squished under my matted shirt. *Ario? Here? I'm hallucinating.* The dehydration is worse than I thought; my brain has mercifully chosen to materialize Ario and his lovely, curly hair one last time before I collapse dead. "ARIO!" the deep voice calls again, closer.

Walls of rustling, eight-foot-high shrubbery surround me. The voice could be anywhere. "Who's...there?" I ask, ragged and squeaking. An agonizing thought arrives too late: Miss Manners knows my boyfriend's name from when she made me delete his pictures.

It's a trap.

"Connor?" the voice returns from behind a knotted shroud. The greenery separates, and a gentle, hulking angel emerges: *Marcos.*

His hair plastered to his forehead, Marcos's baby blue Nightlight tee runs midnight black where it hugs his shoulders. "Connor!" He bounds toward me clutching the only sight more welcome than he is: a bottle of crystal clear water.

"Oh my God, are you okay?" I ask, greedily reaching for the water like a witch who's spotted a pair of ruby slippers. "Can I have some?"

"Yes, it's for you. I had mine already." Whimpering happily, I strangle off the cap and commence guzzling—all my questions can wait until I've licked this bottle clean (questions like where Marcos found water and whether he's a mirage). The bottle empties into a husk, and finally, the ground solidifies under my feet. "Better?" he asks.

"So much"—a belch of water interrupts—"better. I can't believe you found me."

"Yay." Satisfied I'm no longer about to drop dead, Marcos allows his drained, painful expression to reemerge.

"Is Molly with you?"

"No, but she's okay...as far as I know."

"What happened? How'd you get this water?"

"She and I got pretty far when they stopped sounding the alarm for you. I know my way around the forest a little, so I told her I was gonna go back for you. Molly came up with the plan—there was no talking her out of it. She wanted to go to the cabins to get Lacrishia and the Beginners out of there before any staff could round them up. We went to the boys' lodge first, but nobody was there. That's when I got the water out of my pack. The lake was like a ghost town. We couldn't believe it. Really creepy. Then Molly ran ahead to the girls' cabin—there was *no* stopping her—and I said I was going back for you before you dehydrated."

"So, Molly's plan is to take everyone...where?"

"To hide, I think. We agreed that, if I found you, we'd meet up at the waterfall by sunset."

"We still have to get Darcy. They put her in the bunker."

"Yeah..." Neither of us comfortable with this rapidly unfolding crisis, Marcos and I wait in the center of our tropical hedge maze. He softly snaps his fingers. For all his anxiousness, Marcos carries himself as someone all too familiar with having to acclimate quickly to unpleasant realities.

"You came back for me," I say. "You've had to do that a lot today."

"Well," he says, snorting, half-embarrassed, "if you quit causing trouble, maybe I could catch a break."

I meet his eyes, my neck craning upward like I'm in the front row of a movie theater. As I gaze at him, cool breath soothes my burning lungs. "You know, keeping up with my bullshit is full-time work, so I hope you're up for it." I catch his lips wanting to smile, but then a cloud passes over my thoughts. "You had some strong feelings at lunch about staying at Nightlight. Given things changing around here, would you be cool leaving the island...today...with me?"

His lips part, his eyes soften. The hope in my question has pricked him painfully, but he recovers with a nerdy giggle. "Don't think I have a choice anymore."

That's not what I asked, dummy. *"Do you want to leave with me?" "I don't have a choice."* Just what a girl wants to hear. But literally, what did I mean by "leave *with* me"? Like every other word that's slithered past my lips today, what I just asked Marcos was unplanned and loaded with chaos.

"Let's get going to the falls," he says. "It's only a fifteen-minute hike, but there's storms rolling in and we're gonna lose light."

"Lead the way, Weezer," I say, not remotely ready to continue hiking on the blisters that used to be my feet. "Hey, did you...call out the name Ario?"

"Oh, weird, right? Molly didn't want me running into the jungle yelling 'Connor!' and lead them right to you, so she said to yell 'Ario' instead. She said you'd know what it meant and come running."

Molly. Shady lady. "She thought of everything."

"So...what's Ario?"

Unprepared to be walloped by such an obvious follow-up question, I tug Ario's recorder through my shirt for good luck. "Nobody." Hearing myself say the lie throws another thousand miles between me and my boyfriend. Ario and I are running out of time—now, no longer just because he's leaving for college, but because I'm a different person than I was forty-eight hours ago. And when I get home—if I get home—I'll be even differenter.

I'm no clock, but this was not a fifteen-minute hike. Each step sliced into my pounding, throbbing feet, relieved only when the jungle's encroaching darkness broke away into gray daylight. The rain began halfway through our trip, and when we finally exit the forest canopy, I drink in as much as possible.

For the rest of my life, I'll never be hydrated enough.

The storming sky has become an unassailable wall of granite, marked only by foggy halos encircling the island peaks that rise in the distance beyond Lake Monteverde. Marcos was an excellent guide—he led us directly to the edge of the waterfall dropping half a stadium off the clifftop. The waterfall pummels the lake, spraying outward in a fine mist that's just as agreeable as this rain on my sun-battered face. Scanning left, the high grass smothering the lakeshore continues for miles without a single Nightlight cabin, gray-shirt, or camper in sight. Marcos was right: the sudden absence of human life in this camp is maximum creepy.

"We're the first ones here," I say. "Maybe we shouldn't wait out in the open."

"There's a cavern behind the falls," Marcos says, striking an unexpectedly rugged pose as he points confidently toward our destination. Clutching his wrist for support, I follow as we mount the long, slanted rocks leading to the falls' base. It's a risky voyage. Rain, mist, and lapping lake water have turned the rocks slippery; Marcos's wide-legged stance keeps him dependably upright, but my teeny chicken legs won't stop wobbling until we come face-to-face with the waterfall.

I follow Marcos through the roaring curtain of water, and inside, a cavern welcomes us. The falls provide a soundproof cloak against the world outside, allowing only scant flecks of daylight into the grotto. Marcos flicks open his lighter, and a small flame illuminates a ledge in front of us: a shimmering, black-green rock shelf rises to my chest, and from it, a slope continues upward into darkness.

"We should climb it," I say. "It'll be a safer hiding place."

"What if there's no room up there?" Marcos asks, the flame shivering in his hand.

"Then we come back down and wait for everyone. I can check it out on my own..."

"You're not going up there without me." Soaked head to toe, he regards me through rain-spotted glasses, and a strangely comforting version of my anxious pins and needles fill my hands. We're in the worst trouble imaginable, but this boy I just met refuses to let me out of his sight. Another difference between him and Ario.

Marcos leads with his lighter, and we ascend the incline until it plateaus. It doesn't take long. Beneath us by only ten feet or so, the back of the waterfall remains visible. Up here, a low-ceilinged sanctum extends much farther back than I expected, like the roots of a tooth, ending in a naturally circular chamber. "Whoa," Marcos says, spinning his flame around the space. The ground is flat and the walls are craggy but unobtrusive, so our sanctum resembles a small, bare bedroom. "When the storms get bad, the lake floods," Marcos continues, alight with excitement. "But that ledge and this hill would keep this place totally dry. We could hide here forever."

"That'd be nice," I say hollowly. I'd love nothing more than to seal myself away in this sanctum with some snacks, my laptop, a good Wi-Fi signal...and Marcos. But the world won't disappear that easily. People are trying to kill us, and Molly is still out there in the wild.

"Someone else has been here..."

More energized than alarmed, I spin around toward a flame that has grown suddenly larger. Marcos ignites a tiki torch—the same ones that stand guard outside Ambrose Chapel. The torch erupts against the cavern wall, spraying the chamber with a campfire glow. Boyishly proud of his discovery, Marcos beams, but where his heart has lifted, mine weighs heavier.

It's another Winner's Wall.

Instead of pictures, our sanctum's black wall is covered with chalk-drawn hearts, and at the foot of the wall lies a pile of powdery-white limestone. "Have you ever seen this before?" I ask, approaching with the same awe and trepidation as when Marcos brought me to the Winner's Wall. He doesn't respond. His smile fallen, he presses his hand to one of the chalk hearts. Inside it are four letters: MK + CR. "Initials?"

Each batch of initials is different: TB + KW, KS + DA, MR + AS. On and on, they fill dozens of hearts, climbing the cave into darkened corners that even our tiki lamp can't reach. "I think campers come here," Marcos whispers. "They've come here for years. Where Nightlight can't find them. They sneak off...Nobody needs to know what they do. They loved each other."

My heart shatters. The teenagers of Nightlight's past found this sanctum, kept each other company through dark times, and commemorated the victory by leaving their initials like carvings in a lovebird's tree. Through loneliness. Through torture and endless invasions of privacy. Nightlight tried to snuff it out, but love grew. Love found its way to the island, and this sanctuary made it possible. Whoever first transcribed their initials into a heart started a chain reaction that led to an entirely different Winner's Wall. In the cabin, the Winner's Wall of "successful" Nightlight graduates is a depressing monument to control and domination. But this wall is an anthem of wild, unchained resistance.

What happened to them? Wherever these couples are now, even if they eventually fell back into Nightlight's program, this wall is proof that they fought. Fallen soldiers in the war against Nightlight.

My throat snaps shut as, among the fray, my fingers find familiar initials: RH + DD.

RH for Ricky Hannigan? But who is DD? Some sad-eyed, handsome boy who held Ricky and kissed away his traumas: being betrayed by his cousin and torn from the life he was supposed to have—a life that had nothing to do with Nightlight or his rotten family? What happened to DD? Did he marry a woman and have kids? Do his kids have kids? Did he eventually confess the truth and move in with a man, and now every few years, his heart pinches with the memory of this cave?

This sanctum is unbearably heavy from the weight of so much time. I can't stomach looking at another batch of initials; no matter what story I invent for them, it ends in tears. Maybe some of them got out. Someone *has* to have gotten out.

"Do you see the initials *SP* anywhere?" I ask, silently mopping tears with my wrist.

"I don't think so," Marcos says, searching. "Why?"

"Stanley Packard. The Reverend. If he used to come here as a camper, then he knows it's a good hiding place and we're not safe." Marcos hunts the wall of hearts before reporting no secret love life for *SP*. "Aw, poor Reverend. Maybe if he'd gotten some, he wouldn't have become so murdery."

"Yeah..." Marcos chuckles with a twinge of dread.

"No cave kisses for him. He wanted to be *good*."

The Lovers' Wall behind me, I watch the falls crash below, hypnotized until Marcos speaks again: "I don't want to be good."

Unexpected excitement floods my chest and thumps against Ario's recorder. I turn to find Marcos watching me like a dog watches someone eat. His waterlogged shirt sticks like peanut butter to his torso, exposing a strip of brown, lightly furry skin above his hips. The torchlight traces a golden outline along his curves as he heaves shallow, nervous breaths. I struggle not to stare—it's been a complicated enough day as it is. I can't mess around with a boy who thinks we're supposed to end up with girlfriends, no matter how kissable he may be.

Or how wonderfully heavy he'd feel on top of me...

"What do you mean, you don't want to be good?" I ask.

"You don't know what I mean?" he asks. My heartbeat slows to a crawl.

"You can't say it?" Marcos's watery eyes pick apart my resolve piece by piece. "Say it."

"The Reverend's dad was a reverend, then he became one. My dad's a reverend too. I can't do this anymore. My chest..." Wincing, Marcos grips his soggy shirt.

"Are you okay?" I ask, advancing.

"It hurts. I pray before I go to sleep, and I pray that sleep will do it. I'll wake up different. But when I wake up, my chest still hurts. I'm still here. I'm still *me*." Marcos's throat closes, and all that comes next are squeaks. I close the gap between us until the redwood-tall boy looms far above me. Wiping back tears, he narrows his eyes. "I've been here seven months. It hasn't been fun, but things were calm. Things were bad, but they made *sense*. Then you came, and in *one stupid day,* everything gets scary and worse and nothing makes sense anymore."

I can't believe it. Somehow, I managed to make the kindest boy in the universe glower at me like I'm roadside trash. Everyone on this island is either dead or running for their lives because of me. I just want Marcos to look at me again the way he looked at me this morning—smiling, with a toothbrush sticking goofily out of his mouth.

"I'm sorry," I say, defeated.

"You should be," he says. But his expression softens as his warm paw lands softly on the base of my neck. Electricity snaps the spot where he touches. My neck jerks and my eyes want to wince at his touch, but I order them to stay put. I don't want to startle Marcos—*I don't want to stop what's going to happen. What needs to happen.* His fingers slide up my neck, through my sopping hair. My legs weaken, but he holds me in a firm, careful grip. "You little criminal."

He lowers himself on me, and my lips welcome his.

CHAPTER THIRTY-TWO

CM + MC

No one can touch us.

In this cave, guarded by the falls, I've finally found the privacy I need to be what I couldn't be for Ario—sexual. After our first kiss, Marcos and I know what comes next and we know what to do. His hands swirl over my body—my back, my cheeks, my hips—with frantic greed; in seven months, he hasn't touched another boy beyond a handshake. His lips engulf mine, feasting like a man gone psychotic from prolonged hunger. His bristly chin scrapes against mine, but I welcome it; the abrasions are divine. I can't explain it—sex has always been simultaneously intoxicating and uncomfortable, but Marcos's touch doesn't burn me. The balance of my emotions is tipping so rapidly toward ecstasy that I wonder if this is sex at all. Maybe I'm just delirious from dehydration.

We may be inexperienced, unknowledgeable, and terrified of what doing this *means*...but AT LAST, none of that matters. The urgency is everything. I'm not embarrassed to be doing sex wrong with Marcos because Marcos is on my same playing field. Skill means nothing. Instinct is driving us.

Ario's breath was light and minty, but Marcos tastes riper— *richer*—like bootstrap leather and charred meat. Ario never went anywhere without a spritz of cologne, but Marcos—to be blunt— smells nasty. I hadn't noticed when we were farther apart, but pressed against me, Marcos stinks like he's spent the day running around in 100-degree humidity. His sticky, pungent musk reminds me of rutting animals in captivity, which only swells me harder against his leg.

I'm a cliché, but I don't care. I don't care! I DON'T CARE!

Marcos is fully erect beneath his shorts, invitingly warm, even though I'm already dizzy from the heat. Without warning, he throws strong, paint-can-round arms under my knees and hoists me off my feet. My legs instinctively close around his back. Huffing, he walks me to the cave wall, pushes me against the rock, and resumes devouring my mouth. The maneuver isn't graceful—Marcos grips me clumsily, kisses messily, and the rock jabbing into my back already hurts—but even as my thoughts spin further outside of my grasp, I refuse to do anything that might end this moment prematurely.

"You lifted me...like I was nothing," I gasp.

"I saw it on TV," he whispers, becoming the gentle, nervous preacher's boy again. "Thought it would be fun to do." Our eyes deadlock, and a thrilled laugh escapes me; my internal roller coaster, slowly climbing, takes its first plunge into pandemonium. Marcos grins sheepishly, but one blink later, the starved lion returns. "I've been dying to pick you up all day."

"What else d'you want to do?"

Still cradling me against the stone, Marcos presses his lips to my ear and whispers his wish list, each sinful instruction spilling down my neck with cool, hissing delight. It's unnerving to see him like this, to hear him talk this way—not frightened, no finger-snapping, no well-mannered mother hen. *This newer Marcos is a Grade-A freak.* And I am too. We grew up in hostile, religious homes, and all the while, these nasty little thoughts spun, taking root, building their nests...now unleashed, thanks to the privacy of our fairytale cave.

Unleashed onto each other.

"I want to do everything with you," I breathe as he gnaws eagerly at the nape of my neck. His teeth scrape an inch above the leather string of Ario's recorder. However we left each other, Ario was slipping away from me. I was frustrating him—and then resenting him. I was scared of being alone, so I didn't do anything about it. I didn't do the right thing and let him go. I needed Ario. Needed his attention and validation, not a partner. I needed him... but I *want* Marcos. A faint part of me, vanishing further with each stroke of Marcos's palm against my cheek, still clings to the reality that Ario is my boyfriend. *Is this cheating?* It is. But circumstances have changed. So much—so much my heart can't even accept the reality of how startlingly different my life has become. *Am I even the same Connor from yesterday?* No. That Connor died the moment my mom told Briggs to be careful with me as he lugged me away to this horrible place.

I'm something else now, the Reverend said, and I understand.

This new Connor knows things now. I can't ever be with Ario again. His unknowing touch would be alien to me. I could live with Ario for fifty years, and he would never discover the grim, knowing beast hibernating in my chest—now awake. Marcos has already found my beast. His own beast led him here. Boyfriend loyalty is strong, but to be seen—to be *known*—is stronger.

Swallowed by a guilt as numbing but omnipresent as novocaine, my allegiance abandons Ario, the boy who did nothing wrong, and allows Marcos, this new traveler, inside.

Ten minutes later, tingly and pleasantly tired, I linger by the sanctum's edge and watch Marcos clean himself in the waterfall below. He's even more nude without his glasses, which lay folded on the cavern ledge. The falls cascade down his face like oversized tears...but he's smiling. In a rainy corner of my mind, I've been worrying what would happen if we hooked up. *Would he beat himself up? Pretend it never happened? Get angry and attack me? Beg the Reverend for forgiveness?* So far, he's done none of that. He's remained fully present, validating everything we did together—and everything it meant—by simply staying and smiling.

Revolutionary.

"Come here," he says, reaching with a flapping, summoning hand. I'm similarly bare to the elements (except for Ario's pendant), but I approach Marcos as un-self-conscious about my body as I've ever been. My bare feet, agonizingly knotted from jungle running, slap across the cavern's shallow puddles until I close my hand inside his.

After we shake ourselves dry, we dress in our shorts but nothing else; neither of us are eager to jump back into the sweat-drenched Nightlight shirts we discarded hastily around the cavern. Curled beside the torchlight, Marcos rests my feet in his lap and grinds into them with his thumb, firing shock-combos of pain and relief up my legs. A strip of wilting black hair drips handsomely down his glasses as he concentrates. His wood-beaded bracelet with the small, embedded crucifix brushes my ankle, summoning a devilish smirk in me over how thoroughly we've corrupted each other.

He plunges his knuckle into my arch, and my leg responds by dancing into the air. "There's your trouble. I've got a trick my abuela would do."

Marcos closes his fist, his bicep expanding as it recoils to strike. "Wait—what are you doing?" I ask, wincing prematurely.

"Relax. You'll feel amazing after." *BOOM.* His knuckles collide with my tender, pulsating arch, instantly rupturing the knot the way dynamite levels a dam. "How's that feel?"

"Holy shit," I moan. "That worked."

"My abuela used to—uh, y'know, my grandma—"

"I know what *abuela* means," I say, winking. "I've seen the cocoa packets."

"My dad's always on me about talking English every single syllable all the time. My abuela would tell him to...well, it basically means *shut up and mind your business*." He chuckles before walloping my other arch with another grand slam. The relief is night-and-day.

"What does she think of you being here?"

"She's not...super all there anymore. Few years ago, Dad built a guest house for her, and, y'know, it keeps her out of a nursing home." A draft blows through the sanctum as a shadow passes over Marcos's blissful expression. "My dad lies. He lies all the time, so he's probably got her thinking I'm at boarding school or something..."

I shouldn't have dragged reality into our hideaway, but if Marcos is anything like me, the memories of his grandma might be jagged but he enjoys reliving them.

"My grandma was my best friend," I admit. "If she hadn't died, none of this would've happened to me." My throat clamps shut, unwilling to let me continue. "She died really suddenly, and then everything went bad. She would've never let my mom do this...get this way...let the Reverend get to her."

My hands slap a shield over my face, and I'm terrified to open my fingers and find Marcos looking pitifully at me. I don't think he'd pity me—I just don't want him knowing these things yet. How relentlessly, hideously trashy my DNA is. How fragile I am. I need him to believe that I'm strong enough and smart enough to get us off this island without falling to pieces over my Goddamn mother. "I'm sorry you lost your grandma," he says. "But I'm glad you came here." When my fingers finally separate, Marcos is scanning the cavern. "What if we just...stayed?"

"In the cave?" I sniff, pondering the blankness of the sanctum. There isn't even food.

"Well, what else? I go back to Texas and you go to Illinois? This way here, I can always see you." Marcos smiles with no teeth, only dimples. For all of his family turmoil and months at Nightlight, his handsomeness remains open, unlined, and hopeful.

And it obliterates my heart.

"I want to tell you something," I say, my stomach lurching with a truth I've put off way too long. But Marcos deserves it. "Right before I came to the island, I had a boyfriend."

"Okay, that's okay," he says rapidly. He isn't heartbroken—worse, he's courteous about it. A kind boy angry with himself because he should've known this was too good to be true.

"He gave me this recorder. His name is Ario."

"It's okay."

"No, I'm not done—"

"It's really okay—!"

Marcos withdraws his feet from my lap, ready to rush back to his depressing reality, but I clutch onto his leg. "Marcos, *stay*. He's leaving for college. I think it's over—it's...it's over. Ario didn't...he doesn't have any idea what's really going on with me. He knew—and he tried to be cool with it—but he'll never *get it*. He couldn't. The total nightmare I lived with. My negative, messy life scared him. And after all of this with Nightlight—if I make it out alive—yeah, maybe

I could go back to him...but if he didn't understand me before, he's *really* not gonna understand me now."

Marcos's leg relaxes back into my lap. His fingers snap once, the click echoing throughout our sanctum. "...I'd understand you."

"I'd understand you too. I don't know what kind of shit show we're going home to. I don't know how we're escaping this island. I'm not even sure how far we're gonna get out of this cave...but if you're okay with it, I'd like to take you on a date. Where we both put on suits or really bougie sweaters or...wear whatever you want, but I want to date you." I ramble so fast, my throat catches at the end. "Do you want to go on a date with me?"

"Yes, please."

"You'll date me, a man?"

Marcos's expression freezes for a brief, frightened second as a lifetime flashes before his eyes—everything saying *yes* will invite into his world: dating a man, kissing a man, holding a man's hand, the bars, the flags, the confessing, the screaming, the crying, the ultimatums, the hope for more—and then the warm dawn of his smile appears. "I will date you, a man. After what we just did, I'm gonna need to do that again."

My heart runs laps around my chest. I'm not lying anymore—I'm gay and everyone's going to have to deal with it. And I'm with Marcos, a boy at my own speed. Ario—bless him—will move to college and find a grown-up boyfriend with no family drama (*best of luck there*), and I'll be okay with it. Because I'm not escaping for Ario anymore. I'm escaping for me.

I'm going to hustle Marcos onto a boat and away from this shitbox for good. And if he and I can escape Nightlight, we can take on anything.

I collect a shard of limestone from the cavern floor and hunt through the wall of hearts for an opening. In a gap between UB + CR and PS + JH, I draw a new heart waiting to be filled. As soon as I finish scrawling CM + MC, his arms come from behind and wrap my chest like an octopus. I shut my eyes as he holds me and sways.

"Drew said we're less of a target if we're together," I whisper.

"We're together," he says, kissing the top of my head.

A third voice echoes from behind us: "Um..."

Marcos whips toward the voice like a crack of lightning and leaps in front of me. Except I refuse to let Marcos take whatever punch or shot this staff member is about to deliver. I jump from behind him, into the center of the torchlit sanctum...

It isn't a staff member. At the top of the incline, Molly huddles shoulder to shoulder with Lacrishia and all six Beginners.

"Ah, shit," Molly winces. "This is awkward."

CHAPTER THIRTY-THREE

THE SPEAR

Somewhere, floating out there in the universe, Drew's spirit is cackling. This is his revenge on Marcos and me for spying on *his* private love session. Eight gawping faces stare back at us, two shirtless boys in the most vulnerable moment of our lives. Mud stains track across Molly's dampened shirt, while at her side leans a tree branch taller than she is; the branch's greenish hue ends abruptly at a bare, blond tip that has been sharpened into a spearhead. I spy three more spears scattered among the crowd, but their owners' faces don't register—I'm too hot with embarrassment.

"We've been standing here for a minute," Molly admits. "Sorry."

"What did you see?" I accuse. Before any of the stunned on-lookers can reply, Marcos blurts, "NOTHING!" and his warm fingers depart violently from my waist. As he bolts toward our shirts piled in the corner, a piece of my heart cracks off like a chip in a coffee mug. *So, this is what it felt like for Ario when I pushed him away?* I deflate at the possibility that it's my cosmic punishment for Marcos to drop me like a pan of scalding oil; that the oasis I've been luxuriating in has been a cruel illusion, now meeting reality dead in the face. I glare at Molly, my disappointment pivoting to rage: "Why didn't you say something?! JESUS. Is there nowhere on this island where people don't invade your privacy left and right?"

"There wasn't a good time to speak up," she replies, agitated. "Your backs were to us, and it looked like you were crying. Anyway, here we are, at the waterfall, on time, as planned, as you should have expected."

Of course, Marcos and I knew we were meeting the group around sunset, but I figured we would've at least heard them coming. Sadly, Karaoke Bill said it best: queers sneak around, padding silently as cats.

While I shield my bare chest like an actress caught without her top on in a sex comedy, Marcos collects our shirts. He chucks me mine so powerfully, it might've been shot out of a cannon. I slip the shirt over my head, but giggling erupts as it unfurls past my waist like a flag and my arms disappear inside wide, drooping sleeves. Marcos tossed me his by accident. He has my small one crammed halfway to his tummy by the time he realizes his mistake. I admire how adorably trapped he is, his arms squeezed into my sleeves, but the fun is short-lived. Beyond irritated, he growls and scrambles his way out of the fabric prison.

I can't help dreading that the object of his agitation is me. I slide Marcos's shirt over my head, intoxicated one final time by his unique musk. *Who knows if I'll ever get close enough to smell him again?*

The Beginners, on the other hand, are having a wild time—their first laugh in months. Toward the back of the huddle, Christina and Anke whisper to each other through cupped hands; Jack stares in wide-eyed fascination; Lacrishia clutches a spear in one hand and tiny Owen in the other, both of them in silent agreement to avert their eyes until we've finished dressing; finally, Alan and Vance snicker the loudest, a pair of delighted smiles plastered onto their cheeks with the certainty that, yes—Marcos and I boned each other on this very spot less than ten minutes ago.

"Alan and Vance, you keep laughing, damn it!" Marcos growls, instantly blowing away their grins. Everyone straightens as faces fall all around the cave. No one's ever heard Marcos talk this way—a fatherly, scolding boom. A voice in line with his size. *I like it...but I don't like it.* What he and I did in this sanctum uncaged something in Marcos: a neglected, underfed animal, its teeth now bared to the world. I felt it in his touch, and it didn't unsettle me at the time because—*twist*—I was enjoying myself. But I've seen this group scared into silence only twice before: with Briggs and the Reverend. They have this power too.

What if Marcos isn't out of the woods yet?

Our oasis officially desecrated, Molly steers the conversation away from Marcos and me and toward what the hell it is we're going to do next. In the three hours since we escaped Miss Manners's firing squad, Molly educated Lacrishia and every last Beginner, no matter how young or shell-shocked they were, on what is known and what is not known: the Reverend murdered Drew because of what he knew about the deaths of former camper Ricky Hannigan and his husband, Rigo.

And we're all next if we don't exit stage left pronto.

Delivering justice to Ricky and catching his killer is a dream drifting further out to sea with each passing hour, almost disappearing over the horizon under the gravity of Drew's murder—and how easily Nightlight could convince our families that our deaths weren't suspicious at all, that we were simply little lost lambs who hanged ourselves. Tragedies beyond help.

My mom would believe it. She'd bury me and live her whole life next to the Reverend, never once looking cross-eyed at him.

Escape must happen TONIGHT.

"Our number one priority is getting Darcy out of that bunker,"

I say, expecting the crowd to be with me on this one. Yet more than half of the people staring back at me flinch.

"We've been talking about that," Lacrishia speaks up, no more than a polite mewling at first as the sanctum's torchlight washes over her. "The priority is getting the kids off the island first."

"I absolutely disagree—" I say.

"I understand, but..." Lacrishia starts timidly.

"These kids are only a few years younger than us, and they know their way around this island better than me or Molly. We have to stick together."

"Connor, nobody wants to get Darcy out of that hellhole more than I do—"

"Really? 'Cuz it sounds like—"

"YES, I DO!" Lacrishia's rage leaps from her, no longer restrained by her overwhelming politeness. Panic lacerates my chest at how badly I seem to have upset her. Her own eyes widen, as if frightened by her outburst. Nevertheless, she doesn't retreat. An awkward hush falls on the cave, and the campers stiffen as Lacrishia takes a wide step toward me. "Believe me," she says, "I don't want Darcy in that pit, either. But she and I talked about what if something like this happened, where someone needed to be left behind. This is damage control, and we need to get off this island to let people know what's happening. Then we come back for Darcy."

"After what happened to Drew—"

"Darcy can take care of herself—I've seen it in action—and these people think they've got everything under control now. I know this camp."

"And I know the Reverend." It's my turn to step closer to Lacrishia's spear. Her lips harden, but my expression softens. She has to know what this man is capable of. "I know him. He's cornered and suspicious. And he's smart. And he can be in your head at any time. He killed Drew." A few Beginners suck in sharp breaths. I don't want to scare them any more than they already are, but I have to get this out. "He killed him, just for trying to give us information about Ricky. Miss Manners said so. Now, the Reverend's got Darcy. Lacrishia, if we leave, he will kill her and disappear." Molly and the Beginners look to Lacrishia for guidance...but her stony gaze collapses. "I had the chance to leave Nightlight, but I stayed. Because I know the Reverend, and I couldn't trust any of you would be safe with him. We're escaping the island tonight—all of us. Nobody gets left behind."

A tear flickers down Lacrishia's face in the torchlight, and she whispers, "Could she...What if he already...?"

I shake my head, confidently. I've never been more confident of anything. "If the boat is still here, if the Reverend knows we're still here, he won't hurt her. He'll think there's still the possibility he can force things back to normal."

"Let's have a vote," Lacrishia says, slapping back her tear with frustration. "Hands up for leaving now and coming back later for Darcy."

Hesitation consumes the cave. Eyes dart left and right as a smattering of unsteady hands try to rise against an onslaught of fear. I don't blame anyone. These children have been traumatized by abusers for months, and now the abusers have begun killing. Leaving while we're ahead is the sane choice. In the end, only Anke, Christina, Molly, and tiny Owen raise their hands fully. With grim inevitability, Lacrishia asks who is in favor of saving Darcy from the bunker first. She raises her own hand, followed quickly by myself and

Jack, a hesitant raise from Alan and Vance, and to my joy—Marcos, lost in thought apart from the group as he stares through the drape of falling water.

Lacrishia kisses Owen's straw-colored hair as he begins to weep again. She shushes him before addressing the crowd: "As much as I'd love to see certain folks in jail, we're only grabbing Darcy. No investigating, no trying to capture anybody, and only use the spears for protection."

"About those spears," I say. "Whose idea were those?"

"Moi," says Molly, raising her hand. "Lacrishia had a Swiss Army knife hidden away that she snuck from one of the lunch ladies. So I cut these bad boys out of the driest branches I could find. I made them pretty rushed, but they'll get the job done."

"*The job*? Have you used them on anyone?"

"Not yet."

The air hardens into paste as the entire cave realizes Molly is prepared to shank someone if it comes to it. But my initial shock dissolves. Molly might be the only one giving our situation the appropriate weight: Nightlight has already killed one camper, and they've fired very real bullets at three others. A bloody spear is not only reasonable, it's been a long time coming.

"We'll find the bunker along the lakeshore," Lacrishia says soberly, a welcome counterweight to the rising climate of savagery in the cave. "It's a ten-minute walk past the boys' cabin on the north side of the island. If we leave now, we can make it before dark."

"Marcos, we need your keys," Molly says, less of a request and more of an accusation (*Are you with us or not?*).

"He wants to help," I say on his behalf, but Marcos has retreated further into himself along the cavern wall, giving only a solitary nod for confirmation that he heard us. The rest of my sentence was going to be, *He wants to help because we're supposed to go on a date when we get home.* But all that could just be silly wishing. I don't understand what his big deal is: yeah, it was awkward everyone found us half-naked together, but if he's this angry and embarrassed over campers knowing about us…how's it going to be when we get home?

IF you get home, Major. First things first.

"Lacrishia, what about the boat?" I ask. "Do we know any weird surprises about it? Like, is it easy to motor?" Outside, distant thunder regurgitates unpleasant memories: *Briggs and his team, all seasoned men, struggling to pilot the boat through a dark storm.* Are we going through all this trouble just to drown at sea? My dad taught me sailing, but I was ten and this motored patrol boat will be a totally different story.

"It's a simple craft." Lacrishia nods, dabbing the sweat under her eyes. "I've driven something slightly smaller, but Darcy is the real captain."

"It's a good thing we'll have her with us," I reply cheerfully. Relentless optimism is the only defense against this looming aura of doom. If I'm upbeat, it'll be contagious to the others.

Fake it 'til you feel it, Major.

"The trick will be timing," Molly adds. "We scouted the bay before coming here. About an hour ago, Miss Manners boarded the boat with some staff randos and took off."

"Yeah, and Karaoke Bill lost his shit," Jack adds, sharing a wicked smile with Alan and Vance. I'm unable to connect the dots about why Bill would care enough to make a scene about the boat making a supply run, but Molly clarifies:

"He thought his family was going to be on the boat. Remember that letter he got? Anyway, no one showed, and he just—"

"Lost. His. Shit," Jack repeats, and the Beginners nod vigorously with fiendish delight. A collective cackle ricochets off the cavern walls with such fearsome power, it awakens my own starved animal. *Good*, the voice growls. *Let Bill know what it feels like to have your family ditch you in the dirt.*

"The boat ride from Nightlight to mainland Costa Rica is an hour, give or take," Lacrishia says, clearly anxious over the villainous detours our conversation keeps taking. "So basically, in half an hour, Ramona is gonna dock—"

"Good riddance—" Alan mutters, but Lacrishia raises a silencing finger.

"She's probably going to call Drew's family and let them know Nightlight is going to take care of everything, blah, blah, blah. She definitely doesn't want anyone coming to Nightlight to see for themselves. After that, the staff will turn the boat around and return here. That means in two hours, we need to have Darcy and be ready to rock."

The jocular attitude in the sanctum vanishes. Pins and needles invade my bloodstream over the idea of two hours. In two hours, we'll know if we're heading home...or if we're dead meat. At least Miss Manners is out of the picture—and Karaoke Bill is distracted with his own family drama.

"Well," I announce, stepping into the crowd, "who's ready to go home?"

Molly corrals Marcos and the Beginners into taking a final swig of water from their backpack canteens, and I guzzle the last salty bits from the trail mix Alan shared with me. As I tear open the plastic to lick the remains like a scavenging raccoon, Lacrishia summons me toward the chalk hearts on the wall, the torchlight igniting her flyaway hair with angelic warmth.

"I'm sorry I had to go against you like that," I say, "but I'm glad you're in charge."

"Me too," Lacrishia says, regarding the cavern wall with melancholy. She caresses my newly drawn *CM + MC* heart. "He'll be a great boyfriend, if that's what you want." I groan without meaning to. Rebelling against violent zealots somehow feels less of a problem than navigating my optimism over whether Marcos will want anything to do with me after we escape. Lacrishia squeezes my wrist, kindly, as if she knows the detour my heart is currently taking. "He's sweet, and he's got eyes for you. He's private, but...you can push him. You gotta be patient, but you gotta push him—but you gotta be patient." Lacrishia see-saws her hands in the air as if balancing a scale. "Gonna be a lot of this."

It's bizarre that I've become the one who has to be patient and push a nervous boyfriend. Ario tried to balance this with me...hopefully, I'll be more successful. After a tough swallow, I ask the only question that matters: "Is he worth it?"

Mischief sparks in her eyes as she whispers, "You sampled the goods, you tell me."

"Lacrishia!" A scandalized giggle fit takes us over, but she quickly oscillates back to dire.

"I gotta ask a favor. When we get to the bunker, I need you two boys to go inside for Darcy."

"Aren't we all going?"

"The bunker's too tight. Bill lives there, they use it for storage, there's cages. Everything is dark and crowded, and I'm a big girl."

"...Marcos is a bigger boy, though."

She chuckles, admitting defeat. "There's no damn room, and to tell the truth, it scares the shit out of me. It triggers the hell out of my claustrophobia, and I'm worried I won't be able to help her the best."

"Um...sold."

"Darcy made me promise that if it was ever between saving her and getting these kids off the island, I'd leave her be and come back for her later, but...I gotta be okay breaking that promise." Without any need to search, she taps another heart etched into the rock: DC + LS. *Darcy Culpepper and Lacrishia Sims—another couple who enjoyed the all-too-brief privacy of the sanctum.* Urgency floods her eyes. "We've been messing around this camp, gathering evidence, for way too long. It's time to get her out."

"Don't worry. We'll get her."

Lacrishia closes my hand around the damp, coarse broom handle of a spear, but my body rejects every horrific thing it implies. I push it back, but Lacrishia insists, securing her hand over mine. "You're all talk," she says, "unless you're willing to do the thing. You might not like it, you might not think you can, but there's nobody between us and these monsters. They know we're coming, but what they don't know is what we're willing to do."

"I'm not gonna—"

"You're in charge of these kids, same as me."

"The Beginners?"

"The *kids*. I'm not saying you have to run out there, stab the first staff member you see. I am saying that I need you to go into a dark, scary bunker where the Reverend and Bill and Briggs are hiding and bring back my Darcy so we can all go home."

"I promise. I'll do it."

Lacrishia releases her grip, leaving me holding the jagged, twisted spear. In a single move, as if she's done it a million times, she plucks the torch from its hold in the cavern floor and joins the others. The young woman who could hardly speak above a whisper this morning turns to me, the flickering flame cleaving her face in two: half in shadow, half a hellish red.

"If they put you to the test," she says, "kill them."

CHAPTER THIRTY-FOUR
CAMP'S OUT

"This is escalating quickly," I say, leaving the waterfall—and my scant few happy memories of Nightlight—behind.

"Are you talking about the spears?" Molly whispers. "Or what you and Marcos got up to in the cave?" Molly doesn't need an answer, and I don't supply her with one. Both topics—particularly Lacrishia's directive to *"kill them"*—are twisting my intestines. How could Molly switch from camper to *Lord of the Flies* so easily? She's been ready to scrap from minute one, choking me with a branch as soon as we landed.

I wish I saw things that clearly.

The rain has died off into mist, giving the air itself a physical presence—billows of fog rise off the lake and float low, just above our heads, like ghosts.

Death hangs over Nightlight.

Queasily, I join Molly in assisting the campers down the slippery rocks jutting out of the lake. Lacrishia goes first with Owen, who clings to her like a baby kangaroo, his eyes blaring open in constant alert. Vance grips Molly's hand on his way down to solid earth, breathing in slow, deliberate bursts as if he were in labor. Next, I help down pale, frail Alan, who accepts my hand as daintily as an eighteenth-century courtesan. As he descends the rocks to the lakeshore, Alan flicks bashful glances my way—he hasn't held another boy's hand since arriving at camp. Maybe ever. Jack, as tiny as Owen, has none of that boy's trepidation. He doesn't wait for any helping hand, instead hopscotching off the stones and landing with Olympian grace. The Beginner girls, Christina and Anke, follow Jack's lead—gripping each other, they scamper to shore with considerably less success. Christina's long legs plunge into the lake up to her knees, but she refuses help from anyone but Anke.

Last one out is Marcos. At the foot of the falls, he stares back through the veil of water, like he's heartsick at having to leave our sanctum behind. It's something out of a coming-of-age movie, but they're the only words I have to describe how rattled I feel—how *changed*: Marcos and I went inside the sanctum as boys but are leaving as men. Marcos gazes through the falls, as if he's searching for the young boy he left inside who's wearing his face.

A version of us will always live in that cave. A version of Ricky is also hiding there. A version of Ricky who didn't know how bad it was about to get for him. I don't know how bad it's about to get for me either.

When Marcos finally turns his back on the falls, our drooping faces sync, almost telepathically: *back to reality.* I hesitate before raising my helping hand to him. Holding my breath, I watch him make the decision whether to reach for me. *If he doesn't, if he descends on his own, he's only going to drift further away from me.* After another moment's consideration, his hand envelopes mine like warm, rising bread dough, and through some miracle, I don't burst into grateful tears, sobbing, *"I can't do this without y-y-you-ou-ou-ou!"*

As Marcos hops to shore, Molly rushes toward the group huddle forming along the high grass. Before we join the others, I tug Marcos behind and let him off the hook for having to say it first: "I'm gonna miss our cave too." He squishes my hand and shuts his eyes against an emotional riptide. "You still owe me a date, remember?"

"I'd love to go with you," he whispers, his voice thickening. "Let's just get out of here first."

"A few more hours, okay? Then we're gone."

Brandishing a tiki torch, Lacrishia is already mid-instruction when we reach the huddle: "The light will basically be gone by six. Judging what I can from this sky, that's in less than an hour. This means Miss Manners has already reached the mainland and is about to come back on the boat. Now...we're gonna stick tightly together on our way to the bunker—stick to each other like an amoeba. If I'm right, we won't run into anybody on the way. If we do, if there's any trouble, you'll hear me, Molly, Marcos, or Connor yell, 'Run.' You hear one of us yell 'run,' the amoeba splits apart,"—she snaps her fingers—"and you run into the jungle and regroup at the bay. I'm gonna be clear: if we yell 'run,' nobody goes into the jungle alone. Use the buddy system. Owen with me, Molly with Jack, Alan with Vance, Christina with Anke, and Connor with Marcos. I'll lead with the torch. Marcos, you take the rear—" At the mention of *rear*, Vance snorts and shares a catlike glance with Alan. Marcos's hand grows ten degrees hotter in my grip. "That's enough, boys. Marcos, you're in the back to make sure we don't lose anyone and to check if we're being followed."

"Question," Molly says, raising her spear. "Why don't you think we'll run into anyone?"

"Because they know we're coming," I say. "By now, the Reverend knows we know how Drew died. And after my scene with the birth certificate, he knows I won't leave unless our whole group is intact, so he's gonna let us come to him."

The sidelong glances darken across the huddle. I'm pretty sure everyone is regretting siding with me over Team Abandon Darcy. Lacrishia nods: "He's right. Any of you get scared and think about ditching the group, like maybe things would be better if the camp could just go back to how it was…there's no going back. Camp's out."

Without another sound, ten queer, shivering bodies hoist ten backpacks and begin the expedition north along the lakefront, toward the bunker, Darcy, and the Reverend…

Our journey passes in unnerving silence for minutes before the enormous staff cabin appears. Three times the size of our own lodge, the stilted cabin lords imperiously over Lake Monteverde. Not a single lamp is lit inside, even as the sun dies behind the overcast sky. Technically, it isn't sunset yet, but the isolation of the lake has grown so dark, my eyes cling to Lacrishia's flame at the head of our caravan. The island is more sound than sight at this point: cooing night birds, chittering insects, and the roar of the falls behind us— growing fainter with each uneven step along the beach.

No one speaks as the amoeba of campers creeps around the edge of the staff cabin. Two Jeep Wranglers sit parked out front, splattered in mud the color of creamed coffee. Although both of them are empty, finding the Wranglers startles me; they appeared too suddenly in the dark, harmless but nevertheless unwelcome, like finding a spider in your bathtub.

"No one's inside them," I whisper, tightening my grip on the spear. "No one's there…"

The staff cabin behind us, Alan's feather-light, southern voice calls as he and Vance scoot closer: "Connor! We wanted to ask…" The boys' eyes ping-pong between each other, nervous but tantalized.

"What?" I ask.

"You two…did it?"

Through the curtain of terror suffocating my brain, these boys have somehow managed to irritate me. They've been giggly and obsessed with Marcos and me all day, and now that we're running for our lives, this is what they're concerned about? *Oh, please,* I scold myself. *You're just as boy crazy as they are.* Marcos would hate hearing me admit to this, but he's five campers back, so I don't see the harm. "We sure did," I say, eliciting dramatic, silent movie-style gasps from the tweens.

"So cool," Alan says.

"What was it like doing it with him?" Vance asks, all business.

My eyebrows scrunch again, and I reply, "Um…I'll leave the sex talk to your mom."

"Yeah, she's gonna get right on that." Vance rolls his eyes. "I didn't ask what *sex* is like, I asked what having sex with *Marcos* is like."

I whip sideways so violently, I nearly stop the whole caravan in its tracks. These thirsty little demons. "You mean…how does he kiss? Does he smell sweet or dirty? What's his butt like? How's his dick? Those sorta details?" Speechless, the boys bob their heads in urgent, Morse code messages of *Yes, please! Those details! Hand them over!* I grin and whisper, "None of your damn business, jellybeans."

Satisfied, I double my pace, weaving ahead of Molly and Jack while Alan bickers with his friend: "You had to be sassy. We were gonna get the whole story out of him!"

An eternity later, Lacrishia stops our march outside the girls' cabin, which is identical to ours, except their outdoor shower block is to the left and ours is to the right. Anxious, confused whispering rises as Lacrishia separates from the amoeba and mounts the small, patchy hill toward the showers. Torch-first, she enters the enclosure and reemerges a few seconds after.

"Jack," she summons, and Jack approaches like a dutiful soldier. "I need a squirrel."

"You want it all?" he asks, understanding.

"We're not coming back. Get the whole enchilada." Without further instructions, Jack shuffles toward the shower block like the rabbit that bears his name. "Jack, you need my torch?"

"I could do this in my sleep."

He vanishes inside. A breeze sweeps in from the lake, and the Beginner girls and I scrunch our goosebumping arms across our chests. An invisible, creeping heaviness lands on my neck, spinning me 360 degrees to make sure the Reverend hasn't suddenly materialized behind me. There's nothing there but palm trees rocking in the wind. Still, the heaviness lingers—eyes, somewhere in the dark, watching. For now, choosing to stay hidden. *It has to be the grayshirts.* They can see us, they know we're coming, but they aren't satisfied unless they're whacking around our nerves like piñatas.

"You flipping out on me?" Molly asks, clinking her spear to mine like a champagne flute.

I breathe out a long, steady ribbon of anxiety and whisper so the Beginners won't hear: "They're watching us."

Molly's eyes dart toward the tree line, but she soon regains her spear-granted confidence. "Probably..."

Whatever Jack is doing in the shower block, he's kicking around a shitload of water. A heaving splash rollicks against the shower floor, and out trots Jack, dripping like a sponge and lugging a black satchel. Its shiny, rubber surface reflects Lacrishia's torch as the two of them meet each other halfway up the hill.

"That shit is cold!" Jack shrieks, handing the satchel to Lacrishia as she tears open the flap to ransack its contents.

"What did you do?" Marcos asks. "Climb into the shower tank?"

"Yup." We crowd around Lacrishia as she extracts two accordion file folders bound with massive rubber bands. *Evidence.* Lacrishia and Darcy's little spies have hidden their evidence against Nightlight inside the shower tank.

The whole enchilada.

"What's that, some kind of waterproof bag?" Molly asks.

"Yes, ma'am," Lacrishia replies as she sorts through heavy stacks of multicolored paperwork. "They use it to protect phones and valuables and whatnot on the boat. You can thank Vance for swiping that."

The devilish boy beams, the hero of the moment, and awe crashes over me at what these campers have managed to accomplish. This proud warmth, however, is short lived as I remember the watchful eyes. "We're being spied on from the tree line," I whisper to Lacrishia. Her back stiffens.

"Everyone, take off your backpacks and throw them in a pile in the middle," Lacrishia whispers. "Go on." Ten backpacks, each indistinguishable from the others, drop into a pile like we're making a bonfire. In under a minute, Lacrishia divides the evidence folders into six bunches of paperwork and slips them randomly into the pockets of six backpacks. "Nobody look for your own," she urges. "Just take a random bag and put it on."

Lacrishia is a brilliant strategist. If any of the gray-shirts descend on us, we'll split apart and head for the beach. They can't catch us all, and Lacrishia just upped the odds that at least some of the evidence has a chance to make it off the island. But my stomach sinks at the thought of any of these kids being caught by the Reverend...

By the time we reach the bunker, the sun abandons us completely. Twenty minutes have come and gone since we donned our backpacks and traveled up the shoreline, past the vacant boys' cabin and into uncharted territory. The cleared road has also left us; weeds and long grass brush my calves.

The only thing that's stayed with us is the looming presence in the jungle. Whoever is out there, their footsteps are silent but their energy burns as powerfully as fire. My spear slips in my sweating hand whenever I think about them, crouching, waiting for us to drop our guard.

At last, the bunker materializes in the night. It's just another cabin, only smaller and more dilapidated; it wades halfway into the lake itself, tall stilts lifting it above the water like a dozen outstretched fingers. Surrounding the bunker is a cage of overgrown marine roots, tendrils—tinged blood-red—that reach out of the lakebed to choke the building like a squid trying to drag a ship below.

"It's not blood on those roots," Marcos says, clasping my hand (and reading my mind). "They're red mangroves. They grow like that out of the lake, and Nightlight just built the bunker inside."

"That's dramatic." I giggle, relieved that these tendrils aren't painted with the blood of rebellious campers.

"The door's open," Lacrishia says, wringing small gasps from the crowd. Through her torchlight, I search the bunker's peeling front wall for what she's referring to: beyond the tangle of red roots, a bulky, metallic gate rests open on its hinges. "That door is never open."

"It's a Goddamn trap," Molly says.

"It's a trap," I agree. "But we can't leave Darcy. And we've got the spears." Lacrishia swallows hard, still resolved to our plan but with a new coat of dread. Lake water softly laps against the hefty mangrove roots, filling the silence as the group waits for Marcos and me to do what we agreed to do. "It'll be just like Jack getting the evidence. In and out."

Molly's anxious feet won't let her rest. She launches herself toward us: "I'm coming too."

"No," Lacrishia says, raising her torch. "I'm telling y'all, there's no room in there. There's room for two, and Marcos already knows what it's like inside. I don't need two people going in blind."

Molly strangles her spear, resigning herself to wait with the others. "The boat's on its way back," I say, addressing the campers as a group. Their faces contort in the flames; several of them look nauseated with suspense. "Does anyone have a watch?"

"I can tell time good," Alan offers meekly from the back.

"Perfect. After we go inside, you let Lacrishia know as soon as thirty minutes have gone by."

"Why?" Lacrishia asks.

"If we aren't back in thirty minutes, leave us and get everyone to the boat."

Variations of "No WAY" explode from the crowd in a chorus, ending with Marcos groaning, "You gotta be kidding me..."

"I'm not saying, like, we're all dead in there, but Lacrishia is right: *some* of us have to get off this island tonight, and a group of us staying behind stands better odds at living than if we all left

Darcy alone. You all have the evidence, you can warn the right people. Molly, you know the FBI is trying to find this place. Help them find it."

"That's the plan," Lacrishia agrees soberly. After seeming to bite back a chest pain, Molly finally nods.

"In and out," I tell Marcos, squeezing his hand. "Then we go home."

Marcos steels himself, raps his spear against the ground, and nods. He unhinges the lighter from his belt loop, flicks it open, and the path to the bunker illuminates. "Like old times," he says, dimples flaring.

The night we met, Marcos guided me through the darkness with his lighter.

I vault myself onto tiptoes and press my lips to his. The softness is brutally brief.

As we reach the bunker's gate, the mangrove roots (which really, *really* look bloodstained) space further apart, allowing us a pocket of space to slip inside. The gate opens wider with shocking ease. I expected it to creak like a haunted house, but instead, it glides open with such soundlessness that I'm put even more on edge. Before I step inside, Marcos lets out a sharp "Whoa." I stop myself with a jerk and follow his gaze to an iron plate above the gate. The message is Nightlight's familiar greeting: *SURRENDER YOUR SINS*. But this sign has been vandalized with a dark, textured substance glistening in the flame, making it read:

SURRENDER YOUR SONS

"Okay," Marcos says, "that might be blood."

CHAPTER THIRTY-FIVE

THE BUNKER

Acrowded hallway hurtles forward into darkness. Crates of boat-ing and fishing equipment stack on top of each other on both sides of the hall, leaving only a narrow, snaking path ahead. It resembles a self-storage unit after hours: massive, yet somehow claustrophobic. Outside, a generator rattles, feeding power to two bare light bulbs dangling from the bunker's iron rafters. The light is weak, but thank God for them, or else Marcos and I would be creep-ing into a complete unknown. I advance one step at a time—not too slow to give the pins and needles time to paralyze me, though not fast enough to let myself get ambushed in the dark. Anyone could be crouching behind one of these crates. Behind me, Marcos slows. His fingers snap—his fear is taking over. I raise my spear, pitching its pointed end toward the shadows, and Marcos shuffles closer to eliminate the gap between us.

You're safe with me.

A briny, rotting wood stench infests the bunker—no wonder the flowers are dying. Along the left-hand wall, a row of flowerpots house several botanical corpses, each wilted stalk covered in a layer of gray fuzz. Beside the pots, work boots—caked in dried mud—are scattered in a careless line. Karaoke Bill doesn't keep a clean home.

"There's a door," Marcos whispers, thrusting his spear past mine.

Indeed, beyond the pots and shoes, a second door hides under the cover of the bunker's low lighting. "Good looking out," I whisper. "Maybe Darcy's in there?"

"The cages are farther back. Sorry."

It would be against every speck of bad luck I've had this week for Darcy to be kept so close to the exit. We have to push deeper inside. "Keep your spear on that door. I'll walk a bit closer and see if I notice the cages."

"I'm not sure I love that plan—"

"HELLO?" Darcy screams from the shadows at the end of the hall. She's close.

"Darcy, are you alone?" I call back.

"Not really, but it's safe."

"What do you mean, 'not really'—?" I ask, but two steps closer answer my question: at the end of the crate-choked hallway, a man stands facing the corner. *Briggs.* Motionless, he waits against the wall, his expansive bodybuilder's back to us. I swallow my gasp and stagger backward into Marcos so hard, I ricochet off his belly.

"He's taking the wall, he can't move," Marcos whispers, settling a steady hand on my neck. The calm in his voice instantly balances me.

Just as the Reverend ordered, Briggs is still "taking the wall"— the popular Nightlight punishment that, apparently, isn't off-limits once you graduate to staff member. Briggs isn't completely motion-less, however; as we approach, it becomes obvious he's crying. Those shoulders like boulders bounce at the end of each hiccupping sob. He mutters softly to himself, but I can't make out what.

Except I know what—Drew.

With an aching throb in my chest, I soften for Briggs. I can't imagine what he's going through, and the sounds he made when he found Drew at the end of a rope are tattooed onto my frontal lobe.

But Briggs remains an enemy, and I have people to save. I point my spear forward like a javelin and shout, "BRIGGS. It's Connor and Marcos. We're armed! We came for Darcy, that's it, so stay right where you are!"

No response comes from Briggs except continued inconsolable nonsense. Marcos covers me, aiming his spear toward the door with the dying flowers as I advance to Briggs. The vice tightening my stomach turns another crank.

"Get me the hell out of here," Darcy moans somewhere around the corner. "I thought y'all were dead or something."

"Everyone's safe, as soon as we have you," I say, but it's a struggle to hold on to the confidence booming through my chest. I can't make out Darcy's cage, there are shadows everywhere, and where the hell is the Reverend? The worst omen of all, however, is being unable to see Briggs's face. "We're coming up behind you, Briggs. Don't move."

"I did everything—" Briggs says, his throat strangled with crying: the messy, mucus-filled kind. "I DID *EVERYTHING* FOR YOU! MY WHOLE *LIFE*!"

Marcos rejoins me, and we steady our spears side by side as we reach the end of the hallway, which winds left into another narrow path. "Cover Briggs," I order Marcos, pivoting my spear down the next blind alley. Where the last corridor was stacked with life preservers and fishing nets, this one is lined with prison cells—row after row of iron bars, rising no taller than Marcos.

Like circus animal cages.

At the end of the row, Darcy rattles the prison gate trapping her. All things considered, she doesn't look too rough. She's bleary-eyed from Bill's taser (and probably from such prolonged uncertainty), but otherwise, she still has her game face on. "Does Marcos have the keys?" she asks, sweat beading off her shorn hair. "We don't have time."

"Yeah, he's got them," I say. "Marcos?"

"Get 'em off my belt," he says, retreating from Briggs but never once dropping his spear. My heartbeat thudding between my ears, I turn—but as I go, my spear clangs against the cage bars. The reverberations slice through my brain, and in one devastating blink, a hairline fracture splits the head of my spear. The pieces don't fully separate, but a thin, ugly tear is visible even through the dim light.

"No," I groan.

"What happened?" Marcos asks, panicking.

"Never mind that," Darcy says. "They were all here a few minutes ago—Reverend, Bill, everybody. Just get the keys."

Even if the damn spear is busted, it'll still go stabby-stabby just fine, and right now, I'm keyed up enough to do some major damage to a gray-shirt. I'll snap off this spear piece down to a wooden stake and go full Buffy on the Reverend. *Don't corner a country possum like me.* For the second time today, I slink my hand across Marcos's waist—but this time, it's all business. My hand closes around a fistful of keys and unhooks it from his belt clasp.

"I love you, Drew," Briggs whispers to the wall, his crying simmering to a low boil. "I love you, boy..."

"Is he okay?" I ask Darcy as I spool through Marcos's keys.

"No," she says. "Apparently, Drew didn't kill himself—"

"We know," Marcos and I moan together. But Darcy doesn't pause.

"The Reverend came by talking about it like Briggs wasn't even in the room, and now he's been jabbering at the wall for an hour, and I want to absolutely strangle myself—hey, Boss, you even know what key you're looking for?"

My shivering fingers hunt through the last of the dozen nearly identical keys when I realize: "I don't..."

"Marcos, get over here and open this door! Briggs isn't going anywhere." Marcos shuffles backward, and I hand him back his keys. While he searches, Darcy holds his spear. "How in the *hell* did you boys get sticks like this...?"

"I LOVE YOU!" Briggs screeches without warning, and startled, Marcos's key ring clatters to the floor somewhere in the dark. He retrieves them easily, but it's back to square one looking for the cage key. I linger two steps behind and study Briggs in profile against the wall—his grizzled, handsome face is caving in on itself. "I'm sorry I never said it before, baby boy, I love you. I promise I'll say it, just please come back...I'll take you out of here. Anywhere, I don't care. I'm sorry I wouldn't let you go home. I didn't want to be alone. I was selfish, and, and, and, and,"—Briggs stutters through his hyperventilation—"and I'll never forgive...please don't be dead. PLEASE."

"Jesus Christ," I can't help but mutter as, once again, Briggs disappears into grief. He's immovable from his position at the wall, as if the Reverend put him under a freezing spell. I can't watch anymore because Briggs's torment is unfathomable—his pain is too naked; it cuts him to the bone. He was so desperate to keep Drew, but Drew was only wallpaper over some invisible wound that's now exposed and infected. All that's left for Briggs is a dead boy and a son who hates him, and he knows it. Cold judgment passes over me. How could Briggs work here, hurt people, and not expect Hell to come knocking on his door?

339

It's the Reverend. It all comes back to the Reverend. We're in his web.

I can't stomach any more, not Briggs's anguish or Marcos trying his millionth key with no success. I march my shattered spear farther down the empty prison cells. This corridor ends at another left turn. *Two lefts?* The bunker is nothing but a circle of hallways, one unsettling turn after another. "What's down here?" I ask.

"Bill's room," Darcy replies, failing to muzzle her growing agitation. "Don't go far. I'll be out of here any second, *hopefully...*"

The vice in my stomach unscrews a quarter-turn. *Bill's room.* This afternoon—a lifetime ago—searching Bill's room for Ricky's Expulsion tapes was our number one priority. Now, the only mission is to survive the night.

Forget the evidence. Just get Darcy and go.

Yet my feet move out of my control, faster and faster, until I'm sprinting around the next turn. This area is separated from the rest of the bunker by a black drape hooked to a tension rod. Beneath the drape, a stripe of cozy, warm light spills out onto my shoes. I reaffirm my grip on the spear and slowly peel back the veil...

A prison cell of a different color. Bill's cell has no iron bars, yet all the other makings of a penitentiary: a green army cot—pristinely tucked—occupies half of the thin square footage, the rest of which is commandeered by a small bookcase of deteriorating hardcover spines. An empty mouthwash bottle lies at the foot of a second, final door—*a closet?* Bill's room is so blandly immaculate, my heart floats downward like a fallen leaf.

There's no hiding anything in here. There's no more Ricky tapes.

*Open the door...*the voice in my head whispers.

Absolutely not. My poor stomach lining can't take the fear, and

I've already strayed too far from my friends. Before I can retreat, though, two brass-framed photographs pull me deeper inside Bill's room. The frames rest on top of the bookcase and are maddeningly small, forcing me to come face-to-face with them before their details register.

But once I arrive, the pictures make sense. Instant, gruesome sense.

The frame on the right is black and white: two young, handsome men wear kimonos. They're embracing. One is Hispanic and razor thin; the other is white, his round face achingly familiar. The man I met in the hospital bed would end up far more emaciated, but it's the same person:

Ricky and Rigo.

Time and breath cease. The frame on the right—*Ricky and Rigo*—plunges an icy hand into my chest and squeezes. History laughs wickedly at the men's smiles: Rigo will die. Ricky will suffer a brutal attack.

Why does Karaoke Bill have a picture of Ricky and his husband? Why was he listening to Ricky's Expulsion tape? Why does he live in this dank, horrible room when the rest of the staff sleeps in a plush cabin near the waterfall?

The frame on the left holds my answer.

It's a family photograph, decades old but well preserved—its colors have barely faded. Bill was clean-shaven then: a healthy man with swooping, blow-dried hair and a hearty smile poses with his wife and young son. The little boy, fair and round faced; the wife, chubby, cheery, and permed. The happiest I've ever seen Mrs. Hannigan.

His name is Bill Hannigan.

And Ricky was his son.

CHAPTER THIRTY-SIX

MR. HANNIGAN

Surrender *your sons,* read the vandalized greeting outside the bunker.

A warning. An order. An admission of guilt?

At one point early in Ricky's life, they were a family, but tragedy tore them apart. Did Bill kill Rigo and massacre his own son? The truth is closer to the surface than ever.

In all the times I brought Meals on Wheels to the Hannigans in White Eagle, I saw no pictures of Bill. Was the memory of him too painful for his wife? Too triggering for Ricky? The FBI came looking for a man they'd been trying to catch for decades—but he was being sheltered on an island, far from the law. Ricky knew it was inevitable I would be sent to Nightlight, so he left me a message that was both a warning and an order: *HELP CONNOR.*

Help catch my father.

Is Karaoke Bill the murderer I've been hunting? Was it him—and not the Reverend—who traumatized Ricky? Questions won't stop swirling through my throbbing skull. Regardless of what I've discovered, leaving this island immediately is the only thing that matters.

"GUYS!" I whisper breathlessly, my alarm catching in my dry throat as I hurtle out of Bill's domicile and back into the patchwork shadows of the bunker hallway. I don't stop running until I collide with Marcos just as he's prying open Darcy's cage. My fractured spearhead cracks as, once again, this useless stick has gotten itself caught between iron bars. I snap off the ruler-length shard and chuck it angrily to the floor, spitting, "Goddamn thing!"

"What's wrong?" Marcos asks.

"Did you find something?" Darcy asks, piling on. Both of them fall into a grave silence as they recognize the inhuman fear eating my brain alive.

"It's Bill," I gasp. "Bill is Ricky's father. I found a picture of them—"

"But Ricky is dead," Marcos protests, the gears in his head clicking rapidly. "Bill said his family was coming tonight."

"I...I forgot about that. I don't know. Whoever's coming, it isn't Ricky. There's a family photo of them in that room!"

"You didn't see any tapes?" Darcy asks, snatching my wrist. "What about that letter Bill got, saying his family's coming? Is it in there?"

"Nothing. Just the picture. Guys...he didn't know what Google was." Both thrown for a loop, Marcos and Darcy scrunch their brows. "I told Bill I would Google something when I got home, and he literally didn't know what I was talking about, like he'd never heard of it."

"Like he's been on an island for twenty years," Darcy says. Her shoulders deflate as the same nightmarish understanding envelopes her. Marcos's finger-snapping fills the bunker.

"He's not like the other staff. He sleeps in this shithole, not the cabin. He never leaves the island, not even for supply runs. I think he did something terrible..."

"Go," Marcos says. "As fast as we can."

Duty has replaced the timid boy in Marcos with the grown man who comforted me in the cave. Marcos's bearish grip seizes my arm just under the pit and launches me headfirst down the galley of prison cells. Clutching spears, the three of us race back the way we came, rounding the corner where Briggs remains locked in his own private purgatory. At first, I lead the pack, but Darcy pulls ahead, deftly weaving between the stacked crates. Marcos leaps over boxes as easily as a jaguar clearing a track hurdle.

Our steel-doored exit waits only another few seconds ahead...

A floodlight batters through the dark with an icy, accusatory beam—like a SWAT team halting our path. Darcy and Marcos throw their hands across their eyes. "I'm not armed," the Reverend says from the darkness behind the light. "I ordered my staff to stand down. I didn't want any of you to get scared and get yourselves lost in the jungle. No one's going to hurt you, so don't do anything stupid with those spears."

I may have shattered mine, but I'm still holding a jagged, three-foot branch, and it'll do the job just fine. I raise my spear in the direction of the Reverend's beam, which overwhelms the bunker with blinding white. "We're leaving, sir," I bark. "Step back and let us through."

"What are you going to do, Connor, kill us?" the Reverend asks, brittle and snide. "People will find out you butchered a defenseless Christian mission. There'll be nowhere to go. Not for you. Not your friends outside. Not even those children. I can already see the headlines: *Queers slaughter the righteous—people with families!*"

"People with families? Like Karaoke Bill Hannigan?"

The bunker falls into stillness. A cold laughter breaks. "Mr. Major, you really are making me sorry I ever brought you to Nightlight. Hats off. *Karaoke Bill Hannigan.* I'm happy you brought him up because that's just what I came to talk about."

With a deafening slam, the Reverend shuts his floodlight,

sinking the bunker into an even blacker darkness than before. As multicolored globules swim past my vision, the stout, raven-like outline of the Reverend appears under the lamp above the exit. Somewhere ahead, Darcy and Marcos linger close to him, too close for my comfort. With one good heave, Marcos could impale the Reverend right through his shriveled heart, and we'd be free.

But how would it look? Could we convince anyone this was self-defense? If this were a TV show, I'd say, "Of course people will believe us!" But after what I've been through today, I wouldn't trust my mom to believe I was in danger if I came home in a body bag.

"So, what do you want?" I ask.

"I want five minutes," the Reverend says, descending the remaining steps to us. Through the shadows, Marcos raises his spear, but halfheartedly; he's done the same math I have. The Reverend approaches Marcos with a long, flat box in his free hand. "Mr. Carrillo, thank you for not disemboweling me and congrats on your new courage."

"Why do you need five minutes?" I demand, refusing to drop my spear.

"Because that's how long my tape runs."

The Reverend's box opens like a briefcase. Two steps closer, the overhead light reveals a cassette player in his hand. Its open slot is empty, but once the Reverend drops his floodlight, he retrieves a tape from his shirt pocket. His gleeful smile never fades. *He's savoring this.* Whatever Bill did, the Reverend is the puppeteer. He enjoys dangling us on strings—me, my mom, the campers, Briggs, Ricky... maybe even Bill himself.

"Miss Culpepper," the Reverend says, "I want Mr. Carrillo to feel like he's still safe and able to protect you all, so I won't ask him to lay down his spear. But will *you* take this tape and read what it says out loud?" Darcy advances like a cat toward a treat, each uncertain step considering whether a deadly surprise is in store. "Oh, will you all RELAX? I'm giving you what you want! Take it!"

Relax? You strangled one of us with your bare hands. I'll keep my guard up, thanks.

Darcy plucks the cassette from his hand at the farthest possible distance. She scuttles backward with her prize, squinting as she reads the label: "The Expulsion of Bill Hannigan."

"You motherf...UGHHH," I growl, every inch of my body exhausted from staying rigidly alert. "You're playing games with everyone. You killed Drew! You forced me to deliver meals to Ricky. You ratted me out to my mom. You made her into this psycho! You wanted me to pretend I was Avery's dad! You tricked everybody! You made all of this happen to me! You lied to the FBI. You covered up everything! Ricky loved you! I read it in your Playbill. Remember? *'THERE IS STILL TIME.'* He took you to plays and tried to help you come out and took you to bars, and you ruined his life! If I had a gay cousin, we'd be best friends, we'd tell each other everything, we'd help each other, and I'd make sure nothing ever happened to him! And you're hiding Ricky's dad! WHY? WHY ARE YOU DOING THIS?"

The bunker returns to silence, except for my anguished lungs choking for air. Somewhere inside me, a fuse has blown and I've fully departed from my sanity.

"Touché," the Reverend says quietly. "I want five minutes of your time, then maybe you'll start seeing things my way."

"Well, play it and get it over with," I bark.

"Miss Culpepper?"

The Reverend raps his knuckles against the player's open

slot, and Darcy rushes the cassette inside—*The Expulsion of Bill Hannigan*—and closes the lid. She retreats to Marcos beside Bill's boots and the dying flowerpots, and the Reverend pushes play.

CHAPTER THIRTY-SEVEN

THE EXPULSION OF BILL HANNIGAN

TWENTY-TWO YEARS AGO

GARY: This is the Reverend Gary Packard, and this is the first and only Expulsion—

BILL: Let's do this some other time, Gare. You're not looking too good...The heat doesn't seem to be agreeing with you.

GARY: The date is November twenty-sixth, 1998. Please state your name for the recorder.

BILL: Gare...I don't think that's a smart idea.

GARY: You have my word this recording will never leave the island.

BILL: Why don't we just have ourselves a solid meal? Eh? Not these fish guts everyone else eats. Let's make it a real Thanksgiving.

STANLEY: We didn't fly all the way down here to have turkey with you, Uncle Bill. Traveling during a major holiday makes sure people are less suspicious of my comings and goings. Thanks to you and Dad, I've got the FBI watching every time I turn my head.

BILL: Who's running this meeting, him or you?

GARY: State your name, Goddamn it. I don't feel well.

BILL: And if I don't?

    <silence>

	Bill. My name is Bill Hannigan.
GARY:	Your son is Ricky Hannigan?
BILL:	What the f—?
GARY:	Ricky Hannigan, who lived at 1612 Havenhurst in Los Angeles—
BILL:	Gary—!
GARY:	—until eight weeks ago?
	<brief silence>
	Is that information correct?
BILL:	YES. You wanna tell me what you think you're doing asking me these questions?
	<long, phlegmy coughing>
	Gare, you need a doctor. Turn this tape off!
	<coughing continues>
GARY:	Stanley...
STANLEY:	It's all right, Dad. Save your voice. I'll take it from here. Uncle Bill, can you confirm the date Ricky left Illinois for Hollywood?
BILL:	Your dad needs to get to the clinic, and this conversation is over.
STANLEY:	Bill, I swear, you stand up from that chair and I'll put you on the first plane to FBI headquarters. Now, my dad is strong enough to make it through a five-minute conversation. Unfortunately, he's not strong enough anymore to run this camp. As of today, he's confirmed with management that I am the new director of Nightlight Ministries. So...remember that when speaking to me.
BILL:	Oh..."Director." I don't care.
STANLEY:	You should. Nightlight is your new home.
BILL:	Excuse me? Gary...?

STANLEY: Whatever promises my dad has made you, I wouldn't count on them. We can't afford to move you again—

BILL: Listen, just get me to San José. I could slip away.

STANLEY: No. I need to keep my eye on you. Those orders come from management.

BILL: And why exactly do I need to be recorded like I'm one of your pole-smoking campers?

STANLEY: In exchange for hiding you, my superiors want a recorded confession.

\<silence\>

And at Nightlight, we call that Expulsion.

BILL: So, if I don't confess...I go to prison?

STANLEY: Shall we begin?

BILL: I...that night, I was drunk—

STANLEY: No. Start at the beginning. When did Ricky leave home?

BILL: Two summers ago.

STANLEY: Up and left without saying goodbye.

BILL: ...That's right.

STANLEY: When Ricky and I were sent home from Nightlight, he never went back to Chicago. He went to a community college in White Eagle—you saw to that. A year later, I enrolled so I could keep an eye on Ricky because that's what I do. Keep an eye on him. He didn't socialize, never dated. He kept to the post-Nightlight program. He worked a video store job, went to school, came home. But as soon as that nursing license was in his hands... poof. Gone.

BILL: Not even a note.

STANLEY: Your confession, Bill, is also my confession. I want you to know that the entire time we were at college, I knew Ricky was faking because...I was faking.

GARY: Stick to the facts, Stanley.

<labored coughing>

STANLEY: It is a fact, Dad. I was faking. I'm faking now—but I'm always in control. Anyway, Ricky abandoned us for California. And when he did, all of your suspicious, mean little eyes fell on me. Maybe you were worried I was gonna follow him...

BILL: But now you're a reverend. You're the "director."

STANLEY: After what I've been put through, no one will question my commitment to Nightlight again.

BILL: You should've left me alone. Should've left Ricky alone!

STANLEY: No jumping ahead. So. Ricky was enjoying his West Coast lifestyle, away from us. During that time, he met a man. What was his name?

BILL: Some Goddamn Mexican—

STANLEY: His name, Bill. I'm requiring you to remember it.

BILL: You REQUIRE me?! ...God Almighty, fine. Rodrigo.

STANLEY: Rodrigo Valdes. Ricky and 'Rigo, sitting in a tree. They moved in together and made a home. But that wasn't enough for Ricky. They wanted a commitment ceremony.

BILL: Have you ever heard of anything so HUMILIATING? Gary—

<low coughing>

STANLEY: Don't talk, Dad. Save your strength.

BILL: Look at your dad. Get him to the nurse, damn it.

STANLEY: Two months ago, Ricky broke his silence and called me—probably in a moment of sentimental weakness. We hadn't spoken in years, but he was so IN LOVE, he had to invite me. Me, only me, from his side of the family. Maybe he thought by seeing him get such a happy ending, it would inspire me to run away too. He was always trying to save me.

BILL: No luck there.

STANLEY: No. Such. Luck. So, Bill, I got you involved. You and I flew out for the big occasion. Please describe Ricky's wedding.

BILL: It was no Goddamn wedding—

STANLEY: I said describe it!

GARY: Stan, is this necessary?

STANLEY: I told you to save your strength!

BILL: The wedding was on a beach.

STANLEY: Which beach?

BILL: Santa Monica. There were...streamers. And colored lanterns along the boardwalk. They hadn't bothered to get a permit; not that anyone would've allowed one for such a circus. They were rushing everybody along. It was almost sunset and so damn hot for October.

STANLEY: What were they wearing?

BILL: Robes. I don't even know what kind. Fitted robes. Japanese shit.

STANLEY: Who was there?

BILL: Their friends. Rodrigo's mother, the poor woman.

STANLEY: Poor woman. And where were you and I?

BILL: Hiding. In our suits, we hid.

STANLEY: We surprised Ricky. I brought you along to stop the ceremony and convince him to come home. But you didn't do that.

BILL: No.

STANLEY: What did you do?

BILL: I hugged him. I drank on the plane, and...I was just so happy to see him again, I wasn't thinking. But Ricky, he was scared to find me standing there. His whole life, I've never seen him that scared. He asked if I'd come to watch him...

STANLEY: Get married?

BILL: Whatever. He asked if that's why I came. I said, "If this is what you want, if this is what you're choosing over your family...go ahead. I'll watch."

STANLEY: And what did your son say to that?

BILL: He said...

           <swallowing, whimpering>

           He said..."Thank you, Dad."

STANLEY: What was it like to watch Ricky marry a man?

BILL: Can I please take a break? My head's feeling like it needs water...

STANLEY: No. We're so close. Tell me what it felt like.

BILL: I can't—

STANLEY: What it felt like for ME was strangely interesting. Like being out of my own body. Their vows...so cheesy, so much silly crying. They weren't getting REAL married; this was playacting a wedding, but still...something hypnotizing was happening. I was so used to seeing Ricky in his bad times. His rage and fear. The blankness of the post-Nightlight years. But now, here he was—on a beach, with a sunset, touching this man's hand and looking at him while everyone was looking at them. Every private secret weighing him down his entire life was suddenly public and gone. Crumbled. Flown away into the ocean like it was never there.

BILL: I need water.

STANLEY: After the wedding was over, where did we go?

BILL: A bar.

STANLEY: After the bar, where did we go?

BILL: Ricky's apartment.

STANLEY: You took something out of the trunk of your rental. What was it?

BILL: A crowbar. You know all this! Just tell the story yourself and let me have a drink...

STANLEY: Rodrigo died instantly, didn't he?

BILL: ...Yes...

STANLEY: There was a full minute where I realized what you had done, but Ricky hadn't yet. He was in the next room. It was the longest, worst minute in the whole wide world. I screamed. What did I scream?

BILL: "Run...Ricky."

STANLEY: Did he run?

BILL: No.

STANLEY: No, not when he saw Rigo lying facedown in blood. He didn't even fight you.

BILL: I was so drunk...

STANLEY: You had one gin on the plane and one in the bar. That's not even half a Christmas.

BILL: I was drunk! I didn't know what I was doing!

STANLEY: But you know now?

BILL: Yes!

STANLEY: What did you do?

BILL: I took a crowbar that I bought while you were looking at Marilyn Monroe's handprints in cement, and I beat him up with it. Again. Again. He begged me and you begged me, but I couldn't stop...

STANLEY: You bought that crowbar BEFORE the ceremony. You planned this—

BILL: I didn't. I swear to God, you have to believe me. Please believe me. He's my boy; my son and I left him on the carpet...How is he? Please, tell me how he is.

STANLEY: Let's just say you've changed his life.

BILL: I was drunk out of my mind—

STANLEY: How drunk were you when you killed the patrolman at the Nevada border?

<silence>

You made it pretty far on your own, I'll give you that. But as it turns out...while I was at the hospital with my cousin, still in my suit stained with his blood and Rigo's blood and your blood and mine...turns out, you were already on a private plane heading here. The island.

GARY: Stan—

<hard coughing>

You don't need this part—

STANLEY: You already found help from my father, your wife's big brother. So protective. So eager to HELP.

<harder coughing>

Imagine my shock when I brought Ricky home again and found Aunt Sharon bullied and silent. My uncle vanished. My dad explaining to me that, besides the horrible thing done to that highway patrolman...justice had been served to Rigo and Ricky.

BILL: How do I know they won't track me to Nightlight?

STANLEY: There's no public record Nightlight exists. Or of our family's connection to it.

<ragged coughing>

GARY: That's enough recording, Stan. Did you get everything management asked for?

STANLEY: Oh, Dad...management didn't ask for this. This was for me.

BILL: No, but you said—

STANLEY: I lied. Just like my father has lied to everyone. Why I was told, blood still under my fingernails, to "SUCK IT UP" and go along and if I didn't, "IF YOU DON'T DO THIS FOR US..."

But now it's time for me to look after Nightlight...and look after you, Bill.

BILL: Gary—

<coughing>

Gare, are you gonna let him talk like this?

STANLEY: Dad doesn't have much time left. In fact, tragically, he passed away today.

GARY: What?

STANLEY: He coughed himself unconscious—

GARY: Stanley?

<ragged coughing>

STANLEY: Dad collapsed on our little red bench and rolled right off the cliff.

<loud clatter>

BILL: What are you doing? He's got a sick lung!

<punching, deep wheezing, and then a loud, final thud>

STANLEY: Now, Bill...

<panting>

He's dead. How did you feel watching that? Helpless? Frozen? You know, I always thought that if I was ever in a crisis, I'd spring into action to help. Nah. When you beat Ricky, all I could do was watch. Just like you watched me beat my dad to death just now.

BILL: Oh Jesus, oh Jesus, oh Jesus.

STANLEY: You have choices in front of you. If you kill me, the staff will think you killed me and Dad both. If you play anyone this tape to expose me, they'll know you're a fugitive.

BILL: Are you...gonna kill me?

STANLEY: Not at all. I'm honoring Dad's final wishes. You're going to spend the rest of your life with me. Right here. Happy Thanksgiving.

\<The tape recorder clicks off.\>

CHAPTER THIRTY-EIGHT

THERE IS STILL TIME

TODAY

The air in the bunker stiffens, and the spear dips in my limp hands like a rope given too much slack. We stare at the Reverend, caught between pity and terror now that we've been drawn into the same conspiracy of silence about what happened to Ricky and Rigo. They were married for only a few hours before Bill Hannigan ripped the world out from under them. And the Reverend—little Stanley—for all his love of Ricky, for as much as he tried to stop his uncle's attack, betrayed his cousin one last time and hid Bill from justice. A trail of death has followed this family like droplets of water follow you out of a pool.

Rigo. Ricky. Drew. I can now add a highway patrolman and the Reverend's father to that list.

"I'm still not sure why I did this," the Reverend says as he slips the Expulsion tape back into his shirt pocket. "Record Bill's confession, I mean. I think I just wanted to hear Bill and Dad say it out loud. Admit the whole rotten thing. I needed to hear it, so I knew I wasn't crazy and imagining it. I was worried that, over time, the heat would lower on some of these memories, and I couldn't let that happen." He runs a shaking hand over the pearls of sweat dotting his receding hairline. "Ricky's wedding made me feel awful, but it was also beautiful. I didn't want to forget the beautiful parts."

"'Telling the truth is addictive once you get the taste for it,'" I quote back to him, my jaw locked with tension. "Why did you show us this?"

"I needed you to know," the Reverend pleads, his cool exterior shattering with volcanic power. "I needed *someone* to know."

"You killed Drew to shut him up, but you needed me to know?"

"I killed him so I wouldn't have to kill you. I thought it would get Briggs back in line and stop the leaks and scare you enough to stop, but you kept pushing. You wouldn't take my offer to just marry that Goddamn girl and leave, you're too stupid and stubborn! I thought that when I took you to Nightlight, you'd just mind your own business and be too busy worrying about getting back home, but you pushed and PUSHED. Ricky knew what he was doing planting that seed in your head. You're exactly like him. Things are so...simple for you."

Hot spittle flies from the Reverend's lips, but Marcos—my immovable sentry—holds his spear between me and the Reverend. I can't imagine what it would feel like to marry Marcos...and lose him the same night. "They were only married for a few hours," I growl.

"A few hours together can feel like a lifetime," the Reverend replies, his black eyes narrowing. "You and Marcos know how important—how vital—only a few hours can be." Marcos and I point our spears, alert again as Darcy takes another step toward the door behind her. "My staff informed me you two were headed to the falls, and the other campers didn't reach you for another hour. An hour of bliss. I didn't get my storybook waterfall romance like you or Ricky or Miss Culpepper or EVERYONE ELSE, but I know what goes on in that cave."

"You don't know—" Marcos begins, but the Reverend descends on him, allowing the point of Marcos's spear to graze his heart.

"Mr. Carrillo, don't make me an idiot! I saw the way you moved to protect Connor, I see the disgusting hickeys splattered all over your neck—*animals*—and pardon me, but unwashed faggot sex has a *very* particular scent and it's all over you."

I lunge forward, unthinking, until my spear is one jab away from the Reverend's eye socket. He doesn't blink. "Call him a faggot again," I stammer breathlessly. "Do it again and I'll run this through your eye."

"Connor," Marcos warns, but I said what I said.

"It's getting real in here," the Reverend chuckles, unfazed. "You think stabbing a man of God will play well back home—?"

"You think I care anymore what anyone on this shithead planet thinks?!"

"Oh, Mr. Major," he purrs, vaguely impressed, "now we're talking. Now you finally see where I'm coming from."

"We're leaving the island NOW. You got your five minutes. Step aside."

The Reverend grits his teeth, sweat dropping faster and faster down his cheeks. "I would love to, but you're forgetting one thing. BILL!"

On a *click*, the door opens behind Darcy, and Karaoke Bill floats inside. "Oh, shit," she yelps, grabbing Marcos's spear and swinging it toward our new guest. I continue holding my own spear at the Reverend, but Bill consumes my full attention. No matter how hard I strain, I can't recognize Ricky in his father's sun-beaten face. Matted with filth like a dog in the rain, Bill's wounded eyes flit left and right. "What're you all staring at?" he asks, defensive but swallowed in shame. "I paid my time. I've been stuck in this prison longer than any of you have been alive, so stop your staring!"

"Bill, that's no way to talk to Connor," the Reverend admonishes. "All summer, he took care of Ricky and Aunt Sharon. Hot meals every weekend."

My lip twitches as Bill pivots the heat of his focus onto me. "I heard about that." Bill softens at the mention of his son. "I'm...so grateful to anyone who looks after my Ricky."

How could he say that? The same man who brought a crowbar to his son's wedding, murdered the groom in cold blood, and then beat his son into the floor. And for what? Embarrassing him? Running away from a dirtbag family? I'm impressed Ricky put up with any of them for as long as he did. And now Bill is "so grateful" I took care of him? A couple decades running around on a paradise island, doing whatever he wanted, and suddenly he has perspective?

The Reverend let this monster near queer kids knowing what he was capable of—my mind can't even process it.

"I did what you asked and waited," Bill tells the Reverend. "Now where's Ricky? You said he'd be on the boat tonight, but nobody showed."

"What?" I ask, close to laughing. Marcos and Darcy exchange doom-filled glances, clearly not sharing my morbid sense of humor. Bill's gone off the deep end and, in his delirium, thinks Ricky is still alive and somehow able (and willing!) to make the journey here. Clearly, whatever this letter from home was, Bill misunderstood.

But the Reverend is similarly grave. "I'm so sorry," he says. "I mixed up my information. Ricky is already here." Bill and I freeze, our mouths drooping open, but where I can feel my color is draining, Bill grows golden with anticipation. "It's been such a hectic day that I lost track. He's here, in your room."

"Why didn't you say something?" Bill asks, leveled by an

untamed glee. Marcos, Darcy, and I curl into tenser and tenser shapes with each bout of nonsense spoken.

"Ricky can't be here," I insist.

"Ah, Bill, he's confused," the Reverend says, reaching out his arm. "Please show Connor your letter, and then we'll all go see Ricky together."

I share Bill's overwhelmed agitation at the Reverend's ability to keep stringing us along as we languish in suspense. But as soon as Bill hands me his crinkled letter, I push out the world and read:

July 16

Dad,

It took a while, but I finally read your letter Stanley gave me. Stanley has been good to me and Mom. He pays for whatever I need (not to make you feel worse, but I need a lot). I'm happy he's been kind to you too. I've been thinking about what you asked, and I think I'm ready. The next time Stanley comes to see you, I'll be with him. I want to be your son again.

Love,

RICKY

The letter is typed, but the handwritten signature is wildly, unevenly scrawled. Ricky's signature. The ink has smudged—probably from rain. Possibly Bill's tears. The walls crowd me as the letter's date registers: *July 16*. But Ricky died on the twelfth. He couldn't have written this. He can't be here.

The empty bed. You never saw his body, Connor, and you never went to the funeral.

It's a trap. Ricky is alive, and all of this has been a show. The pins and needles surging through my blood crystalize into ice as I numbly hand Bill's letter back to him.

"Mr. Major," the Reverend says, "lead the way to Bill's room. Let's say 'hello' to Ricky."

With a single flutter of his wrist, the Reverend takes advantage of my shock and plucks the spear out of my hands. I flinch as the Reverend lowers the spear to my neck, and he turns to Marcos. Needing no verbal command, Marcos immediately surrenders his spear to the Reverend. Our weapons disappear with several clatters into the shadows behind the dead flowers, and Darcy groans, as if she expected this. Defeated, motored only by curiosity, I march the group back down the corridor. Marcos and Darcy stick to my sides like peanut butter, craving as much space between them and Bill as possible. We pass Briggs, still sobbing by himself in the darkened corner. He reaches pleadingly for the Reverend's sleeve, but the director rips his arm free. "Not *now*, Ben," he says, sneering. "Your punishment isn't over!"

As I pass the cages, somebody's foot tramples the broken shard of my spear, and in the dark, it skids away to places unknown. We arrive at Bill's sparse bedroom, resembling a prison cell even more in the light of the truth. Ricky and Rigo smile from the frame on Bill's shelf. *How could you do this to me, Ricky?* I wonder as my eyes fall on the closet door.

The door—Ricky is in there.

"Bill, you might scare him," the Reverend advises, hanging

behind and blocking our escape. "Mr. Major, you and Mr. Carrillo should bring him out. He's just behind that door."

While I suck in what could be my last breath, Bill crumbles into joyful tears. "Ricky, it's me!" he cries. "I've been waiting for you!" My knees weaken, forbidding me from taking another step closer to the closet. I desperately need things to start making sense.

After a few snaps of his fingers, Marcos charges past me to the closet. He's braving this first for me; I could kiss him. He turns the knob, but then hesitates—none of us are prepared for what's inside. It opens wide, but from my position, all I can see is Marcos's backside. When he faces me again, he's covering his mouth in shock. I abandon Darcy at Bill's cot and sprint to Marcos.

In the dark, empty closet, Ricky sits on a shelf. *An urn.* A decorative blue vase that I don't have to open to know it contains the remains of Ricky Hannigan.

In the midst of my unrelenting panic, a calming thought pokes its head inside: Ricky didn't trick me. I'm not happy he's dead, but at least the ground under my feet is solid. Ricky passed away one week ago...which means he didn't write that letter.

The Reverend tricked Bill.

"Ricky, I'm sorry!" Bill calls from the hallway. He doesn't know yet. He hasn't seen. "I've thought of you every single day. EVERY SINGLE DAY. Rigo too. I keep your picture at my bed. It was such a beautiful day. I'm so sorry. Twenty-two years, and I'd change everything. If I could time travel and stop myself. If I could *time travel*, Ricky, you don't know how many times I dream that I time travel and do it differently and give Rigo back to you and we're all a family again, but then I wake up and I'm in Hell." As Bill rambles, Marcos and I lock eyes on Ricky's remains. All of Bill's apologies and hopes for the future fight and lose against the finality of the urn. "Oh my God, please don't be scared to come out. I won't hurt you. I'm sorry I hurt you. Please, let me see your face again."

The Reverend orchestrated this perfectly. He wrote that letter tricking Bill to set up this exact moment. The moment I'm about to deliver.

"Bring Ricky out," the Reverend orders, boiling over with glee. "Let him say 'hi' to Dad."

Marcos and I wear masks of fear until I whisper, "Hand him to me. I'll do it." Ricky's urn is heavy and cold, and it requires superhuman determination not to drop him. I return to the crowd, clutching Ricky in both hands, and Darcy is the first to understand—she mutters furiously under her breath. I reach the hallway's shadows, where the Reverend is grinning from his wicked accomplishment. Bill's tear-streaked face is harder to read. He scoffs at the urn, but that amusement dies off into silence.

"I'm sorry," I say against my better judgment. Sometimes evil deserves a sorry.

"As promised," the Reverend says, "here's Ricky."

"What's this?" Bill asks, approaching timidly as if the urn were a live, downed power line. Instinctively, I back into Marcos, who stands close behind me for maximum protection. Ricky may be dead, but I'm not letting him anywhere near his dad. "Where's Ricky?"

A cruel sparkle crosses the Reverend's smile. "Bill...Connor is holding Ricky. You do know he died, don't you? Was that unclear?"

My heart squeezes into pulp as realization seeps into Bill one drop at a time. His wet eyes roll toward me. "What does he mean, dead?"

"I mean he's no longer with us. Last week. He hadn't been turned properly, a bedsore became infected, and he...died, Bill. Connor was there, weren't you, Connor?"

My lips open, but only a stunned squeak emerges. Bill's filthy, shaking fingers reach for the urn, but I clench my arms tighter around the ceramic. Marcos and Darcy close the centimeter of space between us, but we can't move any farther back. "This isn't right," Bill mutters. "This isn't...I've been writing to him. He's been writing to me."

"I don't see how writing a letter would be possible," the Reverend scoffs. "Ricky's injuries were too severe." He withdraws a strip of newspaper on the spot and slides it to Bill. "You'll be happy to know his funeral was very well attended."

Karaoke Bill reads what is no doubt the obituary of his son. As he finishes, the newsprint collapses in his fist. "Stop playing games with me!" He flicks the clipping at the Reverend, but the poor man doesn't even come close to hitting him. "There was no Goddamn funeral! Now, my son wrote me just a few days ago. We've been writing each other for months! We discussed everything, EVERYTHING! He forgave me..."

Bill whirls around the crowded hallway, frantically searching our faces, but none of us are Ricky. His heart in shreds, Bill stares grimly at the urn as confirmation spills over him that, yes, his son is dead; yes, the Reverend forged those letters; and no, there was no forgiveness. In under thirty seconds, Bill ages thirty years. Purple veins line his glassy eyes. His son is gone. Bill isn't going home, or anywhere, ever again.

A choking, almost silent cry floats out of Bill. The tension finally shatters when a nasty, shrieking laugh erupts from the shadows.

"I've waited SO LONG for this," the Reverend laughs, rubbing away tears. "Running Nightlight all these years...it was the only way

I could protect these children from people like you, Bill. It's Hell on Earth to pretend you're someone you're not, but at least they wouldn't end up like Ricky and Rigo. That was my mission. But when Ricky died...it all came flooding back. I was done with you, Bill. But you weren't finished paying. Did you *really* think Ricky forgave you? Did that make *any* sense when you read it? Nightlight isn't forgiveness—it's punishment."

"You didn't have to kill Drew," I blurt, holding back my rage. Bill remains blank, but the Reverend charges over to me. Darcy skitters out of his way as he pushes past, and she retreats to Briggs in the shadows. Behind me, Marcos grips my arm protectively—but there's nowhere to run. He and I are trapped against the bunker wall.

"Drew should've known better than to start throwing around how much he knew about Bill," the Reverend says, breathing steam onto my nose. "Do you think that after everything my family put me through, I'd let a few mouthy twinks be the end of me? Let me take the fall for something that wasn't my fault?!"

"I could've shut Drew up," Briggs squeaks from the dark. "You didn't have to—"

"And you didn't have to screw him and leak our private business, but what's done is done!"

"Well, now we know even more than Drew did...so, what happens to us?" I ask. Breath abandons me as my heart clatters against my chest. I'm too small, sandwiched between Marcos and the Reverend's hulking, cologne-soaked mass.

The Reverend chuckles, but it's injected with darkness. "At first, I wanted to keep you from the truth, but seeing how poorly things unfolded with Drew, I have a new plan: Nightlight goes back to normal. You all stay. Drew's death is a suicide. You know the whole

Ricky story, so the prying will stop. If you agree to keep the truth to yourselves, you'll all be safe and we can go about our business."

"What about Bill?"

"What *about* Bill? There's no evidence Bill was ever here. He's a ghost, remember? And now that I've had my fun, I'm starting fresh. Tonight, he's headed to the bottom of the ocean."

Behind the Reverend, Bill remains unbothered. His eyes par-alyzed, he's lost in a thousand different memories and dreams that will never come true. The Reverend could kill him with his bare hands, and I don't think he'd even blink.

Uncertainty hangs in the silence as a hellish, eternal punishment consumes the bunker. Nightlight *is* punishment. It *is* Hell. Run by the Reverend Stanley Packard, a pathetic monster who lives to inflict his pain on everyone else. He doesn't care about justice for Ricky. If he did, he would've turned Bill over to the FBI years ago.

The Reverend feeds on pain, as simple as that.

"There's still time," I say, Ricky's message occurring to me in a flash. Holding Ricky's remains, renewed strength and optimism flow into my heart. "Ricky wrote two messages: one to me, one to you. Ricky wanted you to help us. He still believed in you." The Reverend's pinched, deep-lined expression softens, unlocking a glimpse of the tender—albeit untrustworthy—boy from the Winner's Wall. I have him in the palm of my hand, and I don't miss my shot. "Take us home. Please. Break the cycle."

"I..." he squeaks, but a shadow falls again. "1612 Havenhurst. Los Angeles. That's where Rigo's ashes are. In the garden. Bring Ricky back to him—"

A blood-drenched spearhead explodes through the Reverend's clavicle, stopping an inch from my forehead. The broken shard of my spear ended up on the floor near Darcy's cage, but Karaoke Bill found it and wields it like a stake—and the Reverend is his vampire to slay. I choke on my own tongue as Reverend Packard paws at the wound gushing crimson down his chest. He wipes at it in disbelief, as if more concerned with the stain than with the hole in him. In a swirling tornado of carnage, Bill pulls the shard out of his nephew's chest and drives it through his cheek.

Marcos and I scream—our lungs full of air again—and topple sideways through the curtain into Bill's room. The urn jumbles in my arms, but I won't let go of Ricky. The Reverend howls like an animal caught in a steel trap as his uncle—pin-drop silent—slices into him, over and over, with methodical patience. The Reverend takes four more strikes to his chest before landing with a deafening thud at our feet. His eyes remain open, as round as pools. "Run..." he chokes out, his chin painted red. "Run...Ricky..."

The Reverend's life ends on a gurgle, and all sounds vanish inside a vacuum.

History is about to repeat itself.

In the doorway, Karaoke Bill blocks our exit, his right hand gloved in blood as it clutches the spear shard. He doesn't even need to catch his breath.

The closet is our only option. Marcos and I could run inside, shut it, and block Bill out with our combined weights. But the door is thin and flimsy. Bill could easily kick it in—or worse, ram the spear through it and into us.

"Give me Ricky," Bill orders. "I only want my son. I just want to go home...same as you."

My central nervous system might collapse at any minute. Bill could absolutely kill us even if I handed over the urn. The injustice scalds like oil—Ricky's ashes deserve to be with Rigo's. The Reverend died trying to do one good thing, and that was to help Ricky get home. Away from his dad. But as Death Himself lurches for us, brandishing the world's largest splinter, a poisonous voice in my head returns with some perspective:

Ricky can help you.

"Sorry, Ricky," I whisper, raising the heavy urn above my head. I'm gonna bash Bill's head in with his own kid, and then we're all getting out of here.

Deranged panic sweeps over Bill as he realizes what's coming. "No—!"

I pitch the urn like a shot put, but my fingers know not to let go as Darcy's arm appears in the hallway. She emerges from the shadows behind Bill, who is still fixated on the urn. Darcy lands a black Pez dispenser to his ear. "Hey, Bill," she says.

As he turns, she fires.

A violet arc of electricity rockets through Bill's skull, violently jerking his shoulders like someone is telling him to get a hold of himself. Before I can blink, Bill drops to his knees and into a ball beside his nephew.

Relief pummels my heart so rapidly, I'm at risk for a serious coronary. Darcy smashed Bill's lights out, and she's wasting no time hauling his limp arms behind his back to bind them with handcuffs. "Got you now..." she growls as she works. Bill moans lifelessly—*she didn't kill him*. Marcos and I stay frozen in a statuesque pose; him hugging me, me hugging Ricky's urn.

We're okay. Ricky's okay.

"Oh my God, where'd you get a taser...and handcuffs?" I ask, relishing the *thud-thud-thud* of Marcos's heartbeat on my back.

"A new friend," Darcy replies.

Briggs steps out of the shadows, hunched and sloppy looking, like a remorseful, hungover prom date. Tears and snot stream down his weathered face. "Darcy..." he says, sniffing in a vain attempt to control the fluids racing out of his orifices. "Darcy said if I help you lot get home, you'll"—he implodes on another swell of devastation—"you'll let me come with. I can't stay here anymore. I have to find my son. I need to bring Drew home. I promised him."

My jaw fully unhinges to the floor. Briggs asking for our permission like a guilty little boy. Permission to finally do the right thing.

There is still time after all, Ricky.

"That's the plan, Benji," Darcy says, hopping to her feet. She passes Briggs into the hallway and continues to bark orders. "Pick Bill's ass up off the floor. We got a boat to catch!"

Guess that means Bill's also coming. We've got our man—Nightlight campers, *one*; FBI, *zero*. Before I can deliver Darcy a hearty "Well done!" for saving our lives, she disappears, off to rejoin Lacrishia and the other campers outside the bunker. With Briggs at our side, the trek past the gray-shirts will be substantially easier—either way, camp's out. Briggs hauls a handcuffed Bill Hannigan over his shoulder like a sack of potatoes—exactly how he hauled me out of my house two nights ago.

Or was it three? I need my damn phone back and an enormous nap (preferably with Marcos as the big spoon). "Ready to come home with me?" I ask, facing him.

"Home," he chuckles, as wrung out as a sponge. "Where's that?"

I try to smile, but Reverend Packard's bleeding, empty carcass at our feet won't let me. The man who brought me boomerangs and snow globes—and almost killed me on this remote jungle island—is dead. Unfortunately, he'll have to stay in the bunker a little while longer. We'll make sure someone finds him. I tap the cold pottery holding Ricky's remains and enjoy one more fleece-warm hug with Marcos (with only a faint moment of nausea) before we embark on our final journey out of Nightlight.

Where's home? he asked.

"Not here," I say.

CHAPTER THIRTY-NINE
DEPARTURES

We walk as one, led by fire. Eleven campers, Briggs, and Karaoke Bill—an amoeba of silent, steely eyed pain—travel the wooded path back into camp. Escape is close, but it feels dangerous to hope. Even though the Reverend is dead, Briggs is on our side, and Bill is in our custody (and thoroughly zapped), no one in the group has let their guard down since we departed the bunker. The weight of eyes, just beyond the dark trees, still lays heavily on my back as we march slowly over the Coral Road. When we left the bunker, we were expecting to find gray-shirts surrounding us, but there was no one. Something is wrong. The gray-shirts are waiting for us, somewhere.

It's not over yet.

Miss Manners still has her rifle. Any of the gray-shirts could have a rifle.

We take no chances. The Beginners march along the middle of our amoeba, and around them, we form a protective circle. Lacrishia guards the rear, torch in hand and rotating in circles every few seconds to make sure we haven't been followed. Darcy clasps her hand tenderly. In Darcy's other hand is Briggs's taser, her arm wrapped fiercely around Owen as if he were their lion cub. No longer crying, Owen swivels his head suspiciously, his courage buoyed having his moms finally reunited beside him. Further ahead, Anke, Christina, and Alan fuse together like a chorus line of dancers, sandwiched between Vance and Jack, each of whom wields a Nightlight staff taser (confiscated from Bill and the Reverend). Ahead of them strides Molly, armed with her spear, which she spins from side to side in a roving sphere of protection over the Beginners. Leading the amoeba is pure trouble: Marcos, Briggs, Bill, and me. Briggs guards the front line with a torch, the only weapon we allowed him to hold. The man has at last gone dry-eyed, except for the occasional sniffle when a renewed swell of emotion strikes him. In his free hand, Briggs drags Bill, who has regained sense enough to walk, and who in the glowing darkness resembles a lurching zombie. Marcos and I hold our spears to Briggs's and Bill's backs, with Ricky's urn tucked under my left arm like a football.

I wish Marcos could wrap his warm, sturdy arm around me, but he has too important of a job: primary hostage taker. Should Briggs or Bill get out of line, Marcos does the poking. I told him we'd hug each other plenty once we're safely on the boat.

As we travel, Nightlight sleeps. The entire camp is soundless, save for our footsteps and the tropical wind rushing through the palms. Everything should be proceeding as planned. Before departing, Briggs radioed Miss Manners and the gray-shirts that the Reverend needed all hands on deck at the bunker to handle an unruly Bill. The remaining Nightlight staff replied that they were near the staff lodge and already on their way—confirming the Coral Road would be safe and clear for us to get ahead of them.

The Coral Road *is* empty, but...I can't stop feeling these eyes on me.

"Where's the Reverend?" Alan whispers timidly.

"Hell?" Vance replies.

"What do you mean?"

"What do you think I mean, dumbass? Connor's splattered in blood. So is Bill, and—"

"Will you chickens HUSH?" Marcos snarls, turning back. Instinctively, I raise my spear to Briggs while Marcos is distracted. As Vance urgently defends himself, Briggs, the hulking, former second-in-command of Nightlight staggers onward, unaware Marcos is distracted by the squabbling. We're being extra cautious holding Briggs at spearpoint, but he's cooperating willingly. Guilt and regret have crushed him into a ghost—a better human being, but a ghost nonetheless. Briggs and Bill shepherd our escape squad like two of the walking damned: vacant, shackled ghouls ferrying souls out of the underworld.

Until Alan spoke, no one who hadn't been present for the bunker drama asked for details. What they did see was Karaoke Bill and me, covered in blood, the Reverend nowhere to be found, and Briggs lying for us on the radio. The sharper (or less naive) campers like Molly, Lacrishia, and Vance put the pieces together on their own, and the others kept quiet with the promise that everything would be explained on the boat.

Out of the next bend, the watchtower rises up, revealing the cul-de-sac courtyard of Pura Vida, each classroom lit with a single porch light. Not a soul—a ghost town. Hairs prickle on the back of my neck as I spot the chopped remains of Drew's noose swaying in the breeze at the top of the tower. Briggs sucks in a brave breath.

"Jack," Darcy orders, "clear us."

"Copy that," Jack replies before breaking from the amoeba and darting toward the watchtower at a sprint. Alan, Marcos, and I hiss at him to stay put, but Jack only takes orders from the Moms. The caravan pauses at the base of the tower and watches in awe as Jack, forgoing the shattered ladder, shimmies to the top like a koala mounts a tree. He reaches the bird's nest in under a minute, and I hold my breath, praying Miss Manners and her horrible rifle are long gone.

The tip of his ponytailed little head briefly emerges from the basket, followed by shuffling and the muted *shink* of a blade. "Oh my God," I whisper to myself, imagining what the hell that sound was and if Miss Manners caught him. A dreadful moment later, Jack reappears to the crowd—Miss Manners's rifle slung across his back by a leather strap—and he scurries down.

"It's empty," Jack informs Darcy, casting the rifle into the darkened woods and retaking his place in the amoeba. "Oh, and I'll trade you." Jack produces a long rusted blade—the one Bill had jammed into the side of the bird's nest ledge—flips it around, and presents the hilt to Darcy. She trades Jack her taser as her fingers close powerfully around the dagger.

Spears, tasers, torches, and knives. We're collecting weapons as nonchalantly as characters in a video game. *You're gonna need them*, a voice in my head reminds me.

"Anyone on the path ahead?" Darcy asks.

"Torchlights at the chapel," he reports. "But they always keep them lit. All clear."

"Let's hustle! Halfway there."

Jack gives his spare taser to Christina, who wields it like a Harry Potter wand, and we're off again, passing the signpost for *Chapel* and *Clinic*. The classrooms of Nightlight receding behind us, we walk with brighter, brisker steps. Some of our worst memories of this island are literally in our rearview, and hope lies ahead. However, when we pass Ambrose Chapel, my insides twist again. The ash-colored giant looms within the copse of trees, circled in torch flames like a Satanic altar. "Hey," I whisper to Marcos, angling my head toward the chapel. "You think you'll ever go to church again?"

"I don't know," he moans, defeated. "Don't ask me that right now. But if you're asking me right now, I'd say…I need to think about it." It warms me to hear Marcos describe my exact thoughts so perfectly. It's going to take time to bleach Nightlight—and for me, the Reverend's chapel back home—out of the idea of church.

Back home. So close.

Through the torchlight, flecks of blood appear across my wrist. The Reverend's blood. The man who booped my nose and scolded me for drinking too much coffee—I'm leaving him dead and rotting in a boathouse. How can I possibly explain any of this to my mom? Or the town? Every soul in Ambrose worshipped him, literally. However, any concerns about the future, my mom, or my return home meet a horrible brick wall when we reach the rattling generator outside the clinic:

It's everyone.

Every surviving Nightlight staff member waits with torches, tasers, and spears of their own across the expanse of the Coral Road. Ten of them—Miss Manners, the tattling Archie, four squat but muscular gray-shirts, the sun-weathered captain I recognize from the boat, even the three lunch ladies.

Miss Manners, at the head of the pack, asks, "Leaving so soon?"

The amoeba disperses, but no one flees or disappears into the jungle's edges only a few feet away. As if subconsciously linked, we reform into a line, led by our fiercest warriors: Marcos, Molly, Darcy, and Jack—their weapons extended. Lacrishia remains in back, swiveling again to make sure we aren't about to be ambushed from behind. "Don't let anything happen to this," I tell Alan, handing Ricky's urn to the trembling boy. Nodding, he retreats, backing away into Anke. In under a second, I shove Christina and Vance behind Karaoke Bill and direct them: "If he moves at all, blast him." Charged with a new fire, Vance and Christina press their tasers to the old goat's back. He flinches, but otherwise sways in place. My duties delegated, I point my shattered half-spear and approach Miss Manners. The gray-shirts lower their spears to strike, but Miss Manners raises her hand to halt them.

Everyone remains at attention—Marcos still holding Briggs—as Miss Manners and I advance on each other at the center of the two opposing hordes. Weaponless, Miss Manners's shredded, filthy lemon dress flaps in the wind, but the effect is of an imperious, mad queen. We meet each other and smile.

"Nice spears," I say, finding my nerve just in time.

"The boys saw yours and thought it was a fine idea," she says. "You look a mess."

"Sorry, I've got Reverend on me."

Miss Manners's lips tighten as she peers over my shoulder at Bill, Briggs, and the rest of her predicament. "I knew I was right not to trust that call from Briggs. What exactly is going on here?"

"You're in peril, Carol," Vance hollers from the back.

Unamused, Miss Manners sneers and attempts to regain her pageant composure. "I take it y'all are leaving and bringing Bill with you?" I nod. "Good idea. This place could use a reboot."

"We'll see," I say, refusing to retreat from her even a millimeter. "First thing, you're gonna step aside and let Briggs and my very fine boyfriend, Marcos, into the clinic to fetch a few things before we shove off. Boys!"

Marcos frog-marches Briggs to the clinic's raised stilts and waits by my side. *My boyfriend.* In the harsh lamplight of the clinic porch, Marcos's strong, sweating arms hold Briggs at bay so confidently, I almost feel faint. His heart must be beating so fast, but he's committed to getting us off the island and isn't about to falter, not even in the face of Miss Manners and her talons. Briggs, on the other hand, can't look anyone in the eye.

Miss Manners pivots herself sideways to let them through and waves to the gray-shirts to do the same, orders they follow without question. I raise my spear to cover Marcos as he leads Briggs up the clinic stairs. As Briggs passes Miss Manners, she hisses, "I knew you'd flop on us. Your boyfriend's waiting for you in there. He smells *realllllll* nice."

Behind me, several people gasp. As Briggs begins to crumple, I shout, "Marcos, keep him moving!" Marcos abides and hustles Briggs inside, who moans all the way. Ignited and activated, I meet Miss Manners face-to-face again. "What should we talk about while we wait? Whatcha gonna do tomorrow with no campers here?"

"Welp," she says, not backing down. "You're taking our only boat off this island, so not a whole lot."

"Don't worry. We'll make sure people know *exactly* where to find you."

She grins with perfect lipstick and not a drop of sweat. "I cannot wait for you to try."

"Eager to get to prison?"

"No, Connor, I mean I can't wait for you to tell everyone. I want you to tell them everything, as many people as possible. Because I can't *wait* for that curtain to fall in your eyes when you realize what I've been trying to tell the Reverend for years: no one cares. A cover-up was always the wrong move, I've been saying it from the jump. You bring Bill back, somebody's gonna pay that man's legal fees. They'll say, 'He's been stuck on that island twenty-two years, no trial, he's suffered enough.' And Bill will be out on the street, same as you, free as birds."

A bone-deep chill erodes my marrow as Miss Manners's hypothetical invades the darkest corners of my mind.

"Y'all need to understand optics," she continues. "This is why the Reverend messed up. Why it was a mistake to have Nightlight run by former campers. You're all queers. And queers think the world runs on their little dramas, those anxieties that mean everything to you and not a darn thing to us." Behind her, the gray-shirts chuckle cruelly while Archie trembles, as stung as the rest of us. "Bill's gonna be on TV. I'll make sure he's a hero."

"And I'll make sure everyone remembers he's a cop killer," I say. "How's that for optics?"

Miss Manners cringes as if she's just chewed something nasty. "Bill, if you hadn't killed that patrolman—"

"But he did, Blanche!" Vance shouts triumphantly behind Bill, who's still swaying and drooling in place. "He did kill the patrolman!"

"My name isn't Blanche or Carol!" she says in a fit.

"She thinks I actually think her name's Blanche." Vance and Alan sputter with private, uncontrolled laughter. "Oh my god, pathetic—"

Miss Manners sizzles, the boys so much more successful at getting under her skin than I was. "THE POINT," she roars, "is we always come back tougher and harder than before. We're cockroaches."

"Oh, and you think we're not?" I ask, closing the gap between us and bringing the splintered end of my spear against her bare shoulder. The gray-shirts raise their spikes and hover them in place, one lunge away from my skull.

Neither Miss Manners nor I blink.

The clinic door clangs open on Marcos's strong kick, and the gray-shirts retreat. My boyfriend shuffles down the stairs with his spear in one hand and a large, bulging duffel bag in the other. "Got it all: everyone's passports, phones, and money," he reports as Briggs emerges gripping the limp, black body bag of Drew's remains. The beast lumbers down the stairs with his ill-gotten love, his own eyes red and damp as he holds the boy in both arms, as if presenting a sacrificial offering to the crowd.

It's so ugly, I can't even watch or attempt to find meaning in it. It's meaningless.

My heart pumps no blood, only venom, and I'm tired of this place and these people. "Get out of our way," I order, but nobody flinches.

Rough soil crunches as two of my friends flank me from behind: Molly and Darcy, waving a spear and a small, rusted machete. "Maybe you didn't hear him," Molly says. "My friend tends to mumble. He said, 'MOVE.'"

Miss Manners seethes, her lemony-cute chest pumping with hatred. She clicks her crimson talons, as if longing to give Molly one more good swipe.

"Move," Darcy orders. "Or you'll get moved."

"You said it yourself, you got nothing to lose," I say, shrugging.

With that, Miss Manners takes a long, deliberate step backward, and her army of gray-shirts and baffled lunch ladies follow her, providing a clear path onward into darkness. Remembering my arrival from last night, the clinic is the first sign of life on the island. The journey to the beach will require us to leave the beaten path and enter raw wilderness.

Our amoeba reforms without another word. With Briggs's arms full, I claim his torch and lead my pack away from Nightlight for good.

The moment we set eyes on the beach, several people burst into tears—and not the ones I expect, either. Darcy bubbles over, almost hyperventilating into Lacrishia's shoulder, as she explains, "I haven't—I haven't seen this since the day I got here." Lacrishia pets her girlfriend's head as her chest heaves in an attempt to corral her own unexpectedly frantic emotions.

"You okay?" I ask Marcos, rubbing his back as he nods, sucking in long, deep breaths of his own. For Molly and me, this beach was yesterday. For lifers like Darcy and Marcos, it's a moment they couldn't even allow themselves to dream about, it was that impossible and painful.

Molly takes Darcy's blade from her and chops the open-shelled patrol boat free of its bungee cords. With the smooth ease of a swing set, our vessel slides off the wooden ramp and onto the shoreline of the crescent-shaped bay. No one pauses for sentimentality—Molly and Darcy scramble up the back ladder first and straddle the transom as they scoop Drew's body bag out of Briggs's arms. "Careful please," he mutters as they set Drew delicately on the deck and then accept Lacrishia, Owen, Anke, Christina, Alan, Vance, and Jack up the ladder next.

Marcos and I wade into the shore up to our ankles, and the

gentle, lapping water soothes every ache. We keep our spears on Bill as Briggs climbs aboard next.

"Up you go, Bill," he groans, reaching for him. "Finally leaving the island."

"Is my son on board?" Bill asks in a dreamy haze. I confirm that Alan is still holding Ricky's urn, but the boy is clearly itching to be rid of the thing and the continuous ghoulish stares from Bill. Briggs hoists Bill up to the deck with enormous difficulty as the old man, so vibrant this morning, has become brittle dead weight under the thrall of the taser.

As Marcos supervises the prisoner transfer, I keep my spear trained on the island's tree line. I don't trust Miss Manners, not even for a heartbeat. If she or any of the gray-shirts get a change of heart and come charging onto the shore, I'll be ready to skewer them. Yet the tree line remains dark and ghostly quiet. Even if someone were watching us, I'd have no way of knowing. Our only light comes from the single torch we left behind in the sand, just beyond the entrance signpost:

NIGHTLIGHT MINISTRIES
SURRENDER YOUR SINS!

I smirk at the message. *I beat you.*

Marcos taps me, and then he and I—the last survivors on the beach—ditch our spears and clutch each end of the hull to shove our escape vessel into the lapping surf. The boat is stubborn, but I'm scrappier. Marcos and I smile at each other through wet hair as we make headway, me wading up to my thighs (and Marcos up to his knees). Finally, the boat tears free of the rocky shallows, and the motor kicks alive. Fighting the surge of the splashing engine, Marcos lunges for the ladder and yanks his entire heft out of the bay. Gripping the ladder with one arm, he reaches for me in the waist-deep water. His bicep rippling in the moonlight, I gaze—a pile of goop—at his hand.

A warm, confident hand that will defend me to the bitter end.

And here we are, at the bitter end.

I grunt, dog-paddling after the boat, and leap for Marcos. His hand closes around mine as the boat picks up speed and drags me through pitch-black open water. *We ride together into the ink-black drink!* Marcos pulls me from the sea, and my free hand finds the ladder. "Got you," he says, beaming.

Both of us clutching the stern, we kiss. A sopping, breathless kiss. A kiss of survival.

The island sinks behind us.

We beat you.

CHAPTER FORTY
ARRIVALS

THREE DAYS LATER

here's shockingly little to say. In the spot where Ricky's hospital bed used to be, his urn now sits on the coffee table between Mrs. Hannigan and me like a chessboard awaiting our first move. The old house in White Eagle creaks in the summer wind flying through the cracked living room window. She's chosen to leave it open—in the days since our highly public escape from Nightlight, people have started throwing eggs and stones, so I can't blame her for not being thrilled to see me.

When I arrived alone, Mrs. Hannigan didn't get up. She lay immobile, melted into her recliner, her exhausted, puffy eyes waiting for the horrible moment I'd call with a burning desire for answers. Actually, I have no desire. I've already learned all I care to know about Ricky, his father, his cousin, or any other relation.

"Did you kill him?" she asks me.

"No," I reply, not remotely offended. It's not the first time I've been asked this question since I returned. "Your husband did."

"I'm glad he's dead. You'd have been in your rights to kill him if you did."

"What about your husband?"

"He's where he belongs."

"Where do you think Ricky belongs?"

The brittle chill of our conversation breaks apart as our eyes find the urn. Mrs. Hannigan shudders at the sight of it and smooths back her white, wispy permed hair. "I've held on to Ricky too long," she says, gathering courage. "His home is somewhere else."

I stand and gather the urn. "I was hoping you'd say that."

Ricky's remains belong with Rigo's at their home in Los Angeles. I don't know how or when I'll be able to get him there, but I'm going to succeed and I can't trust anyone else with the job. My heart is as empty and weightless as a scooped-out melon rind, so I leave Mrs. Hannigan without saying goodbye. All I came for was permission.

The old woman's eyes, so tired of it all, drift nearly imperceptibly toward the bureau of framed photographs that Ricky's hospital bed used to obscure. The pictures, conveniently, maddeningly absent of Bill Hannigan, that rabid dog, taunt me with their hope. In the frontmost frame, two young children, boys, one slightly smaller than the other, embrace on a dock at the end of a grand lake house. A dull ache grips my chest like an old war wound: I'm convinced these boys are Ricky and his young cousin Stanley Packard. They're soaking wet in their swim trunks, pure joy in their eyes, unmarred by time, unaware of the savage future waiting for them.

They were friends.

The cruelty singes my lungs black. My eyes burn with tears. They're dead. They don't need to be, this didn't need to happen. I wrestle with the unfair weight and constraints of time—I'm furious at my body for not being able to instantly travel back in time, right now, and rescue those boys on the dock.

"Why couldn't you have just let them alone?" I whisper darkly. Without waiting for an answer, I leave.

Surrounded by her picture frames, Mrs. Hannigan calls after

me, "I did my best, you know. I did my best. I did my BEST." She repeats this on a loop, almost a mantra to herself, because I'm clearly not listening and I don't stop walking. I leave her alone, the only surviving member of the Packard-Hannigan family, save for Bill. Her brother is dead by her nephew's hand. Her nephew, son, and son-in-law are dead by her husband's hand. She did her best, but what's her best when the men of her family have massacred each other like a pack of lions?

I fight a twinge of guilt as I hug Ricky tighter—he probably wouldn't have wanted me to treat his mother this coldly, but I have many difficult conversations ahead of me today and I can't spend all my energy on a ghost.

"One down, two to go," I say as my driver pulls her sleek, government-issued sedan out of the Hannigans' sloping driveway and toward the rich part of White Eagle.

"*Starting route to 731 North Orchard Court,*" the GPS says, and my breath vanishes. I grasp the knotted bamboo of Ario's recorder beneath my tank top and press it to my lips.

I'm not ready for this at all.

"Hey, Meals on Wheels, I'm proud of you," Agent Elms says as she turns onto White Eagle's main thoroughfare, past the bookstore where Ario first punched his number into my phone. Agent Elms is exactly as I remembered her from the day Ricky died: decked in an impeccable black suit, with short, severely parted blond hair draping to one side. "*The look of a power lesbian,*" all the news sites have said about her, from LGBTQ media to the right-wing hatemongers. They all bow to the chic queer power of Special Agent Diane Elms—the woman who finally brought Bill Hannigan to justice.

"Proud of me?" I ask.

"For how well you've been keeping it together."

"Not crying is something to be proud of?"

"That's not what I meant. I'm sorry—"

"No, I'm sorry. I just..."

"Escaped a place that forced you to act like a manly man?"

I chuckle dully as I summon the strength to look at my phone. I've allowed myself one glance every hour—the notifications were too much, so I shut them off. Friends, family, supportive strangers, and strangers who wish I was dead all message me around the clock from every possible avenue. There's no keeping up with it, but the only thing I want to see on my phone right now is yesterday's Instagram post.

The post—eleven smiling, triumphant Nightlight survivors taking a selfie on the bow of our escape boat—couldn't be posted until everyone's families had been notified. But once it hit, it struck like a pipe bomb. In less than thirty-six hours, the pic has gained over three million likes. Vance texted the group chat that that's almost as much as Beyoncé's *Lion King* promo. Perspective.

Sadly, our turmoil didn't end when we escaped the island.

After two hours at sea, we reached mainland Costa Rica and were shuttled to San José by local authorities. The Costa Rican government put us up in a hotel, but it became clear that we were once again prisoners. No one was allowed to leave the hotel or discuss anything about our situation with anyone except our families. For two days, frantic emails and phone calls pinged between the hotel and the American embassy until this tangled mess could be sorted out. It turns out Nightlight's island wasn't leased by anyone in the Packard family, but instead a dummy LLC called *Nightlight Management*. As I expected, all listed means of communicating with Nightlight Management had been disconnected.

Somehow, Miss Manners had gotten to her bosses a message to go dark.

At the end of the first day, the U.S. embassy got their way and Molly, Darcy, Lacrishia, the Beginners, and Drew's body were sent home to their families. Briggs, Bill, and I continued to be held, since we were the most central to the Nightlight catastrophe and it still needed more sorting out. Marcos refused to leave me—he told his parents he'd stay until I was released. With Briggs and Bill in custody, Marcos and I had the luxury hotel to ourselves, and we spent the most beautiful two nights of our lives together: we showered in a real shower, put on bougie resort wear we bought in the gift shop, and had our first dinner date. The privacy of our cave sanctum paled in comparison to the privacy of our hotel suite...with a king bed.

I miss him so much, I feel like a reanimated corpse—shuffling and mumbling around but otherwise vacant. Marcos's soaked, golden retriever face smiles at me from our Instagram post, and I have to shut my phone again.

"*Your destination is on your left,*" the GPS sings, and my searing pain turns to nausea.

Ario Navissi waits for me at the bottom of his family's grassy hill. His curly black mop is a bit longer than when I left him, but otherwise, it's the same magnificent boy: Apollo with the evening summer sun making his skin shimmer like gold paint. His twelve-year-old sister Trini, no older than Christina or Anke, fidgets next to him and constantly adjusts her bug-eyed glasses. Oddly, seeing

Trini warms me more than Ario—she actually knew about Nightlight before any of us.

"Take your time, love," Agent Elms says as I set Ricky carefully on my seat and meet the Navissis.

"This is gonna be so much worse than I imagined," I mutter to myself as Ario runs to me, those large, furry arms outstretched—those arms I would've killed to be wrapped in four days ago. His hug swallows me. He pecks at my neck, panting, "Oh, my God, sweetie," before kissing me firmly on the lips. I go slack in his arms. I don't pull away, but I don't kiss him back with any energy. I simply let it all unfold. It's nice—so nice—but it's a shirt that no longer fits. This kiss feels like ten times the betrayal my kiss with Marcos was.

Ario senses the disturbance immediately and pulls back, his doe eyes glistening. "I'm sorry," he says. "I should've been there to return your texts."

"It's okay," I whisper, brushing away his tear. "You didn't know."

"I should've just come and got you, but I was sca...I should've..."

"You didn't know," I repeat, letting my own tears come. It's been long enough since I've cried, and I've earned them.

"What happened to you over there? They're saying a million things, but I don't know what to believe—"

"You can pretty much believe it all." The traditional news has more or less gotten the story correct, as fantastic as it is, but it's the fringe outlets that are out to muddy the waters and make everyone doubt our stories. At the mention of news, Trini approaches as cautiously as a kitten. "Hey, Trini!" I pull the girl into a hug, but she remains stiff and deadly serious.

"Drew's aunt sent all her supporters an email," she says. "He really didn't make it?" Trini deserves the truth. I shake my head and fight another crumbling wave of pain. Trini hugs me again, for real this time. "Thank you for bringing him home," she whispers.

Strength floods my heart—finally, a witness to what's actually been swirling through my head. Dry-eyed, Trini claps my shoulder one final time before running inside and leaving me with a vastly more labyrinthine crisis—Ario. *Do it now, Major. Like a Band-Aid, right off.* "I can't see you anymore," I hear myself say.

Ario drops his head in pain, but nods agreement anyway. "That guy I saw you with on TV...?" he asks.

"Marcos."

"I don't blame you. I'm going to college soon—"

"It's not that."

"'Cuz I messed up texting?"

"It's not that, either."

"What then? It's only been a few days."

Clarity comes to me. Trini's strength has given me enough life bar energy to find it. "It was only a day, but things just changed. You have this whole house, this whole family, and you know that this will always be your home no matter what. And I'm about to get in this car"—I point at Agent Elms in the sedan—"and go see my mom, and I don't know what the hell is even going to happen there. And you've always known this is my situation, but you wanted so badly for me to be a normal boyfriend with a normal situation. I'm gonna be chaos for a long time, maybe forever. It's too much pressure for me, and it's not fair to you." Ario's chest heaves with mighty, shallow breaths, and it's time I finally said it: "It was totally dangerous to make me come out."

"I thought you'd be happier..."

"You wanted a public relationship. An Instagram relationship.

You didn't want rules and boundaries and the closet again, and you totally deserve that. But you shouldn't have demanded that of me."

"I'm not a bad guy!"

"You're not. But...when did you first know I was missing?" Ario blinks, baffled by the question, but the wheels click together eventually. His lips turn white and refuse to speak. "It was when I texted you from the hotel in Costa Rica, wasn't it? After it was all over."

"It was only a weekend, Connor—"

"My last text to you was 'I think she wants to kick me out.'"

"You're *always* saying that—"

"And then I didn't text again for two days?!"

"I thought she took your phone again!"

"You didn't come by to check?!"

"Your mom scares the SHIT out of me, Connor! No, I didn't do that! I'm an eighteen-year-old Muslim who had sex with her underage son, and she's a MAGA lunatic! She could've called the cops on me right there. I'd be DONE, no college, nothing!" We stand at the base of his hill, huffing furiously, tearfully at each other. "I'm sorry, but I got scared."

"She's crazy, I know it. A week ago, I would've told you she'd never try to arrest you or whatever, but what do I know what she's capable of now?"

"I'm sorry—"

"I'm setting you free. No more chaos." I tug the recorder pendant off my neck and present it to him as a bounty for the death of our relationship.

"Connor, don't." He waves me off, refusing to touch it. "If you hand me that, I'm gonna scream." He skips backward up his hill, motorized by an unseen anxiety that's spiraling out of his control. "Please keep it. I ruined everything."

"ARIO." The bass resonates through my voice and settles him exactly how I wanted. "You didn't ruin anything. Your recorder kept me going in a way I can't ever explain. I'm always gonna care about you and nothing'll change that."

At the top of his hill, Ario thrusts both hands into his pockets and holds them there, wracked with tension. All he can do is nod. "Please be careful. I read all those comments, and the people out there...they don't want you to tell your story. You have to be *so* careful."

As soon as Ario disappears inside, I return to Agent Elms like a warrior finished with another brutal kill. She rolls down her window and gazes at me coolly through expensive shades. She makes me smile—I can't put my finger on why. "DRAMA," she sings.

That's why.

"Diane, I saved the drama for my momma," I say, hopping into the passenger seat. Ricky's urn returns to my lap as I buckle in for the home stretch. As we peel out, I can't look back at Ario's home—not at the destructive wake I've left. Or he's left. Or really, that my mother has left. I never even considered she might be capable of making legal trouble for Ario—but it makes sense. His whole hands-off attitude to me after my coming out blew up makes terrible, horrible sense.

Our fifteen-minute journey from White Eagle to Ambrose is a single country road of open fields, but each mile feels like another step closer to the end of the world.

The only glance at my phone I allow myself is to reread Marcos's last text: a selfie of the two of us—mud-splattered, rode hard, and put away wet—in the lobby of our hotel the night we arrived. He captioned it *Icons* ♥ .

Once more, my heart squeezes through a vice. I miss him like a limb. A lifetime has passed in the twenty-four hours since we said goodbye.

On our second day in luxurious Costa Rican custody, Special Agent Elms and her partner Agent Rhodes descended like savior eagles into the hotel. While they battled the local government over permission to charter a boat to find the island, Marcos and I remained sequestered. When we weren't passing time with each other, we passed the time YouTubing the Hannigans. I had no idea how massive Ricky's tragedy had actually been. *60 Minutes* devoted an entire special to the unsuccessful manhunt, spawning a 2001 made-for-TV movie, which is impossible to find online because it was so maligned. Back then, Mrs. Hannigan wouldn't cooperate, so too many details of the attack remained shrouded in mystery, leaving filmmakers to get offensively creative filling in the holes. Two decades came and went, and the Hannigans faded into history—even among those who experienced it firsthand.

When Agent Elms and I were first alone in the San José hotel, she hugged me. A tsunami of grateful tears consumed her. Bill Hannigan was her first case after graduating the Academy; she'd fought an ugly, uphill battle to keep the case alive in the Bureau's minds, but now here were these kids handing her the Devil on a silver platter. She'd become the first of many crying people to ask if they could hug me. Strangers even cry on me. All the time. They just walk up and cry. Bill's violence cut through hundreds of thousands—millions—of people like a rusty blade, slicing and infecting anyone who heard the story. Bill's victims number so much higher than his initial three. That's what a hate crime does: it reaches out, through space and time, and touches you with a greasy hand. You can still feel its touch long after you think you've wiped it off.

It took Agent Elms until the end of our second day to secure permission to send a team to the island. As we all feared, they found Nightlight empty. All records burned beyond recognition in the fire pit in the woods. The Winner's Walls in both cabins picked clean. Most horrifically, the Reverend's body was nowhere to be found and the bunker scrubbed of evidence. Somehow, Miss Manners was able to reach management and get them to rescue her and the remaining staff. In exchange for immunity from charges of child endangerment, harboring a fugitive, and complicity in Drew's death, Ben Briggs named every single Nightlight employee in his deposition to the FBI, but they're all as good as ghosts now—especially Miss Manners. Ramona Hayward doesn't even exist. At least, it's not her real name. She was last spotted in an airport in Moscow but has since vanished.

Just like that, Nightlight fled into the shadows like locusts.

On the morning of the third day—today—we returned to the United States. Special Agent Rhodes extradited Bill to California, where he is awaiting arraignment for the murders of Ricky Hannigan, Rodrigo Valdes, and Officer Clark Prescott. Cleared of all charges, Briggs returned to Colchester. I hope he finds his son.

With no other business in San José, Special Agent Elms and I boarded a flight to Chicago and Marcos waited for his later flight to Dallas/Fort Worth. Our goodbye was impossible, utterly impossible. It made no sense that I couldn't go where he was going, and he couldn't come where I was headed. Separating from that hug was the shittiest thing I've been put through all year, and that's saying a ton. As of this moment, as Agent Elms drives me home, Marcos only landed half an hour ago and is facing a five-hour drive to his family in Lubbock. I'd give anything to be on that miserable Lubbock drive with him rather than approaching the massive, unsubtle Christian billboards outside of Ambrose.

"Keep your head down, honey," Agent Elms snaps, but stupidly, I do the opposite.

CONNOR IS LYING, reads the graffiti across the billboard of a baby, which used to be an anti-abortion ad.

"Surrender your sons," I remember with fire in my eyes. I pull the urn closer.

Agent Elms slams on the gas and zooms me past the next two billboards, which I don't bother to read. Ambrose, Illinois, reveals itself in all its picket fence, small town fakery. These familiar roads have become alien. Like Mrs. Hannigan said about Ricky, this isn't my home anymore. But it has to be. I've got one more year under Marcia Major's roof, however I'm going to manage that. At least at Nightlight, I had Marcos, friends, and a driving purpose.

My mom couldn't meet me at the airport because ever since the news broke, our house has been swarmed with media and she's terrified to step outside. She had to call in sick to work. This was fine with me, as Mom would've never allowed me to wrap up business with Ario and Mrs. Hannigan. This way, I've delayed the inevitable for a few more hours.

"Welp," Agent Elms says, decelerating her sedan to a more small town-friendly speed. "Someone definitely let it slip you're coming home."

It might as well be the Fourth of July—and I'm the only float in the parade. The entire town of Ambrose gathers along the sides of every street, some even squatting in deck chairs, to witness my arrival. There are no smiles, only scowls. Ambrose greets me like a row of hawks perched on a branch.

"Don't slow down," I blurt.

"I have to. That's all we need is to mow down a pedestrian," Agent Elms says, frustrated as she detours down a smaller avenue. But the town is waiting for us there too. Diane throws the automatic locks on the sedan and I swivel around to look at the faces, desperate to find someone mildly happy to see me alive.

There's no one. Not even as we pass my old middle school. The office secretaries, Clair and Maryann, wear enormous sun visors as they gawp at the return of Connor Major: OG trouble.

Some people won't ever be convinced, not with all the evidence in the world. *Nightlight Believers*, they're called: people—cults, basically—who not only believe my friends and I are lying about what happened to us, but that we're murderers. Sinful, fame-hungry liars, who realized who Karaoke Bill was and decided to profit off his capture. According to the most fanatical believers, I personally gutted Reverend Packard and killed Drew with my bare hands. The more detailed theories get really gruesome. Some even deny that Reverend Packard is dead at all. Miss Manners knew what she was doing disposing of him. No body, no crime.

All the evidence we have is my Nightlight shirt stained with his blood.

Around the next turn, people camp outside of Sue's Diner, that beloved place that's three abandoned railway cars converted into a greasy spoon over half a century ago.

My heart lifts.

Alone among the crowd stands Sue—ancient, pink haired, and gripping her oxygen tank. In her other arm, Sue shakes a picket sign that reads *Sue's Diner believes Connor!* She cheers our sedan as we pass. Two men holler at her to sit down, but she merely swings the sign in their direction and shouts, "BANNED!"

"You can't do that!" complains a woman at the other end of the crowd.

Sue swings the picket in her direction and spits, "BANNED!"

I cackle as Sue forgets all about her jeering former customers and returns to waving her sign at me. It's as delicious as any milkshake I've ever drank. My good luck streak continues as Agent Elms takes a shortcut through River Drive—my beautiful, amazing friend Vicky Woodbine waits on her front porch. "He's here!" she cries, little Avery sticking out of the Björn on her chest like a wild mushroom. She and her parents leap from their lawn chairs and together they wave their homemade banner: *The Woodbines believe and LOVE Connor Major!*

There's too many sour-looking neighbors lurking around for us to stop, but I slap my hands against the window in a furious wave to Vicky's family. Weeping, I chicken-peck my loving, heart-exploding texts to Vicky, but it all comes out as autocorrected gobbledygook.

It's going to be okay. I don't need everyone to believe me if I have the best of them.

One final turn later, and we're on Fifth Street, careening past the sprawling farmhouse estate of the richest family in two counties: the Packards. A single smokestack rises out of the processing plant behind the Reverend's two-story brick manor. With no one to live there, the iron gate remains locked across the four-car drive. Attached to the gate is an unending billowing of bouquets and remembrances.

I can't make room in my heart for sympathy for the Reverend—not today.

I whip my head forward to the end of my road. Where the farm-house ends, the endless fields of soybeans begin. On the right is a vast plot of land with only a single home in the center—mine. The lawn is choked with cameras, and Agent Elms can't get any closer than a block away because too many news vans have boxed us out.

"You escaped an island of murderers," Agent Elms says, throw-ing us into park. "This is nothing." I deep breathe the pins and needles out of my arms as I weigh taking Ricky's urn out of the car with me. I won't run the risk of someone stealing such famous re-mains out of Diane's car, but if people swarm me and I drop Ricky...

"I'm ready," I say, clutching the urn as if it were my own child.

"Whatever happens,"—Diane reaches tenderly for my wrist—"don't let her see you sweat."

We exit into the storm, Diane as my bodyguard. As we approach the front lawn, she waves her FBI credentials as if it were a talisman to ward off wicked spirits, but it only whips them into a greater frenzy. Arms lunge for me. Microphones are thrust. Questions are shouted. Flash after flash explodes as I quietly, gravely, climb the walkway to my mother.

The showdown everyone has waited for.

Will she be a Nightlight Believer or a Connor Believer? Will the next year of my life be fear or love? I don't know if I want the answer. Who could possibly want the answer?

Would you?

Pale and gaunt, Mom peeks at me through the curtains. She's waiting. I *believe*. I believe in love. On my next breath, I take the plunge, turn the knob, and arrive home.

CONNOR'S ULTIMATUM

FIVE MONTHS LATER

I text my mom *Merry Christmas* the moment I hear the knock. Like a cat, I curl and stretch luxuriously under my down blanket before welcoming my boyfriend inside. A pinch of spice hits the air as Marcos enters balancing two enormous mugs of coffee. They've been sweetened with the gingerbread-flavored syrup I've been guzzling like cough medicine lately. "Merry Christmas," he says, decked out in dachshund pajama bottoms and handing me a cup before flopping onto my queen mattress.

"Gedmorningmurrychrissmiss," I croak as I bring the life-giving nectar to my lips. Spiced coffee smashes the pleasure center in my brain like a carnival mallet. After that, Marcos's lips close around mine, and the only thing I can do is shut my eyes and moan happily. Beneath the smiling dachshunds on his pajamas, a stiffness rises and meets my leg. He sets his coffee on the nightstand and rolls on top of me. My neck flinches, almost stopping my breath. Even after all this time away from conversion therapy, a boy's touch still hurts at first. Marcos says the same happens to him, but he pushes through.

"Later?" I ask into his mouth. "When we're in the car?"

"I know the house rules," he says, nibbling my lower lip before disengaging. "I'll be good." He's gotten a lot better at kissing me in places where we might be interrupted—and I want him to keep up that growth—but I'm staying in this house under good graces and neither of us want to jeopardize that. Honestly, it's energizing just to be near each other again. At the end of such a violent, tumultuous year, this much uncomplicated joy feels jinxy.

"How was it in the guest room?" I ask Marcos.

"So cozy," he says, snuggling closer. I swear, if he gets gropey again, I won't have the willpower to stop him.

"I love that you're here. I can't believe you're really here...You're sure you're okay not being with your family for the holiday?"

Guilt smothers my heart, but not a drop of sadness appears behind his black frames. "Nope." He smiles and pokes my chin. "I'm with you."

Marcos's mother and grandmother are the reason he's still able to live at home. Our departure from Nightlight created a nightmarish public fiasco for many families, especially Marcos's dad, the Reverend Tyson Carrillo—a local megachurch celebrity. The relationship between Marcos and his dad is as tense as ever, but now that the world is watching, Reverend Carrillo has agreed to play nice. The two Mrs. Carrillos, both fiercely protective of their young prince, successfully integrated Marcos back into his old high school so he could redo his senior year and get back on track to becoming valedictorian.

Upbeat as always, Marcos doesn't mind that most of his friends left Texas for out-of-state colleges or that people whisper about him. All he wants is to graduate and be accepted into a college close to me. It's the only thing making our distance bearable. He asked me to be his prom date in the spring, and I'm not ashamed to say I booked my flight instantly. How could I pass up the opportunity when his homecoming picture stirred up so much FOMO? I've spent many lonely nights with pics of Marcos in his homecoming suit—a candy-red blazer, black slacks, and loafers with no socks. The way his surf-wave hair rose up and then tumbled down his forehead is seared into my corneas. It was such a nuclear explosion of handsomeness, even Ario messaged me: *DAMN*.

We live in wildly different places, but Ario is aggressively trying to get a double date going for us and his new boyfriend, Calvin (who is literally a Chicago cop dating a college freshman, but whatever, no judgment). Weirdly, I'm not opposed to this plan—if it ever materializes. The memory of dating Ario is like an echo of an echo. On my dresser, his recorder hangs off the lid of Ricky Hannigan's urn. I kiss two fingers to the urn (my morning ritual) and pull on a tank top and jogger sweats. My gold glitter nail polish is chipping; I need a touch-up after the holiday.

Back on the bed, Marcos spreads out like a snow angel. "A new *Nightlight BB's* just dropped!" he yelps, already queuing the video on his phone. Agitation briefly sweeps into my chest as I check my notifications: nothing yet from Mom regarding my *Merry Christmas* text, but indeed—Alan and Vance have added a new episode.

I miss everyone being in one place.

"Who's their guest?" I ask, cannonballing back to bed, into the warm nook of Marcos's arm.

"Jack," he says, and we both "Aw."

Alan and Vance both live in Virginia within ten minutes of each other. Following our return, Alan's parents relocated closer to Vance's family to help ease their son's depression. It worked wonders—both boys are inseparable; they're freshmen at the same high school, and last month, they launched a viral web series called *Nightlight BB's* where they perform in drag as their hyper-confident alter egos, Beatriz (Vance) and Belinda (Alan). The wigs are cheap, but their makeup is impeccable.

"*Jack Singer,*" Vance says, flipping through notecards with red satin gloves. Between the queens, Jack straddles a bar stool in Vance's family's posh basement den. "*You've got the name of a man who would pick up Lana Del Rey in a convertible outside 7/11 before driving into the desert.*"

"*Yep,*" Jack agrees, as beguilingly direct as ever. Jack keeps a low profile in Minnesota, save for a popular Instagram of gamer stuff, a new girlfriend, and updates on his transition. Now twenty-five days on T, his sharp cheekbones are dotted with acne. "*Being on T is amazing, but it hasn't been exactly like I thought. Like, I thought I'd have a beard already, but it's been way less* Teen Wolf *and more, just, zits everywhere.*"

"*Yes, men are very greasy,*" Alan says with sensitive, Oprah-like understanding as he brushes a strand of strawberry blond wig from his lips.

Luckily, most campers have families who rapidly turned a corner as soon as the Nightlight news broke. Molly took a page from *Nightlight BB's* and leveraged our situation into minor internet celebritydom: now fully out at home, she records "roughing it" videos where she does *Man vs. Wild* shit in the Arizona wilderness with her girlfriend (and no supplies), cooking whatever she finds with whatever she can find. She once barbecued roadkill with a scrap of tinfoil, and it made everyone (including me) very upset—but it got her an REI sponsorship, so who am I to judge?

The other campers actively avoid the spotlight. Anke, Christina, and Owen are out in their various Midwestern homes, but Owen—youngest and littlest—worries us. I don't have many details, but there was a suicide attempt after school started. He went back to regular classes, but apparently, his mom has taken to sleeping outside his door to listen for signs of him trying again. His parents don't want him socializing with other campers (and they'd probably rather forget anyone ever heard of Nightlight), but at least they let him speak to Lacrishia. She flies out when she can.

"*Belinda, what did your mom do when she first saw you in makeup?*" Jack asks.

"*She said, 'no,'*" Alan responds to a gale of laughter.

"*She said, 'no'?*" Vance cackles.

"*Yeah, oh my God, just 'No.' Like I was asking.*"

I giggle into the fleshy, furry nook of Marcos's arm, and the knots of tension in my neck unwind. Nearing the end of the video, Marcos is already typing his comment about how much we loved it, how Jack is the greatest, and how flawless the boys look. I can't handle accidentally reading any troll comments, not after the insane one I read last week—the one I haven't been able to pry out of my mind.

Don't think about the comment. Breathe in your through your nose, out through your mouth.

While Marcos drops his compliment, I avert my eyes from the comments section and sneak another peek at my notifications: no response yet from Mom. She's probably not up yet. She sleeps in on holidays.

"*Okay gurr, who's our guest next week?*" Alan asks.

"*We're off to New York City, Mama,*" Vance replies. "*Know what that means?*"

"*MOMS!*" the three boys cheer.

The Moms, just as they had at Nightlight, instantly found a way to thrive on their own terms. Lacrishia was already eighteen when we escaped, so as soon as we landed, she was on a train to New York, couch-surfing the entire fall while she started online courses at Columbia. Darcy made peace with her dad in Long Island, but as soon as she turned eighteen, she bolted to Washington Heights, where she and Lacrishia share a studio that's cramped but one hundred percent theirs.

Despite our radically different home lives, all former campers are united by a common refrain we're told: *"Your parents belong in prison!"* Maybe they do and maybe they don't, but the simple fact remains that all of us were brought to Nightlight underage—you'd be amazed what parents can get away with in the name of "deciding what's best for their kids." Our parents joined together under the same deluded, self-serving lie—that they had no idea what was actually going on at Nightlight, or of the camp's connection to Bill Hannigan. To our parents, this was supposed to be a wholesome religious retreat, one they were legally free to enlist us in. Conversion therapy bans exist in many states for minors, but they're secular. Religious reasons still persevere over any law.

So, why don't we hate our families? Why have so many of us come back home?

The nice answer is it's not so easy to simply cast off the family you've known and loved your whole life.

The not-so-nice answer—in some ways, the real answer—is many of us *do* hate our families. Or mistrust them. It just isn't good business to cut them off, especially when you're young. There's still colleges and cars and phones and beds and bills that need paying. And our parents *will* pay. We play nice and exchange our love for this payment, some of us more consciously than others.

Do I hate my mom? No.

Do I resent her? Yes.

I'm not as cutthroat on the subject as, say, Molly is. Me, I still believe in my mom. It's painful stitching, but I still choose to believe.

"I'm starving," I say, sliding off the bed and into my Toms.

"Everyone's awake downstairs," Marcos says. "I forgot, but she asked if you wanted pancakes."

Even though my stomach is a roiling acid bath, pancakes would be appreciated. I check my notifications one more time. Under my *Merry Christmas* text is the thing I've been waiting for: typing bubbles. Finally, my heart can breathe. "She's writing back!"

"Who is?"

"My mom!"

"Your mom?" Marcos's grin collapses into pure dread, but my positivity can't be snuffed out. *I believe. I BELIEVE.* After twenty agonizing seconds of typing, the call comes. Every drop of blood in my body hardens into ice—*she's calling me.* "Connor, wait, don't—!" Marcos blurts, but I've already accepted the call.

I had to.

"Momma?" I ask. Silence on the other end. "Mom? Are you trying to talk? I can't hear you."

She doesn't speak, but her silence deepens into labored, staccato breathing, interrupted by occasional steady breaths. *She's smoking again.* After twenty seconds of nothing but Marcos staring back, horrified, Mom's voice comes, raspy and soft: "What are you doing texting me?"

My heart bangs against my chest. "Why? It's...Christmas, Mom."

"You trying to embarrass me? You haven't done enough of that already?"

"Embarrass...? No, I—"

"Call to tell me I'm scum? On the Lord's birthday? Not enough for you to tell the fake news I'm scum, you gotta do it to my face? On the LORD'S DAY? A day I might finally be able to get some peace? You don't got ANY sense at all, Connor! You're CRUEL!"

"Momma, but—"

"How could I have raised...how...? Such a cruel...don't you know I can't ever, EVER forgive what you did? Don't you? Doesn't anybody understand that?!"

I grip my phone until my hand becomes a claw, and all I can hear is my thudding heart. "You have to believe me." Silence again. A puff of smoke hits her receiver. "Mom. You have to believe me. Me. Not someone else. *ME.*" Another puff. "I could've died, Mom. People died."

"Connor..." she says. "I know...because you killed them."

My belief in my mother finally meets a brick wall.

Marcos calls out to me, but the only sound in the room is my dull, slowing heartbeat. Agent Elms was right. The last time we saw each other, she warned me never to reach out to my mom again, but I had to. *It's Christmas.*

In the initial days following our escape, the people who cried to me in public were crying about Ricky. Or Drew. As time went on, the crying became about me. About how my mother cut me off. The world watched as I was chucked out like a diseased animal.

Whatever our problems used to be—me being gay, whatever—it's about her guilt now. She's too stubborn, too ingrained in her own righteousness, to ever believe me about anything that happened on the island. She'll believe any conspiracy theory if it protects her from the truth. She believed I was Avery's dad against all evidence. And now she's graduated to a worse theory.

Her hospital became unbearable with too many people knowing what she did to me, so she moved. Last I heard, she's holed up somewhere in Vegas, exchanging cash for coins at casinos. A desert far away from any knowledge of her past.

Or any memory of me.

It feels like I'm still on the island. Like I never escaped. My therapist helped me understand that my conversion therapy goes beyond the borders of Nightlight—that the world is my island. I was in conversion therapy before the island, and I'm still in conversion therapy today. The point is control, and for years, my mother has tried to control me, my behavior, who I am, what I do. That's why my pain didn't end when the Reverend died. It was my mom. It was always my mom. She controls me, even after disowning me. After everything she's done, I still texted her *Merry Christmas*.

Merry Christmas, I texted.

"Murderer," Mom replies and hangs up.

I regain consciousness on the floor. I can't breathe. Hysterical, body-wracking sobs clog my nostrils as I battle the familiar storm. My throat emits childish, choking noises as Marcos climbs on me and pets my cheek. "It's okay," he soothes, grappling with his own panic over what's happening. "You're okay. We won't let anything happen to you. You're safe. Jesus, Connor, why'd you have to text her?"

Christmas was me and my mom's special time. It's warm and yummy and makes her miss my grandma. I thought...maybe...I could reach her today. But the woman who took off my socks and warmed my feet after coming in from the snow isn't the same person anymore. She's something else now. Like it did to the Reverend, and to me, Nightlight changed her.

Mom loved me. Then she got lost. And the more I chase after her, the likelier I'll get lost too.

Thunderous footsteps approach outside until my bedroom door blasts open on its hinges. Marcos leaps off me to meet the blond, middle-aged woman striding inside—the only person besides Marcos who calms my heart purely on sight. "Evelyn, I'm sorry, the coffee spilled over there," Marcos confesses rapidly, snapping his fingers *click-click-click.*

"BooBoo, it's just coffee," Evelyn tells Marcos as she races over to me on the floor. "What happened?"

"His *mom* called him." Marcos swallows the words he would rather use to describe my mom, the woman responsible for the four days I spent homeless in Chicago.

Evelyn's cool, manicured touch pets my hair in long strokes, but she is far less picky about her words than Marcos. "I'm gonna kill her," she growls.

"Evelyn..." Marcos warns, but he's too late. Her five-year-old daughter wanders into the room to gawp as I gulp manic breaths.

"Did Connor fall down and hurt himself?" the girl asks.

"No, Daisy, he's just sad," Evelyn says through her rage. "Can you go tell your dad to keep stirring that pancake batter and we'll be right down?"

Daisy scoots away as she's told, and Marcos throws open the light-blocking shades in my room to let in the California sunshine. The patch of palm trees outside my window performs a magic spell that instantly balances my breathing. After spending half a year at Nightlight, Marcos can't stand the sight of palms, but they bestow literal life on me.

"It's my fault," I whisper, but Marcos and Evelyn shout "NO" in unison.

"You're an angel to still believe in her," Evelyn says, reading my *Merry Christmas* text.

"Drew should be here," I moan, miles away and getting more lost by the second. "I should've...I could've helped..."

"Shhhhhhh," Evelyn says, stroking my hair. A frantic tear escapes her.

Evelyn Schreiber saved my life. Actually, Ario's sister did. If she hadn't made me fork over ten dollars to hunt down Drew, my information would've never appeared on Evelyn's mailing list. My memories of those August nights I spent sleeping on a bench by Lake Michigan are midnight-dark and, with each passing day, decline steeply into the realm of obscurity where we tuck away our worst traumas. After Mom threw me out, I'm not sure why I didn't reach out to Marcos or Ario or Vicky or Agent Elms or my dad or Molly or the other campers. All I had was Ricky's urn—entrusted to me. I was lost, just Ricky and me, wandering the city. I was embarrassed to let anyone know what happened. I was Triumphant Connor, destroyer of conversion camps. A victor. I had my happy ending, and it was supposed to stay that way. How I could be so lost again? Worse than before? Part of me even wondered...maybe I *was* a murderer, forcing Drew to give up the secrets that got him killed.

After my third night on the streets, someone anonymously posted a picture of me sleeping under a bench—me, the famous boy from the boat. The one who helped catch the monster. Evelyn tried calling my number from the GoFundMe list, but my mom had disconnected my phone, so Evelyn hopped on a plane from LA to Chicago. On day four, she found me. And she wasn't alone. Ario,

Vicky, and Marcos were there. Each of them had been looking for me for days (Marcos even flew in from Texas), without any luck until they paired up with Evelyn, who had the resources and know-how to contact local shelters and trace my directionless path around the city.

Finding the four of them standing over me was like some impossible dream. Accepting hugs all at once from the people I truly love who truly love me sent me into inconsolable wails. No one was mad at me, like I worried they might be. Evelyn didn't blame me for Drew. Ario didn't hate me for Marcos. Vicky didn't hate me for destroying her Avery lie. Marcos didn't ask why I hadn't tried to reach him.

I was loved, and it saved me.

Marcos shushed me and said that everything was okay as he took Ricky's urn (*"I've got him, you can let go."*). "Where's Avery?" I asked Vicky as she clutched my cheeks in both hands.

"With my mom, don't worry," she said, nostrils shimmering with tears.

"He needs you—"

"I know, but I needed to be here. Okay?"

My rescue squad stayed with me for two more days in the city. Evelyn rented us hotel rooms, and we didn't do much except hang out and return to normal. It was beyond bliss, but eventually, we needed a long-term plan.

And that's when Evelyn took me in as if I was her son.

I'm currently in the middle of my senior year because of her; I'm killing it on my college applications because of her; and I haven't lost my damn mind because of her. Weeks after I moved into her home in West Hollywood, my dad (a day late and a dollar short, as usual) found out what happened and halfheartedly offered to let me live with him in England. But I turned him down and a deal was made to let Evelyn foster me until I graduate. I like living with Evelyn, and I refuse to be an ocean apart from Marcos.

Evelyn lost her last shred of hope when her nephew didn't make it back alive. Sometimes, it feels like she needs me as much as I need her.

My episode on the floor now soothed, Evelyn kisses my head and returns downstairs to the sound of sizzling pancakes. Marcos brings me next to him on the edge of the bed. I kiss him, but the throbbing pulse of my mother's call turns up the volume on every one of my miserable feelings. I tap my skull before finding the right words: "It's raining in here."

To Marcos's enormous credit, his expression never dips into pity. He summons his best dimples and says, "Can't rain forever. I love you."

Neither of us have said this yet. Everything remains on mute, but around the corners of the thunderheads in my mind, golden light blossoms. "Are you saying that because I'm being messy trash right now?"

"I love you," he repeats flatly.

"You're just saying that because—"

"I love you."

Soft hands cup my cheeks, and the swaddling sensation releases more golden light into my brain. We still haven't found the right balance of medication for me, and I don't know how long it'll be before the clouds reconverge and swallow the light, but for this minute, I feel it. "I love you," I tell him. "It's so kind of you to visit me in my loneliness."

He grins, cheerful enough for the both of us. "It's kind of you to visit me in mine."

We kiss, but the longer it lasts, the deeper my heart sinks. I still have a job to do, and I've put it off for way too long. "Go with me somewhere," I whisper, breaking the kiss.

He sighs. He knew this was coming.

———

After pancakes, Marcos and I excuse ourselves without explaining our destination. If we had, Evelyn would've thrown herself in front of the door to stop us. It's not that she's controlling, she just knows that certain things—and certain places—set me off, especially when I'm already vulnerable. But the morning of a major holiday means LA will be empty, and I've been waiting five months for the right amount of privacy to do what I need to do.

As expected, West Hollywood is a ghost town. Marcos drives his rental car down Santa Monica Boulevard, its spray-painted, rainbow crosswalks still littered from Saturday night's festivities. The closer West Hollywood gets to Beverly Hills, the more gay bars dot the landscape. Not that I've gone inside one—Evelyn made it clear that should my curiosity get the better of me, she personally knows every bartender and drag queen in town and they will text her the moment I'm spotted. "I know you think you'll have fun," she warned, "but if I hear you snuck in, I'll be there faster than the cops."

Evelyn jokes, but what she's really worried about is losing me. After our escape, I've become quite well known, especially in queer-dense neighborhoods like this. One picture of me drinking, underage, and surrounded by dancing men, and I'll be on the first plane to England.

But I've never been tempted to go inside. I just like to drive past and see everyone enjoying themselves. It helps to be around joy.

"Is someone gonna notice us?" Marcos asks, turning onto Havenhurst Drive.

"Maybe," I say, hugging my backpack tighter. "But we promised."

The lushly green street tightens my chest—we're close.

Street parking is easier on holiday mornings. Everyone's asleep. I've driven past this block countless times in the three months I've lived in California. I've only had the courage to walk in the building once, and my pins and needles made sure it was a brief visit. Marcos takes my hand as we consider the luxury apartment building hunching like a grave marker at the top of a stone staircase: 1612 Havenhurst. Ricky and Rigo's apartment. The site where Karaoke Bill committed one of the most monstrous domestic crimes of the twentieth century. The place where Rigo's ashes lie in a garden surrounding a spitting courtyard fountain.

"You're home," I whisper to Ricky's urn inside my backpack.

Marcos doesn't try to talk me out of it. He clasps my hand and leads me toward the haunted house, one stair at a time. The building's open archway leads directly into the courtyard of bungalows; they haven't gated it off to the public—yet. People still live here, and it's not right to have them constantly ambushed by sobbing queers and allies on a grim pilgrimage to the Hannigan murder site.

Past a row of mailboxes, the massive garden fountain waits for Ricky. Large-paned California windows lie open all around us to tempt in a morning breeze. We'll be seen if we linger, so I unzip the backpack without ceremony, uncork the ceramic lid of the urn, and return Ricky to Rigo's bedside. It only takes a few persistent taps of the urn before he's dusted around the greenery evenly. Luckily, building maintenance already removed many of the bouquets and "Always in Our Memory" placards people laid out after Bill's arrest. There were hundreds this summer, but it's since died down to a small handful.

"They're together now," Marcos whispers, rustling his fingers through my hair.

I nod but can't speak. My chest hurts too badly. After my mother's call, I can't pretend not to know what Ricky must have felt like living here—far away from his dad, hidden and safe until the Reverend ruined everything. I can't bring myself to look into the ground floor window that used to be the Hannigan-Valdes home. Ghosts live there. According to witnesses that night, Ricky begged like a toddler as Bill beat him. They all agreed it's a sound they'll never forget.

I can hear it happening. The attack. It plays loudly in my mind like some horrible echo. Except Marcos's face keeps replacing Rigo's.

Marcos...dead...I won't ever see him again...

"Get me out of here," I hiss, returning the empty urn to my bag. Marcos has been waiting to hear me say that. He hoists me to my feet, and shepherds me out of the crime scene, back to our car.

"Turkey time," he says as we buckle ourselves in and speed away, leaving Ricky and Rigo to their much-needed rest, just as the Reverend wanted. This began with a request from a dead man and it ends with a request from a dead man. I'll keep the urn as a reminder of what it cost to get Ricky and me home. Ricky didn't live on Bill's terms and I won't live on my mom's. I block her number, and for the first time—more than when we captured Bill, more than when we set sail on the boat home—I truly feel like I've escaped Nightlight.

But Nightlight has not escaped me.

I swipe over to Instagram and find the viral post of the eleven of us escaping the island. With vice-like concentration, I hold my breath and scroll to one of the comments I've left unanswered. I've told no one—not Agent Elms, not Marcos, not Evelyn, not any of the campers—of what I found waiting for me in the comments last week. I couldn't, not until I knew how I was going to respond. It's not a comment from my mother; it's from a person with even darker intentions.

Semriss Mann reads the name of the AVI-less account. Their comment is written in impenetrable Russian—Cyrillic, to be exact. It only took me a day to work out the anagram: Semriss Mann.

Miss Manners.

Ramona Hayward, Miss Manners, whatever her name is, is part of Nightlight Management. This is the second time Semriss Mann has taunted me on social media. Last month, I was DM'd a blurry screenshot of a signpost along a cement wall in some unknown frozen tundra. The sign, also written in Cyrillic, bore an inscription identical to the Instagram comment. I ignored the DM because I get dozens of random, foreign language messages every day, but when this message repeated, I couldn't help but investigate. As soon as I translated the message, I understood. The thing I've always dreaded, the thing I should've expected, is now confirmed reality:

"Surrender your sins."

Miss Manners sent me a photo of this exact message written on a snow-covered wall somewhere in Eastern Europe. There are other Nightlight camps. With kids just like me, like Marcos, like Molly, like Drew, like Ricky, like all of us, right now...trapped.

Finally, embracing Ricky's urn, I find the clarity and courage to reply to Semriss Mann in English: *See you soon.* I seal the comment with a lipstick kiss emoji and hit send. The thrill of striking back at Miss Manners, my first strike of many to come, wakes my heart out of the deep sleep of depression. The evil is still out there, and must always be fought. Nightlight is a hand that reaches beyond the island. It's a poison that leaves no one unscalded or unchanged. This began with Ricky, but we are all Ricky. And I'm more than ready to take them on, whatever it takes, as long as it takes.

Yet for now, there's Christmas to enjoy with Marcos. I'll tell him in time, and Agent Elms, and anyone else who will listen. We'll take these people on together.

As we return to Evelyn's, heading down the boulevard Ricky and Rigo called home years ago—to buy groceries, to go to parties, to feel the sun together—Marcos's hand finds mine.

And somehow, there's no more pain.

ACKNOWLEDGMENTS

Just as Connor Major couldn't escape Nightlight on his own, I depended on many others to get this book into the world. I began writing what would eventually become *Surrender Your Sons* in 2013. That's over six years. A serpentine journey of setbacks, rejections, and revisions that took me from rough concepts to the shelf of your local bookstore.

My first and biggest thanks is to my editor, Mari Kesselring, who took a chance on a weird, darkly funny book about queer trauma. It was a mixture that scared away many people, but I'll be forever grateful to Mari, Ashtyn Stann, Megan Naidl, and the entire Flux team for seeing this through.

I can't speak about being given a chance without thanking my agent, the great Eric Smith, whose positivity never wavered that Connor and the gang would find a home in the end. *Surrender Your Sons* was always about Connor versus the Reverend on an island conversion camp, but beyond that, this manuscript existed in multiple, radically different forms. In fact, it began as an adult fantasy novel set in the 1980s. Connor and the Reverend were British and battled each other with mystical superpowers (not a joke—don't ask). It was...not ready yet. Some tough love was required. In 2016, that tough love came from Eric, who rejected one of these early versions, but reached out a few months later reminding me to hang in there. That belief was like a match in a hurricane for me. Thanks is also due to Connor Goldsmith, who convinced me to make this YA, and to Alyssa Jennette, who convinced me to remove the fantasy elements. Sometimes when agents reject you, you learn your best lessons.

When you're starting out with a book that's good but not quite there, those Early Believers mean everything. Thank you to the support of Nena Smith—if she believes in you, you'll never lose. To Brian Centrone and Casey Ellis, who published my first short story in their collection *Startling Sci-Fi*—thank you for that first step into a larger world. To Evan DeSimone and Alanna Bennett, thanks for showing up to my first event. To Andrew Smith, Nathan Burgoine, and Alim Kheraj, thanks for the interviews about my book opinions. In the time before I sold anything, it made me feel like a real publishing fancy lady.

Thanks to Lisa Amowitz, my mighty mentor in Pitch Wars. We may not have sold our version, but it got Connor out of Britain and into the Illinois farmlands. To the Pitch Wars class of 2016, what an incredible club to be a part of: Kosoko Jackson, Ernie Chiara, Mary Dunbar, Anna Birch, Jenny Howe, Gwynne Jackson, Maxym Martineau, Sarah Van Goethem, Ian Barnes, and Annette Christie, to name a few. And of course, Brenda Drake for setting it all up.

Six years. A million versions. This means I've had my share of beta readers, but I'd be sunk without them. Thank you, Sam Glatt, Becky Kirsch, Cat Griffith, Paul Anderson, Marcus Kaye, Lizzie Partridge, April Griffith, Todd Lampe, Paul Kirsch, Tiffany Rose, David Abramovitz, Jack O'Brien, Ben Fowler, Kyle Stevens, James Pearson, Tatianna Carr, Eli Alperin, Ben Matthew Empey, Max Wirestone, Jessica Cluess, Jay Coles, Mark O'Brien, Josh Martinez, Grace Li, Caden Gardner, and Mary Ann Marlowe. You read some of the sketchiest detours this story has taken and found the core things to love about it. That's all I could ask for.

You can't publish a book without friends. There's too much waiting, uncertainty, and anxiety baked into the process for an author to survive without emotional support. My frantic, tearful phone calls to besties like Ian Carlos Crawford and Russell Falcon kept me laughing when my brain wanted to wallow. Drew Factor is not just a friend, but a watcher on the wall: he's the only human being other than me to have read every version of this story. Sorry I had to kill your namesake, Drew. Mike Chen was an indispensable fount of knowledge about the book submission process, on which there are very few articles or books written. Thank you to the patient ears of Amanda Santos, Wendy Heard, Mathew Rodriguez, Thomas Williams, and the TeamRocks Slack channel. Thank you to my *Twin Peaks* fan group—Keith, Michael-Vincent, Robert, and Marianna—whose lively discussions kept me going during agent hunting. Thanks to Garrard Conley for his vital insights into the horrors of conversion therapy. Thanks to an old friend, Kelsey Famous, who years ago—the week before I came out to my family—suggested the next thing I write should be about a boy finding his way home.

The YA community has inspired me for years while *Surrender Your Sons* incubated. It can be tough. There are a lot of big personalities, new ideas, and a persistent need to hold everyone accountable for themselves (what a concept!), but there are no finer people in publishing. Thank you, Dahlia Adler, Aiden Thomas, Rob Bittner, Cody Roecker, Rachel Strolle, and Claribel Ortega, for your enthusiasm. Thank you, Fabian and Kai—titans of European YA—for being two of the most fabulous Insta stars I know. Thank you, Terry Benton, not just for your belief but for fighting every day to forge your own way in this business. Thank you, Ryan La Sala, Corey Whaley, Cale Dietrich, Lev Rosen, Adib Khorram, Shaun David Hutchinson, Alex London, Tom Ryan, and Julian Winters, for shepherding brave, wonderful queer boys through your magnificent fictional worlds.

The next three names are going to make me cry. Caleb Roehrig: my first hero-to-friend transition, I wouldn't be writing without your work to guide me and I wouldn't know what to do with myself without our texts. Kevin Savoie: my salty little brother, my fellow Illinois kin who knows that Pepsi is better than Coke, and one of the fiercest writers I know. Phil Stamper: my de facto manager, my sage adviser, my Jack Donaghy (a reference you finally get!), and a superstar in the making. Gonna get even cornier here and acknowledge that in the weeks before I sold this book, I fell—and fell hard—and I was not pleasant, but you three caught me. Thanks is also due to the Househusbands of YA—Jonathan Stamper-Halpin, Uldis Balodis, and Damian Alexander—for allowing your men's phones to keep going off all day with my deluge of messages.

A publishing secret is that most authors need a day job, and I'm lucky enough to have one of the best there is. To my ATTN: branded team, thank you for keeping me laughing and employed while I cobbled away at this book on nights and weekends: Nacho, Nick, Liv, Krisha, Ziona, Hoy, Nanea, Eric, Perdita, Allen, Austin, Zach, Ashley, Doody, Anand, Ally, Jesse, Clare, Tom, Jem, Jen, Dylan, Hannah, Collin, Ramirez, Tiffer, Taylor, Pasquale, Charlie, Paul, Chenelle, Mynor, Warren, Bailey, Lynn, Lyndsay, Yimu, Tony, Cole, Adam, Jireh, Cameron, Dennis, Allie, Aimee, Michelle, Stacey, Hilary, Kevin, Devon, Silva, Casner, Dee, Matthew, Jarrett, Samantha, Craig, Evelyn, Leo, Natalie, Donny, Delaney, Mia, and, of course, Frankie—who was there when I got the call that I'd sold this book.

This book is about the dark side of family, but I'm exceedingly grateful that I wrote from imagination, not memory. Thank you to my brilliant mom and dad, Pam and Mike Sass, and my supportive in-laws, Mike and Maria Russo. My apologies if anyone ever wrongfully assumes I wrote you into this book! Thanks also to the people who make my family so wonderfully full: Stephanie Russo, Erik and Maggie Sass, and my nieces, Charlotte and Kennedy.

Last but not least (ope, crying again!), "thank you" does not begin to cover how important my little family is to me. Day in and day out, through the darkness of writing *Surrender Your Sons* and the strain of getting it published, I always had a warm, loving home to return to. My dogs, Marty and Malibu, never left my side as they curled up at my chair while I wrote. My husband, my heart, Michael: whenever I needed my characters to tap into strength and humor in the face of adversity, I drew from you.

A final thank you to Connor Major: We've spent the last decade together, and I'm so proud of you for holding on. I finally got you off the island, just like I promised. I will miss writing you, but now you get to hang out with new friends, our readers.

It was so kind of you to visit me in my loneliness.